Jenny's Grace

PAT NICHOLS

JENNY'S GRACE by Pat Nichols
Published by Armchair Press
ISBN: 979-8-9860519-1-8
Copyright © 2022 by Pat Nichols
Cover Design by Elaina Lee
Edited by Sherri Stewart

Available in print from your local bookstore or online.
For more information on this book or the author visit:
https://patnicholsauthor.blog
Printed in the United States of America
Jenny's Grace is a work of fiction. Names, characters, and
incidents are all products of the author's imagination or are
used for fictional purposes. Any mentioned brand names,
places, and trademarks remain the property of their
respective owners, bear no association with the author or
publisher, and are used for fictional purposes only.
Library of Congress Cataloging-in Publication Data
Nichols, Pat.
Jenny's Grace / Pat Nichols

Books by

Pat Nichols

Women's Fiction

Willow Falls series

The Secret of Willow Inn
Trouble in Willow Falls
Star Struck in Willow Falls
Bridges, Books, and Bones

Butler Family Legacy series

Big Secrets, Little Lies
Truth and Forgiveness
New Beginnings

Contemporary Romance

Jenny's Grace

To Julia, whose smile warmed our hearts. Your time with all who loved you
ended far too soon.

Chapter 1

Jenny Collins peered at her car's gas gauge, dangerously close to empty. If she hadn't been speeding three months earlier, that cop wouldn't have pulled her over and unleashed an avalanche of trouble. Fired from her job. DUI school. Thirty-six-hours behind bars. How had everything gone so wrong? She'd only downed two glasses of wine. Well, maybe three. Plus, a couple of shooters. Now just shy of three hundred dollars in her purse, cancelled credit cards, and an over-drawn bank account, she had to make a decision. Fast.

At the next exit, she pulled off Interstate 20, turned toward Madison, and drove into town. After backing into a parking space on South Main, she eyed the brick buildings lining the street—none were taller than two stories. She'd never lived more than a few miles from a big city teeming with skyscrapers. Maybe she should've stayed in Atlanta and found a way to pay her back rent instead of moving out before dawn. Too late to second-guess her decision now. Besides, if she worked for six months and kept her expenses low, she'd save enough money to attract an investor, open her own restaurant, and prove she was nothing like her mother.

Jenny shouldered her purse and waited for a pickup to pass before climbing out and making her way to the brick sidewalk shaded by budding trees. A symphony of chirping birds and a gentle spring breeze accompanied her as she meandered past the post office to the corner. When the traffic light changed, she dashed across the street, and walked inside a two-story brick welcome center.

An attractive, elderly woman greeted her with a smile. "Welcome to Madison."

"How'd you know I'm not from around here?"

"I'd remember a pretty girl like you. How may I help you, sweetie?"

Jenny fingered a brochure touting Madison's history and tourist attractions. "Do you know of any openings for an experienced chef?"

"Can't say I do, except for Lou. She needs to hire someone to help out in her coffee shop. It's up the street and around the corner. Lou's place is open 'til noon."

Not exactly what she had in mind. She could pound the pavement hoping to find an opening or spend another twenty for gas and try the next small town. Best to save the cash and check out the lead. "Thanks for the scoop."

"My pleasure, and welcome to Madison."

Jenny returned to the sidewalk and walked a block and a half. As she approached Lou's Coffee Shop, a movie-star handsome young man with sandy blond hair and expressive blue eyes walked out.

She smiled.

He held the door open. "If you're looking for a great cup of coffee you've come to the right place. Best spot's at the end of the counter."

"Good to know." Jenny breathed in the subtle scent of musky aftershave, then glanced at his left hand. No ring. Their eyes met. Maybe she'd found the perfect guy for a short-term fling. After all, four months had passed since her last romance. Bad idea in a small town where everybody knew everyone's business. "Thank you."

"My pleasure."

Her shoulder brushed his chest as she walked into the coffee shop and tuned into the lively chatter. The rich scent of fresh-brewed coffee mingling with cinnamon and vanilla made her mouth water and her stomach grumble. Eyes followed her as she moved to the end of the counter. She hung her purse on the back of the vacant stool and eyed the black and white checkerboard floor tiles and Formica tables. A definite fifties vibe.

"You're new in town." A thin, elderly woman set a cup of coffee on the counter—her quintessential gray hair pulled into a tight bun, reading glasses perched halfway down her nose. "I'm Lou Johnson, owner of this establishment."

"Jenny Collins. Pleasure to meet you."

"Do you want to doctor yours up, Jenny, or do you prefer black?"

"Cream and sugar, please."

The man sitting cattycorner to Jenny nodded toward Lou. "My friend serves the best coffee in Georgia, plus a healthy dose of local gossip."

"Don't fill this pretty young lady's head with nonsense, George." Lou placed a paper napkin beside Jenny's coffee. "What brings you to town, honey?"

Desperation. "The history. The small-town atmosphere. Actually, I'm planning to stay awhile." She aimed her thumb toward the window. "I noticed your help-wanted sign."

"I posted it two days ago after my assistant went into labor three weeks early."

"This could be your lucky day, Ms. Johnson." Jenny planted her forearms on the counter. "I'm a professionally trained, experienced chef."

"Are you now?"

"You might be familiar with some of the restaurants showcased in my extensive portfolio."

After Jenny rattled off a list of previous employers, Lou eyed her for a long moment. She pulled a pen from her apron pocket, scribbled a note on a paper napkin, and pushed it across the counter. "That's what I can afford to pay for your help in my kitchen. Plus, you'll keep all your tips."

Jenny stared at the number. Small town, small paycheck. If she accepted, she'd have to scrimp to save any money. Besides, waiting tables didn't suit her image.

"If you're willing to show up before the crack of dawn and help serve customers after we open, you have yourself a job, honey."

Jenny arched her brows. "Don't you want to interview me or at least read my recommendation letters?"

"Lou has a keen nose for character." George pushed his empty plate away. "She obviously thinks you're a good risk."

"He's right." Lou pushed her glasses up her nose. "In my seventy-plus years, I've learned a thing or two about people. What do you say, Jenny? Should I take that sign down or leave it up?"

Maybe she should hold out for a job that paid a lot more and didn't require shlepping food to customers. Although, working mornings meant she'd have afternoons free, and tips would provide immediate cash. "You have yourself a new chef, Ms. Johnson."

"Everyone calls me Lou. Knock on the shop's back door at four tomorrow morning. For now, what can I bring you? On the house."

"What's the most popular item?"

George snapped his fingers. "Hands down, Lou's cinnamon buns."

"Then a cinnamon bun it is."

Lou plated a large bun drizzled with vanilla icing and placed it on the counter. "I want your professional opinion."

Jenny cut a small piece and savored the aroma before tantalizing her taste buds.

"What's the verdict?"

"Best I've ever tasted."

Lou patted her hand. "I have a notion we're fixing to get along like family."

Hopefully, not the insane family she'd escaped years earlier.

George cradled his coffee cup in both hands. "Where do you hail from, Miss Jenny?"

"Here and there. How about you?"

"Born and bred in Madison. I've been retired for twelve years, and still show up right here every morning. Except for occasional out-of-towners, I'm well acquainted with Lou's customers."

"Well then." Jenny leaned close. "How about clueing me in, so I can provide top-notch service to all these fine folks."

"And earn yourself some good tips to boot."

Jenny grinned. "We're gonna get along great, George."

Late in the morning, after Jenny charmed customers with southern hospitality and well-laced compliments, Lou poured herself a cup of coffee and ambled over. "Seems the newest member of my little team is quite the flirt. Mind you, honey, I'm not complaining. If you're as good in the kitchen as you are working a crowd, business is likely to boom."

Jenny noted the twinkle in Lou's eyes. "You're one sharp lady."

"I have my moments. Where are you staying?"

"I don't know yet. Any suggestions on someone who can help me find a decent rental?"

"Gibson Realty. Sam, the owner's grandson, is a top-notch agent. You passed him on your way in. He's one of Madison's most sought-after bachelors. I can't count the number of young ladies who've tried and failed to reel him in."

Maybe he also preferred short-term flings. "Lots of guys and gals in my generation enjoy the single life."

"Sam was engaged a couple years back."

"To a local girl," added George. "She broke it off a month before the wedding. Darn near tore Sam's heart right out of his chest."

Lou thumped George's arm. "And you call me a gossip. You go on over and talk to him, Jenny."

"I will." She shouldered her purse and slid off her stool. "I'll see you tomorrow morning, Lou."

"Tell Sam I sent you."

Jenny waved over her shoulder as she walked out. Following a short walk, she stopped under a canopy and fingered gold letters outlined in black on a window reflecting the park across the street. *Gibson Realty*. She removed a small bottle of perfume from her purse and spritzed behind each ear.

The plump, pretty woman sitting behind a desk motioned her inside.

Had she seen the perfume ploy? Jenny squared her shoulders and walked in.

"I'm Mary. If you're looking for the best realtor in town, you've come to the right place."

"So I've heard."

"Mr. Gibson Senior is out, but his grandson is in his office. I'll let him know you're here."

Jenny's pulse accelerated as she anticipated officially meeting the most eligible bachelor in Madison.

Chapter 2

S am Gibson swiveled his executive chair, faced the dark blue wall behind his desk, and laced his fingers behind his neck. While eyeing an oil painting depicting the sun rising over the ocean and waves crashing on a cliff, his mind drifted to the stranger whose shoulder had brushed his chest. A head shorter than his five-foot-ten-inch frame. Sun-streaked, silky brown hair. Mesmerizing hazel eyes. Why hadn't he asked her name? Didn't matter. She was probably passing through town. A knock preceded his door opening. He spun his chair around.

Mary peeked in. "A pretty young lady needs your assistance."

"Show her in." He hastened to the door.

The stranger strolled toward him.

His breath caught as he extended his hand. "We meet again. I'm Sam Gibson."

She flashed an enticing smile and accepted his hand. "Jenny Collins. It's a pleasure to meet you officially."

His eyes lingered on hers as he breathed in the delicious scent wafting around her. Who was this intoxicating woman? He released her hand and pointed to a plush-leather easy chair. "Please, have a seat."

She sat and crossed a leg over her knee, revealing three inches of thigh below her denim skirt. "Gorgeous office." She pointed to the wall behind his desk. "I love the painting. It's so inspirational."

"My sister selected it." Sam diverted his gaze and moved to his desk chair. "She claims it represents new beginnings."

"Perfect choice for a real-estate office." Jenny leaned forward and ran her fingers along the top of his mahogany desk. "Is this beautiful piece a real antique or a masterful copy?"

Interesting. She recognized quality. "The real deal. It belonged to my great-grandfather. He founded Gibson Realty."

"Which means you're following in the family business."

"After Grandpa retires, I plan to open an office in Athens and make Gibson Realty the top agency in Central Georgia." What prompted him to share details with a total stranger? Except she didn't feel like a stranger. "How can I help you, Ms. Collins?" He kept his gaze firmly planted on her face.

"I'm new in town and need a place to rent." She tilted her head and fluttered her lashes. "Not too expensive, and on a month-to-month basis."

Why month-to-month, and what did she consider not too expensive? He noted the rhinestones on her denim jacket. It didn't look cheap. "You've come to the right place. Do you prefer a house or an apartment?"

"The latter. Close to downtown. Furnished. One bedroom's fine."

"Let me see what's available." He tapped his laptop keyboard. "I found two excellent properties." He turned the screen toward her.

She focused on the options for a moment then stood and moved to an array of black and white photos arranged on the side wall. "Are you the photographer?"

"My grandfather shot those. They represent a few of Madison's historic homes."

"Lou said you're a top-notch real-estate agent who knows how to satisfy customers."

"She's my number-one fan."

"I begin working at the coffee shop tomorrow. At the moment, I'm a bit low on cash."

"How much are you prepared to spend?"

Her eyes met his. "A hundred for the first month."

Sam clenched his teeth to keep his jaw from dropping. Maybe he should suggest she rent a pop-up tent.

"Recently I had some unexpected expenses." She returned to the chair. "I have a portfolio full of recommendation letters and references."

She wouldn't offer references if she had something to hide, would she? Besides, Lou trusted her enough to hire her. "I can't promise anything, Miss Collins—"

"Please, call me Jenny." She flashed a smile. "The moment I walked into this beautiful office and our hands touched, I sensed I'd come to the right place, Mr. Gibson."

His eyes locked on hers. "Sam." What was it about her? The way she tilted her head and fluttered her lashes? The attraction seemed more than physical. Maybe it was her vulnerability. Unlike the blonde who broke his heart, this stranger needed him, or at least his expertise. One fact he couldn't deny—he had to come through for her. "I'll do everything I can to find you a place to live."

"Thank you. For now, I'd best be on my way." She stood.

He dashed to the door.

She tilted her head and touched his arm. "Do you mind if I stop by tomorrow around noon to find out when I can move into my new place?"

Sam swallowed. "That'll work." He escorted her through the reception area and held the front door open.

"Until tomorrow, Sam." Her shoulder brushed his chest again as she moved past and turned toward Main Street.

He remained in the doorway watching her stroll up the block. Where had she come from and how had she ended up in his town?

"My, my." Mary's voice dashed Sam's musings. "You promised a minor miracle for the pretty-as-a-peach lady who claims she's poor as a church mouse?"

"You heard, huh?"

"Why do you suppose she's broke? Maybe she came to town straight from jail or she lost all her cash gambling in a casino. My cousin over in Mississippi had the same thing happen to her. She had to beg my aunt for rent money."

Sam's eyes remained focused on Jenny. "Your imagination is running wild."

"What are you planning to do?"

"Find Miss Collins a place to live."

"Doggone near impossible unless you supplement the rent with your own money."

"What happened to your faith in my problem-solving skills?" He closed the door.

She smirked. "You realize she used a well-rehearsed approach to lure you like a big fat catfish?"

"I won't mind if you take the afternoon off and go on home." Sam escaped to his office, closed the door, and breathed in the lingering scent of Jenny's intoxicating perfume. He couldn't deny the fact that Mary had nailed the truth.

He dropped onto his chair. Now what? An apartment was out of the question. Maybe someone would rent her a room. He made a dozen calls. No takers. He had never let a client down, and he wasn't about to start now. Especially a beautiful woman who was counting on Gibson Realty. On him.

Sam drummed his fingers on the desk and racked his brain for a solution. Someone somewhere must have spare space to rent. He stopped tapping and stared at one of his grandpa's photographs. Was it possible? Sam grabbed his phone, dashed to his car, and drove four blocks. The moment he pulled onto the driveway beside his grandpa's two-story, white-columned home, mountains of doubt erupted. He stared at the detached double-car garage and second-guessed his scheme. Had he let his emotions override his common sense? Maybe he should have checked Jenny's references. Too late now.

He slid out and climbed the stairs to the two-room apartment serving as his family's dumping ground for discarded furniture and boxes of junk. Dust and cobwebs accentuated the musty odor in the main room anchored on one end by a small kitchenette.

"Are you looking for something particular?"

Sam whipped around toward his grandfather's deep voice laced with a southern drawl. "Hey, Grandpa."

"I remember the day your newlywed parents moved in here. Your grandma, God bless her soul, was thrilled to have her son and his bride living a few yards from our back door. No one's lived here since."

"Maybe it's time that changes." Sam sneezed.

His grandpa's brows raised. "What do you have in mind?"

"We have a new client who needs a reasonably priced apartment."

"Let me guess. She's one of our town's pretty young ladies who has her eyes fixed on winning you over?"

"She's a chef, new in town. I figure there's no use letting these rooms stay empty when they're prime to generate a bit of profit."

His grandpa's grin deepened the lines around his seventy-six-year-old blue eyes. "Appealing to my pragmatic nature, are you?"

"Is that a yes?"

"Do you trust her?"

"Lou hired her."

"That's good enough for me. When does the mystery lady want to move in?"

Sam swiped his hand across the dust-laden oak coffee table. "Tomorrow afternoon."

His grandpa brushed his fingers through his thick white hair. "Well now, since our newest client seems to have you wrapped around her little finger, we'd best start fixing up the place."

"I'm glad you're on board." Sam pulled down the stairs to the overhead attic. "We'll start by stashing everything she won't need up there."

"Good thing I'm taking the day off." His grandpa rolled up his sleeves and hoisted a box up to his shoulder.

Five hours, one pizza, and four beers later, grandfather and grandson stood in the middle of the main room and admired their work. "How much rent are you planning to charge?"

"I'll figure that out after she receives her first paycheck."

"A stranger without rent money." He clasped his hand on Sam's shoulder. "All I can say is this woman *must* be something special."

"She's a client, nothing more." The moment the words tumbled off his tongue, Sam suspected they sounded as insincere to his grandfather as they did to his own ears.

Chapter 3

Fifty dollars poorer, Jenny donned her white chef coat, pulled her hair into a ponytail, and checked out of the motel. One more night paying for a room would drain too much from her miniscule cash stash. If Sam didn't come through, she'd be forced to spend the night in her car. It wouldn't be the first time. She stuffed her duffel into the back seat, drove to Madison, and parked behind Lou's Coffee Shop.

After tucking her cutlery case under her arm, she climbed out and knocked on the door. A lock clicked. She stepped into the kitchen. The mouth-watering aroma of baking bread greeted her while classical music added an air of sophistication to the small, spotless, stainless-steel world. "You've obviously been here awhile."

Lou nodded. "Since three. Do you know how to make donuts?"

"In San Diego I worked in a breakfast diner that specialized in home-made donuts and pastries."

Lou pointed to the case Jenny set on the worktable. "What's in there?"

"My knives."

"You really are a pro. We'll need four dozen donuts."

"I'm on it." Jenny washed her hands and dove into her first assignment. As she shaped the dough—in her mind a far too mundane task for a professionally trained chef—she pictured the menu board she'd noticed on the wall opposite the front door. Best to wait a few weeks before convincing Lou to add new items. "Why the high-brow music?"

"I like it, and I don't cotton to idle chatter while baking. Too distract-ing."

"Sorry." Unaccustomed to silence in a professional kitchen, Jenny split her attention between accomplishing tasks and scrutinizing Lou's routine.

At least her new boss seemed to have mastered efficiency, and she didn't micromanage. For the moment, it appeared the job would work out. Until she found something better.

Five minutes before six, before the sun peeked over the horizon, the aroma of fresh-brewed coffee filled the air, and the tall glass cabinet behind the counter displayed an array of donuts and pastries. Lou switched the music to country pop and unlocked the front door. As if she'd flipped a switch, she transformed from laser-focused pastry chef to easygoing, coffee-shop hostess. "I can tell you know your stuff, Jenny."

"Thanks to a culinary degree and ten years of experience." Jenny exchanged her chef coat for a waitress apron and released her ponytail, letting her hair fall to her shoulders. "One of these days, I'll show you my portfolio."

"No need. I know I hired a pro." Lou held her wrist out and tapped her watch. "Our first customer is due in three, two, one—"

A middle-aged police officer strolled in and set his cap on the counter. "Morning, Lou."

"How's it going, Matt?" She poured a cup of coffee and plated a slice of coffee cake.

"Slow and easy."

"Meet my new assistant, Chef Jenny."

Matt eyed her and tipped his head. "Pleasure, ma'am."

She couldn't risk the law checking up on her driving record. Jenny pasted on her best smile. "The pleasure's all mine, Officer."

George breezed in and plopped beside Matt while two elderly men settled at a table beside the window. Jenny delivered two coffee-filled mugs to their table. "Good morning, gentlemen."

The taller of the two opened a sugar packet. "You're new in town."

"How sweet of you to notice. I'm Jenny."

"What brings you to Madison, Miss Jenny?"

"Friendly people. The small-town vibe."

"I don't know about the vibe thing, but our town's full of friendly folks."

"Just like you two handsome guys. What can I bring you?" Movement outside drew Jenny's attention. Sam. She held her breath.

He strolled in, caught her eye, and signaled a thumbs-up.

She released the air. Did his gesture mean he'd come through for her?

"—one with chocolate frosting."

Jenny blinked. "Pardon me?"

The shorter man grinned. "Seems Sam distracted our pretty waitress."

"He's my real-estate agent." She shifted her weight from one foot to the other. "About your order."

"One donut, chocolate covered. And one cinnamon bun."

"Coming right up." She scurried to the display cabinet while catching a glimpse of Sam settling at the end of the counter. Lou poured him a mug of coffee and struck up a conversation.

Before Jenny had a chance to question Sam, he finished his coffee and walked out, leaving her to speculate what his thumbs-up foretold. When her shift ended, she pocketed her tips and made a beeline to his office.

Mary greeted her. "Welcome back, Miss Collins. Mr. Gibson is waiting for you."

Sam sauntered from his office. "Right on time."

"From your expression, I'm guessing you found the perfect place for me."

"Gibson Realty aims to please."

"Especially pretty newcomers." Mary grinned as if relishing a scandalous secret.

"Our long-time receptionist has a tendency to think out loud way too often." Sam turned his attention to Jenny. "Where are you parked?"

"Behind Lou's."

"Instead of taking two cars, do you mind if I ride with you?"

"Depends on where we're going."

"To check out your new home."

Jenny slipped her hand around his muscular bicep as they strolled out to the sidewalk. "I'll be happy to act as your chauffeur, Mr. Excellent Realtor."

"Just plain Sam will do."

"On the way to my car, you should tell me all about this delightful little town, Just Plain Sam. Starting with the park across the street." Ten minutes later, Jenny turned onto a driveway and parked in front of a double-car garage.

Sam opened the passenger door. "The apartment upstairs is move-in ready."

"Furnished?"

"Not fancy, but comfortable." He scooted to the driver's side and opened the door.

She slid out and eyed a bicycle leaning against the stairs before climbing up to the stoop.

Sam followed close behind. "The door's unlocked."

Jenny stepped into the space warmed by a gentle breeze flowing from open windows on each end of the main room. She turned in a slow circle, drinking in every detail.

"You're welcome to paint the walls any color you choose."

She set her car keys on the glass-and-chrome end table beside a sofa upholstered in blue and white striped fabric. "I think soft yellow or maybe pale blue." Jenny pointed to a cut-glass vase filled with pink and yellow tulips centered on the oak coffee table. "Nice touch."

"From Grandpa's backyard."

Jenny moseyed to the kitchenette and ran her fingers along the Formica-topped dinette table. "Do your grandparents live in the big house?"

"Just Grandpa. Grandma passed on a few years back."

"Were they close?"

He hesitated. "Theirs was one of those rare love stories everyone dreams of, but few ever find."

A faraway look clouded Sam's eyes. Had this man, this stranger given her a momentary glimpse into his soul? "He must miss her terribly."

"He has a lifetime of memories to keep him company." Sam blinked as if returning from a private journey. "Anyway, this is his place."

The wide-plank wood floors creaked as she moved to the bedroom and eyed the double bed covered with white sheets and a blue blanket. A pine dresser and matching nightstand completed the arrangement. "How much rent is he expecting?"

"No charge the first month. Negotiable after your first paycheck."

"I'm not a charity case." Jenny opened the closet then peeked in the bathroom. "I intend to pay a fair-market price."

"I wouldn't expect anything less."

"It's perfect." She faced Sam and fluttered her eyelashes. "Would you mind helping me carry my things up?"

"Glad to."

"Is everything you own in that green car parked in my driveway?" The male voice drifted from the doorway.

Jenny spun around and faced the distinguished-looking man.

"Jenny, meet Paul Gibson, my grandfather and your new landlord."

She approached and offered her hand. "It's a pleasure to meet you, sir."

He sandwiched her hand between his. "Likewise, young lady."

"The answer to your question, Mr. Gibson, is yes. I've found that too many possessions tend to tie me down."

"Please, call me Paul." He released her hand. "I assume you've traveled around a good bit."

"Wherever opportunity takes me."

Sam nudged his grandpa's arm. "How about we help your new tenant move in."

"We're on it."

Jenny held the door open while Sam and Paul hauled a guitar case, picnic basket, suitcase, and duffel up the stairs.

"I think that's everything." Sam set the basket on the table. "For picnics?"

"That's one of the tools of my trade."

His brow pinched momentarily. "One of these days you can explain. For now, I suspect you want time to unpack."

"Do you want me to drive you back to your office?"

"It's only a few blocks from here. I'll walk."

"Thanks again for finding me this place, Sam, and for renting it, Paul. I'll find a way to thank you both."

After the men left, Jenny pulled her suitcase into the bedroom, hoisted it onto the bed, and stared at the blank walls. How long before her past reared its ugly head and forced her to flee from another town? Or worse, drove her to drink?

She forced the questions aside, opened the suitcase, and eyed her cherished chef portfolio. Validation of a successful career cooking for more than a dozen restaurants in five different cities during the last ten years. She fingered the sunflower adorning the cover before placing the treasure on the dresser. Her eyes drifted back to her suitcase and the framed photo—the only picture she possessed of her mother. A beautiful woman before the ravages of alcoholism stole her soul, diminished her beauty, and drove everyone who loved her away.

One of her mother's haunting declarations exploded in her head. "You're exactly like me, Jenny. Pretty on the outside, with a body meant to entice men. But weak and ugly on the inside. Doomed to a life of addiction and misery. Your sister is plain, like her old man. She'll fare far better than you." How many times had those words rolled off her mother's tongue after she'd guzzled a bottle of whiskey, gin, or vodka?

Jenny tossed the picture in the top drawer and covered it with a layer of clothes. Out of sight, out of her thoughts. After unpacking her clothes, she moseyed to the kitchenette, pleased to find enough dishes and basic cookware to prepare simple meals.

A bark sent her dashing to the window overlooking the driveway. Sam was sitting on the deck with his grandpa. A black Labrador retriever lay at Paul's feet. She loved dogs. The bigger the better.

After placing her guitar case and picnic basket on the floor beside an empty bookcase, Jenny dropped onto the sofa and propped her feet on the coffee table. Sam had come through for her big time. She closed her eyes and pictured him sitting at the dinette table, savoring her signature dish. Maybe they were destined to become more than friends. At least until she'd saved enough cash for another new beginning in another new town. Or until he discovered the ugly truth about her.

Chapter 4

S am parked in the lot behind Gibson Realty and climbed out of his late model Lexus as the first hint of dawn crept into Madison. His morning routine had begun five minutes earlier every day since Jenny moved into the garage apartment. If Lou noticed the subtle changes, she hadn't commented. At least not yet.

He unlocked the back door and switched on the lights to his office. The moment he stepped in, images of Jenny filled his head. Was her perfume still lingering or was his imagination on steroids? Maybe he should skip Lou's this morning and focus on work. Except his first appointment was two hours away, and he hadn't had his first cup of coffee.

Sam tossed his keys on the desk and dashed through the reception area to the front door. He covered the short distance to the coffee shop in record time and settled on his favorite stool at the end of the counter. "Morning, George, Matt."

"Fifth day in a row." George dug his fork into a cinnamon bun. "Keep this up and you'll arrive before Lou unlocks the front door."

So much for subtle moves. "Are you keeping a record of my arrival times?"

"Creatures of habit don't change routines without doggone good reasons."

Lou moseyed over and set a mug of steaming coffee on the counter in front of Sam. "Jenny made the coffee cake this morning. Want me to cut you a piece?"

"One of these days you should add a couple of healthy items to your sugar-laced menu."

"Is that a yes or a no?"

"Bring me half a slice." Sam's eyes shifted to Jenny carrying two mugs to the newest arrivals. Even with her back turned toward him, he could tell she was pouring on the charm.

Lou delivered Sam's coffee cake. "When you look past her brazen flirtation, it's easy to see she's a gem."

His eyes remained trained on Jenny. "Put the arrow back in your quiver, Cupid. I'm not in the market."

"Too late. It already hit its target."

"Your relationship antenna is way off base." Sam faced Lou. "I find Jenny interesting, nothing more."

"Of course, you do." She winked and moved to the other end of the counter.

Accustomed to Lou's not-so-subtle attempts to end his bachelorhood, Sam rolled his eyes and turned his attention back to Jenny. There was no denying she came across as an unabashed flirt. And yet, she performed her job with efficiency, paying equal attention to every customer. Based on her accent, she hailed from the south. But how did she end up in his backyard? And why did a stranger he knew nothing about stir his emotions like no other woman since his fiancée walked out on him?

George knuckle-thumped Sam's arm. "When are you gonna invite the pretty lady to dinner?"

"Are you and Lou co-conspirators now?"

"Jenny's fun to talk to and a real looker."

Lou returned to warm Sam's coffee. "George is right. Besides, you're over thirty and still unattached. It's not natural. My precious husband and I were married fifty-one years before he passed on. Best years of my life. You're missing out on the good life, Sam."

"Trust me, being single has its advantages."

"If you're not careful, other guys will snatch all the eligible gals right out from under you."

Sam lifted his mug. "Too bad *you're* not forty years younger."

"You're a good catch, honey, but you couldn't hold a candle to the love of my life."

"Matchmaker one minute, heartbreaker the next." Sam laughed, yet deep down he envied Lou. Like his grandpa, she had found her soulmate.

Three years ago, he believed he had found the perfect woman to settle down with and start a family. Until that doomed relationship cost him an expensive engagement ring, a ton of regret, and a boatload of humiliation.

Lou patted his arm. "Take my advice, Sam, and give love another chance."

Easy for her to say. Her heart hadn't been ripped from her chest and shredded. His attention shifted back to Jenny.

When she turned toward the counter, her eyes found his and lingered. She wandered over and placed her hand on his arm. "Good morning, Mr. Real-Estate Genius."

Sam ignored George's elbow nudge. "How's it going, Jenny?"

"Couldn't be better."

"That's a fact." Lou adjusted her glasses. "Customers are warming up to our gal better than butter on a hot biscuit."

Jenny brushed a lock of hair off her cheek. "Madison is full of friendly folks, most of them good tippers. I've decided to paint my apartment, Sam, to add some color."

"Good idea. Let me know if you need some help."

Jenny's smile evaporated as she pulled her hand off his arm. "Thanks, but I can handle it on my own." She spun around and walked away.

Had his offer to help insulted her or sent the wrong message about his intentions?

"This job is way less than she's accustomed to." Lou topped off Sam's coffee. "I hope another restaurant doesn't steal her away."

Sam noticed Jenny glancing at him over her shoulder. Why were women so confusing? "Maybe you should let her experiment with new menu items."

Lou leaned close. "Maybe you should invite Jenny to dinner."

"And maybe you should find another unattached guy to harass."

Lou winked and patted his arm. "Not as long as you're the best catch in town." She responded to a customer calling her from the other end of the counter and walked away.

Sam tuned into George and Matt's conversation about baseball while watching Jenny work the room. If he invited her to dinner, would she accept or turn him down? Maybe he should find out.

Chapter 5

Lou's comment about *our gal* echoed in Jenny's head. She suspected her boss fancied herself as Sam's one-woman dating service. Like either of them needed help in that department. Maybe Sam showing up earlier every morning for nearly a week had nothing to do with her. What about his offer to help paint? Did he think she couldn't handle the job on her own, or was it a ploy to spend time with her? And why had Sam's fiancée ditched him a month before their wedding? Should she invite him to dinner and find out?

Forget it. She needed to stay focused on recouping her savings. Maybe she shouldn't waste money on paint. Except living in a colorless apartment would stifle her creativity. Jenny approached newly arriving customers and stole another glance at Sam. His eyes no longer seemed to follow her. Maybe he wasn't a good candidate for a fling after all.

By the time noon rolled around, she was eager to capitalize on seven days of generous tips and a month's advance on her salary. After spending more than she'd planned on paint supplies and accessories, she drove to her apartment and hauled her purchases up the stairs.

Three hours later, she stood back and admired the room's transformation. Pale yellow walls. The painting she'd hung above the sofa was perfect—a white vase filled with sunflowers set against a blue background. Not bad for a second-hand Madison Market find. Now she could focus on saving money.

Jenny pulled two fives from her purse, opened her chef portfolio, and slid the cash into the next-to-last plastic sleeve. What about her canceled car insurance? She closed the portfolio, hoping the stab of guilt over a lifetime of misplaced priorities would pass. Except, after everything she'd suffered, didn't she deserve a living space that lifted her spirits? Besides, resolving the insurance issue would take a few more weeks of decent tips plus a new bank account. By that time, she'd find a local agent she could sweet-talk into ignoring her DUI and giving her a deal. In the meantime, perhaps she shouldn't risk driving uninsured.

Jenny poured a glass of orange juice and carried it to the front window. She could walk to work. It was safe enough in a small town. But slow and meant less sleep six mornings a week. As she stared at the driveway below, a memory resurfaced. An image crystalized. She set her glass on the coffee table and dashed down the stairs. The bike she'd spotted the day she'd moved in was missing. Jenny rounded the garage and found it leaning against the wall. A light attached to the handlebars. Perfect for predawn rides. She rolled the bike to the driveway and stared at the gears.

"Six months ago, my great-granddaughter replaced those two wheels with four." Paul strode across the deck with his black Labrador beside him.

"Your great-granddaughter?"

"My granddaughter's oldest child."

"If no one's using it, would you mind if I ride it to work?" What if he asked why a bike instead of her car? "I'd welcome the fresh air and exercise."

"The tires need air." Paul's dog followed him down the steps.

"She's a beauty. What's her name?"

"Duchess."

Jenny squatted and stroked the animal's back, setting her tail in motion. "Nice to meet you, Duchess."

"We raised her from a pup." Paul punched a number into a keypad. The garage door on the left lifted.

Jenny straightened and eyed a late-model convertible backed into the garage. "Nice car." She ran her fingers along the ornament attached to the grill.

"I bought it for my wife."

"You must have loved her a great deal."

"Best woman I've ever known. We celebrated our fifty-sixth anniversary two months before she passed on. Every year I loved her more than the last."

Jenny's bottom lip caught between her teeth. She couldn't imagine a more dramatic contrast to her parents' troubled relationship. Not to mention the toxic, so-called wisdom her mother spouted during some of her more lucid moments.

Forgive.

Jenny startled. "Pardon me?"

"I didn't say anything." Paul's voice drifted from the back of the garage.

Positive someone had spoken, Jenny pivoted and scanned the space around her. No one in sight. A soft breeze rustled the leaves shading the backyard. She smiled. It must have been the wind.

"Found them." Paul emerged from the garage carrying a hand-held air pump and a tire gauge. "This will fix her right up."

After inflating and testing the tires, he gripped the handlebars and raised the kickstand. "Want to take her for a test ride?"

"Good idea." Jenny climbed on, keeping her right foot planted on the driveway while she fingered the shifter.

"Have you ever ridden a seven-speed?"

Another childhood experience she'd missed—owning any kind of bike. "Can't say I have."

"It's easy. I'll show you."

His grandfatherly manner tugged on her heartstrings and quashed her tendency to revert to a well-rehearsed flirtatious response. If she'd had a loving grandfather, maybe he would have rescued her from her parents' madhouse.

"Ready to give it a try?"

"I think so." She lifted her foot, followed his instructions, and pedaled to the end of the driveway. A sense of adventure engulfed her as she turned right and rode by century-old homes, some identified with ornate signs displaying names and circa dates.

She marveled at the lush lawns and manicured shrubbery—a stark difference from her childhood home. Jenny stopped to admire a white picket fence, enhanced by a flowering vine lacing through the slats. A bumblebee flitted from one blossom to another. After she opened her own restaurant, she would buy a pretty house just like this with a big backyard. Maybe she'd even hire a gardener.

A woman walking her dog waved and wished her a pleasant afternoon. A driver approaching from the opposite direction smiled and nodded. Jenny continued exploring the neighborhood, enjoying every moment. When she returned to Paul's driveway, she found him in the backyard, tossing a ball to Duchess.

"Did you enjoy your ride?"

"I did. Thanks again for letting me use it."

"Glad I could help out."

Duchess returned the ball and dropped it at Jenny's feet. She scooped it off the ground and pitched it high. The dog raced ahead and caught it midair.

"Seems my dog has found another new friend."

"So have I."

"What do you think of our town so far?"

Jenny tossed the ball again. "Everyone seems friendly, and Lou's a sweetheart."

"She's a good woman to have in your corner."

They chatted about Madison until he removed the ringing phone from his belt clip and glanced at the screen. "I have to take this call. Why don't we continue our conversation tomorrow?"

"I'd like that." She gave Duchess one more head pat before climbing the stairs to her apartment. Eager to continue the transformation, she opened a can of pale-blue paint and carried it to the bedroom. When she finished the job, she turned in a slow circle surveying her handywork. One more week of tips, and she'd have enough money to buy a pre-paid credit card and use Lou's tablet to order a fancy bedspread and a couple of throw pillows. If she convinced Sam to keep her rent low, she could afford one more little luxury. After that, she'd begin a serious savings plan.

Chapter 6

Following hours of negotiation that forced him to skip his morning trek to Lou's, Sam attached an *Under Contract* sign to the *For Sale* sign in his client's front yard—a block from Jenny's apartment. Maybe he should stop by and check out her paint job. He glanced at his watch. Eleven-thirty. She was still at Lou's.

Back in his office, he pictured Jenny sitting in the chair across from his desk, with one shapely leg crossed over her knee. Her perfume lingering in the air. Why couldn't he go more than an hour without thinking of her? Somehow he had to focus on work.

Sam dropped onto his executive chair, booted his laptop, and opened his emails. After responding to urgent matters and deleting others, one subject line triggered a painful memory. His chest tightened as he opened his bottom desk drawer and removed a framed photo of his ex.

Six weeks before their wedding, Kathy had spent two weeks visiting a college friend in Atlanta. After returning to Madison, she'd seemed detached. Easily distracted. Who could blame him for suspecting she'd met another man. When he confronted her, she flew into a rage, claimed she'd grown bored with small-town life, and declared she needed new adventures. Two days later she left him a note apologizing and wishing him the best. Dozens of rumors surfaced after she moved out of her apartment. He refused to respond to innuendos and questions. Pride kept him from speaking of her to anyone except his grandpa. Maybe it was time to ditch the photo.

Startled by a sharp rap, he placed the photo facedown on his desk. "Come in."

His grandpa strolled in and settled on an easy chair. "Did you forget about our lunch meeting?"

Sam slapped his palm against his forehead. "With the mayor an hour ago."

"I called you. It went straight to voicemail."

He removed his phone from his belt clip. "It's still on airplane mode. I'm sorry."

"Not a problem. I covered for you." His grandpa hiked his ankle on his knee and eyed Sam. "Mind if I give you some advice?"

"About business?"

"Personal."

Sam placed his forearms on the desk and laced his fingers. "Shoot."

"It's time to forget the past and allow your heart to love again."

Despite the difference in their ages, Sam was closer to his grandfather than he was to his dad. They understood each other on a deep level. "All those months after Kathy broke our engagement—" He swallowed the thickness in his throat. "All the stares and pity."

His grandpa fingered his loafer. "A couple of weeks after your dad turned eighteen, he sat your grandmother and me down and asked to borrow money to buy an engagement ring for a girl he'd been dating since summer. They both planned to attend University of Georgia."

"Did you give him a loan?"

He shook his head. "We figured if he couldn't afford a ring, he wasn't ready to make a long-term commitment."

"Smart move."

"A month before their senior year ended, the girl broke up with him and announced she had accepted an offer to attend University of Florida."

Sam scoffed. "Georgia's number-one rival."

"Which stung that much more. Anyway, he spent most of that summer in his room sulking. Then halfway through his freshman year at UGA, he met your mother."

"Lucky for me and my sister."

"And your dad. What I'm trying to say is sometimes the best relationships are those least expected."

Sam stared at his grandpa for a long moment then unlaced his fingers and flipped the frame over. "Good thing Kathy's parents moved out of town last year. Keeps us from running into each other when she visits them." He yanked the picture from the frame and slid it across his desk. "I don't care what you do with it as long as I don't ever have to look at it again."

His grandpa lowered his leg and lifted the photo. "Bet she sold your ring, gained seventy pounds, and married a guy who ended up with a bulging beer belly."

Sam laughed. "Speaking of beer. How about we call it a day and head over to the Chophouse Grill for a brew."

"Great idea. I'll meet you out front in five."

"You're on." The moment his grandpa walked out, Sam tossed the empty frame in the trash and closed his desk drawer. Time to begin a new chapter. Maybe as early as tomorrow.

Chapter 7

Jenny dashed under the awning sheltering the coffee shop's back entrance and shook water from her umbrella. After wiping her feet on the mat, she walked into the kitchen.

Lou looked up from the stainless-steel worktable. "Real gully washer going on out there. Bet you didn't ride your bike."

"You've got that right." Jenny washed her hands while eyeing Lou. Maybe enough time had passed to voice her opinion. "I know you like to work without chatter, but I've been thinking."

"I wondered how long you'd take."

Jenny's eyes widened. "To do what?"

"Offer suggestions."

"You've been expecting me to speak up?"

"From the first day you stepped into my kitchen." Lou leaned back against the counter. "What's on your mind?"

Jenny wiped her hands with a paper towel. "While our donuts and cinnamon buns are delish and perfect for a coffee shop, they're way too predictable. Based on my experience, I'm confident a greater variety would spice things up and increase sales. I'm thinking quiche, served with banana or zucchini bread."

"Now you're a marketing expert as well as a chef?"

Another benefit of a pricey culinary degree. "We could add fresh fruit to please the eye."

"You're suggesting an item more akin to a diner than a coffee shop."

This would take some work. "We could start with two quiche options as daily specials. I predict we'll attract new customers, especially more ladies."

"You're persuasive." Lou swiped a towel across her forehead. "Before you leave for the day, write down everything you'll need."

"Are you giving me the go-ahead?"

"Honey, at my age I've settled into a comfortable routine. At the same time, I'm not too old to entertain new ideas."

"In that case, I also think—"

Lou aimed an open palm at Jenny. "Hang on to your chickens, sweetie. We'll start with the quiches tomorrow and see how it works out before we go jumping into something else. Right now, the clock is ticking."

"Got it." Pleased with her success, Jenny hummed along to a song she recognized. If Lou responded favorably to more of her creative ideas, maybe she'd stay put a bit longer. Besides, she enjoyed afternoons off to meet new people. Especially young men who could afford to buy her dinner. Like Sam. Why hadn't he asked her out? Maybe he preferred blondes. Or after his broken engagement, had he given up on dating?

The music playing in the background changed to a forlorn classical number, conjuring images of Jenny's mother, and sending her mood spiraling toward despair. She couldn't let the melody spoil her good mood. Her thoughts shifted to Duchess and the dog's late-afternoon routine. Her new pal pattering up her apartment stairs, barking once. Her tail slapping the floor as Jenny rewarded her with a treat. Dogs loved unconditionally.

Jenny carried a tray of donuts to the fryer as another song began. More upbeat, it lifted her spirits. She had to admit the atmosphere in Lou's kitchen was less hectic than most. Plus, working in a coffee shop provided one more important benefit. No booze to tempt her in the event a trigger aroused her urge to drink.

Forgive.

Startled, she spun around. Lou slid a third tray of cinnamon buns into the oven. This time Jenny blamed the sound on the exhaust fan and focused her attention on the task at hand.

When six A.M. rolled around, she half expected to walk into the dining room and find Sam waiting at the front door. Instead, he showed up at seven and settled on his favorite stool, a half-hour later than the day before.

Moments after he arrived, a pretty woman dressed in blue scrubs—her sandy blonde hair pulled into a ponytail—dashed inside and headed straight toward him.

Curious, Jenny moved within earshot.

The woman slid her arm around Sam's shoulders. "I knew I'd find you here."

"What brings you in?"

"Curiosity about the temptress who zips around town on a bike and has managed to wrap half the men in town around her little finger. You're wise to stay away from her."

Sam smirked. "When did you shift from ER doc to psychologist?"

The woman nudged George. "Do you mind?" She gestured toward a vacant stool halfway up the counter. "I need to talk to Sam."

George peered around her, grinning. "Be careful, Sam. She's fixing to lecture you on the perils of friendly women."

The woman planted her hands on her hips. "Well? Are you going to let me have that seat?"

"You're a pretty lady, Doc—" George clutched his cup and plate before sliding off the stool. "But way too bossy and opinionated for your own good."

Jenny suppressed a giggle.

Sam laughed. "Good one, George."

"He's old and out of touch." The woman hiked her hips onto the vacated stool. "You need to listen to me, Sam. That woman is a boatload of bad news."

Jenny squared her shoulders and moved toward the end of the counter.

Sam grabbed the doctor's arm. "She's headed our way. Why don't you tell her face-to-face?"

The woman's head jerked around.

Jenny stepped between her and Sam and eyed the woman from head to toe. "Who's the pretty lady who chased poor old George off his stool, Sam?"

"Meet my sister, Dr. Sandra White."

His sister? Interesting. "I see the resemblance. Except your hair is a bit darker than your brother's and your eyes more green than blue."

"She's also five years older than me and under the delusion she's the smart sibling and knows what's best for me."

"Funny." Jenny's lips curved into a bemused grin. "My older sister suffers from the same delusion."

Sam burst out laughing. "That comment deserves a reward. How about dinner? Tonight."

Jenny touched his shoulder and batted her lashes. "Why, Sam, I thought you'd never ask little ole me for a date." She offered her best Scarlet O'Hara imitation. "I'm simply dying to try the Madison Chop House Grille."

"Glad to oblige." He placed his hand over hers. "I'll pick you up at six."

"Until tonight." She squeezed his shoulder.

Sam cleared his throat and released her hand.

Jenny faced his sister. "It's a pleasure to meet another member of the Gibson clan. Please tell your daughter her bike is coming in handy." She winked at Sam before stepping away but lingered to catch the doc's reaction.

Sandra knuckle-thumped her brother's arm. "You asked her out to spite me."

"You're overreacting, sis, and it's one date not a lifetime commitment."

"Maybe so." She waggled her finger at Sam. "When she breaks your heart, don't say I didn't warn you."

Lou wandered over. "Morning, Sandra. Would you like a cup of coffee?"

"No thanks. I'm due at the hospital." Sandra eyed Sam. "We'll continue this conversation later."

"Don't hold your breath."

Sandra slid off the stool and tramped to the door.

Lou refreshed Sam's coffee. "Good for her prodding you to make a move."

"You have hearing like a bat."

"Honey, everyone within earshot heard your little drama play out."

George tipped his cup and moved back to his stool. "Good going, Sam. Lou and I will look forward to an update tomorrow morning."

Sam pulled a ten-dollar bill from his wallet and set it on the counter. "Keep the change, Lou. You'll need it when someone sues you for eavesdropping."

"I'll pay my attorney in donuts and sweet talk I'm learning from our gal." Lou planted her hands on her hips. "And what happened to young folks respecting their elders?"

Jenny suppressed another laugh.

Sam stuffed his wallet in his back pocket and saluted.

Jenny kept her eyes glued on him as he headed to the door. Outside, he paused, faced the window, and smiled.

Her breath caught as a memory of an incident she struggled to keep buried escaped and sent a shiver racing up her spine. A stark reminder why she couldn't let herself fall in love. Not now. Not ever.

Chapter 8

Jenny stared at her image in the bathroom mirror—her bangs brushing her brows, her hair tucked behind her right ear. She stepped back, bringing the tight-fitting, low-cut, sleeveless bodice into view. Maybe the dress was too revealing for a first date. She returned to her bedroom and flung the closet open. Not much to choose from.

A knock drew her attention. She closed the closet and squared her shoulders. The dress would have to do. Her three-inch heels clicked on the wood floor as she rushed to the front door. "Are all real estate agents punctual?"

"This one is. First time I've seen you in a dress." Sam's eyes drifted down her body then back to her face. "Guess I should have worn a tie."

Maybe he wasn't different from every other guy she'd dated. She batted her lashes while touching his shirt's open collar and letting her fingers brush his neck. "The casual look works for you."

He gripped her wrist. "That approach might work for other men, but not for me."

Heat crept up her neck and warmed her cheeks. Had she overreacted? "If that's true, I suggest you keep your eyes focused above my neck."

"Good point. Why don't we start over?"

Maybe she'd misjudged him. "Fair enough."

He released her wrist. "You're lovely in red."

"Thank you. I love your casual attire. It's perfect for dinner between friends."

"I'm glad you approve." He held his arm out. "Shall we?"

She grasped his bicep as they descended the stairs. When he opened his car's passenger door, Jenny started a mental list of his attributes, beginning with gentleman. She slid onto the tan leather seat and waited for him to round the front of the car and scoot in beside her. "Nice ride."

"This is my office on wheels." He backed into the street. "Madison Chop House is one of my favorites. It's known for great steaks."

Jenny glanced at his profile while fighting the urge to run her fingers through his thick hair. "Are you a meat-and-potatoes kind of guy?"

"Hardly."

"I thought...I mean, since you mentioned steak—"

Sam chuckled. "First time I've invited a chef to dinner."

"Seems we're even. I've never dated...I mean, dined with a real-estate agent."

"I reserved a table on the patio." He turned onto Main Street. "If you prefer, we can eat inside."

"It's a perfect night for alfresco dining."

"Are you sure?"

"Positive." She paused. "Your sister is an interesting woman."

"She's more like a mother hen than a sister. What about you? Brothers? Other sisters?"

"Just my sister, Jill. She lives on the West Coast." Jenny turned her attention to the passing scenery. "We haven't seen each other in years."

"Do you miss her?"

"We're not close."

"I suppose that has its advantages." Sam turned right and parked behind the restaurant, then circled to the passenger side. He placed his hand on Jenny's back while escorting her to a table under an umbrella beside a manicured hedge. "The best view is across the street." He pulled out a chair facing Main.

She sat and eyed the white frame house featuring covered verandas stretching across the first and second stories. "The Dovecote House, part of the Antebellum Trail."

He settled across from her. "You've learned a few things about my town."

"It's easier to pay attention from a bike than a car."

Their waitress walked out from a side door. "Hey, Sam."

"How's life treating you, Nancy?"

"Couldn't be better." She tucked menus under her arm and lit a candle nestled in a glass container.

"Meet my new friend, Jenny Collins."

The young woman eyed her. "I hear you're an experienced chef."

"Word spreads fast."

"It's a small town. How's Lou holding up?" Nancy handed Jenny a menu. "You know she's getting up in years."

"No need for anyone to worry about her. She's as spry as a young pup."

"One of these days, she'll need someone to take on more responsibility. Maybe that's why she hired you. Can I start you out with something to drink? A glass of wine, or maybe Sam's favorite beer?"

If she said no, would she raise Sam's suspicions? Or keep him from ordering what he wanted? Maybe she could handle one glass of wine. If she sipped through dinner. Who was she kidding? One glass could destroy everything she had going. "Iced tea for me. Sweet."

Nancy made a note. "How about you, Sam?"

"I'll take a beer."

"Coming right up."

A man with a mind of his own. Another positive. Jenny reached for her menu and focused on the appetizers. "Do you eat here often?"

"Couple times a month with friends. Sometimes lunch with out-of-town clients."

"Do you get a lot of those? Out-of-towners, I mean."

"A fair amount."

Which was she? A friend? A client? A hot date? "I'm curious." She looked up. "Did you invite me to dinner to annoy your sister?"

"Do you think I needed an excuse?"

Jenny shrugged. "That's why I asked."

"How about you? Did you accept to prove you're not easily intimidated?"

"Hmm." How should she respond? "Seems Sandra prodded both of us."

"I'm not complaining."

Jenny tilted her head. "Neither am I."

"With my sister's questionable influence out of the way, we can relax and move on to dinner." Sam plucked his menu off the table. "Starting with what to order."

Jenny stared at him for a long moment. "You're an interesting man, Sam Gibson."

He caught her eye and laughed. "Of all the descriptions a beautiful, mysterious woman wearing red could choose, she goes with 'interesting'?"

A sense of humor, another quality to add to her list. "Maybe by the end of the evening, I'll come up with a phrase more to your liking."

"I'll do my best to give you something to work with."

"I'm counting on it."

A small boy walking across the side street with a young woman stepped onto the sidewalk. "There's Sam, Mommy." He scooted to the table and climbed onto Sam's lap.

"Hey, Billie." Sam tousled his hair. "Jenny, meet my neighbor and the best four-year-old pal a guy ever had."

Billie eyed Jenny. "Does she play catch?"

"Now, that's a good question. Do you, Ms. Jenny?"

Before she could respond, the woman lifted Billie off Sam's lap. "Sorry for the disruption. We haven't seen you in a couple of days."

Sam winked at Billie. "Tomorrow afternoon we'll toss a ball around. Afterwards, if your mom approves, we'll splurge on hamburgers and milkshakes."

The boy's eyes widened. "Can we, Mommy?"

"Of course." She mouthed thank you, before leading her son back to the sidewalk.

Jenny leaned back and folded her hands in her lap. "Are you crazy about all little kids or just Billie?"

"Especially him. His dad is deployed to the Middle East. I'm filling his shoes until he returns."

"Billie's mother is gorgeous. I imagine she's lonely and plenty grateful for your attention."

Sam's eyes narrowed. "What are you insinuating?"

"Don't get all bent out of shape. I'm just saying she's lucky you care."

Nancy breezed out and set their drinks on the table. Her eyes darted from one to the other. "Have y'all decided what you want to order?"

"Have we decided, Jenny?"

His stern tone caught her off guard. Was he struggling with a guilty conscious, or had she crossed a line? She blinked. "What are you ordering, Sam?"

"Prime rib. With a house salad to start. Honey mustard."

Jenny pushed her menu aside. "Make it two. Bleu cheese for me."

"Good choice." Nancy collected the menus and headed back inside.

Sam's eyes probed Jenny's face, then softened. "Are you a meat-and-potatoes kind of gal?"

Change of subject. Good. "When the mood strikes."

He took a sip of beer. "How long have you been a chef?"

"Officially or unofficially?"

"Both."

How much should she tell him? "Way back in my grade-school days, my sister and I often had to fix dinner."

"Working mother?"

More like worked over. "Not exactly. Anyway, we learned how to create meals from whatever ingredients we managed to find on hand. That's how I discovered a natural talent. When my sister graduated high school and moved out, the kitchen became my refuge." Afraid the floodgate would open and allow too much information to gush out, she swallowed the words sitting on the tip of her tongue. "What about you? How did you end up in real estate?"

"Guess it's in my genes. Except they skipped a generation. My dad's a retired attorney. A while back, he and Mom left Madison and bought a house on Lake Oconee."

"Did you ever have a hankering to live in a big city?"

"One time. For a moment." He crossed his arms on the table. "After I graduated UGA—Go Dawgs—Grandpa offered me a partnership."

Good-looking and smart. "I suppose returning to your hometown has certain advantages."

"Sometimes. Are you a city girl?"

"Sort of. I grew up in an Atlanta suburb and graduated from high school thirteen years ago. My parents still live in the same house."

"Which makes Madison close enough to visit."

Not unless someone held a gun to her head and forced her to go. "What do you do for fun?"

"I play a little tennis, and I'm remodeling the house I bought a few years back."

"One of the historic homes?"

Sam nodded. "It's a couple blocks from Grandpa's."

Nancy arrived with their salads. "Bleu cheese for the lady, honey mustard for the gent. Enjoy."

Jenny reached for her fork. Her hand froze halfway to her plate as she noticed Sam's eyes closed, his head tilted down a fraction. Was he praying?

He looked up. "Bon appétit."

"Are you a religious kind of guy?"

"Family habit. Grace before digging in."

"Why?" She shot him a droll look. "Afraid someone might poison your food?"

"That's a pessimistic perspective on faith."

"My parents didn't buy into the whole church-going routine." She winced. Why hadn't she swallowed the comment before allowing it to escape? "Sorry. Sometimes my vocal filter goes all haywire."

"The same description you tagged me with applies to you." His lips curled into a grin. "You're an interesting woman, Jenny Collins."

She stabbed a piece of lettuce. "Now we're both charged to come up with more intriguing adjectives."

"I'm working on it."

During dinner Jenny enlightened Sam on the finer points of her profession. He entertained her with stories about growing up in a small town. While sharing dessert, their forks touched, sending a tingle through her fingers and heat to her cheeks. She pulled her fork away, hoping he hadn't notice her not-so-subtle reaction. "How did you end up buying the house you're living in now?"

"I'd always admired the style and its history. When it hit the market, I grabbed it."

"What's it like?"

"I'll show you as soon as you finish the last bite."

After she swallowed the last forkful of cake, Sam motioned to Nancy. She laid the check on the table. "I hope you enjoyed your first meal at our restaurant, Jenny."

"Delicious. Please give my compliments to the chef."

Sam removed bills from his wallet and handed them to Nancy. "No change needed."

Nancy's face lit with a smile. "Thank you. One of these days you'll make a great catch for some lucky lady."

"Too late, you're already married." He grinned and scooted his chair away from the table.

Jenny swiped her napkin across her lips, while adding *Generous* to her list.

After escorting her to his car, Sam drove a short distance and stopped in front of a two-story home. Landscape lighting cast a warm glow on the siding painted a warm shade of gray. Black shutters accented rows of tall windows. A white picket fence enclosed the corner lot's side yard.

"I've ridden by and admired your home more than once."

"One of these days, if you'd like I'll give you a tour."

"Maybe some Saturday afternoon." She yawned. "Since Sunday mornings I don't have to wake up before the chickens."

"It's a date."

They fell silent until he parked beside Jenny's car. He followed her up the stairs and paused outside her door.

She turned toward him. "Thank you for dinner."

"One last question before I leave. Have you come up with a description more exciting than 'interesting'?"

Her gaze caught his. "How about charming?"

"That works." He touched her arm. "And you are one fascinating woman."

Expecting a kiss, Jenny closed her eyes.

His breath brushed her face like a warm breeze, releasing the delicious lure of anticipation.

"Good night, Jenny." He moved away before his lips touched hers. "I'll see you at Lou's tomorrow morning."

Her heart leapt to her throat. She opened her eyes and waited for him to descend the stairs, then whispered, "Good night, Sam."

Chapter 9

I t took mountains of discipline for Sam to resist dashing back to the landing, drawing Jenny into his arms, and kissing her. The way she looked drop-dead gorgeous in red. At the bottom step, he turned to catch one more glimpse. She'd already gone inside. "Sweet dreams, Jenny." He strode toward his car.

"Join me for a brandy, Sam." His grandpa's voice drifted from the deck.

Sam pocketed his keys, climbed onto the deck, and dropped onto a chair. He glanced at the apartment window, disappointed to see darkness. Duchess planted her muzzle in his lap, inviting a head scratching.

Moonbeams lit his grandpa's shadowy figure as he pushed a snifter across the glass-top table. "How'd your date go?"

"My sister called you, didn't she?"

"Sandra's a caring woman."

"She's more like a meddling nuisance." Light from Jenny's bedroom window flicked on. Was she thinking about him? She'd closed her eyes, expecting a kiss. Maybe she longed to embrace him as much as he ached to hold her.

"Fifty-plus years in real estate has equipped me to read people." His grandpa sipped his brandy. "I've spent some interesting afternoons becoming acquainted with our new tenant."

"I assume you've formed an opinion about her."

"Underneath her charm she's a troubled young woman, carrying a heavy burden on her shoulders."

Jenny's earlier comments about her sister drifted up. "An unhappy childhood?"

"Perhaps in part. I suspect her pain goes much deeper."

The bedroom light extinguished. Sam held his snifter in both hands. "Is this your way of telling me to stay away from her?"

"That depends."

"On what?"

"How much you care about her."

He had no idea how to explain his feelings for Jenny to himself, much less to someone else.

"I remember the first day I laid eyes on your grandma—three weeks after her family moved to town and a week after she celebrated her sixteenth birthday. She was the most beautiful girl I'd ever seen. It sounds corny, but at that moment I knew we were destined to be together for the rest of our lives." He paused. "Your silence speaks volumes, Sam."

"A couple of weeks ago Jenny walked into my life. Broke, and based on your observation, probably broken. Now, she's never more than a thought away. There's something about her."

"When an overwhelming connection between two people happens—one that changes everything—it's important to pay attention."

"She's complicated."

His grandpa set his snifter on the table. "In a way, we all are."

"She's the most blatant flirt I've ever met."

"Most likely self-preservation."

"She's opinionated. Smart." Sam sighed heavily. "Deeper than other women I've known. Yet more vulnerable."

"You'd have to fight for her and break down the wall she's built around herself."

Sam caught a glimpse of his grandpa's expression. His mentor understood better than anyone the damage his fiancée had inflicted.

"You're a good man, Sam. Compassionate. Perhaps Jenny's feet were set on a path leading to the man worthy of her love."

He peered at the dark bedroom window. "Maybe she wants to rent on a month-to-month basis because she doesn't plan to stick around long."

"Give her a reason to stay."

"One dinner, and we're talking about a relationship with a mysterious woman, possibly weighed down with a truckload of baggage."

Grandpa clasped his hand on his grandson's arm. "Chances are she'll break your heart before she understands how much she needs you."

Sam swirled his brandy and stared at the spinning liquid. Maybe he should forget about Jenny and begin dating local women again. His gaze shifted to the bedroom window, now open a crack. Had she heard their conversation? What if his grandfather was right? That divine intervention led her into his life. Only one way to find out. Jump in with both feet. But could he risk another broken heart?

Jenny wandered to the window in her dark bedroom, cracked it open, and breathed in the fresh, cool air. Male voices, too muted to make out the words, drifted from below. Sam's car remained in the driveway. Her eyes shifted to the deck where two shadowy figures sat at the glass-top table. The surface glistened in the moonlight. Had Paul warned his grandson to stay away from her? Impossible. She and Paul had become friends. That didn't matter. Sam was family.

Her mother's warning—uttered countless times over the years—exploded in Jenny's head. 'If you never learn anything else from me, learn this one truth. Men are all the same. They use beautiful women for their own gratification before throwing them to the curb like yesterday's garbage. Or worse. Control them like possessions they're too terrified to lose.'

Sam seemed different. Same thing she'd believed about Max until he proved her wrong. And Tony, the wealthy Los Angeles chef, who'd promoted her to sous-chef for Chez Lemaire—his fine-dining restaurant raved about by all the important people in town. She'd used her southern charm and playful seduction to initiate an affair and move into his luxury apartment. Free room and board. Friends with benefits. Until a well-heeled, well-connected brunette worth millions replaced her. At least his review of her culinary talent held a prominent place in her portfolio and landed her more than one premier position.

What would a fling with Sam do for her, other than tag her as a big-city, wanton woman taking advantage of a small-town guy? "You're right,

Mother." She spat *mother* as if it were foul-tasting medicine acting as flesh-eating acid on her tongue. "I can't let men come too close."

Jenny moved away from the window and slid into bed between the cool sheets. Somehow, she had to find the will to resist anything other than a short-term fling with the town's most eligible bachelor.

Chapter 10

By eight-fifteen, Jenny's bacon and cheddar quiche had sold out, five male customers had sampled her new dish, and her tip income had increased. Despite the successes, another glance at the empty stool anchoring the end of the counter drove her exuberance and pride down a notch. The morning after their first date, and Sam hadn't bothered to show up. Had she said something that turned him off? Why hadn't he kissed her? Maybe dinner had never been a date in the first place.

"Lou's getting kind of fancy with her menu."

"Time for you to find a way out of your rut, George." Jenny refilled his coffee mug. "Tomorrow, I'll save a slice of quiche for you."

"Don't bother. I'd confuse the dickens out of my stomach if I switched from cinnamon buns to some strange kind of pie baked without sugar and fruit and served without a scoop of ice cream."

"One of these days, I'll inspire you to step out of your dietary-comfort zone."

"When it snows on the Fourth of July." He stirred sugar into his coffee. "How'd your date with Sam go?"

"Leave our gal be." Lou set a cinnamon bun on the counter and nodded toward the empty stool.

Jenny couldn't let Sam's absence give George, or any other busybody, the idea she couldn't hit it off with the most eligible bachelor in town. "We had a lovely time and shared a dessert." Her comments spilled out with too much volume and enthusiasm. "He probably slept in this morning, after the late night and all."

Half the folks sitting at the counter stared at her, sending heat crawling up her neck. Was she trying to tag herself as an easy mark? "What I mean is, after we said goodnight at my door—before ten, mind you—he and his grandpa talked on his deck for a long while."

Lou wiped a spill off the counter. "Everyone knows those two gents could carry on about business into the wee hours." Lou nudged Jenny. "Mrs. Perkins is motioning for you, honey."

Grateful for the rescue, Jenny turned away from prying eyes and scooted from behind the counter. "Good morning, you two lovebirds."

Mr. Perkins grinned. "We saw Sam out early this morning, showing a couple the house across the street from us. He's a hardworking young man."

So, that's what kept him from showing up. "Would you like your usual?"

Mrs. Perkins nodded toward the menu board. "I'd love a slice of quiche."

"I'm afraid it's all gone. I'll save you a piece tomorrow morning."

"In that case, we'll take coffee and muffins."

"Coming right up." Jenny returned to the counter, eager to set everyone straight. "You seem to have a handle on everything that goes on around town, George. Any chance you know the couple Sam's showing listings to this morning?"

"Why would I...oh." George's brows shot up as if a light bulb suddenly flicked on. "Whoever they are, they kept him from stopping by for his caffeine fix."

Jenny leaned close. "You catch on fast."

"Glad to oblige."

Thankful for the Perkins' revelation, she delivered their coffee and muffins. "On the house to make up for running out of quiche."

At noon, Jenny flipped the open sign to closed then moseyed to the counter and settled on Sam's stool.

Lou poured herself a cup of coffee. "Banner morning, thanks to your newfangled pie without sugar."

"You've gotta love George's description."

"He's been a close friend as far back as I can remember. He was even god-father to our daughter." Lou slid onto the stool George had abandoned.

"I didn't know you had children."

"Just the one. Sara's a big-time corporate executive. She lives in Texas, and travels all over the world. Unfortunately, she's too ambitious to settle down and start a family. In her opinion, her dad and I wasted our time and talent staying in our hometown. Don't get me wrong, I love her dearly, and I'm proud of everything she's accomplished. We simply have different ideas about success."

"Why only one child?"

"When we first married, we planned to raise a big family. Three or four kids." Her chin tilted down. "For eighteen years I tried to get pregnant. I was pushing forty by the time we got lucky. Seems Sara was the only child we were meant to bring into this world."

Jenny's jaw clenched as she gripped her coffee cup and glared at the mocha-colored liquid. How unfair Lou couldn't have more than one child, while her mother who didn't deserve any gave birth to two.

"Do you want to talk about it?"

Jenny blinked. "About what?"

"The pain you keep bottled up inside."

Could Lou read her mind? "What makes you think I'm hiding something?"

"Honey, managing a coffee shop is akin to bartending. Folks talk. I listen and observe."

Jenny breathed in the sweet aromas lingering around her. "Does your daughter have any idea how fortunate she is to have you as a mother?"

"I suppose she does. Every time she returns to visit, we spend hours reminiscing. What about you and your mom? What memories do you share when you're together?"

"Do you really want to know the truth?" Jenny's nostrils flared. Her right hand curled into a fist. "About my rotten excuse of a mother who's an incurable drunk? Whose greatest talent is verbally abusing her daughters? And my father, her dedicated enabler, who keeps her supplied with endless bottles of booze?"

Lou placed her hand on Jenny's arm, her eyes filled with compassion. "I'm sorry."

Jenny's hand uncurled. "My sister Jill worked part-time all during high school to save enough money to flee to the West Coast and escape the madness. The day after she graduated, she left me—a fourteen-year-old—alone to fend for myself."

"It's tragic how addiction rips families apart."

"Now you know everything there is to know about my ugly past." Fearing tears were on the verge of erupting and exposing the lie, Jenny squared her shoulders and held her head high. "What's done is done. No use dwelling on it. About the quiche experiment, next week I'm thinking broccoli and ham with zucchini bread."

"Sounds like a winner." Lou pulled her hand away, humming as she cleaned the countertop.

Jenny stared at the woman, who in a few weeks had become more of a mother than the woman who brought her into the world. She cringed at the idea of Lou or Sam discovering the truth about the curse she carried in her genes, or the incident that had changed her life forever. She retreated to the kitchen aiming to scrub the surfaces and her soul clean.

Chapter 11

S am glanced at his watch. One-thirty. After hours of negotiation, he managed to convince the seller to offer his clients an acceptable price. He mentally kicked himself for failing to ask for Jenny's phone number. Not showing up the morning after their first date likely sent the wrong message. No use calling Lou. She bragged about leaving her phone in the kitchen, claiming modern technology disrupted her chats with friends. After signing papers and scheduling a closing date, he escorted his clients from his office to the front door.

"I've been dying to find out about your dinner with Jenny." Mary's cheery tone oozed with curiosity.

He stared at her. "How'd you know...my sister, right?"

"If you ask me, Sandra is too much of a mother hen and a worry wart. I always say, 'let love lead where it wants to go.'"

"You're jumping to conclusions—"

"Who do you think you're kidding?" Mary tapped her finger on her desk. "You've been a nervous wreck all morning."

"Working to negotiate a deal—"

"And missing your visit to Lou's."

"Now you're a mind reader as well as a receptionist?" He dug his keys from his pocket. "I'm out of here."

"When you find Jenny, tell her hi."

"What is it with you women?" He dashed from the reception area before Mary could respond. On his way to the back door, he stopped at his grandpa's office. "I closed the deal and am taking the rest of the day off."

"Good going, Sam." He looked up from his desk and winked. "Jenny's probably heading home by now."

No point denying his intentions to the man who could see into his soul. Sam dashed out and climbed into his car. After cruising through town without spotting Jenny, he drove to the garage apartment and found her bike propped against the staircase. Now what? A glance at the living room window showed her motioning him up. *There's my answer.* He cut the engine and climbed the stairs two at a time.

She met him at the door. "Did you sell the house? The Perkins clued me in."

"It took a while, but yeah."

"Come on in, Mr. Real-Estate Mastermind, and see what I've done to the place."

Sam stepped inside and eyed two sunflower-embellished throw pillows on the sofa and a photo album held center stage on the coffee table. He pointed to the painting on the wall above the sofa. "I'm guessing sunflowers are your favorite."

"They are such interesting forces of nature, don't you think? The way the petals turn to follow the sun."

"Nice choice of paint."

"Yellow is a cheery color, like a little bit of sunshine. Have a seat and I'll bring you a glass of lemonade."

"Thanks." He settled on the sofa and eyed the guitar case and picnic basket sitting on the floor beside the bookcase. "How long have you been playing?"

"Since my friends chipped in and bought the guitar for my sixteenth birthday. It's a Gibson." She handed him a glass and set hers on a sunflower coaster.

"Nice friends."

"Along with my knives, it's one of the three possessions I never leave behind."

Sam's eyes widened. "Knives?"

Jenny giggled. "Chef tools, not weapons." She pointed to the picnic basket. "That's number two."

"Another tool of your trade?"

"You remembered. I suppose you could call it my briefcase. I fill it with samples whenever I interview for a job." She tapped her portfolio. "That along with this has opened a lot of kitchen doors."

"So, it's not a photo album?"

"Even better. It's a record of my professional experience and accomplishments."

Sam opened the cover to a culinary-institute diploma inserted in the first sleeve. He flipped through pages displaying recommendation letters, notes from diners, newspaper articles, and photographs of Jenny posing with chefs. "You're obviously way overqualified for the coffee shop."

"Give me a little more time, and I'll convince Lou to expand and offer lunch."

"That'll take some doing."

"Maybe not as much as you think." Jenny flipped past empty sleeves and tapped the handwritten note inserted into the last plastic sleeve. "That's my dream."

"Reserved for Jenny's Place."

"One of these days, I'll become the executive chef in my own restaurant." She pointed to the bills in the adjacent sleeve. "Savings toward the down payment."

"I have no doubt you'll succeed." He set his glass on the other coaster and nodded toward the bookcase, empty except for the cut-glass vase he'd placed on the coffee table the day he and his grandpa cleaned the apartment. "Looks like you could use some items to fill those shelves. If you're not too particular, I can help."

"What do you have in mind?"

"You'll see." He moved to the center of the room, lowered a pull-down ladder, and climbed into the attic. Moments later he climbed down with a large box balanced on his shoulder. "You're welcome to take anything that appeals to you."

"I suppose the vase could use some company." She lifted the lid, revealing items wrapped in newspaper. "This is like Christmas without fancy wrapping paper."

He settled on the sofa, enjoying her squeal with each new discovery. An hour later she finished arranging her newfound treasures and stood in front of the bookcase. "What do you think?"

"You should add decorating to your list of talents."

"All it needs now is some fancy books."

"What do you like to read?"

She shrugged. "I'm not particular. What about you?"

"Mostly suspense novels and thrillers. Although I have read a few of the classics." He snapped his fingers. "I have a great idea. Let's ride over to the Madison Market and find you a couple to display, maybe even read."

"I love that place. It's where I found the painting and throw pillows."

"In that case, we'll make our second date a shopping trip."

"You're an interesting man, Sam." Jenny picked up the glasses off the coffee table.

"Uh-oh, you're back to that bland description."

"You do know the word has more than one meaning." She carried the glasses to the sink.

"I'll accept your explanation as acknowledgement that I'm not a total disappointment."

"Are you fishing for a compliment?"

"Yeah, how am I doing?"

"I'll let you know after our shopping trip." She shouldered her purse. "Shall we?"

He bowed. "Your chauffeur awaits, Miss Collins."

"All you need is a cute little cap and a bow tie."

"Cap maybe." He held her elbow as they moved down the stairs. "Bow tie? No way."

When they arrived at the market, Jenny climbed out the moment he braked and dashed to the entrance. Sam caught up with her and followed her inside. As she bounced among the treasures, delighting in everything she saw like a child during her first visit to a toy store, more questions sprang up in his mind. Who was this woman who had arrived in town broke with few possessions? What had happened in Jenny's past? How much pain had she suffered?

Following two hours of chattering and cooing over merchandise, she selected three leather-bound books. "How about these?"

"Hmm, *The Scarlet Letter, Huckleberry Finn,* and *Great Expectations.* Excellent choices."

"They look expensive and classy."

"They're classics."

She huffed. "I know."

"I didn't mean to insult you."

"You didn't." She tapped *Great Expectations.* "I'll read this one first."

"Good choice." After Sam paid for the books and drove back to her apartment, Jenny raced up the stairs.

He followed and stood beside her while she placed her new treasures on the shelf beside two crystal candlesticks.

"This is the first time a man has given me gifts worth keeping." She stood on her toes and kissed his cheek. "To show my appreciation, tomorrow night I'll serve you my two signature dishes."

Battling the desire to pull her into his arms, he brushed his fingers through his hair. "Want me to bring a bottle of wine?"

"White. But only if you want some. I'll stick with tea."

"In that case, I'll bring beer. How about one more small gesture to thank me?"

Her brows furrowed.

"Perfectly innocent. Exchange phone numbers, in the event something comes up."

"Great idea."

After adding her number, he clipped his phone to his belt. If he stayed longer, he feared giving in to his desire to kiss her. "Time to head home."

"Oh." The hint of a frown clouded her face. "Thanks again for the books."

"You're welcome." He headed to the door. "I'm meeting with a potential client at Lake Oconee early tomorrow, which means I'll miss coffee at Lou's."

"Guess I'll need to fill you in on local news during dinner. Say around five?"

"I'm counting on it." He walked out and descended the stairs hoping he had come one step closer to understanding Jenny and discovering if their paths were meant to cross.

Chapter 12

Jenny counted her tips and dropped the cash in her purse before hanging her apron on a hook in Lou's kitchen. "Another profitable morning."

"Thanks in part to your ingenuity." Lou pressed the dishwasher start button. "Sam missed two days in a row. A good sign real estate is booming."

No point keeping her invitation to Sam a secret. Lou would find a way to coax it out of him. "I'm preparing dinner for him tonight."

"You two make a sweet couple."

"He's a friend." Maybe someday with benefits. The idea of a secret romance with the town's most eligible bachelor both terrified and enthralled her.

"Deep love often begins with friendship."

"So I've heard." Jenny headed to the back door. "I'll see you tomorrow morning."

"Enjoy the evening with your 'friend.'"

Jenny rolled her eyes, stepped out back, and donned her sunglasses before climbing onto her bike and pedaling two miles to the grocery store. Inside, she gathered ingredients for the meal, which until today she'd only used to impress prospective employers. Tonight would her culinary skills prompt Sam to kiss her? Or was he the sort of man who wanted the promise of something more than a short-term fling before locking lips? If that was the case, kissing was out of the question.

Jenny spent the remainder of the afternoon preparing a meal for the man she'd found far more than interesting. Fifteen minutes before his scheduled arrival, she set the table and glanced around the main room. Nothing out of place. She ambled to the bedroom, opened her closet, and peered at her options—chef attire, jeans, casual shirts, three dresses chosen to entice men. At least no one could accuse her of spending money on lavish clothes. Maybe she should dress like a pal instead of a date. She opted for jeans, a blouse, and sandals.

Satisfied with her decision, she returned to the main room and tuned her new radio—another spur-of-the-moment purchase—to an easy-listening station. Too romantic. She switched to a country station. Better. A bark sent her rushing to the door. Before she could stoop to pet Duchess, a car turning onto the driveway perked the dog's ears and sent her padding down the staircase. Moments later Duchess raced back up, darted into the apartment, and sat on her haunches beside the coffee table.

Sam followed carrying two beer bottles. "Seems I'm not the only guest eager to sample your culinary masterpieces."

"Except my canine friend will have to settle for a dog biscuit."

"You've obviously captured one canine heart."

Jenny tossed a treat to Duchess. "She wants to hear more about Pip."

"You're reading *Great Expectations.*"

"Couple of chapters. I assume you've read it."

"In college." Sam popped the cap off one beer and set the other in the fridge. "How many courses have you whipped up?"

"Four."

"Hmm. Maybe I should buy you another fancy book. One for each course. So, what's your opinion of the one you're reading now?"

How could she explain the connection she felt with the orphan when she had two living parents? "It's interesting."

"Is that always your go-to adjective?"

"When it fits."

Sam sipped his beer. "I remember Estella."

"I haven't met her yet."

"She's beautiful, self-possessed. Raised to break men's hearts."

"No kidding." Maybe she'd find more in common with Estella than with Pip. Jenny removed two soup bowls from the fridge and placed them on the table. "The first course is ready."

"My mouth's watering." Sam sat. "Something smells scrumptious."

"Roasted veggies. Have you ever tried gazpacho?"

"Can't say I have."

She dropped a dollop of sour cream in each bowl. "It's my favorite cold soup. Perfect for a warm day." She sat across from Sam and remained silent until he finished his silent blessing. "Let me know what you think."

He dipped his spoon in the bowl and kept his eyes focused on Jenny while tasting. "I can honestly say it's my favorite cold soup."

"Or the only one you've ever tried."

"There is that." He smiled. "Seriously, it's delicious."

"I'm glad you like it." Alarmed by an overwhelming desire to please him, Jenny broke eye contact and plucked her spoon off the table. "How'd your morning meeting go?"

"I signed a contract to sell a four-million-dollar, lake-front home."

"What's it like? The house, I mean."

While listening to his description, her mind drifted to her small, unkempt childhood home—devoid of warmth or laughter. If she had grown up with a mother who loved her daughters more than booze, maybe she'd be free to open her heart and let Sam in.

Sam paused, caught off guard by the melancholy expression clouding Jenny's face. What bitter memories had his comments unleashed? He cleared his throat. "The view from the back deck is worth the price."

She blinked, as if emerging from a long, dark alley. "Why are the owners selling?"

"Divorce settlement."

"Another lousy marriage."

Was that the pain she'd been forced to deal with? "Yours?"

The flicker of a frown creased Jenny's forehead. "What makes you think ex-husbands lurk in my past, which by the way, they don't."

His brows pinched then released. "Good to know." He pointed his spoon toward her. "If the other three courses are as good as this one, I'll definitely buy you another book."

She stared at him for a long moment. "Are you in the mood to barter?"

"It's not out of the question."

"Well then, I hope you'll find my entrée worthy of something larger than a book but smaller than a car."

He noted the sparkle in her eyes. "What's this mystery dish that could end up costing me big-time?"

"I think I'll keep you guessing."

"Such torture." Fascinated by her playful nature, he swallowed the last drop of gazpacho and pushed his bowl across the table. "I'm ready for round two."

Jenny replaced his bowl with a salad. "Enjoy while I finalize the carrot, so to speak." She removed a container from the fridge and stood in front of the stove, blocking his view.

As he breathed in a rich seafood aroma and listened to her humming along with the country tune, he imagined spending a lifetime enjoying such moments of simple pleasure.

She glanced over her shoulder. "Is something wrong with the salad?"

"Nope." He dipped his fork into the greens. "Homemade dressing?"

"Do you think a chef would serve anything store-bought?"

"Uh-oh. Major faux pas." He laughed. "But what do you expect from a guy who has a freezer full of frozen dinners."

"Some folks say the best chefs are men." She removed a pan from the oven, spooned items onto two plates, and placed them on the table. "I'm committed to proving them wrong."

Sam stared at two perfectly shaped crab cakes with sauce artfully drizzled along the side, accompanied by roasted vegetables. "I call that a work of art." He removed his phone from his belt clip and snapped a photo. "Now for the real test."

She propped her elbows on the table and rested her chin on her knuckles. "Almost no filler."

He locked eyes with her while savoring the sweet, succulent taste. "They're incredible."

Her face beamed. "I spent months perfecting the recipe."

"Definitely worth the effort." While continuing to relish the entrée, Sam punctuated their conversation with well-placed compliments. With his last bite, he laid his fork across his plate. "Hands down, you could go toe-to-toe with any male chef in the universe and come out the victor."

"Are you saying the meal is a worthy bartering tool?"

"That depends."

Her brows raised. "On what?"

"Your dessert."

"You drive a hard bargain." She transferred two small dishes from the fridge to the table. "My version of crème brulée."

He lifted his spoon.

"Wait." She lit a small torch, aimed it at the custard, and created a perfect caramelized layer. "Time for the final bargaining chip."

He tasted. "So far, so good."

When he'd swallowed the last spoonful, Jenny tapped her fingers on the table. "What's the verdict?"

"I have one question." He leaned forward. "What's bigger than a book but smaller than a car?"

"A television." Jenny finished her dessert. "Now we're even. Dinner for three books." She tilted her head. "You know I'm kidding about the TV."

"You could become my personal chef and cook more delicious meals."

Jenny fanned her face with her fingers. "Oh, my." She fluttered her eyelids, her southern accent exaggerated. "How you do carry on about my little ole cooking skills."

He burst out laughing. "Dinner with a comedic chef. How lucky can one guy get?"

Duchess sprang to her feet and barked.

Jenny stroked her back. "I think she deserves another treat."

Sam grinned. Maybe one day she'd say the same about him. "I'm guessing she's in the mood for a walk. Want to join us for a moonlight stroll?"

"Sure. Why not?"

He pulled her chair away from the table while summoning every ounce of will power to resist leaning down and kissing the nape of her neck.

Chapter 13

Jenny scooted behind the counter to plate a cinnamon bun and peeked at Sam sitting in his usual spot, chatting with George. Were they talking about her? Four days had passed since the dinner in her apartment and he hadn't asked her for another date. Relief collided with disappointment and played havoc with her emotions. Hadn't he found her appealing? Was that why he didn't try to kiss her? Or had her bartering banter pegged her as a gold digger? Impossible. She'd made it clear she was joking.

Sam caught her eye and winked.

Sensing her cheeks were seconds from turning multiple shades of pink, Jenny dashed to a table to deliver the bun and focused all her energy on smothering customers with compliments and tip-worthy service. By the time Lou flipped the open sign to closed, Jenny had come to the only logical conclusion. Sam had relegated their relationship to the casual-friendship category. She carried a tray of dirty dishes toward the counter.

Lou peered up while spritzing cleaner. "You seem preoccupied."

"Probably the weather, which is perfect for a bike ride."

"You go ahead. I'll finish cleaning up."

"Are you sure?"

"Positive. Now scoot on out of here and enjoy this gorgeous afternoon."

"On one condition. You let me do all the cleanup tomorrow."

Lou wiped the counter dry. "You're obviously accustomed to bartering."

Jenny's eyes narrowed to a slit. "Did Sam tell you about the television?"

"What television?"

Uh-oh, big mistake. "Nothing." Jenny carried the tray to the kitchen, set the plates in the dishwasher, and walked outside. While breathing in the fresh air, she climbed onto her bike, and rode through downtown. She pedaled past a woman pushing a baby stroller and diverted her eyes. At the corner she turned onto Main Street and headed north until Madison Drug came into view. A good place to clear her head. She parked her bike on the covered veranda and swiped her palm across her damp forehead.

Inside the iconic building, a young woman holding a toddler's hand smiled while brushing past her. A sudden urge to quench her parched throat sent Jenny scrambling to the lunch counter to order a Coke. After draining half the liquid in one long slurp, she carried the large paper cup to an aisle displaying an array of gift items. Lou had a birthday coming up. Maybe she could save enough money to buy her something special or at least borrow from her meager savings.

Jenny downed the rest of her drink, returned to her bike, and rode home where she found Duchess sprawled at the bottom step. "Are you looking for a treat or a belly rub?"

The dog yawned, wagged her tail, and followed her up the stairs.

Jenny rewarded her canine friend with two biscuits before plopping onto the sofa.

Duchess sprawled on the floor beside the coffee table.

"Are you ready to hear more about Pip?" She reached for *Great Expectations*. With her hand inches from the cover, she glanced at the wall beside the bookcase. Following a double take, she gasped. A large flat-screen television wrapped with a pink ribbon hung in the space above her guitar. She bolted to her feet, grabbed the envelope taped to the ribbon, and ripped it open.

A token of my appreciation for treating me to the most delicious dinner I have ever experienced. I hope there's more to come.

Sam

Flurries of guilt pulsated in her chest. He hadn't asked her for a dime's additional rent, or for that matter anything at all. Instead, he'd bought her an expensive gift. Why? Was he one of those men her mother had warned her about? This called for a face-to-face confrontation.

Duchess barked. Her head cocked.

"Not with you."

Jenny dashed down the stairs and climbed onto her bike. Her anger escalated as she rode into town and stormed into Gibson Realty.

Mary looked up. "Are you fleeing an angry swarm of hornets or a mob of robbers?"

"Is Sam in his office?"

"Sorry, honey. He worked at home today." Her brows lifted. "If there's a problem, maybe I can help."

"This is between me and Sam." She stormed out and sped toward his house. A horn blasted as she cut in front of a car.

The driver shook his fist at her.

"Sorry." She forced her mind to focus on the road until she reached Sam's front yard. A couple strolling on the sidewalk waved. The moment they passed, she stomped onto the porch and pounded her fist on the door. Twice.

The door opened. Sam stared at her. "What's wrong?"

"What do you expect in return?" Her tone was harsh. Her voice loud. "Tell me the truth, Sam."

He grabbed her hand and pulled her inside. "Do you want the neighbors to think I'm assaulting you?"

She yanked her hand away.

He shut the door.

"You want me to sleep with you. Is that it?"

"What in the devil are you talking about?"

"Trading a television for sex. Why else would you give me an expensive gift? And what did you mean by 'I hope there's more to come?'"

"More dinners." He glared at her. "I can't believe you think I'd try to buy my way into your bed." He spun and stalked into the living room.

She followed. "How did you expect me to react?"

"I don't know." His eyes grew fierce. "Maybe with a little gratitude or a modicum of trust?" His tone edged with disgust. "If I go rip the television off the wall and give it to a woman who doesn't think I'm some creep bartering for sex, will that make you happy? You tell me. Is that what you want?"

Jenny's chin dropped to her chest. Her cheeks burned. "I'm sorry. I didn't mean—"

"It's a gift. Or if you prefer, a perk for a tenant. Nothing more."

She lifted her chin. Tears erupted and tracked down her cheeks.

Sam brushed them away with his fingertips.

His touch sent a wave of desire coursing through her, followed by a shudder of shame and regret.

He clasped her shoulders. "I don't know how many men have hurt you, or if you'll ever find it in your heart to trust me. But I'm not giving up on you."

Her body tensed. What did he mean by not giving up? Was he falling in love with her? It didn't matter if he waited a lifetime, she would never be good enough for him.

Sam gazed into Jenny's eyes, troubled by the pain and suffering they revealed. What could he say to keep their relationship from falling apart? If he told her he was falling in love with her, would she refuse to see him? Or worse, leave Madison? He released her shoulders. "What do you want me to do, Jenny?"

She broke eye contact and sniffled.

He waited.

She folded her arms across her chest. "I want us to remain friends."

Sam shoved his hands in his pockets. Would she ever want more? "If that means hanging out and enjoying each other's company—with no strings attached—I'm all in."

"Then we have an understanding." She paused. "About the TV, can it stay in the apartment?"

Why was he attracted to such a complicated, confusing woman? "Like I said, it's a gift. So, yeah, you can keep it."

She unfolded her arms. "One more thing I need to know."

Now what? "I'm listening."

"How much rent do I owe?"

"That's Paul's decision, not mine."

"Ask him and let me know tomorrow." She spun away from him and headed toward the door.

Sam waited for the door to close before turning toward the window. His heart ached as he watched her climb onto her bike and pedal away. He pressed his fingers to the back of his neck to ease the tense muscles. Somehow, he had to find a way to tear down the wall she'd built around her heart.

Chapter 14

Jenny's eyes darted to the coffee shop window for the umpteenth time. Why hadn't Sam shown up? Most likely because her outburst and accusation disgusted him. Maybe he'd spent the morning tossing her belongings to the curb and changing the lock on her apartment door. Who could blame him after she'd acted like a fool?

"What's today's flavor?"

Jenny blinked and stared at her customer. "I'm sorry. What?"

"The quiche. What's in it?"

"Ham, tomato, and Swiss cheese. Served with zucchini bread."

"Even better than last week's special."

"It's a customer favorite." She peered at the window. If Sam came in, should she pretend like nothing happened? "Do you want coffee or juice with the quiche?"

"Coffee."

"Coming right up."

For the following two hours Jenny struggled to stay focused on her customers. By the time noon rolled a bundle of knots had taken up residence in her gut. She slipped into the kitchen and gripped the edge of the worktable. Maybe the time had come to move on and land another job in another town. Another state.

Jenny released her grip and leaned back against the counter. Who was she kidding? She couldn't afford to change jobs until she'd saved more money. A ringtone sent her dashing to her purse. She pulled out her phone and stared at the screen. Kelley Bristol, her high-school friend, now a renowned psychologist. "Hey, Kelley. Sorry I've missed your calls."

"I never know what time of day to reach out, given the crazy hours you work. Anyway, I'm free tomorrow morning. How about meeting for breakfast and catching up?'

"The thing is…I moved to Madison a few weeks ago. It was kind of sudden. You know me and new opportunities."

"My friend the nomad. Tell you what, I'll come to you—"

"I'm working six days a week until noon."

"Then we'll make it Saturday. I'll drive over and we'll spend the afternoon together. We'll have lots to talk about."

Would she ask too many questions? After all, Kelley knew about her occasional binges, but not about her DUI or its consequences. "As friends, or patient and psychologist?"

"Whichever you need."

"Then, friends. Meet me at work, Lou's Coffee Shop. I'll save you a slice of quiche, our new specialty."

"It's a date."

Lou peeked in the door. "One of our regulars is asking for you."

Jenny eyed the clock. Five after twelve. The coffee shop was officially closed. "I have to go, Kelley. I'll see you Saturday." She dropped her phone in her purse and swung the door open. The stool at the end of the counter remained empty. Relief fused with disappointment swept through her.

Lou caught her eye and nodded toward the wall opposite the counter. "He's waiting over there."

Sam sat at a corner table. Alone.

Jenny's pulse accelerated as she closed the distance. She breathed deeply to slow her pounding heart. "Did someone spill coffee on your favorite stool?"

"We need to talk." He motioned for her to sit.

"The coffee shop closed five minutes ago."

"I know."

She hesitated. "What's going on, Sam?"

"Not until you sit down."

Curiosity won out over apprehension. She sat across from him and studied his expression, searching for some kind of clue. Maybe he wanted an apology. "I'm sorry I caused a scene yesterday."

"I'm over it." He leaned forward. "This morning Grandpa and I talked about the apartment."

Sweat erupted and trickled between her shoulder blades. "Are you evicting me?"

"Why do you always assume the worse?"

"I wouldn't blame you." She stared at the envelope. "I'm not exactly the ideal tenant."

"Do me a favor. Stop with the crazy talk and open it."

She wiped her damp palms on her jeans, peeled back the flap, and removed a folded sheet of paper. "Is this a lease?"

"Month-to-month agreement. Two hundred due on the first of each month."

The small amount would make it easier for her to stockpile more cash. "That's not a lot of money."

"It's more than zero." Sam handed her a pen.

"Did you tell Paul about my meltdown?"

"Does it matter one way or the other?"

Had he, or hadn't he? "I don't want him thinking some out-of-control lunatic is living on his property."

"He wouldn't have signed an agreement if he had any qualms about you."

Jenny's gaze slid to the contract. "How much past rent do I owe?"

"That's up for negotiation."

"More bartering?"

"If that's what you want to call it."

She glanced at his face, relieved to see the hint of a grin. What could she offer without sending the wrong message? Her forte. "In that case, I propose home-cooked Sunday dinners for you and Paul for the next three weeks?"

Sam chuckled. "That will drive my sister nuts."

"Invite her and her husband. I can cook for four as easily as two."

"Five, including you, as our guest."

"You've got a deal." Jenny signed the paper. "Can I bring you a cup of coffee?"

He nodded. "Any quiche left?"

"Couple of slices."

"Bring two. One for me, the other for you."

She tilted her head. "Only if you let me pay. As your friend."

"You drive a hard bargain."

"Do we have a deal?"

He leaned back. The corner of his eyes crinkled with an engaging smile. "Today, breakfast is on your dime."

Chapter 15

Footsteps striking Paul's kitchen floor startled Jenny as she slid a baking pan into the oven. She spun and caught Sam's sister, Sandra, staring at her, holding a glass of wine in her right hand, her left hand propped on her hip. "I noticed five place settings in the dining room. Is it customary for a hired chef to participate in a family dinner?"

Jenny cringed at Sandra's contemptuous tone. "Preparing a meal is my way of thanking Paul."

"For what? Letting you live virtually rent free in my parents' first apartment, or allowing you to wheedle your way into our family?"

"If my presence upsets you that much, I'll serve dinner and disappear."

"And have Sam blame me for kicking you out? No way I'm giving you the upper hand." Sandra moved the glass to her lips.

"I don't understand what I've done to make you dislike me?"

Sandra lowered her glass. "You show up in town from who knows where, with virtually nothing to your name, and set your sights on my brother."

"He's my real-estate agent—"

"Do you have any idea how many young Madison women from good families want to marry him? He could have his pick of any one of them."

What about the blonde who broke his heart? Had she come from one of those so-called good families? Fearing a remark she'd regret was seconds from escaping through clenched teeth, Jenny willed her lips to curve into a smile. "I hope you like beef Wellington."

"Changing the subject won't erase reality."

Sam wandered in. "Is my overbearing sister giving you a hard time?"

"We were enjoying a friendly chat about your hometown. If you'll gather everyone at the table, I'll serve the first course."

Sam nudged his sister's arm. "When you taste Jenny's food, you'll swear you've entered culinary heaven."

"Uh-huh." Sandra spun and disappeared around the corner.

Sam shook his head. "My brother-in-law has the patience of Job to put up with her moods."

Jenny shrugged. "Love excuses a lot of bad behavior."

"Uh-oh, what did she say to worm her way under your skin?"

"Don't go reading anything into an idle comment."

He held his palms up. "Guilty as charged."

She noted the twinkle in his eyes and smiled. "Truce."

"Now that I'm back in your good graces, I'll gather the troops for chow."

Jenny studied Sam's broad shoulders and muscular arms as he walked away. How would they feel wrapped around her, pulling her close? She swallowed past the dryness in her throat and carried a soup bowl to the mahogany buffet in the dining room.

Paul sat at the head of the table. "First time since Christmas we've enjoyed a meal in here."

Ted, whose dark hair and olive skin hinted of Italian heritage, pulled a chair out for Sandra. "As well as the first time a professional chef prepared a meal for us."

Sandra spread a napkin on her lap. "Have you forgotten all the delicious meals Grandma served?"

"Her casseroles and desserts were the best in Georgia." Ted settled beside his wife.

Paul eyed Jenny, his brow pinched. "Where's your bowl?"

She glanced at the table setting beside Sam. "I need to keep a close eye on dinner. Do you mind if I join you for the entrée?"

"We're counting on it. Before you escape, I'll say grace."

Jenny bowed her head. When Paul finished, she scooted to the kitchen to keep his heartwarming words from playing havoc with her emotions. She leaned back against the counter and let her eyes wander around the pristine space featuring cherry cabinets. A stark contrast to her parents' dreary kitchen, with worn linoleum flooring curled at the edges and dirty dishes piled in the sink. Torn curtains hung askew at the window offered a view of the weed-infested backyard. She couldn't summon a single memory of her family gathered around the table to enjoy a meal together. Disgusted by her mental pity party, Jenny focused on finalizing dinner.

"You missed all the kudos." Sam deposited empty bowls in the sink. "The soup earned you an A plus."

"You mean bisque."

"Seems I have a lot to learn about fine dining. Can I give you a hand?"

"Actually, yes." Jenny placed a beef Wellington on each plate beside garlic mashed potatoes and asparagus drizzled with Hollandaise sauce. "Help me carry these to the table."

"At your service, Ms. Amazing Chef."

She removed two plates from the counter. "You're stealing my line."

"Borrowing." He balanced the remaining three.

"Don't drop them."

"Not to worry. My first job was waiting tables."

"A man of many talents." She followed him to the dining room. After setting the plates down, she remained standing. "The steak is medium rare. If you want it cooked a bit more, let me know."

Paul cut into his. "Looks perfect. Sam, seat our guest and pour her a glass of wine."

"No thanks on the wine." Jenny sat and spread her napkin across her lap. "I never drink when I'm in charge of dinner."

Ted picked up his fork. "And I've never tasted bisque as delicious as yours."

Sam chuckled. "My brother-in-law is an important attorney who knows the difference between soup and bisque."

"Don't let Sam kid you. Underneath his southern-boy charm, he's a walking dictionary." Ted popped a piece of beef in his mouth. "This is definitely a prime cut and delicious." He nudged Sandra. "Try a bite, honey. I guarantee it will change your eating habits."

Paul grinned. "My granddaughter isn't exactly fond of meat."

Jenny eyed Sandra. "Sorry, I didn't know."

"My brother isn't always a wiz on details, unless they pertain to real estate." Sandra cut a piece of asparagus. "I'm curious about your background, Jenny. Where did you live, and what did you do before you moved to our town?"

Should she tell her about DUI school and watch her drop her fork? Jenny swallowed a bite of potatoes. "Atlanta. Before that Nashville, San Diego, San Francisco—"

"Based on your accent, it's obvious you're a southerner. Do you have any siblings?"

Did Sandra quiz all of Paul's guests like a prosecuting attorney? "An older sister."

"What about your family? Where are they from?"

Sam cut a piece of beef. "Besides being a brilliant doctor, my sister is big into tracing ancestry."

Paul swallowed a bite. "In my opinion, digging into the past is a waste of time. It's better to focus on the future."

"Knowing our genetic history helps us better understand who we are. So, Jenny, why don't you enlighten my brother and grandfather on what you know about your family history?"

Okay, she asked for it. Jenny wiped her mouth with her napkin while keeping her eyes glued on Sandra. "We're a small, highly dysfunctional clan of misfits. I've never met my maternal grandparents and only saw the other set once before they fled someplace south of the border. Most likely to escape the law. My mother drinks too much. Her sister lives in a commune someplace out west. My old man, an only child, stocks the kitchen with liquor, then drives a truck to stay away from home as much as possible. My sister hightailed it clean across the country to escape the crazy house. And me? I'm the family wanderer."

Silence filled the room until Paul roared with laughter. "Now, there's a family tree worth knowing about."

Sam pointed his fork at Sandra. "I told you she's the most intriguing woman in Madison."

"Way to go." Ted grinned as he tipped his wine glass toward Jenny. "You saved my beautiful wife hours of painstaking research."

Sandra's face turned six shades of red. "So shoot me for wanting to know more about this woman you all find fascinating."

"Lighten up, sis. We're playing with you."

"I don't blame her, Sam." Jenny reached for her fork. "After all, you have such an upstanding family, and I'm an outsider."

"You're welcome in my home any time, my dear. About this meal." Paul smacked his lips. "This beef is good enough to make a big dog break its chain."

Duchess popped up on her haunches and barked.

"What'd I tell you?"

Sandra managed a smile. "I have to admit it is tasty."

"I'm glad you approve." Jenny glanced sideways at Sam, trusting her revelation would provide a valid reason for him to ditch any romantic feelings.

The conversation shifted to careers, dogs, and small-town versus big-city life. After indulging in dessert, Sam helped Jenny clear the table and load the dishwasher. "The cake alone made up for your past rent. Which doesn't mean you're off the hook for two more meals."

"For a party of two, three, or five?"

"Three. My sister has already learned everything she needs to know about you."

Jenny pressed the start button. "What about you, Sam? Are we still friends?"

"Best buds, unless you decide you want more." He placed his hands on her shoulders.

Her skin tingled beneath his touch. She pressed her palm to his cheek. "You're the best pal a girl could ask for. One day a woman worthy of your love will come along and melt your heart."

His eyes remained locked on hers. She pulled away and dug her fingernails into her palms to keep tears at bay. One fact had become crystal clear. She cared enough about Sam to resist luring him into a romance that could never last.

Sam's eyes narrowed. The way Jenny's body stiffened triggered an avalanche of confusion. Did her sudden move mean she could never be that woman? Or was she hiding her true feelings? He suppressed the urge to demand an answer.

"Thanks for helping me clean up." Jenny placed a knife into her case and snapped it shut. "I'll leave you to enjoy your family."

If he asked her to stay, would she?

"I've been awake since three." She yawned. "I'm ready to call it a night."

There's the answer. "I understand."

She tucked her knife case under her arm, kissed his cheek, and walked out to the back deck.

Befuddled by mixed messages, Sam sighed and scratched his head.

"You do know your wandering tenant is a shameless tease."

Sam turned and faced Sandra. "Give it a break, already."

She moved close and placed her hand on his arm. "I'm not trying to interfere in your life—"

"You could have fooled me."

"It's just—" Sandra's tone softened. "I love you and don't want another woman to break your heart all over again."

"Jenny and I are friends."

"I saw how you looked at her." She pulled her hand away, her tone sharp again. "All googly-eyed."

"What man wouldn't?"

"I'm simply saying you deserve better."

"Better than what?"

"You are one stubborn man."

Ted wandered in. "You're scheduled for a double shift tomorrow, sweetheart. It's best we head on home."

"After eating all that meat, I doubt I'll get a good night's rest." Sandra followed her husband to the sliding glass door while waving over her shoulder. "Don't come crying to me when that chef rips your heart out and stomps it to bits."

"My sister, the ER doc slash drama queen." Sam shook his head and wandered from the kitchen to the den where he found his grandpa sitting in a vintage leather club chair, holding a brandy snifter.

"Grab a drink and join me."

"Might as well." Sam moseyed to the bar and poured a glass. "Jenny's one talented chef."

"Indeed, she is."

"What's your take on her comments about her family?" Sam sat on the leather sofa. "Exaggerated or spot-on?"

"More spot-on. Maybe even understated."

"I can't imagine life without a close-knit family." Sam swirled his brandy. "Even one with an opinionated, bossy big sister."

"Sandra means well." His grandpa took a sip. "I suspect Jenny has a distorted view of loving relationships. That's probably why she blew up over the television."

"At least she signed the agreement."

"Which gives you more time to win her over."

Sam swallowed a sip of brandy. "If I figure out what sets her off."

"One thing is certain, it's impossible for men to fully understand women's moods. All those years your grandma and I were together, she still confused the dickens out of me. Not often, mind you. But enough to make life interesting."

"Jenny seems to have mastered the art of confusing the opposite sex. Did I tell you tonight's dinner plus two more are payment for past rent?"

"We came out on the plus side of that deal."

"Indeed we did."

"It's still early." His grandpa nodded toward two chairs flanking a small table holding a chess set. "Are you up to a challenge?"

"If I'm remembering correctly, I beat you last time."

"Which makes this a grudge match."

Sam popped up and selected the chair facing the white chess pieces. He released a chuckle as his grandpa settled across from him.

"What's tickled your funny bone?"

"Chess is the perfect analogy for my relationship with Jenny. Every calculated move has the potential to lead to disaster."

"Or if played smart, to victory. You make the first move."

Sam eyed his grandpa. "With Jenny or the game?"

"Both."

Chapter 16

Jenny scooped a two-dollar tip off the table and dropped the bills into her apron pocket, pleased she could add a few more bucks to her miniscule savings. She sighed and stacked the dirty dishes. On the way to the kitchen, she glanced at Kelley sitting at the counter chatting with George and Lou. With her long blonde hair cascading over her shoulders and her sunglasses pushed to the top of her head, she looked more like a model than a doctor. At least her friend had arrived after Sam had gone.

Jenny backed into the kitchen and set the dishes in the sink. How much should she tell Kelley about the real reason she fled Atlanta? Or that moving back to that city last year after fleeing ten years earlier hadn't been such a good idea? She filled her lungs, then slowly released the air and returned to the dining area.

Lou removed Kelley's empty plate and nodded toward Jenny. "Thanks to your friend's creativity and charm, business is better than ever."

"She's one smart lady." Kelley pushed her cup to Lou.

Jenny moved to Lou's side and eyed her friend. "Have these two told you everything there is to know about Madison?"

"We held back a few bits of information." Lou refreshed Kelley's coffee. "Besides, it's fun watching an honest-to-goodness psychologist trying to analyze my old pal."

"I can't knock a free brain-probing session." George set his elbow on the counter and rested his chin on his fist. "Have you figured me out yet, Doc?"

"Let's see. You're charming, sociable, and handsome."

"Is that all you can come up with?"

"If I told you more, I'd have to send you a bill." Kelley leaned close to him. "At my rates, you'd already owe me a couple hundred bucks."

He laughed. "I don't need a degree to know you're loaded with gumption."

Lou nudged Jenny. "Why don't you take off and show your friend around town before George chews her ear off."

"Are you sure?"

"The crowds have thinned, so you two go on and enjoy the day."

"Give me a minute." Jenny dashed back to the kitchen. She hung her apron on a hook and slung her purse across her chest then returned. "Chef Jenny aka tour guide at your service, Dr. Bristol."

Kelley laid a twenty on the counter and slid off her stool. "Thanks for the coffee and delightful company."

George snapped his fingers. "You're smart and generous to boot. If you ever get a hankering to live in a small town, you're welcome to move here and set up shop. There's plenty of interesting brains to probe."

"Best morning chat I've had in a long time." Kelley lowered her sunglasses as she accompanied Jenny outside. "I could spend all day talking with those two."

"I suspect George and Lou gave you an earful about Madison's population."

"Enough to pique my interest about the town's history. I'll save that lesson for another visit. Today I want to enjoy this gorgeous weather and catch up on everything going on in your life."

Jenny shrugged. "There isn't that much to tell. I show up at work before dawn and leave at one." She spoke to a passerby as they rounded the corner and walked up Main.

"You and Lou seem close."

"She's more like my mother than my boss. Which is why I haven't looked for another job. Soon I'll convince her to expand to a lunch venue." At the intersection, Jenny greeted a middle-aged woman by name, then stepped into the street. A car horn blasted. Her heart exploded against her ribs. She bolted back to the curb.

Kelley touched her arm. "Are you okay?"

Jenny blinked away a painful memory. "I'm fine." She stepped off the curb again and greeted a woman crossing from the opposite direction.

"You've obviously met a lot of nice people."

Jenny nodded. "Life in a small southern town."

"Seems like a great place to settle down."

She ignored the comment as they continued walking up Jefferson. Jenny pointed toward the antique store at the next corner. "That's where I found the perfect painting for my apartment."

"Let me guess. Sunflowers."

"You remember."

"You didn't respond to my comment about settling down."

"I didn't think I needed to." They crossed at another intersection and strolled beside the wrought-iron fence enclosing Town Park.

Kelley nodded toward the buildings across the street. "Gibson Realty, where Sam works, right?"

Jenny halted. Her eyes narrowed. "What have you heard about him?"

"According to George, you and the most eligible bachelor in town are—as he put it—courting."

"George needs to mind his own business."

"Based on your reaction, I'm guessing you and Sam are more than casual acquaintances."

Jenny resumed walking. "It's complicated."

"Why? Because you're a short-term-fling kind of gal?"

"Something like that."

Kelley looped her arm around Jenny's elbow. "Do you mind if I give you a word of advice?"

"Like I could stop you."

"It's okay to let your guard down and follow your heart. Besides, it wouldn't hurt you to settle down in one place longer than six months."

"Sam and I are friends—"

"Have you forgotten I'm a psychologist trained to read people?"

"The park is a nice place to visit." Jenny pulled away and raced ahead.

Kelley caught up with her. "Not even you can outrun your emotions forever."

"You don't give up, do you?"

"I care about you, Jenny. You've been running away far too long. You deserve to find true happiness."

"Fairy-tale endings don't exist for women like me." Jenny pointed to the building on the other side of the park. "Did you know every room in the Madison Inn is named after one of the town's historic homes?"

"You're wrong."

"It's true, I've walked inside."

Kelley elbowed Jenny. "You know I'm not talking about the inn."

"How about we change the subject."

"For the moment, but I'm not letting you off the hook."

They meandered into the park and sat on a circular wall surrounding a decorative pool featuring a fountain and statue. Jenny swirled her fingers in the water. "Most days I ride through here on my way home."

"To the apartment Paul Gibson and his grandson fixed up for you?"

"Good grief." Jenny rolled her eyes. "What else did George tell you?"

"Enough to know Sam's one of the good guys."

"That doesn't matter." Movement caught Jenny's eye. She turned as Sam escorted a man and a woman through the park entrance.

He sent the couple in the opposite direction before approaching. "Good afternoon, ladies."

Jenny shaded her eyes and lifted her chin. "Are you happening by, or did Mary see us walk in here?"

"My new clients asked about the park. Mary cinched the deal." He hiked his foot on the wall, leaned down, and extended his hand. "I'm Sam Gibson."

Kelley pushed her sunglasses up and accepted. "Kelley Bristol. Jenny and I go back a long way."

Sam released her hand and propped his forearm across his knee. "It's a pleasure to meet someone from her past. Have you been to Lou's Coffee Shop?"

"I spent the last hour chatting with Lou and George. He pointed out your official spot at the counter."

Jenny fidgeted. How many more tidbits had George spilled?

"It's where I catch up on all the local news. Did you try Jenny's quiche of the week?"

"I did and loved it."

"She's quite a gal."

Kelley's head tilted. "Lou or Jenny?"

"Both. I'm glad I had the chance to meet you, Kelley."

"Same here, Sam."

He straightened and lowered his foot. "Sorry I have to run, but I'm on a mission to find the perfect home for the Andersons. Next time you're in town, I'll treat you and Jenny to dinner."

"I'll hold you to it."

Sam flashed a smile then headed toward his clients.

Jenny's heart pounded as her eyes followed Sam.

"That handsome, charming man is wild about you," whispered Kelley.

"So now you're a romance expert?" Jenny popped up and moved to the path leading to the park's side entrance.

"You aren't denying it."

"Like I told you twenty minutes ago, it's complicated."

"If you ask me—"

"I didn't."

"Too bad, because I'm going to tell you something you need to hear." Kelley wrapped her arm around Jenny's shoulders. "You can't let your past continue to keep your heart locked up inside."

The devastating past she'd never revealed to anyone. The reason she could never let herself fall in love. "I have an idea."

"You're changing the subject again." Kelley sighed. "Okay, I'm all ears."

"I'll treat you to a late lunch after you meet the real love of my life."

Kelley chuckled while lowering her sunglasses. "Let me guess, a four-legged furry friend."

"Her name's Duchess. She's a lovable black Lab."

"You're still a pushover for big, lovable canines."

"Always." For good reason. Dogs never expected more from her than she could give.

Chapter 17

Two weeks after Kelley's visit, Jenny pedaled from the coffee shop along Jefferson Street to the Town Park entrance. She climbed off her bike and walked it to the octagonal gazebo anchoring one corner of the massive outdoor space. Dark clouds rolling in from the west promised rain and welcome relief from the summer heat. She lowered the kickstand and stepped into the gazebo.

A beetle crawled up a white column toward a spider perched in a web. Not on her watch. She flicked the pending victim with her index finger, sending it flying away from an unsuspecting doom. A tabby she recognized from previous treks through the park sprang onto the railing and settled three feet from her. "Hey there, kitty." The cat yawned, stretched, and sprawled on its belly. "Am I invading your space or are you looking for company?"

Thunder rumbled in the distance. "Seems we need to make a decision. Either stay here or flee to better shelter."

"I'd say that depends."

Startled by Sam's voice, Jenny spun around. "Are you stalking me and my feline friend, or did you happen to walk by?"

He moved beside her. "You've become a creature of habit."

"Guess it's time to change my routine." His arm brushed against her shoulder, sending a quiver surging through her limbs. She edged away.

"I want to run an idea by you."

"I'm listening."

"You know Lou's birthday is three weeks away."

"It's hard to imagine she's about to turn seventy-five." Jenny flicked another unsuspecting insect off the column. "Anyone who meets her for the first time would swear she's sixty-something."

"Grandpa and I want to throw her a surprise-birthday party and invite her closest friends."

"You're talking about half the town."

"We'll limit the number. The thing is, we need a woman's touch. Someone who loves Lou as much as we do. Which makes you the perfect person to help us plan and implement the big event." Sam leaned back against the railing. "We're meeting at my house for dinner and want you to join us."

Jenny's eyes drifted to a wasp flying straight into the spider's web. Following the television fiasco and their agreement to remain friends, he hadn't invited her to dinner. Although they bantered every morning at Lou's, and she had fulfilled her promise to prepare two more meals for him and his grandpa. "Is this a ploy for another fancy meal?"

He folded his arms across his chest. "You can't help yourself, can you?"

"Like you said," she mocked, "I'm a creature of habit."

"Fact is, I'm grilling steaks and potatoes and Grandpa's bringing the salad and dessert. So, why don't you drop the attitude and show up as our guest."

She parroted his stance. "AKA free party planner and caterer?"

"Another accomplishment to add to your portfolio."

Why couldn't she resist a snarky response? "Will you pen a letter touting my skills?"

"Why not?" Sam unfolded his arms. "What guy wouldn't want to write a recommendation letter in place of a love note?"

Jenny breathed in the musky scent of his aftershave and fought to keep her arms from unfolding as she imagined his muscular arms pulling her tight against his chest and his lips seeking hers. Her shoulders curled inward. Her mouth went dry. "What time tonight?" Her voice came out raspy.

He remained silent for a long moment. "How long are you planning to ignore the feelings we have for each other?"

She dropped her arms to her side and stared at the floor. "You don't understand."

"You're right. So, please try to explain."

Jenny hesitated. "There have been other men."

"What's the big deal? We're both in our thirties. It's logical we have pasts."

She couldn't reveal the incident she had spent years trying to escape. That night. The blinding light. The pain. "I care about you, Sam. It's just—"

"What are you afraid of?"

Raindrops assailed the roof, followed by a flash of lightning and a loud thunderclap forcing them to move to the center. The cat jumped off the railing and curled around Jenny's legs. She stooped and gathered the feline in her arms. "I'm not suited for a serious relationship."

"Not suited? Is that your way of telling me I'm not good enough for you?"

If he only knew. She stroked the cat's back as memories surfaced of four-year-old Billie climbing onto Sam's lap. "You'd best find a woman who wants to settle down and raise a family. Instead of an ambitious chef destined to work an insane number of hours running her own restaurant. Maybe more than one. Besides, we agreed to friendship, not romance."

Sam closed his eyes and pinched the bridge of his nose. "According to my sister, men often act like fools. Seems I'm proving her right."

"That character flaw isn't exclusive to the male population."

A cool gust of wind roared through the gazebo, sending goosebumps popping out on Jenny's arms.

Sam wrapped his arm around her. "Are we still friends?"

She leaned against him, wishing that long-ago night had never happened. But it had. "For now."

"Fair enough."

The rain pelted the gazebo and sent water cascading over the side. For a moment, she imagined spending the rest of her life in Madison. With Sam. Until another lightning bolt and thunder clash shocked her back to reality. No matter how hard she tried to forget the past, it would never stop haunting her.

Hours after the storm passed, Sam removed a baking dish holding three marinated filets from the fridge and set it on the counter. "If Jenny bothers to show up for dinner, promise to kick me if I say something stupid, Grandpa. Like she's driving me crazy. Or I can't stop thinking about her."

"You need more patience."

"She has deep feelings for me. I can see it in her eyes. The problem is one wrong move could send her fleeing to another town, and out of my life forever."

"Stay focused on your friendship." His grandpa clasped Sam's shoulder. "When she's ready, she'll find her way into your arms."

"What makes you so sure?"

"Faith." A chime echoed through the house. "I'd call that a confirmation."

"You're a true romantic."

"So are you. Now go welcome the mysterious woman who's charmed her way into your heart."

Sam dashed to the foyer and gripped the handle, determined to play it cool. He pulled the door open, keeping his focus on Jenny's face. "I hope you're in the mood for the best grilled steak this side of the Mississippi."

Her head tilted. The hint of a grin toyed with the corner of her lips. "Better than my beef Wellington?"

"We'll let Grandpa judge, after he treats us to his store-bought apple pie."

She crossed the threshold. "There's a combination to tease a chef's appetite."

And hopefully begin to melt her heart. Sam pressed his hand to her back and led her to the kitchen.

Paul greeted Jenny with a hug. "Thanks for agreeing to help us." He released her. "Sam and I are smart enough to know that planning a shindig for one of Madison's most popular citizens needs a feminine touch."

"I'm glad to help."

Sam removed three steaks from the fridge. "I prefer mine slightly north of rare. How about you, Jenny?"

"Perfect."

He pulled a bottle of red wine from a chiller mounted under the cabinet and set it on the counter beside three stemmed glasses. "How about a toast?"

"I uh...never developed a taste for wine."

"Not a problem." He removed two cans of ginger ale from the fridge and filled the stems. "Here's to our party-planning trio." And if he played his cards right, to the beginning of a relationship beyond friendship with the most amazing and frustrating woman he had ever met.

Chapter 18

Jenny scanned the guests gathered in Paul's backyard whispering as they moved among white cloth-covered tables with candles nestled in mason jars serving as centerpieces. During the weeks she, Sam, and Paul had gathered to plan Lou's party, she'd enjoyed the sense of belonging. The laughter. The playful teasing.

Duchess scampering from one attentive guest to another brought a smile to her face. The prospect of walking away from everyone she'd grown to love made her heart ache. Yet she feared that time was fast approaching.

At Sam's signal, the guests fell silent. Paul opened the French doors leading to the deck. Lou, radiant in white slacks and a long-sleeved red tunic, stepped out, her silver hair draped in soft curls to her shoulders. A touch of makeup erased years from her face.

Her friends welcomed the guest of honor with shouts of 'surprise,' followed by a rousing crescendo of cheers. Lou pressed her right hand to her chest. A smile lit her face. She clung to Paul's arm while he escorted her down the steps to greet guests rushing toward her.

Sam stood beside Jenny. "Seems we pulled off a surprise."

"This is the first birthday party I've ever planned." She nodded toward a tall, pretty woman, clothed in a designer dress and sandals. "Wait 'til Lou sees who flew in from Europe."

The crowd parted as Sara, carrying a bouquet of roses, approached Lou. "Happy birthday, Mom."

"Oh, my stars. My daughter has come home."

As the two women embraced amid resounding applause, the tears Jenny had struggled to hold back escaped and trickled down her cheeks. "They love each other the way mothers and daughters are supposed to." Had she said that out loud?

Sam touched her arm. "You know Lou considers you her other daughter, which is the second reason why you should stay in Madison."

Yeah, she had uttered the words. Jenny sniffed and dabbed her cheeks. "What's the first?"

"Grandpa needs the rent money."

"Silly me." Jenny nudged his ribs with her elbow. "I figured the first was because you'd miss your best buddy."

"Hey, you pack a powerful jab." He leaned close. His breath warmed her cheek. "And yeah, I'd miss you. Almost as much as Duchess would miss her daily trek to your door."

He had no idea how much she'd miss his smile. His touch. Their coffee shop banter. Yet Sam was one big reason why she couldn't stay. She swallowed the lump rising in her throat. "It's time to feed this crowd. Do you want to help me uncover the goodies?"

"At your service, Chef Jenny, or should I say first-class caterer and party-planner pro?"

"Are you practicing for the brilliant letter you promised to write for my portfolio?"

He snapped his fingers. "I almost forgot. You want a recommendation instead of a love note."

She patted his cheek. "Good memory."

They lifted a cloth off the long table, revealing an array of appetizers. Sam grabbed a bacon-wrapped date and popped it in his mouth.

"Are you my official taste tester?"

He swallowed. "I might need a second bite to form an honest opinion."

"One per customer, buddy."

He winked. "You know I could sneak up to your apartment and grab an extra."

"Hmm, maybe I should recruit a more reliable helper."

"Too late, I'm your man."

Her shoulder brushed his arm. His statement was far more accurate than he would ever know.

"Before it's time to refresh the food, you need to meet our birthday gal's daughter." Sam slipped his arm around Jenny's waist and ushered her through the crowd to the guest of honor.

Lou pressed her palms together. "Thanks to Paul and you two, I feel more like fifty than seventy-five. What's more amazing, this party was a complete surprise. Even old George managed to keep it a secret." She reached for Jenny's hand. "I want you to meet my daughter."

Sara turned. "You must be Jenny. Based on Mom's letters, you've succeeded in convincing her to expand her rather limited concept of coffee shop menus."

"All she needed was a little nudge." Jenny smiled. "Your mother is the most amazing woman I have ever met."

"Indeed, she is." Sara sandwiched Jenny's hand in hers. "Sometimes I worry about her working too many long hours. I'm glad you're helping her."

"Believe me, she works circles around me. Besides, the coffee shop keeps her young."

"Exactly what I keep telling my worrisome daughter." Lou patted Sara's arm. "Will you scoot over to that big cooler, honey, and find me something to sip on while I chat with these two? A nice cold beer if there are any."

Sam nodded. "Your favorite brand."

"One brew coming up."

The moment her daughter walked away, Lou embraced Sam then Jenny. "I imagine you two are the reason she agreed to fly halfway around the world. She's the only family I have left, other than you two. So, thank you from the bottom of my heart."

Sara returned carrying a beer wrapped in a paper napkin. "The food looks amazing, Mom. Why don't we claim a table before they're all taken?"

"Not before I hug all my friends."

Jenny touched Sara's arm. "You can stay with your mom. We reserved a special table for you."

"Good." Lou's smile widened. "I want to spend as much time as possible with my girl before she leaves."

"You have me for three whole days."

"We'll make the most of every moment."

An image of her mother sprawled on the kitchen floor, unconscious from a drunken stupor, crept into Jenny's mind. Sara had no idea how lucky she was to have a loving mother like Lou. "Tell you what, I'll cover for you at the coffee shop until Sara leaves. My personal birthday gift for you."

"Thank you for your generous offer. Every time I return for a visit, I have to share Mom with the entire town."

"I'm glad to help out." Jenny swatted a gnat away from her face. "Besides, with the kitchen all to myself, I'll have a chance to add something fun to the menu."

Lou laughed. "If Jenny had her way, we'd serve all sorts of fancy breakfast fare."

"Don't worry. I promise not to experiment with more than one dish."

"Let me guess. Eggs Benedict."

Jenny snapped her fingers. "Thanks for the suggestion."

"If she needs help waiting tables," said Sam, "I'll pitch in. That is, if Chef Jenny doesn't object to me keeping the tips."

Jenny thumped his arm. "It takes more than a pretty face for folks to ante up."

"Like not spilling coffee on their shirts or dumping food in their laps?"

Lou giggled. "As long as you stay out of the kitchen, Sam, my coffee shop will survive."

"So little confidence in your favorite customer."

"Maybe I ought to reconsider my opinion." Lou patted Sam's cheek. "After all, I hear you grill a first-class steak."

"The best in Madison."

Jenny nodded. "That is a fact. Now I need Sam's help to keep the buffet table filled."

"Demoted from master chef to errand boy." He snapped his fingers. "A guy can't catch a break."

"It's difficult to find good help these days." Jenny playfully shook her head as she grasped Sam's arm. "I'll pay you with extra goodies."

He grinned. "I suspect your definition of goodies is different from mine."

Lou laughed.

Sensing heat easing from her neck to her cheeks, Jenny released his arm. "Typical guy."

He leaned close. "You're extra charming when you blush."

"Like anything other than warm weather could pinken my cheeks." She diverted her eyes and headed to the buffet table.

Sam followed. "Nice touch, giving Lou more time with Sara."

"I'm holding you to your promise to wait tables."

"Anything for two of my favorite gals, or should I say friends."

Two hours after the party began, Paul blew a loud whistle, quieting the crowd. "Turning seventy-five is a milestone worthy of a celebration." He walked to the reserved table and held his arm out to Lou. "Come with me, birthday gal."

"Oh my, what does this handsome man have in mind?"

"Something special." He escorted her to a large object sitting on the grass, covered with a black cloth. "As far back as many of us can remember, you have brightened our mornings with excellent coffee, delicious pastries, and friendly conversation. In many ways you personify what small-town life is all about. Therefore, you deserve a memento to mark this important occasion. Something to remind current residents and future generations how much you mean to Madison."

With exaggerated flair he swept the cloth away, revealing a wrought-iron bench matching those in Town Park. He pointed to a plaque attached to the back. "Dedicated to Lou Johnson, our friend who inspires us all to live life to the fullest."

Lou ran her fingers over the bronze plate. "I'm astounded and humbled."

Sam sidled beside Jenny. "Congratulations. Your bench suggestion is a huge hit."

"She deserves the recognition."

His arm brushed her shoulder. "Next Saturday night, how about going to a concert in the park with me?"

Was he asking her for a date? "Invite Paul to join us, and I'm all in."

"Are you afraid to be alone with me?"

Terrified. "I wouldn't call surrounded by hundreds of people alone."

"Good point." Sam shoved his hands in his pockets. "Is Grandpa still part of the deal?"

"How about we make it a foursome."

"Why?" Sam nudged her. "Are you planning a round of golf before picnicking?"

"I don't think Duchess can swing a club."

"Two guys, a gal, and one canine. Definitely can't call *that* a date."

Her point exactly.

Chapter 19

Determined to avoid giving Sam the slightest clue about the feelings locked in her heart, Jenny stood on her toes and assessed her attire in the bathroom mirror. Jeans. An oversized white shirt tied in a knot at her waist. A red ball cap touting Madison's history. She stared at her feet, clad in white tennis shoes. Perfect.

A loud knock prompted one more peek at her image before she scooted through the bedroom and opened the door. "Right on time."

Sam removed his ball cap and swept his hand through his hair. "Do you mind if we walk to the park? Traveling on foot beats searching for a parking spot."

"I'm game." She followed him down the stairs where his grandpa waited.

"You two young folks are in for a treat tonight." Paul clipped a leash to Duchess's collar. "The band's playing music from the fifties and sixties. Other than forties big bands, they're the best songs ever written."

Sam laughed. "Be prepared for Grandpa's rousing game of 'name that tune.'"

"And the artists," added Paul.

Jenny pulled her ball cap close to her brows. "What's the winning prize?"

"Bragging rights."

"Which belongs exclusively to Grandpa." Sam slung three canvas bags holding folding lawn chairs over his shoulders. "We'd beat him if he'd ever agreed to a competition featuring music from the twenty-first century."

"And lose my competitive edge?" Paul retrieved a cooler off the bottom step. "No way."

Jenny gripped Duchess's leash and headed up the driveway sandwiched between grandfather and grandson. "The next time a country-western band shows up in Madison, I'll challenge both you guys."

They turned onto the sidewalk and eased into a jovial debate about oldies versus contemporary music. When they arrived at the park, Sam placed the chairs close to the pavement encircling the fountain. Jenny sat in the middle with Duchess at her feet.

Paul set the cooler beside his chair. "This is the perfect spot if the music puts our feet in the mood to boogie."

"Back in the day, he and Grandma were quite the dancing pair."

"You bet we were. There's nothing more romantic than holding the woman you love in your arms, moving to your favorite song."

Jenny's heart warmed at the sight of Paul's blissful smile and faraway stare.

A young girl climbing into her mother's open arms caught Jenny's eye. Why hadn't her mother cared enough to nuzzle her neck? She couldn't remember either parent ever speaking words of endearment to her or Jill. Another reality, far more devastating, wound its way to the surface. That fateful night.

Jenny forced her eyes to shift to an elderly woman, her shoulders bent forward, pushing a walker across the grass. An image of her own future played in her mind—a lonely old lady dying and leaving behind a room full of cats and bitter memories.

"Ginger ale or water?" Paul's voice broke through her trance.

"Water." She paused. "Make it a ginger ale."

He handed her a can.

Grateful for the distraction, she popped the tab and let the cold liquid slide down her throat. "How many concerts in the park have you attended, Paul?"

"Too many to count. This is the first since my sweet wife passed on."

Jenny set her ginger ale in the cup holder. "I imagine she's smiling down on us."

"Pleased such an exceptional young woman has come into our lives. The music's about to begin. Are you ready to challenge the tune-naming master?"

"You're on." She turned toward the stage.

The leader welcomed the crowd. After introducing his band members and promising a fun evening, the four-man crew launched into the first rousing number.

Paul tapped his foot to the music. "Do either of you recognize that tune?"

"Based on the lyrics," Sam snapped his fingers. "'Let's Go to the Hop'?"

"Close. 'At the Hop'. Who recorded it?"

"I don't have a clue."

Jenny shook her head. "Neither do I."

"Danny and the Juniors, late fifties."

Sam nudged Jenny's arm. "Told you he's an oldies fanatic."

By the fourth song, Paul had racked up a lead of four to zero.

Number five perked Jenny's ears. "Hold on. I know that one. Johnny Cash. 'Walk the Line.' It's also the title of a movie about his life."

"Score two points for the pretty lady." Sam chuckled. "One for the extra details."

Jenny had watched the film more than once. The story of a gentle, tormented soul, driven to addiction by hurtful words and painful memories. Why hadn't her father ever attempted to help his wife recover, like June Carter helped Johnny? Maybe he'd tried and failed.

Pressure on Jenny's knee drew her attention.

"Are you okay?"

Jenny stared at Sam's hand as she pictured the scene from the end of the movie, with the family finally whole. Happy endings were for other people. "The song brought back memories."

The number ended. Another began. "Okay, you two youngsters, five seconds to name that tune."

Sam shrugged. "Again, I don't have a clue."

"Jenny?"

"Nope."

Paul tapped his foot and sang along with the opening line. "Why do Fools Fall in Love."

"Age-old question." Sam lifted the tab on a ginger ale.

"Frankie Lyman." Paul slapped his hand on his thigh. "Score six for me, two for Jenny."

She popped up and tossed her ball cap on the chair. "Come on, Grandpa, and teach me a few dance steps."

"I'm a bit rusty." He eased off his seat. "But willing."

Sam slung his arm over the back of his chair. His eyes trained on the two people he couldn't imagine losing as they slid into an empty slot among the dancers. Why had Jenny reacted to the Cash song? What tormenting line had she walked? Would she ever trust him enough to share her deepest secrets?

He marveled at his grandfather's stamina as he led Jenny through two more rock-and-roll numbers. When the fourth began, Sam bolted to his feet, yanked off his ball cap, and dashed across the grass. He reached his grandpa and Jenny seconds before the first line. "Mind if I cut in?"

"Just in time. These old feet are about to give out." Paul placed Jenny's hand in Sam's.

He slid his arm around her waist. "This is one number I know. 'I Only Have Eyes for You.' Grandma and Grandpa's signature song."

"That's why he hesitated."

"It reminds him how much he misses her." Sam pulled her close. The world around him seemed to drift away the moment she melted into his arms and placed her hand on his shoulder. He breathed in the fresh scent of shampoo and soap as they moved to the music, their bodies in sync. When the tune morphed into another slow number, she didn't pull away.

He nodded toward a couple dancing with a young girl sandwiched between them, clinging to their necks. "See that little family of three? The parents are buddies from high school."

Jenny flinched.

He noticed and drew her closer.

At the end of the song, she pulled away, her eyes glancing up. "This is the first time I've danced since my high school prom." Her smile dissolved as her brows furrowed. "I need a break. Too much ginger ale."

He yearned to understand what lurked beneath the surface as he watched Jenny weave through the crowd. Back at his chair, he removed a bottle of water from the cooler.

"Did you lose Jenny?"

"Bathroom break."

Paul fingered his wedding ring. "Did you notice how she reacted to 'Walk the Line'?"

"Maybe the song or the movie sparked memories of her mother's drinking problem."

"Jenny needs more time to heal, Sam. Don't give up on her. She's worth waiting for."

Jenny stared at her image in the bathroom mirror and breathed in Sam's scent clinging to her collar. The warmth from his body lingered, their hearts beating as one was still fresh in her mind. His comment about his friends dancing with their daughter cut deep. Why did she dance with him and blur the line between friendship and romance?

"Hi, sweetie." Mrs. Perkins moved from a stall to the sink beside Jenny. "Watching you and Sam reminded me of Paul and his precious wife. Back in the day they loved to cut a rug. My sweet husband claims he has two left feet, which makes luring him on a dance floor near impossible." She finished washing then dried her hands. "You go back out there and show us old folks that young love still exists."

"Sam and I are friends."

She patted Jenny's arm. "Enduring romance always begins with friendship."

"What I mean is—"

Mrs. Perkins winked. "I understand. No need to explain." She turned and walked out.

Jenny gripped the sink's edge. What did Mrs. Perkins understand? She wiped sweat from her upper lip. Somehow, she had to quash any speculation two innocent dances might have unleashed on the small-town population.

Chapter 20

Images of Jenny danced in Sam's mind as he stared unseeing at his email inbox. Frustrated, he swiveled his executive chair toward the wall behind his desk. He gazed at the sunrise painting. The sky lit with bright shades of orange and red. A powerful wave crashing against a cliff. A month had passed since he held Jenny in his arms, dancing to his grandparents' song.

"Having a hard time focusing on work?"

"My sister claims this painting represents new beginnings." He turned and faced his grandfather. "I'm no closer to softening Jenny's heart than the first day she walked into this office."

His grandpa dropped onto a chair facing the desk.

"She sat right there where you're sitting, full of life and playfulness. Plying me with smiles and compliments. Batting her eyes like a temptress pegging me as an easy target."

"Don't tell me you're giving up?"

"How would you have reacted if Grandma treated you the way Jenny treats me?"

"You mean like a close friend?"

"Six days a week I see her at Lou's. She agreed to have dinner with me at a restaurant twice. The second time I drove her home, she wouldn't let me walk her up the stairs. If I tried to kiss her, she'd accuse me of stepping over the line." Sam drummed his fingers on the desk. "I'm running low on patience."

His grandfather crossed his leg over his knee and plucked a piece of lint off his trousers. "I never told you about the time your grandmother and I separated."

"You're kidding, right?"

"It happened a couple months after our second anniversary. She was four-months pregnant. Happy. Full of life. Eager to welcome our firstborn into the world." A pained expression clouded his face. "One day, while carrying a basket of laundry down the stairs, she tripped and fell. She broke three bones. When she discovered she'd lost the baby, she plummeted into deep depression blaming herself for killing our child. Nothing I could do or say consoled her. She packed a bag and moved back in with her parents." He paused. "She refused to see me or take my phone calls."

Sam stared at his grandfather. "I had no idea."

"I wrote her dozens of letters, telling her how much I loved her. Pleading for her to come home. I left them in her parents' mailbox. She failed to respond. I didn't have a clue what to do, until one day the truth punched me in the gut. My wife couldn't return to our house and face the memory, the guilt over-and-over again. I put a for sale sign in the front yard and drew up a contract on another house."

"Where you live now?"

He nodded. "Three weeks after I moved in, the doorbell rang. I found the woman I loved standing on the porch with tears streaming down her cheeks. In a flash, I pulled her into my arms." His eyes reddened. "She begged me to forgive her. I kissed away her tears." His voice cracked. "At that moment, my love for her reached a new depth. We spent every day for the rest of our lives together. Until this world released her to her eternal home."

Sam studied his grandfather's pinched brows and the deep lines around his eyes.

"Love like mine and your grandmother's is worth fighting for, Sam. No matter the pain or the time it takes."

Sam longed for a relationship like his grandparents'. A loving wife. A couple of kids. "I don't know if Jenny and I will ever have what you and Grandma had."

"Given enough time, I believe you will."

"Because you have faith?"

"You should try a little."

Sam considered the challenge. "Not a bad idea." He stood and stretched.

"Are you heading to Lou's?"

"I don't want to miss my daily caffeine fix." Sam walked into the reception area.

"Hold on a sec." Mary moved her cell phone away from her ear and eyed Sam. "You're going to Lou's kind of late, aren't you?"

"What makes you think that's where I'm heading?"

"Tell Jenny hi."

He walked outside, welcoming the hint of autumn in the air. Eager to see Jenny's smile and hear her voice, he quickened his pace. When he reached the coffee shop, he headed straight to the corner stool. "How's it going, Lou?"

"Busy morning." She poured him a cup of coffee.

He glanced at Jenny, chatting with a young couple he didn't recognize.

"What are you in the mood for, Sam?"

Another dance with the woman he loved. "A donut. No, make that quiche, if there's any left."

"We still have a couple of slices."

George set his cup on the counter and nudged Sam. "Jenny talked me into trying a piece this morning."

"No kidding? How did she manage to steer you away from a cinnamon bun?"

"She made the crazy dish with fruit."

Sam chuckled. "So, what's the verdict?"

"It's sweet, almost like a real pie. No broccoli or spinach."

Jenny wandered over. "Did George tell you about his new culinary adventure?"

"Seems you made a believer out of him."

She nodded. "Until next week when I make the pie with crab or shrimp."

George shook his head. "You come up with the craziest ideas about what makes good eating before noon."

Jenny laughed.

Sam eyed her. Seemed she was in a good mood. Maybe it was time to test the water again. "Speaking of eating, I'm in the mood for Italian. Want to join me for dinner tonight at Amici's?"

"I suppose spaghetti or lasagna would hit the spot. I'll meet you there at six, and I'm paying."

Success. "In that case, I'll order dessert."

"We'll share one, my choice."

"You're on." Maybe he was winning her over one step at a time.

Lou tapped Jenny's arm. "How about fixing quiche for Sam."

"Coming right up."

She placed a slice of quiche, banana bread, and a strawberry on a plate and delivered it to him. Their eyes locked. He tasted the quiche. "Another example of your amazing cooking skills, Jenny."

"Glad you approve."

"One of these days, she'll make someone a mighty good wife," said George.

"Her culinary talent is way beyond domestic. Someday she'll open her own restaurant. If we're lucky, right here in Madison." Sam held out hope she'd agree, until she blinked, turned, and walked away.

Chapter 21

Jenny wandered into the coffee-shop kitchen. Would accepting Sam's dinner invitation turn into a huge mistake? Except for the night they danced in the park, they'd settled into a comfortable relationship devoid of any hint of romance—thanks to her efforts to keep Sam at arm's length. And he had agreed to let her pay for tonight's dinner. Besides, friends sharing an occasional dinner while supporting local restaurants was the neighborly thing to do. Right?

Jenny counted the morning tips, relieved she'd accumulated enough cash to add to her savings *and* pay for dinner. She dropped the money in her purse and checked her phone. Two missed calls from her sister. Odd. They hadn't spoken in months. And it was three hours earlier on the West Coast. Something must be wrong. She pressed the number, praying nothing had happened to either of her nieces.

Jill answered at the first ring. "He's dead, Jenny."

The hair on the back of her neck raised. "Who?"

"Our father."

Jenny clutched her chest as guilt consumed her. She hadn't spoken to him in years. "When? How?"

"Three weeks ago. Seems he suffered a fatal heart attack. Their next-door neighbor tracked me down."

"Did anyone arrange a funeral?"

"Of sorts." Jill paused. "Our mother should have died first."

"Have you talked to her?"

"Until that call, I'd come close to erasing her existence from my memory. Besides, what can I do from California?"

Jenny leaned back against the wall and slid to the floor. "So, the answer's no."

"Someone needs to make sure her power and water haven't been shut off for lack of payment. Are you still in Tennessee or have you escaped to another town?"

If she said Alaska or Canada—someplace far from the south—Jill wouldn't expect her to go. "For all we know, she's sprawled out on the kitchen floor, rotting away."

"According to the neighbors, she treks to the mailbox every couple of days. You haven't answered my question."

Jenny released a heavy sigh. "I'm an hour away."

A moment of silence. "I know it's a lot to ask. Problem is, there isn't anyone else."

"I know."

"Then you'll go?"

"Seems I don't have a choice."

"Promise to call me from their house and tell me what you find?"

"I will." Jenny ended the call and wrapped her arms around her shins. The idea of facing the woman who had caused her a lifetime of grief unleashed a wave of nausea. Why had her older sister saddled her with the burden of dealing with their mother? Because she had moved thousands of miles away from Georgia. That's why.

Lou carried a tray of dishes into the kitchen and set it on the counter.

Jenny pushed off the floor and grabbed the counter to ease the dizzy sensation threatening to throw her off balance.

"What's wrong, honey?"

"My father died."

Lou's eyes widened as she pressed her hand to her chest. "I'm so sorry. What can I do?"

"There's nothing, really. I'm leaving for Norcross to check on my mother as soon as I ride back to my apartment and get my car keys. Will you tell Sam and apologize about dinner?"

"Of course, and it's okay if you need to take a couple days off to grieve."

"It's better to stay busy." She released her grip and grabbed her purse. "I'll see you tomorrow morning." Jenny dashed out back and rode her bike to her apartment. Seconds after she climbed off and lowered the kickstand, Sam's car pulled onto the driveway.

He climbed out and rushed to her side. "Lou told me. Why don't you let me go with you and keep you company?"

She couldn't bear to let him see where she'd come from. "Thanks, but I need to do this alone."

"I understand." Sam drew her close. "No matter what happens, I'm here for you."

Fearing she was moments from melting into his arms, Jenny pulled away and dashed up the stairs. She stepped inside before tears erupted and spilled down her cheeks. Why did he make it so easy to fall in love with him?

Jenny wiped her tears and waited for Sam to back out of the driveway before grabbing her keys and dashing to her car.

By the time Jenny parked in her parents' mildew-stained driveway, a tangle of knots gripped her stomach. She clenched her fingers around the steering wheel and stared at the shadows falling across the lawn, long ago given way to weeds and patches of red clay. Overgrown shrubs shrouded the front façade, rendering the living-room window virtually useless. Should she back up, drive away, and pretend the woman didn't exist? Except she did. And she'd promised her sister.

Jenny stepped out and trudged to the sidewalk, careful not to trip on the uneven concrete. Her pulse accelerated as she stepped onto the landing and rang the bell. No response. She rang a second, then a third time. No one could blame her for not trying. She spun away from the door. A creak sounded behind her.

"Jenny?"

She froze. *Run.* She sucked in air and dug deep for the courage to stay and face the woman who had given her birth. Her pulse pounded as she turned and stared at Dorothy Collins. The once-beautiful woman had become a slave to addiction and a wasted life. Her bloodshot eyes were lost in dark circles. Her hair disheveled. Her mouth and forehead furrowed with deep lines.

"Hello, Mother."

"You know about your old man kicking the bucket, don't you?" Her words slurred.

"Jill called."

"Figures." She stood aside. "You might as well come in."

"I can't stay long." Jenny stepped inside. Her nose crinkled at the stench of alcohol seeping from her mother's pores.

"Where'd my oldest daughter end up?"

"On the West Coast."

"Long way from Georgia." Her mother stumbled into the living room, and dropped onto the faded couch—stained from a lifetime of careless spills.

Jenny skirted the papers littering the floor and sat on a straight-back chair opposite her mother. Disgust overwhelmed her as she eyed one empty and two partially-filled bottles sitting on the end table beside two glasses. Nothing had changed.

"The first heart attack hit Henry a year ago. His days were numbered, but he kept working. You want a drink?" Her mother poured whiskey into the empty glass and pushed it across the coffee table.

The overpowering desire to drown her memories compelled Jenny to reach for the glass. As she pulled it close, fingerprints on the surface churned her stomach. She swallowed the bile erupting in her throat and set the glass beside a pile of unopened mail littering the coffee table. "Are those bills?"

Her mother shrugged. "Probably."

"Do they need to be paid?"

"Everything's on autopay." She guffawed. "My husband died believing I'm not good for much of anything."

Jenny shuddered at the sight of her mother's fingers gripping the glass and lifting it off the end table.

"Long time ago, I had dreams. I even took a job stripping in a fancy men's club to earn money for college. I was beautiful back then. Desirable." Her slurring escalated. "My mother drank herself to death after her old man abused her. For years. It destroyed her when he ran off with a younger woman."

Was her mother delusional? "First time I've heard that story."

"Genetic curse."

"As far as I know, Jill doesn't drink."

"She's not like you and me. I could've had my pick of men. Some rich and powerful. Even had a fling with a highfalutin attorney, 'til I found out the bum had a wife. He wouldn't leave her. Said a divorce would ruin his reputation."

Her mother's revelation unleashed mind-numbing shock mingled with uncontrollable curiosity. "How did you end up with our father?"

"Met him at a bar after my shift. We drank 'til the wee hours. I ended up in his bed that night and the next. He bought me pretty things, so I stayed. When I told him I was pregnant, he said he'd marry me. He swore he'd pay for me to go to college. I planned to stick around 'til I got educated." She guzzled half her drink. "By the time I realized he'd lied, your sister was on the way. After she was born, the booze trapped me, bought and paid for by a man who'd shackled me with invisible chains and a kid."

Her mother drained the last drop and refilled her glass. "I could've had a good life." She swallowed a gulp and shook her finger at Jenny. "Take my advice and don't let any man trick you into falling in love. When you can't give them what they want, they'll throw you out with the garbage. Or break you until no other man wants you." Her head bobbed. "Use the bums. Take what you want from them and move on."

Jenny shuddered. "Some men are good."

Her mother's eyes grew lightning-fierce. She filled the glass again and downed half the contents before slamming it on the side table. "You're a fool. Bound to end up like me." She glared at Jenny. "One more beautiful woman...stuck." Her shoulders slumped. Her eyelids drooped. "Ruined." Her chin dropped to her chest. Her jaw fell slack.

Jenny cringed at the sight of her mother, passed out cold. Drool escaped the corner of her mouth and trickled down her chin.

She closed her eyes and pressed her fingers to her temples as childhood memories erupted. Climbing onto the couch with a children's book in hand, yearning for her mother's touch. Watching her drink glass after glass of strange-smelling liquid. Feeling confused by her mother's foul and hateful words. Jill taking her by the hand and leading her to their shared bedroom.

Jenny lowered her hands and eased off the chair. She backed out of the room while keeping an eye on her mother. Uncontrollable curiosity directed her feet to the bedroom hallway. She eased down the narrow space until she reached the last room on the right. Her room. She swallowed and walked in. Sunlight filtered through dirt-encrusted windows. Mounds of dust covered every surface and polluted the air. The room hadn't changed since the afternoon her mother had chased her from the kitchen wielding a butcher knife. The day she packed a duffel and escaped through the window. The last time she'd set foot in this house.

Curiosity continued to trounce her impulse to flee. She moved across the hall and stared at the closed door she and Jill had been warned to never open. Other than strange noises, she'd spent a lifetime wondering what lurked inside the mysterious room. Jenny glanced down the hall. No sign of her mother.

She curled her fingers around the knob and eased the door open. A gasp escaped her throat as the odor of urine and cheap perfume forced her to cover her mouth and nose with her hand. Her jaw dropped at the sight of the unmade bed and dirty clothes lying in heaps on the worn, soiled carpet. Dust swirled in the draft from the ceiling fan.

Jenny gawked at framed photos of her mother cluttering the dresser—a shrine to the woman before the ravages of alcohol stole her beauty and warped her soul. The only photos displayed anywhere in the house. Unable to pull her eyes away, her emotions teetered on the seesaw of gut-wrenching anger and pity for the woman who had given her life. Broken. Abused. Wallowing in self-pity.

Fearing the scene in front of her offered a glimpse into her own future, Jenny backed out of the room. She eased down the hall and tiptoed to the front door. Her heart thumped wildly against her ribs as she stole one last glimpse of the woman she had grown to despise.

Jenny dashed to her car, slid onto the driver's seat, and gripped the steering wheel until her knuckles turned white. Anger collided with disgust as she glared at paint peeling off the garage door. Her eyes drifted to a giant wasp nest anchored under the eave.

She pried her fingers off the steering wheel, plucked her phone off the seat, and pressed Jill's number. After relaying her experience—omitting her mother's bedroom shrine—she ended the call. Following one last glance at the front door, she backed into the street and drove aimlessly, tormented by reality. If her mother had pushed a clean glass across the coffee table, she would have given in, maybe even joined her in a drunken stupor.

Jenny braked for a red light. Her phone rang. She glanced at the screen. Sam. She couldn't talk to him. Not now. A neighborhood bar on the corner caught her eye. A horn blasted behind her. Green light. Jenny drove through the intersection. The bar's open sign flashed and beckoned her. She turned right at the next corner, circled the block, and drove into the bar's parking lot.

She dropped her phone and her keys in her purse and stared at the front door. Memories of that night twelve years earlier wrestled its way to the surface. All she needed was one drink to relieve her parched throat and dull the pain. Then she'd drive back to Madison before dark.

Chapter 22

Jenny ran her finger around the rim of her fifth martini, courtesy of the man perched on the stool beside her who reeked of cigarettes and sweat. Months of sobriety had been shattered by her mother's spiteful rhetoric. She stared at her image in the mirror opposite the bar. Who was she kidding? Deep-rooted guilt, not her disgusting mother, landed her here. She lifted the glass and tilted it toward the mirror, spilling half the contents before swallowing the rest in one long gulp.

A hand squeezed her thigh. "That's it, baby. Drink up and I'll show you a good time."

She jerked her head toward the man. Her jaw set, her eyes narrowed. "Back off, buster." Her words slurred. "Before I land a nasty left hook clean across your disgusting mug."

He jerked his hand away. "Why, you stupid little—"

The bartender gripped the man's arm. "The lady isn't interested, buddy. You'd best pay the bill and move on before you do something you'll regret."

"Only thing I regret is wasting time and money on that ball-breaking tease." He slapped two twenties on the bar and stalked out.

Jenny pushed her glass across the bar. "Now that I'm buying, I'll switch to wine. White. House brand."

"That guy was right. You led him to the slaughter."

She tilted her head and fluttered her eyelashes. "In addition to my handsome hero, are you also my judge and jury?"

"That approach won't work on me, honey."

"Tough guy." She crossed her arms on the bar, vaguely remembering Sam uttering a similar retort. "My name's Jenny. What's yours?"

"Does it matter?"

"I suppose not, Mr. Barkeep."

"Name's Chuck. About the wine, can you pay or do you need to wait for another chump to wander in and foot the bill?"

"Do I look like I'm broke?"

He shrugged. "How should I know? When you walked in, I didn't peg you as a tease."

"Looks are deceiving." She reached in her purse and pulled out a handful of bills. "How much will this buy me, tip included?"

"Maybe you should go on home."

"Are you refusing to serve a paying customer?"

Chuck shook his head as he removed a wine stem from an overhead rack and filled it half full. "I don't care if you continue to drink yourself into a stupor." He held the glass at arm's length. "But if you want me to serve you, hand over your car keys."

"Why? Are you planning to steal my trusty ride?" She hiccupped.

"I don't let my customers drive drunk and put themselves and my business at risk."

"Huh. A bartender with a conscience." Jenny stared at him for a long moment. "You drive a hard bargain." She chuckled at her play on words then dug her keys from her purse and sent them skidding across the bar. "Do you have some peanuts to go with the wine?"

He stashed the keys under the bar, pushed the wine glass toward Jenny, and filled a small dish with mixed nuts.

She swirled the wine before taking a sip and glancing behind her. "Two customers besides me. How can your waitress make a living with business this slow?"

"Don't worry, after five o'clock you'll have plenty of victims eager to fund your habit."

What habit? She could put the glass down and walk out anytime she chose. Except he held her keys hostage. The same way Sam held her heart. The notion of him or Lou wandering in and finding her out of control burned her cheeks. She wasn't worthy of Sam's or Lou's love. Why not stay and drown her shame? Like her mother predicted.

Jenny aimed her thumb at the stool beside her. "I'm counting on you to warn the next guy who lands his butt beside me."

"Do I look like your guardian or your daddy?"

She looked away. "My father just died."

"I'm sorry."

"No big deal. I hadn't seen him in years."

The hours passed as Jenny continued to sip wine, bantered with Chuck, and watched him tend other customers. Three men had settled beside her and offered to buy her a drink. Eager to prove her key confiscator wrong, she refused. By the time the afternoon light gave way to darkness, the alcohol she had consumed sought an explosive escape. She stumbled to the restroom and hung her head over the toilet.

Drenched in sweat, she staggered back to the bar and begged for her keys.

Chuck leaned close. "You're in no condition to drive. Either call someone to come pick you up or I'll call for a ride."

She glared at him. "I could have you arrested for theft." Her head spun.

"The cops will thank me for keeping you from killing someone."

"Fine." She dug her phone from her purse. Three missed calls. One from Lou. Two from Sam. Her cheeks burned.

"What's your decision?"

"I'll make the call." She stared at the short list of favorites. Only one option would do. She pressed the private number.

"Hi, Jenny."

Tears flooded and dripped onto the counter. "I'm in trouble, Kelley."

"Where are you?"

"I—" She couldn't remember the name of the bar, much less the street. Her chin dropped to her chest as she handed the phone to Chuck. How many times would she fall off the wagon before she faced the truth? Alcohol was her master.

The rich scent of strong coffee nudged Jenny's eyes open. She blinked and stared at the unfamiliar bedroom awash in shades of beige and pale blue.

"Welcome back among the living." Kelley sat on the side of the bed. "You had quite a night."

Vague memories filtered through the fog muddling Jenny's mind. Her friend and a man guiding her out of the bar into the cool night air. Passing out in the backseat of a moving vehicle. The keys she'd given over to the bartender. "Where's my car?"

"In the driveway. My husband drove it home."

Jenny squinted at sunlight streaming in through the window. "What time is it?"

"Seven-thirty."

"Oh my gosh." She pushed off the pillow. "I have to call Lou and apologize for not showing up to work."

"No need. Sam called her."

"What?" Jenny's head pounded with pain as she swung her legs over the side of the bed. "How'd you talk to Sam?"

"I answered your phone last night."

Her shoulders slumped forward. "What'd you tell him?"

Kelley handed her a mug. "That I'd convinced you to visit an old friend and stay the night."

Jenny gripped the mug with both hands to stop the trembling. "Did he believe you?"

"He seemed more worried than skeptical."

"Thanks for covering for me."

"That's what friends do. He promised to call Lou and clue her in. Sam also told me about your dad dying and you dropping in on your mother."

Memories from the visit filtered through the haze. "Seems I didn't suffer enough punishment growing up with that woman."

"You did what any daughter would do." Kelley pointed to Jenny's clothes neatly folded on a chair. "Clean and fresh. While you shower and dress, I'll fix you a hot breakfast."

"Don't you have patients to tend to?"

"Not until ten." She stood and moved toward the door. "You'll find everything you need by the sink."

Jenny carried the mug to the bathroom and stared at her bloodshot eyes and pale skin. She peeled out of Kelley's pajamas and turned on the shower. When steam drifted from the stall and fogged the mirror, she stepped under the hot water and scrubbed her skin, hoping to wash away every trace of alcohol and regret. After blow-drying her hair and dressing, she shuffled into the kitchen and sat on a stool at the island. "Nice house."

"With a giant mortgage." Kelley placed a plate of scrambled eggs, banana slices, and a muffin on the counter beside a glass of orange juice.

"Is this Dr. Kelley's cure for a hangover?"

"Eggs for protein, bananas and orange juice for potassium. The muffin because it's yummy."

"You're a nutritionist and a shrink?"

Kelley sat beside her friend. "At your service."

Jenny swallowed a bite of eggs and glanced at her friend. "You're avoiding the ugly elephant in the room."

"You mean, how you ended up nearly passed out in a bar?"

Jenny closed her eyes, waiting for the wave of nausea to pass. "You have no idea what it was like coming face-to-face with my mother after all these years."

"You suffered from an alcohol-use trigger."

"Proof I'm not addicted. Right? Besides, last night was the first time I'd had a drink in months."

Kelley searched Jenny's eyes. "Which proves you have an enormous reservoir of strength until confronted with a situation too painful to deal with. What you need is someone to help you resist temptation the next time your mother or anyone else ignites your urge to drink. So please promise to call me before giving in."

"Who says there'll be a next time?"

"I'm just saying if there is, you don't have to fight it on your own."

Jenny bit into the muffin as the bitter taste of reality sent bile racing to her throat.

"Are you okay?"

She sipped her orange juice to wash away the bitterness. "There's a lot you don't know about me."

Kelley reached for Jenny's hand. "You'll never find peace until you release the secrets you keep locked up inside. Whenever you're ready to talk, I'll listen. As your friend not your doctor."

How could she tell Kelley about the things she had done? The people she'd hurt. The fate she'd sealed. "Forget what I said." She pulled her hand away. "It's not a big deal."

The lie lolled on Jenny's tongue like a bitter pill refusing to slide down her throat. Last night she had crossed the line and broken her resolve never to drink again. She had let herself lose control. Maybe she should reveal the truth to Kelley. No. Not now. Maybe never.

Chapter 23

Hours after returning to Madison, Jenny stared at the bottle of wine sitting on the dresser—purchased in a moment of weakness on her way home from Kelley's. How long before her resolve gave way again? An hour? A day? The world seemed to spin around her as she summoned the courage to slide the bottle back into the bottom drawer beside its companion.

While the prospect of abandoning people she had grown to love ripped a hole in her heart, she accepted reality. She had to leave Madison before another incident or painful memory sent her sidling up to a local bar to order a drink. Then another and another, until the alcohol numbed her pain and destroyed her reputation.

A single bark lured Jenny to the door. The sight of Duchess staring up at her failed to bring a smile. "You understand I have to leave before anyone discovers the truth." She motioned her canine friend inside and tossed a dog biscuit high. Duchess caught the treat midair. "I'll miss our afternoon visits."

She schlepped across the room and dropped onto the sofa.

Duchess plopped her head in Jenny's lap.

She stroked the dog's muzzle while racking her brain for a logical reason to leave town. Something everyone could respect and accept. Her eyes drifted to her chef portfolio. Only one explanation made sense. Tomorrow she would lay the groundwork and leave the day after. Quick. Like ripping off a bandage.

Following a restless night and a challenging morning, Jenny flipped the open sign to closed and gathered dirty dishes off a table. Exhausted and struggling with angst over her pending task, she tripped on the way to the kitchen and dropped the plates.

Lou stooped to help her pick up the pieces. "Do you need to take a few days off and recover from your father's passing?"

"No." Jenny peered around the empty coffee shop. It wasn't too late to change her mind about leaving. Yes, it was. "We need to talk."

"Now's a good time." Lou straightened. "What's on your mind?"

Jenny set the broken plates on the counter and choked on the lie ready to roll off her tongue. "I've been offered a job as a sous-chef."

"Second in charge. Which lucky Madison restaurant is fixing to steal you away?"

"This is the hard part." Jenny's nostrils flared as she struggled to release the words. "It's in another town."

Lou hiked onto a stool. "How far away?"

She pressed her hand to her gut and avoided eye contact. "Charleston. South Carolina.

"I see." Lou paused. "Have you told Sam?"

Jenny shook her head. "I wanted to tell you first."

Lou reached for her hand. "Are you positive that's what you want?"

"It's an opportunity I can't pass up." She swallowed the acrid taste of deceit. "For my career."

"Madison couldn't hold on to my Sara, either. You know, one of these days I'll take a notion to retire. When that happens, I'd be proud if you'd return and take over. Maybe expand our little coffee shop and serve lunch."

Jenny eyed a lipstick-stained coffee cup on the counter beside a half-eaten donut. "I can't imagine you sitting in a rocking chair on your front porch, watching life pass you by."

"What I'm trying to say is I hope you find your way back home. But even if you don't get a hankering to return, I'll always count you as my second daughter."

Jenny choked back tears. "I'll treasure our time together forever."

"Me too." Lou embraced her.

"I have to find Sam and give him the news."

"You'll break his heart."

Tears erupted and spilled down Jenny's cheeks. "In time he'll forget me."

"No, honey, he won't. But he'll find a way to survive." Lou dabbed Jenny's tears with her fingers. "When are you leaving?"

She sniffled. "Tomorrow morning."

Lou hesitated. "Since this is our last day together, I want you to come to dinner at my house."

"I don't know—"

"The invitation isn't up for debate. Five o'clock."

She owed Lou that much. "What can I bring?"

"Just your sweet smile and a big appetite."

Jenny plucked a paper napkin off the counter and blew her nose before carrying the broken plates to the kitchen. After taking one last glance around, she fled out the back door and climbed onto her bike. During the short ride, she drank in the view to burn the images into her memory. When Gibson Realty came in sight, her pulse pounded. How could she tell Sam without falling to pieces? Maybe she should leave him a note, like she had done with other friends she'd abandoned. Except she counted him as far more than a friend, and Lou knew she intended to tell him face-to-face. She climbed off her bike, wiped sweat from her upper lip, and walked into the reception area.

"Hey, Jenny." Mary's cheery tone added to her angst. "Are you looking for Sam?"

"Is he here?"

She nodded toward the left. "He's in the conference room with his grandfather."

"I'll come back later."

"No need. Believe me, they'll welcome the interruption." She hopped up, guided Jenny down the hall, and stuck her head in the last doorway on the left. "A pretty lady wants to speak to you, Sam." She nudged Jenny inside then slipped away.

A grin lit Sam's face. "What a nice surprise."

Paul stood. "Do you want me to leave you two alone?"

"No. Please stay. "Jenny's heart thumped against her ribs.

"Pull up a chair." Paul sat back down.

"Thanks, but I'd best remain standing."

"What do you think, Grandpa? Is she afraid we'll put her to work, or does she want a quick getaway?"

"Maybe we'd best ask her. Which is it, Jenny?"

"I...have something important to tell you."

"Uh-oh." Sam's brow pinched. "Bad news?"

"Not exactly." She repeated the story she'd told Lou. "I'm leaving first thing in the morning."

"I don't understand." Sam rose to his feet. "Why would a restaurant in a town full of chefs offer a job to someone who lives hundreds of miles away?"

"Did it occur to you that I have a good reputation?"

"What did you do, Jenny?" Sam's tone came across as harsh, almost accusatory. "Send out resumes, or call every chef in Charleston begging for a job?"

"That's not what happened."

Sam gripped the edge of the conference table and leaned forward. "What's the name of this restaurant you're so all-fired eager to run off to?"

Jenny fought the urge to flee as she scoured her brain for a logical response. "It could be one of several. A lot of executive chefs own more than one restaurant."

"Is that why you wanted a month-to-month lease? So you could leave with a moment's notice?"

"It's not that I want to leave."

Sam's eyes narrowed. "Then why are you? And what happened to opening your own restaurant?"

"I'll have a better chance in Charleston."

Sam dropped back onto his chair. "If you'd have asked, I would've given you the money."

"I need an investor, Sam. Not a donor."

"Don't be too hard on him, Jenny. Your decision comes as quite a shock. I think it's appropriate to say you're welcome to return home any time."

"I'll miss you both." More than they would ever know. Tears welled in Jenny's eyes.

"We'll stay in touch with letters and social media." Paul lifted off his chair and moved close to Jenny. "Whatever works. After all, Duchess will want to know what's going on with her favorite pal."

Her skin turned to gooseflesh as she glimpsed Sam's downturned mouth, his eyes dull and empty. She had stabbed him in the heart without warning—like the blonde who'd abandoned him. At least she wasn't breaking an engagement or even a romantic relationship. And she had never promised to stay. "I don't want to hurt you, Sam. In time you'll see this is for the best."

"For who? Me? Lou? Or are you only thinking of yourself?"

"That's not fair."

"Have you even bothered to tell Lou?"

She nodded. "Before I rode over here."

Mary stuck her head in the door. "Your one o'clock appointment...is here. Is everything okay? You three look like your best friend went and bought the farm."

"We're all peachy keen." Sam's voice dripped with mockery. "Right, Grandpa? Chef Collins?"

"I'd better go." Jenny brushed past Mary and dashed outside seconds before guilt and shame released a torrent of tears and gut-wrenching remorse. At least she'd given Sam a valid reason to forget her and move on with his life.

Sam swiped his hand across the conference table, sending a stack of papers fluttering to the floor.

"Oh, my gosh." Mary gawked. "Is someone dying?"

"Nothing that dire. I'll fill you in later." Paul faced her. "Right now, go apologize to Sam's appointment and reschedule for tomorrow."

"Yes, sir." She walked out.

His grandfather faced Sam. "You were mighty tough on Jenny."

"What did you expect me to do? Wish her well? Thank her for charming her way into our lives before running out on us?" He stalked to the window overlooking the back parking lot.

"You love her too much to give up on her now."

Sam's hands fisted. "Why don't you tell me when I should give up. After she's gone for six months? A year? A decade?"

"You need to leave the door wide open, and give her a reason to return."

"She cares more about advancing her career than coming back to Madison."

His grandfather plucked Sam's vibrating phone off the table. "Lou's calling. Want me to answer?"

"Put it on speaker."

"Hey, Lou."

"Has Jenny been by?"

"She left a few minutes ago."

"How's Sam taking the news?"

"About how you'd expect."

"That bad? I want to run something by you both." She explained.

"Clever ploy."

Sam spun away from the window. "What makes you think your insane idea won't backfire, Lou?"

"We have to try."

"You two do whatever you want. But count me out." Sam bent to scoop the papers off the floor.

"Don't worry, Lou. I'll talk sense into my stubborn grandson." He ended the call and leaned back against the conference table. "You can't let Jenny leave thinking you don't care about her."

"Do you expect me to put on an act, and pretend she hasn't cut me to the core?"

"Twenty-seven letters. That's how many I wrote to your grandmother before she came back to me."

Sam tossed the papers on the table. "I'll think about it."

"Think long and think hard, because two futures hang in the balance."

Chapter 24

After packing clothes from three dresser drawers, Jenny opened the fourth and removed her sweaters, exposing her wine stash. One drink to calm her nerves wouldn't hurt. She carried the bottle to the kitchenette, removed the cork, and filled a juice glass. Her hand trembled as she stared at the golden liquid, inches from her lips.

The glass slipped from her hand and fell to the floor, shattering on impact. Jenny grabbed the bottle and tipped it over the sink. "You're not taking me down. Not tonight." After willing her hand to remain steady until the last drop disappeared down the drain, she tossed the empty bottle in the trash and cleaned up the mess.

With ten minutes to get ready, she returned to the bedroom, flung open her closet, and stared at the one unpacked item. Her red dress. Why not wear it during her last night in town. She shoved memories of her first date with Sam aside, slipped it on, and grabbed a dog biscuit.

Jenny met Duchess on the stoop. "Maybe after I'm gone, another lady or a guy will move in and give you treats." Her canine friend followed her down the stairs. When she climbed into her car, Duchess tucked her tail and padded onto the deck. "You know we won't see each other again, don't you, girl?" Jenny whispered while eyeing the dog pawing the sliding glass door. Following the scene in the conference room, she couldn't bear facing Paul or Sam. She backed out of the driveway, drove to Lou's, and parked on the street in front of the two-story, frame home.

Angst held her soul captive as she stared at the three-foot-high white picket fence, lush lawn, manicured shrubbery, and islands of colorful plants. Maybe this wasn't such a good idea. Except she owed Lou a proper goodbye. Before she could change her mind, Jenny climbed out and rushed up the front walk to the covered porch. A hollow sensation assailed her chest as reality hit home. Tonight, she would set foot inside Lou's home for the first and last time.

Lou opened the door before Jenny knocked. Her hair flowed free. She wore the same outfit she had worn for her surprise birthday party—white slacks and a long-sleeve red tunic. "Welcome to my humble home." A dog with silky black and white fur stood beside her. "Meet my Border collie, Buttons."

Jenny stooped and patted the dog's head.

"She's older than me in doggie years. My, what a pretty dress."

Jenny straightened. "Everything else is packed."

"Perfect choice for tonight." Lou stepped aside and motioned her into the front hall.

Jenny breathed in the sweet aroma of cinnamon and brown sugar wafting in the air. "Let me guess, homemade apple pie."

"My grandmother's secret recipe. She was such a dear lady. Come on, I'll show you her picture."

She followed Lou through an arched opening into a cozy parlor. Buttons yawned, moseyed to the corner, and curled up on a fat pink pillow. Lou turned toward the wall and swept her arm in a wide arc. "Meet my family."

Jenny gazed at the space on both sides of the arc, covered with framed photographs. "So many pictures." She touched a photo of a younger Lou standing in front of the coffee shop smiling.

"The day I opened my place all those years ago."

"It still looks the same." Her eyes drifted to a pretty woman, a handsome man, and a young girl gathered around a cake. She traced her finger over the glass. "Is this you and your husband?"

Lou nodded. "Celebrating Sara's third birthday."

"Would you believe there isn't a single picture of me and my sister or anyone else in my parents' house?" Except those she'd discovered in her mother's bedroom.

"I guess some folks aren't into photos. Tell you what. Tonight, I'll take a picture of us and add it to my wall of memories."

"Me?"

"Of course, honey. After all, you're as much family as anyone."

Words and thoughts collided with the sting of reality. She was hours from running away. Again. Would it ever stop?

Lou grasped her hand and led her to a sofa facing a brick fireplace. She sat beside Jenny and poured lemonade from a pitcher into one of four tall glasses sitting on a silver tray. "Freshly squeezed."

Jenny ran her fingers over the sofa's smooth floral fabric while eyeing an eclectic collection of candlesticks on the mantel flanking a painting—a white-washed country church set in a field of green grass. "Pretty picture."

"My father's work. Everyone considered him quite the amateur artist. He gave most of his paintings away to friends and neighbors."

"Do you paint?"

"Just walls. My talent hails from Mom. Cooking and gardening. I spend my afternoons tending my flowers and loving on Buttons. Staying busy keeps my joints from stiffening up. After dinner I'll show you the rose bushes in my backyard."

A doorbell chimed.

Buttons' ears perked.

"Hope you don't mind. I invited a couple of special guests to join us." Lou patted Jenny's arm. "I'll be right back."

What was Lou up to? Jenny faced the arch. Her breath hitched at the sight of Sam clutching a bottle of wine, and Paul carrying a gift bag stuffed with yellow tissue paper.

"We couldn't let you leave without giving you a going-away party." Paul placed the bag on the wingback chair catercorner to the sofa and hiked his hip on the arm.

Sam handed Lou the wine, then moved to the fireplace. He placed his left foot on the hearth and planted his forearm on the mantel. "You look nice, Jenny." His tone lacked emotion.

Lou set the wine on the coffee table and settled beside Jenny. "How about taking a picture of Jenny and me, Sam, before I end up with cabbage or chicken stuck in my teeth."

"Glad to." He removed his phone from his pocket.

Lou wrapped her arm around Jenny's shoulder. She slid her arm around Lou's waist, her lips on the verge of quivering.

"Okay ladies, big smiles. Pretend old George walked in carrying a half-eaten quiche." His eye caught Jenny's. "Wearing a Speedo, black socks, and sandals."

Both women giggled.

"That's a good shot." He snapped the photo.

"Now, I want a picture of the three people who pulled off a birthday shindig that'll go down as one of Madison's finest." Lou nodded toward Paul. "Go over there with Sam."

Paul held his arm out to Jenny and escorted her to the fireplace.

She stood between the two men.

Lou aimed her phone. "Arm in arm, like lifelong pals."

Jenny's muscles tensed as their arms interlinked. Sam's musky aftershave elicited memories of her cheek pressed against his neck. Why had Lou invited them to dinner? Was this really a going-away party, or a ploy to convince her to change her mind?

"Now picture George like Sam described him."

Jenny breathed deeply and slowly released the air, forcing her heartbeat to slow.

"Perfect." Lou lowered her phone, then filled two more glasses with lemonade. "Why don't you give Jenny her gift before I serve supper."

"Good idea." Paul motioned toward the sofa.

Jenny's throat constricted as she skirted the coffee table and settled beside Lou.

Paul placed the bag on her lap. "Go ahead. Look inside."

She removed the tissue, pulled out a framed photo, and stared at the four of them posing at Lou's birthday party.

"We don't want you to forget your friends when you become a famous, world-class chef." A grin warmed Paul's face as he nodded toward the bag. "There's one more item."

Jenny reached in and removed a cell phone.

"Pre-paid," said Sam. "To replace yours when the minutes run out. It's programmed with our numbers, so we can all stay in touch."

"I—" The words froze on the tip of Jenny's tongue. The lie she had told stuck in her throat. How could she abandon the three people who meant more to her than she dared admit?

"Seems we've left our gal speechless." Lou pressed her palms together. "Sam, you escort our guest of honor to the dining room and pour the wine. The corkscrew is on the sideboard. Paul, come with me and give me a hand in the kitchen."

"At your service."

Sam picked the bottle off the table. "Guess we'd best follow Lou's instructions."

Jenny walked beside him as they crossed the hallway to the dining room.

"I'm sorry for acting like a fool earlier today." Sam moved to the sideboard and cut the foil off the wine. "No one has the right to criticize you for wanting to advance your career." He glanced at her before removing the cork.

Had he bought her fabricated story? Jenny moved to the front window and stared at the front lawn. The splash of liquid pouring into a glass broke the uncomfortable silence. "Does that mean you're not here to talk me out of leaving?"

"I'd be lying if I said I won't miss you." Sam moved beside her. "If things don't work out in Charleston, you'll always have a home here."

If only she'd met Sam years ago...instead of Max. She choked on the bitter taste of remorse. "Your comment means more than you can imagine."

"I don't know who broke your heart, Jenny—"

"Please." She pressed her fingers to his lips. "Don't say any more."

He swallowed. His eyes reddened.

Jenny clenched her lower lip between her teeth. She couldn't bear to see him fall apart. "This move is best for everyone."

Footsteps struck the floor behind them. "Lou's outdone herself with this feast." Paul's voice boomed. "Fried chicken. Mashed potatoes. Black-eyed peas."

Jenny broke eye contact, then pulled her hand away from Sam's lips and spun toward the table. "An honest-to-goodness southern feast."

"You bet." Paul set a tray on the sideboard and transferred serving dishes to the table.

Lou carried a bowl and platter. "Plus, coleslaw and cornbread. We old folks will sit on this side of the table and you young'uns across from us."

Sam cleared his throat. "You're the boss." He pulled a chair out for Jenny.

After Paul said grace, he lifted his glass to offer a toast.

The world stood still as Jenny stared at her wineglass. Why hadn't she told Sam not to fill hers? Too late. Go along. Pretend to sip. She reached for her glass.

"To Jenny and a future bright with promise."

She curled her fingers around the stem and touched the glass to her lips. One tiny sip. To ease the pain in her heart. As the smooth buttery wine slid over her tongue, images of the bartender holding her car keys hostage exploded in her head. Somehow, she found the courage to set the glass down.

Sam's arm touched hers as he passed her a bowl.

Her breath caught. Desperate to ignore the wine and avoid any discussion about her move to Charleston, Jenny spooned buttery mashed potatoes onto her plate. "Your cooking talent obviously exceeds donuts and cinnamon buns, Lou."

"Wait 'til you taste the chicken. It's an old family recipe, and better than the Colonel's."

Paul laughed. "Maybe you should change Lou's Coffee Shop to Lou's Café."

Jenny held her breath. Did his comment precede a plea for her to reconsider her decision?

Lou nudged Paul's arm. "Why go changing a formula that's worked for years."

Jenny released the air. "Lou's right. Besides, if she spent more time in the kitchen, George and Sam would miss their daily dose of local news."

For the remainder of the meal, their conversation remained jovial, without a word about Charleston. After finishing her last bite of peach cobbler, Lou released a yawn. "Sorry. It's an hour past my bedtime."

Paul reached for Lou's plate. "I'll help you clean up to give Sam and Jenny time to say goodbye."

"No." Jenny pushed away from the table.

"Jenny's right, Grandpa." Sam stood. "We should leave now." He grasped Jenny's hand.

She trembled.

He kissed her fingers.

Her pulse pounded.

His eyes lingered on hers. "I hope you find what you're searching for."

She choked back tears.

Sam released her hand and walked out without looking back.

Paul eased beside Jenny. "We're all here for you when you need us."

"I know." Her voice was barely above a whisper.

He kissed Lou's cheek. "Thanks for inviting us."

"My pleasure." She escorted him to the door.

Jenny traipsed to the window. Tears spilled at the sight of Sam climbing into his grandfather's car. The desire to run after him and tell him she'd stay compelled her to take a step toward the door.

Lou returned to the dining room, carrying the gift bag. "I'm too tired to mess with cleaning up tonight."

The urge passed. "Are you sure?"

"Positive." Lou handed Jenny the bag. "Besides, if you stay any longer, I won't be able to hold back my tears."

Jenny embraced her. "I love you, Lou."

"I love you too, honey." She pulled away and wiped a tear from Jenny's cheek. "Promise we'll stay in touch?"

"I promise." Her shoulders curled as she headed to the front door, walked out to the cool night air, and closed the distance to her car. She paused at the driver's side and caught a glimpse of Lou standing at her dining room window. Jenny burned the image into her memory before climbing into her car and pulling away from the curb.

When she turned onto Paul's driveway, a sigh of relief escaped. Sam's car was nowhere in sight. Jenny climbed out and spotted the bike propped against the staircase. She'd miss the early morning rides through the quiet streets. Fearing she'd change her mind about the move, she dashed up the stairs. Shallow breaths escaped as she rushed to the bedroom and lifted the remaining bottle of wine from her dresser. She twisted off the cap and downed a long swallow. Somehow, she mustered the courage to screw the cap back on and place the bottle back in the drawer before collapsing onto her bed and crying herself to sleep.

Chapter 25

F ollowing a night riddled with nightmares, Sam's eyes eased open and adjusted to the dark. He glanced at the clock beside his bed. An hour before dawn. Why hadn't he swallowed his pride and begged Jenny to stay in Madison? Desperate to talk to her before she drove out of town and his life, he threw aside the sheet, and swung his feet to the floor. Ten minutes later, he turned onto his grandpa's driveway and rolled to a stop beside the empty space. He pounded the steering wheel with his fist while staring at light shining through the apartment windows. Movement to his left caught his eye. He lowered his window.

His grandfather leaned down. "She left a half hour ago."

"Gone." Sam's shoulders slumped. "Out of my life forever."

"Not necessarily."

He stared at his grandfather. "Your unfounded optimism won't erase reality."

"Come with me. I want to show you something."

Surrendering to curiosity, Sam released a deep sigh and traipsed up the stairs behind his grandfather.

"Go in and take a look around."

"What's the point?"

"Humor me."

He shook his head, crossed the threshold, and turned in a slow circle. Nothing seemed out of place. The painting, sunflower throw pillows, and coasters Jenny had bought remained. Half expecting her to saunter in from the bedroom, he moved to the bookcase. The displayed items appeared as he remembered them. "She obviously doesn't think much of the gifts I bought her."

"Keep looking."

Sam squinted. "One book's missing. Big deal."

"Beside the bookcase."

His eyes drifted to the television before sliding to the space below. Stunned, he squatted.

"Now what do you think?"

He opened Jenny's guitar case and ran his fingers over the Gibson. "This is one of her three prized possessions. I can't imagine her leaving it behind."

"Whether she left it consciously or unconsciously, plus with everything else she failed to take with her, it's a sign she intends to return."

"Have you forgotten that we can ship anywhere?"

"I don't expect she'll ask us to send anything to her."

Duchess sniffed the guitar, whimpered, and sprawled on the floor beside Sam. Her head dropped to her paws. Sam stroked her back. "What makes you so sure?"

"Gut feeling. Plus, the way she looked at you last night."

Mental images of Jenny—beautiful, enticing in the dress she had worn during their first dinner together—tugged at his heart. He had summoned every ounce of self-control to keep from gathering her into his arms and begging her to stay. "You said it took twenty-seven letters to entice Grandma back home?"

"Yep."

Sam pushed up and plucked *The Scarlet Letter* from the bookcase. "We should leave the apartment as she left it." He placed the book back on the shelf.

"My opinion exactly."

Jenny struggled to keep from exceeding the speed limit as she drove past the last exit to Augusta and crossed over the Savannah River. Her mind wandered back to last night. The camaraderie. The laughter. The sideways glances stolen at Sam. Why hadn't he tried to change her mind about leaving? Had he accepted the new reality, or put up a good front?

By the time she exited Interstate 20 and cut over to I-26, the sun had penetrated the morning mist. Somehow, she had to find a job before she depleted the funds available on her prepaid credit card or was forced to dip into her savings. Again. Why hadn't she spent less and saved more?

She turned on the radio, scanned to a country station, and forced her fingers to tap to the beat until she arrived at the outskirts of Charleston. A sign advertising low weekly rates beckoned. She turned into the motel parking lot.

After prepaying for a week at the extended-stay property barely worthy of a two-star rating, she unlocked the door to her ground-floor room and scrunched her nose at the piney odor of cleaning fluids. Her shoulders slumped at the sight of drab gray walls, stained carpet, and cheap furniture. A far cry from her cheery apartment back in Madison. At least the so-called kitchen came equipped with a stovetop and a mini fridge. She opened the curtains and stared at the oil-stained parking lot. No point wallowing in regret.

Jenny schlepped to her car and popped the trunk. Her hand froze half-way to her picnic basket. Something didn't seem right. She dashed to the rear window and peered inside. No sign of her guitar. Had someone stolen it when she stopped for gas and headed to the restroom? She squeezed her eyes shut, trying to remember if she had locked the car door. Her mind drifted to the last moments in her apartment.

She leaned back against the door, slid to the pavement, and buried her face in her hands. One of her most valuable possessions—left behind. Maybe forgetting served as a sign she needed to let go of the past and focus on the future.

"Are you okay, Miss?"

She glanced up at the middle-aged man standing over her. "Yeah. Long drive. Guess I'm tired."

"I know what you mean." He extended his hand and helped her to her feet. "Do you need help carrying your bags in?"

"Thanks for offering, but I can manage." She waited for him to pass on by before hauling her bags and picnic basket across the walkway and into the dreary room. A sigh escaped as she pulled *Great Expectations* from her duffel and placed it on the small round table marred by scratches and water stains. One of these days, she would find out what happened to Pip and Estelle.

Jenny reached back in the bag and removed the photo taken at Lou's birthday party. Her little family of four, who would live on in her memories. She placed the picture on the dresser. When she finished unpacking, she settled on a chair in desperate need of restuffing and pulled up a list of fine-dining restaurants on her new iPad—another extravagant purchase. An hour after logging on, she tapped her finger on the name topping her hand-written list. Le Champagne. Eager to move on to step two in her three-pronged plan, she returned to her car to search for a grocery store. Tomorrow she would complete step three.

Chapter 26

B efore the sun crept over the horizon, Jenny's phone alarm nudged her awake. A car engine revved. She blinked. A sliver of light peeked around the edge of the drawn curtains. Had Sam pulled onto Paul's driveway in the wee hours of the morning? A pang of regret kindled as her fingers gripped the scratchy sheet, and reality broke through her mental fog. That brief season in Madison had come to an end. She crawled out of bed and slogged to the kitchenette, then popped a pod in the coffee maker and focused on the task at hand. When finished, she donned her favorite chef coat and equipped her picnic basket for her first—and if all went well—only interview.

Jenny transferred the cash from her portfolio to a motel envelope. After hauling her enticements to her car and locking the money in her glove box, she drove into Charleston and found a parking spot on Meeting Street. She checked her image in the visor mirror. "Time to turn on the southern charm."

With her basket looped over one arm and her chef portfolio tucked under the other, she hastened to the middle of the block, entered Le Champagne Restaurant, and headed straight to the kitchen.

A woman looked up from the prep table. "We don't open 'til five, Miss."

"I'm here for my interview with Chef André."

The woman shrugged and nodded toward the left. "He's in his office."

"Thank you." Jenny held her head high and moved to the closed door. Hoping she hadn't lost her touch, she knocked.

"*Entrez.*"

Showtime. Inside the tastefully decorated office, she set the basket on the desk. "It's a pleasure to meet the South's finest chef."

André's chin lifted. His brows arched. "And you are?"

She extended her hand to the man with slicked-back dark hair and skin tone that appeared more Latin than European. "Chef Jenny Collins."

"If you're seeking a position, Mademoiselle, I am not currently hiring." She suppressed a smile at his over-the-top French accent.

Jenny dismissed the comment with a shrug and placed her portfolio in front of him. She flipped to the first page. "As you can see, I received training in one of the country's finest culinary institutions. Please review my credentials while I prepare to delight your taste buds."

He stared at her. "I must say, your approach is unique."

Plus, well-rehearsed and most of the time effective. She opened the picnic basket revealing a royal blue lining. Sensing his eyes remained fixed on her, she laid a white linen place mat, a gold fork, and a matching spoon on the desk. Next, she removed an insulated container and peeled off the lid. With exaggerated flair, Jenny lifted out a white porcelain plate displaying a perfectly formed lump-crab cake. She placed it on the mat and drizzled her signature sauce along the side.

Jenny moved a chair close to the desk. "Please, take a seat."

"You have piqued my curiosity." He moved from his desk chair.

"Bon appétit, Chef André."

He dipped his fork into the crab cake. "Almost no filling." He swallowed one bite and took another. "Impressive."

"Thank you. It's one of my two signature recipes."

"And the other?"

Jenny removed a second insulated container and used her culinary torch to create a perfect caramelized top layer on her crème brûlée.

"An excellent French dessert."

"You will find my version quite unique." While he sampled, Jenny touted her accomplishments, with emphasis on her sous-chef position at Chez Lemaire in Los Angeles. "Are you familiar with Chef Tony?"

"A French restauranteur with an excellent reputation."

"As you can see, I have the experience needed to fill a spot in your fine restaurant."

André returned to his executive chair and flipped to another page in her portfolio.

Jenny remained standing with her hands clasped behind her back while anticipating a positive reaction. When he paused to read Chef Tony's' recommendation letter, sweat trickled down her back as memories of her more-than-professional relationship with the man surfaced. Another brief time in her nomadic lifestyle.

Chef André closed the cover. "You have captured my imagination, Chef Jenny." He pronounced her name with the emphasis on the last syllable, laced his fingers, and stared at her for a long moment. "My dining room is small, attracting a sophisticated clientele. Reservations are booked months in advance."

Time to massage his ego. "Which speaks to your incredible talent and ingenuity." She pressed her hand to her chest. "I will consider it a great honor to work for a man who has mastered his craft with such brilliant finesse."

His chest puffed. "I only hire the best, and at the moment I am fully staffed."

She winced inwardly. That didn't work.

"However, I am less than satisfied with one of my line chefs." He unlaced his fingers. "I will give you five days, without pay, to work in my kitchen and prove you are the better choice."

How dare he suggest she work for free, with no guarantees! Should she pack up and walk out? Her eyes drifted to the array of framed awards displayed on the wall behind his desk. Landing a position at Le Champagne would open a lot of doors. Maybe even lead to an investor.

"If you're considering whether to accept my offer, perhaps you are not up to the task."

No way she'd let Mr. Exaggerated French Accent intimidate her. She unclasped her hands. "Shall I begin today or tomorrow?"

Chapter 27

Sam's eyes shifted from the blank sheet of paper lying on his desk to the pile he'd wadded and tossed in the waste basket. He had no idea whether Jenny moved to Charleston to advance her career or escape a painful past. All that mattered was giving her a good reason to come back to Madison. To him. He grabbed his pen to take another stab at writing his first letter, this time as a friend. When he finished, he folded the page and placed it in his top drawer. All he needed now was her address.

Eager for a cup of coffee, he walked out of his office and dashed past Mary before she had a chance to comment. Outside, he eyed the dark clouds moving in from the west and stepped up his pace. At least the weather accurately reflected his mood. When he arrived at the coffee shop, the help-wanted sign in the window tugged on his heartstrings. Maybe the job had played a role in Jenny's decision. After all, her talent and experience far exceeded Lou's requirements. He walked in and spotted his sister, dressed in scrubs, sitting on his stool. Not in the mood for a lecture or confrontation, he took a step back.

Sandra caught his eye and motioned him over.

No need trying to sneak out. She'd chase him down and tackle him to the sidewalk if that's what it took to coerce him to listen. Might as well stay and find out what she was up to. He released a heavy sigh and meandered to the counter.

George swiveled. "Morning, Sam."

"How's it going, George?" He settled on the stool beside his friend.

"Fair to middling. Think it's gonna rain today."

"Good assumption."

Lou set a coffee-filled mug on the counter in front of Sam. "It's about time you came in."

"Busy morning." He glanced sideways at his sister. The last time she'd showed up at his morning hangout, her accusations prompted him to invite Jenny to dinner. Too bad that wouldn't happen this time.

Sandra pushed her cup forward. "How about a refill, Lou."

"Coming right up, Doc." She grabbed the coffeepot and poured. "Are you going on or coming off duty?"

"Off. I hear Jenny moved out of the apartment yesterday before dawn. I can't say I'm surprised."

George leaned on the counter. "Won't be the same around here without her."

Sandra emptied a sugar packet into her coffee. "You do know it's impossible to keep a perpetual wanderer tied down for long."

Sam clutched his mug in both hands. "Are you gloating?"

"I'm just saying it's best she moved on."

"Best for who?" He glared at his sister.

"Look, Sam." Sandra sighed. "I didn't come in to argue or upset you."

His eyes narrowed to a squint. "Then why are you here?"

"To make sure you're okay."

He couldn't tell her his heart ached for Jenny or that he had spent the last two frustrating hours attempting to write his first letter to her. The way he'd labored over every word. "I'm fine."

"Good to hear. Because I love you and only want what's best for you." Sandra slid off the stool and moved to her brother's side. "We have a new nurse on staff who's dying to meet you."

So that was her ploy. Hook him up with another woman so he'd forget Jenny. "You know I don't go on blind dates."

"She's a gorgeous redhead."

"Hey, Doc." George nudged Sandra's arm. "Does she like older men?"

Lou laughed. "You mean ancient codgers."

Sam guffawed. "Now there's a worthwhile idea. Setting the redhead up with my pal, George, the most eligible bachelor in town."

Sandra huffed and yanked her hand off Sam's arm. "You three are a barrel of laughs. My hilarious brother will pay for my coffee, Lou. Make sure he tips you well."

"He always does."

"Thanks for stopping by, Sis."

"Ugh." Sandra rolled her eyes, turned on her heel, and stomped out.

Lou topped off George's coffee. "Your sister means well, Sam."

"In an irritating sort of way. Any word from Jenny?"

"Not yet. Can I bring you some coffee cake or a warm cinnamon bun?"

"No thanks. I'm not hungry."

Lou leaned close. "I saw how Jenny stole glances at you during dinner at my house. One of these days she'll find a reason to come back to Madison."

"Same comment Grandpa made."

George elbowed Sam. "That guarantees it'll happen."

"I heard Jenny left yesterday."

Sam turned toward the woman's voice.

"Morning, Madge." Lou smiled at her.

The plump, seventy-something woman with pink cheeks and dancing eyes clutched Lou's help-wanted sign. "Hey, George. You're looking good."

"You know what they say about old codgers."

"No, but I'm sure you'll tell me." Madge placed the sign on the counter. "It's been two years since my dear husband passed. I'm finally ready to come back to work."

Lou tilted her head. "Are you sure?"

"Positive."

"Well then, you have yourself a job."

"Welcome back, Madge."

"Thanks, Sam." She nodded toward the empty stool at the end of the counter. "Why'd you switch seats?"

"Temporary move." One good thing about Madge taking the job, she wouldn't remind him of Jenny. He turned toward Lou. "I think I'll take a slice of coffee cake after all."

Chapter 28

By midnight, Jenny had worked the entire shift, identified her competition, and cozied up to the sous-chef—a pleasant-looking young man. She had also learned that Chef André valued his reputation as a demanding perfectionist. Exhausted, yet pleased she hadn't lost her touch, she drove back to the motel with her shoulders squared and her head held high.

The moment she entered the dark, dreary room, gut-wrenching loneliness soured her mood. In five-and-a-half hours, the delicious scent of coffee and fresh-baked breakfast breads would sweeten the air in Lou's Coffee Shop. Morning regulars would wander in. George would devour a cinnamon bun. Sam would occupy the corner stool, sip his coffee, and banter with Lou about local gossip. Life in Madison would continue. Without her. Too bad. She had made the decision to move on and start over in another new town.

Jenny trudged to the bathroom, turned on the tub spigot, and peeled out of her clothes. As soon as steam filled the tiny space, she slid into the hot water. It wouldn't take long to make new friends and forget how much she loved Sam and the warm sensation that surged through her every time he touched her.

She closed her eyes and forced her mind to shift to what promised to turn into a job after working free for a week. If it paid off, the position at Le Champagne would enhance her reputation as a gifted chef. Charleston was the perfect town to open her own restaurant. Lots of tourists and locals with plenty of money to invest in a new venture. Somehow, she had to find a way to meet André's clientele.

Jenny opened her eyes and cringed at the sight of a bug crawling up the wall. In the morning she'd demand the manager spray her room. When the water cooled, she eyed the threadbare towel hanging on a rack. Why had she left the luxurious towels she'd purchased in the bathroom back home? Because this is what she deserved. A grungy motel room. Groveling for a job. Jenny gripped the silver chain hanging from the faucet with her toes, yanked the plug from the drain, and climbed out.

After drying, she tossed the poor-excuse-for-a-towel over the edge of the tub and slipped into pajamas. To keep her bare feet from touching the soiled carpet, she pulled on a pair of socks before walking out of the bathroom and heading straight to bed. Jenny pulled the flimsy bedspread off the bed and tossed it across a chair. She also should have brought her new comforter.

The air conditioner cycled off with a clunk. The moment she slid between the sheets, memories from the life she had left behind played in her mind. She grabbed the remote, turned on the television, and flipped mindlessly through the channels.

Her eyes drifted to the clock on the dresser—three A. M. Lou would arrive at the coffee shop any minute, eager to bake and spend another morning with lifelong friends. Loneliness returned with a vengeance and sent rivers of regret racing through her. Jenny grabbed her phone off the nightstand and pressed Lou's number.

"Jenny, it's good to hear from you. Are you waking up or going to bed?"

"The latter."

"How's your new job going?"

"Really good. I finished my first shift tonight."

"I imagine your boss has already discovered the wisdom of hiring you out from under me."

If Lou only knew the truth. "How's Sam doing?"

"He puts on a brave front, but he misses you like crazy."

Jenny bit her lip to prevent the rush of words she feared would unleash a torrent of tears. "Have you hired someone to replace me?"

"An old friend. As soon as you're settled, you need to give Sam your address."

Why couldn't he refuse to let her go and move on with his life? "I'm not sure that's a good idea."

"You promised all of us you'd stay in touch."

Another big mistake.

"Everyone asked about you. Lots of folks miss your smile and cheery ways."

At least all the people she had befriended would remember her as friendly, fun-loving Jenny. The talented chef who rode her bike through town and greeted everyone she passed, and not the woman whose friend rescued her from a drunken binge.

"They're all counting on you finding your way back to Madison."

She couldn't give Lou false hope. "Tell everyone hi for me and that I'm loving my new job."

"I will."

"And tell Sam to give Paul and Duchess hugs for me." She ended the call with renewed determination to relegate the friendships, the joy, and the love she had found in the quaint Georgia town to her growing collection of distant memories.

She switched off the television and shifted her focus to André's challenge, hoping she had moved one day closer to landing a plum job and eventually achieving her dream.

Chapter 29

Sam sat at his office desk and stared at the folded handwritten letter he had finished three weeks earlier. His first attempt to stay connected to Jenny. Now that he had her address, he could mail it. He drummed his fingers. How would she react? Would she respond? Write back? Maybe he needed one more read-through. He unfolded the single page and stared at the words.

Dear Jenny,

I hope your new job is going well. If your boss doesn't promote you to sous-chef, I'll write a convincing recommendation about your crab cakes and fancy pudding. Yeah, I know it's crème brûlée. I learned a thing or two from you.

In case you haven't heard, Lou hired Madge the day after you left. She worked at the coffee shop before her husband died. She's around Lou's age with a wicked sense of humor and a laugh that shakes the walls. Everyone who comes in half asleep leaves wide awake. Watching her flirt with George adds a big dose of humor to my morning caffeine fix. He claims they had a fling back in high school before he met his wife. In case you're wondering, he flirts right back. It's like I'm an extra in a crazy sitcom for seniors. Who knows? Maybe they'll end up together.

Mrs. Perkins complains about Madge's quiche, which thus far is the same every week. She says it doesn't compare to yours and wants you to send Lou your recipes. Although, I suspect it's more a problem with the chef than the ingredients. The good news is Lou's still baking cinnamon buns and breakfast breads.

Well, that's all the news I have for now. Stay well and if the mood strikes, write back.

Your pal,

Sam

Satisfied he had written a neutral letter, he folded it, slipped it into a stamped envelope, and headed out of his office. Grateful Mary hadn't arrived, he exited and turned toward Main. During his walk to the coffee shop, he dropped the letter in a mailbox and checked the pickup time. Three o'clock. Maybe Jenny would read it before the end of the week.

After arriving at Lou's and finishing his second cup of coffee, Sam eyed Madge bantering with the Perkins. He still missed watching Jenny work the crowds. The way their eyes met for brief moments. He turned his attention back to Lou and pushed his mug across the counter. "One more fill-up."

She topped off his coffee. "Do you want another slice of banana bread?"

"One's plenty."

Lou set the coffeepot on the warmer. "Has Jenny communicated with you?"

"Not a word." Sam stirred sugar into his coffee. "You?"

"Nope, except for the one phone call and the text with her address. I can't say I'm surprised. Professional kitchens are demanding."

"You seem to take the workload in stride."

"I'm only open mornings and spend half my workday relaxing and chatting with customers. Jenny's a full-time chef, most likely pulling twelve-hour shifts five or six days a week."

"Maybe burnout and exhaustion forced her to jump from one job to another."

Lou leaned close and locked eyes with him. "Don't give up on her, Sam." Her voice was barely above a whisper.

"Have you been conspiring with Grandpa?"

"Once Jenny sorts her life out, she'll realize she's in love with you."

"There you go playing cupid again, or more appropriately, matchmaker for the hopeless."

"Such pessimism." Lou reached across the counter and thumped his arm. "I'll keep on matchmaking until you two are a happily married couple ready to celebrate your first anniversary."

George leaned forward. "Kind of hard to do long distance, don't you think?"

Sam shook his head. "How do you manage to tune into every conversation?"

"Can't help it. For an old buzzard, I have a good set of ears."

"That he does." Lou grinned. "Back to Jenny. Have you sent your first letter?"

Why had he revealed his letter-writing campaign? "I mailed it on the way here."

"Good. Your first step to bringing her back."

"She'll come back when and if she decides this is where she belongs." Sam drained his coffee and laid a ten on the counter. "So don't push it, Lou." He slid off his stool and walked out.

Lou's eyes followed Sam as he turned toward his office. She understood how his heart broke a little every time he sat at the end of her counter and watched Madge cater to Jenny's customers.

George shook his head. "That boy has a bad case of love sickness."

"Something in my bones tells me Jenny misses him as much as he misses her."

"Do you honestly believe she'll show up again, or were you trying to make Sam feel better?"

"Truth is, I don't know. That won't stop me from doing everything I can to encourage her to find her way back home."

"What kind of mischievous plan are you cooking up?"

"You know me too well, George." Lou removed his empty plate from the counter.

"Are you gonna answer my question?"

"All I can say is Sam's not the only person who understands the power of the written word."

Chapter 30

The first letter from Sam arrived four days after Jenny moved into a tiny studio apartment on Market Street. She dropped onto the green-and-white-striped, rented sofa bed and stared at the legal-size envelope. Her chest tightened as she slid her finger under the flap and removed the single sheet of Gibson Realty stationery. What if he begged her to return or told her he loved her? She unfolded the correspondence and read the words he'd written.

Her shoulders slumped as she attempted to read between the lines. It seemed he didn't miss her much after all. Wasn't that what she wanted? She placed the letter in her dresser drawer on top of the envelope holding her savings. Her eyes drifted to the photo taken at Lou's birthday party. Jenny traced Sam's smile with her finger. He deserved a response. She plucked a Le Champagne postcard and pen off the dresser. Not much space to write. Perfect.

Hey, Sam. All's well here. Love working at Le Champagne. Lots of high-class locals and well-to-do tourists. Keep me posted on the George-and-Madge drama and tell everyone hi for me.

Jenny.

She stared at her words. Short and sweet. Not a hint of how much she missed him. After dressing for work, she rode the elevator to the ground floor and donned her sunglasses. During the seven-block stroll to the post office, too many sights reminded her of Sam. Maybe she should have responded with more than a postcard. Next time. If he bothered to write again.

Hooves clopped the pavement behind her. She slowed her pace and eyed a tour guide standing at the front of a horse-drawn covered carriage. Two couples occupied the first row. A family with two young children filled the bench behind. The little girl sitting on her daddy's lap waved. Jenny waved back. That's what Sam deserved. A sweet wife. A couple of kids. Fun vacations. Tons of happiness. Eager to mail the postcard and head to work, she stepped up her pace. If she accepted South Carolina as her new home, Georgia and Sam would one day become a distant memory.

An hour after Jenny arrived at work, André summoned her to his office. He had fired the last chef invited to his inner sanctum. Had she ticked off his sous? Or had a customer complained about an appetizer she'd prepared? Sweat popped out on her upper lip as she crept in, stood in front of his desk, and watched him flip through a stapled document.

He pushed the document aside and made eye contact.

She clamped her arms to her sides and mentally prepared to defend herself and counter any unfounded accusations.

"I've kept a close eye on you and must say you have proved your value as a line chef."

Hoping the next word tumbling off his tongue wasn't but, she swallowed. "Thank you, sir."

"For the past few months, I've contemplated expanding my influence through an upscale catering venture. I would oversee the business." He leaned back, keeping his eyes trained on hers. "However, my plan would require an individual with the brains to manage the day-to-day operation and the savoir faire to serve and impress Charleston's elite clientele."

Jenny blinked. Did he consider her a viable candidate?

"The position would be equivalent to a sous-chef."

Better salary and another accomplishment to add to her portfolio. She had to jump at the chance. "Without presuming what you're thinking, may I suggest that I'm the perfect person for the job?"

"Perhaps." He eyed her for a long moment. "However, I must know for certain. Therefore, I will give you one week to develop a strategy to launch the business. Based on the quality of your work, I will make a decision."

She stared at his smug expression. Did he want her to create a plan then steal it as his own? Except he *had* hired her after she worked free for a week.

Chef André tapped his fingers on his desk. "Of course, if you are not up to the task—"

Jenny squared her shoulders and took the bait. "What are you looking for?"

"Imagination. Business savvy."

"One week?"

He stopped tapping. "That's the offer."

She had enough experience to understand that the potential payoff made the risk worth a shot. "I'll return seven days from today with a plan that will blow your socks off."

"Such an unrefined phrase."

Heat crept up Jenny's neck. "What I meant to say, be prepared for a first-class plan."

"We'll see. By the way, this conversation is strictly confidential."

"Understood."

"Good. Now, back to work." He dismissed her with a hand flick.

Jenny returned to her workstation amid glances from other chefs. The sous sidled over. "Is there a problem?"

"Everything's fine." Except she had made a commitment she had no idea how to deliver. For the remainder of her shift, Jenny struggled to focus on the tasks at hand. By the time she left the restaurant, her shoulders and head ached from the mounting stress and escalating insecurity.

She trudged into her studio apartment and peeled out of her work clothes. Pulling eleven-hour shifts six days a week, how could she possibly find the time and energy to develop even a half-decent proposal? Much less an idea worthy of a promotion. Maybe she should call it quits.

No way she'd back out and give André the upper hand. She brewed a pot of coffee, booted her iPad, and sat at the tiny kitchen table. An hour later her jaw clenched as she stared at the blank screen. She had to talk to someone. Kelley didn't know beans about restaurants. Sam understood business, but she couldn't wake him at three in the morning and risk unleashing an array of complicated emotions.

One option remained. She reached for her phone and pressed the number for the only other person she could trust.

"What a pleasant surprise." Lou's voice lifted her spirits.

"I hope you don't mind me calling."

"You can call me any time, honey. What's on your mind?"

"I sort of need some professional advice and didn't know who else to turn to. Other than the chefs I work with, I'm surrounded by strangers." Jenny took a deep breath before sharing Chef André's challenge.

"How long have you been awake?"

Jenny counted on her fingers. "Nineteen hours."

"Goodness gracious, honey. Before you do anything, you need to sleep."

"I don't have time—"

"Nonsense. You can't tap into your creativity when you're plum worn out. So, get some shuteye and call me when you wake up. Then we'll talk."

"You work 'til noon and I'm due at the restaurant at one."

"Set your alarm for eleven. I'll make time."

"Are you sure?"

"Positive."

Jenny scooted away from the desk and stumbled to the bed. "You're a lifesaver, Mom."

"You're way beyond tired." Lou chuckled. "And you just called me Mom."

"I did?"

"Not that I'm complaining. Now, say good night."

"Good night, Lou." Jenny set her alarm, plugged her phone into the charger, and crawled into bed. As she pulled the sheet up, visions of catering fancy affairs for Charleston's elite released her tense muscles and lulled her into a deep sleep.

At eleven, Sam folded his arms over his chest, leaned against the wall in the coffee shop kitchen, and stared at Lou's phone. His sense of shame for secretly listening to her conversation with Jenny paled in comparison to his desire to hear her voice. Only his grandpa and maybe Lou understood the hope he clung to—that he would give her a reason to come home.

Lou's phone rang.

She glanced at Sam then pressed the speaker icon. "Right on time. Were you able to sleep?"

"Eight hours."

Hearing Jenny's voice for the first time since Lou's going-away party touched Sam's soul. How he longed to gaze into her eyes and run his finger along her cheek.

"Good. Now, let's talk about a plan."

Sam kept his eyes focused on the phone while listening to Jenny and Lou brainstorm ideas that would keep her in Charleston. Why couldn't she open her own catering business right here in Madison? He'd loan her the money, with no strings attached.

"Thanks, Lou. You're a lifesaver."

"The credit is all yours, Chef Jenny. I simply helped you tap into your creativity."

"If this doesn't impress the dickens out of my boss, nothing will."

Lou smiled. "Remember to show him you're a professional."

Jenny giggled. "You mean instead of a flirtatious southern chick who needs a gimmick and fluttering eyelashes to persuade?"

Lou laughed. "Not my exact words, but close enough."

"All right, I'll rely on my skills. By the way, how's Sam doing?"

"Nothing's changed." Lou's eyes met his. "He's still the handsome young man who shows up at my counter every morning."

"Is he dating anyone?"

Sam shook his head.

"As far as I know, he hasn't abandoned his bachelor status."

"Maybe he'll find someone soon. Tell him hi for me."

Lou nodded. "I will."

"Thanks again for all your help and encouragement."

"Any time, honey."

Jenny ended the call.

Sam shoved his hands in his pockets. "Her boss is a fool if he doesn't jump on her idea."

"Success might give her the sense of accomplishment she needs to find her way back to you."

"Or stay away forever." He pushed away from the wall. "Thanks for letting me eavesdrop."

Lou placed her hand on his arm. "I still believe everything will work out the way it's supposed to."

"Maybe it already has." He spun and walked out of the kitchen.

George peered at Sam. "What kind of scheme are you and Lou cooking up?"

"What makes you think something underhanded is going on." Sam bristled at his own snarky tone.

"What has you all riled up?"

"Sorry, George. Guess I've had one too many cups of coffee. I'll see you tomorrow." He headed straight to the door and strode out. Heavy rain clouds peppered with distant thunder mirrored his somber mood. Why had he fallen in love with such a difficult woman? Grandpa called it fate. Thus far, fate had lost its way. Maybe Sandra was right about fools holding out hope for hopeless situations. Except his grandpa hadn't given up on the woman he loved. Neither would he. Sam stepped up his pace and headed straight to his office. It was time to write letter number two.

Chapter 31

Six days after brainstorming with Lou, Jenny folded the second letter from Sam—short, sweet, and neutral like all the rest. She placed it in the drawer on top of Lou's letter, the one that gave a hint of Sam's feelings and kept her emotions in turmoil. Maybe that was her plan. Jenny grabbed her purse, tucked her iPad under her arm, and headed for the elevator.

Ten minutes later—an hour before the kitchen staff was due to arrive—she entered Le Champagne's elegant dining room and found Chef André sitting at a table beside a window facing the street. He motioned her to sit and pointed to a pitcher of water and two glasses.

Jenny pushed her sunglasses up, sat across from André, and placed the iPad on the table. "As you requested, I prepared a plan to launch your newest venture, beginning with a name suggestion." She wiped her damp palm on her pants and pulled up her presentation's first page—Le Champagne Prestige Catering—scribed in gold letters.

"Interesting name. What else do you have?"

She resisted the urge to wield her fine-tuned feminine wiles and held his gaze. "In a city filled with exceptional dining experiences, your restaurant is recognized as one of the finest. Therefore, your catering business must stand out as the crème de la crème. The only choice for a clientele accustomed to the best. One that requires a launch to captures the imagination." She paused.

"I'm listening."

She filled a glass and swallowed a sip of water to moisten her dry mouth. With one shot to land the job, she had to make it count. Jenny scrolled to the second page and continued her thirty-minute presentation, ending with estimated costs and future projections. "As you can see, the investment has the potential to position you as Charleston's premier caterer."

André stared at her for a long moment, his expression unchanged. "Stay here." He pushed off his chair and disappeared into the kitchen.

Jenny tapped her foot. She had spent every ounce of energy she could muster preparing a near-perfect proposal. All on an average of four hours of sleep for six straight nights. And he didn't have the decency to even acknowledge her work? What more would it take to impress him? She slammed her iPad face down on the table. Her boss would end up with one gigantic fight on his hands if he attempted to implement the plan without offering her the job.

Her foot tapping accelerated as she stared out the window at a passersby. Her plan would impress the socks off every Charleston restaurant owner. She should walk out right now and go straight to a competitor and pitch her idea. That would put arrogant André out of business before he had a chance to cheat her. Who was she kidding. The man was a respected member of the community and she was a mere newcomer. A nobody.

Footsteps struck the floor behind her. She turned.

"Come with me."

Jenny tucked the iPad under her arm. "Where are we going?"

"You'll see."

She followed André to the sidewalk and lowered her sunglasses. They walked past the restaurant and turned right at the corner. Halfway down the block, he fished a key from his pocket and unlocked a door to an empty storefront. "I own half the buildings on this block."

Curiosity battled anxiety as Jenny followed him into the space filled with tables and chairs.

"A low-end restaurant occupied this space before the owner closed up and moved to Florida. I'm designating it as Le Champagne Prestige Catering's headquarters." He removed a single sheet of paper from his pocket, unfolded it, and set it on the table. "I need your signature." The executive chef who held her future in his hands removed a pen from his pocket and handed it to Jenny.

She raised her brows. "On what?"

"A contract. I'm hiring you to set up and manage the business."

"Really? I mean, thank you. I won't let you down." She signed.

"We'll initiate your launch in three weeks."

"That soon?"

André's eyes narrowed. "Do I need to withdraw my decision?"

"No, sir."

"As of now, you are relieved from your line-chef duties." After pocketing the contract, he handed her a credit card. "Every morning I expect you to provide detailed records of your expenses as well as your progress." His French accent disappeared. "If you exceed your proposed budget, the funds will be deducted from your pay. Any questions?"

"Yes, sir. No, sir. I mean, I understand."

"Good." He slapped the key on the table and walked out.

Jenny collapsed against the back of the chair and pressed Lou's number. The call went straight to voicemail.

Her finger hovered over the second name on her favorites list. If she considered Sam a friend, didn't he deserve one phone call? Her finger tapped the number.

"Hey, Jenny."

She pictured him sitting at his office desk with the sunrise painting behind him. "How's everything going at Gibson Realty?"

"About the same. What's up"

"Has Lou kept you up to date about my plans?"

"If you're referring to the catering challenge, she has."

"Today, I landed the job."

"I wouldn't have expected otherwise."

She closed her eyes, envisioning his smile. "It's a great opportunity, if I manage to pull it off."

"You will." He paused. "The coffee shop regulars miss you."

What about him? Did he miss her? "Even George?"

"Especially George. My old pal still complains about you skipping town before he had a chance to enjoy another slice of your crazy fruit-free pie."

She didn't dare admit how much she missed bantering with George, Lou...and him. "Sounds like all is well at the coffee shop."

"Other than Madge replacing you, nothing's changed."

"Tell everyone hi for me."

"I will. It's good to hear your voice, Jenny. Congratulations on the new job."

"Thank you, Sam."

"You can call me anytime."

Her heart ached as she ended the call and tucked her iPad under her arm. She stepped out to the sunshine hoping her new role and time would diminish her love for the man she had left behind.

Sam tossed his phone on the desk. "When is our new beginning, Jenny?"

"Are you expecting an answer?" His grandpa strolled in and sat across from him.

"Everything's falling in place for her in Charleston. Which makes luring her back to Madison tougher than ever."

"She needs more time."

"She's moving on without me." Sam swept his hands through his hair. "Jenny Collins is the most complicated woman I have ever met. I don't have a clue if my letter-writing plan will work."

"Sometimes you have to let go to hold on. She has to deal with her issues before she can find her way back to you." His grandpa glanced at his watch. "I'm meeting a new client for lunch. Want to join me?"

"No thanks." After his grandfather left, Sam lifted a photo off his desk—Jenny sitting across the table from him at Town 220 Restaurant. Her chin rested on her knuckles. A smile lit up her entire face. Her eyes were full of life and more than a touch of mischief and mystery. Jenny Collins was a beautiful, strong-willed, intelligent woman. He longed to hold her, kiss away every hurt she kept hidden, and spend a lifetime making her happy. "I love you too much to give up without a fight, Jenny." He set the photo down, pulled a sheet of stationery from his desk, and penned letter number three.

Chapter 32

J enny parked the Le Champagne Prestige Catering van at the end of a dock, gripped the steering wheel, and stared out the windshield. Tonight her future and André's investment hung in the balance.

Valerie—her feisty, blonde assistant who looked more like a young movie star than a chef—reached across the console and tapped her shoulder. "Do you need a pep talk?"

"In two hours, seventy-six of Charleston's most distinguished residents will climb aboard a fancy boat and seal our fate. Truth is, I don't have a clue how to impress people accustomed to the best money can buy."

"You've worked in plenty of restaurants that cater to well-to-do clientele."

"In the kitchen, not out front."

"Folks on tonight's guest list aren't all that different from you and me."

"Except they're rich and have sophisticated taste."

"Quit worrying, already. You know our appetizers are to die for." Valerie unbuckled her seat belt. "Better yet, André's one of *them*. Which means he knows how to schmooze. Did you know that his family dates back a couple generations? They're not mega-rich but way more than comfortable. That little tidbit is beside the point. Right now, our servers are waiting to help us haul everything on board. Which means it's time to get this gig going."

Jenny thumped her arm. "You're kind of bossy."

Valerie opened the passenger door. "Someone has to take charge 'til you find your mojo." She climbed down, rounded the rear of the van, and swung open the double doors.

Jenny peered into the visor mirror. Valerie was right. The guests were ordinary people who happened to have tons of money and boatloads of clout. They were also the reason André's new business existed. She needed to get a grip and make this one memorable launch.

She stepped from the van and smoothed her white chef coat with her name and the company embroidered below her right shoulder. Her eyes fixed on the anchored hundred-foot luxury vessel. "That is one big boat."

"It's called a yacht." Valerie loaded a tray onto a three-tier catering cart.

Jenny followed her and three hired servers as they wheeled three carts up the dock to the gangway. She stepped onto the aft deck at the same moment André strolled out from the main salon. His white slacks and Hawaiian-style shirt made him look more like a rich, party goer than a demanding executive chef.

The tanned gentleman accompanying André lowered his designer sunglasses from his thick white hair and moseyed to Jenny. "Welcome aboard Lady Catrina, named after my late grandmother. I assume you're the aggressive young woman who sweet-talked my assistant into transferring your call to me."

"Yes, sir." Jenny eyed his white shorts and matching polo shirt. "It's an honor to meet you, Mr. Wallace. Thank you for lending us your magnificent yacht."

"I couldn't resist hosting an elaborate event on my old pal's dime."

André placed his hand on the man's shoulder. "First time you come begging for my catering services, I'll double our prices and recover my entire investment."

"Like you need the money."

Jenny's eyes followed the two men as they settled on blue and white cushions covering the U-shaped bench hugging the boat's railing. Surely Mr. Wallace understood that Le Champagne Catering was her brainchild, and that André merely paid the bills.

"Earth to Jenny." Valerie tapped her arm. "We need you inside."

"I'm coming." She entered the luxurious salon, awash in white, gold, and shades of blue. "Every person on our guest list could fit in here at the same time, with room to spare."

"Lifestyle of the rich and famous," mumbled one of the servers.

Valerie motioned toward a woman arranging wine bottles and glasses on the marble-top bar anchoring one end of the massive space. "I imagine the top-shelf wine she brought cost André a pretty penny."

"She's eager to attract a high-end clientele to her new wine bar, so she's donating everything."

"Your boss owes you a big fat bonus for pulling that off."

Jenny glanced over her shoulder at André schmoozing the yacht's owner. "I'd settle for a little credit."

"Don't count on it. Even though this is all your doing—with a little help from me—we're nothing more than worker bees in Chef André's kingdom. The way I look at it, he's providing us with decent jobs and an opportunity to mingle with the city's upper crust." She leaned close. "Which is the best way for us to meet single rich men."

Jenny laughed. "Did you take this job to go on fishing expeditions?"

"I'm not planning to spend the rest of my life cooking for strangers. So, yeah. Don't tell me you wouldn't jump at the chance to catch some wealthy guy."

"All I want is a financial investor to bankroll my own restaurant."

"Good for you, girlfriend." Valerie leaned close. "By the way, thanks for hiring three hot young guys to serve this crowd."

"What happened to your snag-a-rich-guy plan?"

"Doesn't mean I can't enjoy eye candy while I'm hunting." Valerie nodded toward one of the servers heading their way. "He's the one I have my sights set on."

The muscular young man eyed Jenny. "We're ready to go to work, Ms. Collins."

After giving the staff instructions, Jenny directed every detail. At seven o'clock a base player and a saxophonist joined the pianist seated at the white baby grand and began playing smooth jazz. The waiters held trays of appetizers, ready to circulate. The wine-bar owner uncorked bottles. André and the yacht owner stood at the gangway welcoming Charleston's elite aboard.

Jenny's breathing accelerated as guests gathered on the deck and in the salon. All seemed eager to chat, as if they couldn't wait to talk about everything going on in their privileged world.

When the captain maneuvered the yacht away from the dock and aimed toward Charleston harbor, Valerie stepped beside her. "It's time for you to work the crowd and promote the heck out of our new business."

Jenny squared her shoulders and held her head high. She approached the first woman who hadn't blatantly ignored her and stumbled through a rehearsed elevator pitch.

The woman leaned close. "Don't let these snooty folks intimidate you, sweetie." Her southern accent hinted of humor. "They're a bit pretentious, but as harmless as little old dragonflies. You just march right up and tell them all about your new venture."

"Thanks for the advice."

The woman patted her cheek. "Trust me, you'll charm the socks off them."

It didn't take long for Jenny to settle into a comfortable routine using subtle flirtation and tons of southern charm.

Valerie moved close, balancing a tray of stuffed dates. "Now you're working it."

"I finally found my mojo." Jenny spotted André popping an appetizer in his mouth while socializing with his peers. His eyes flicked over her before he turned away, as if associating with the staff was beneath his dignity. She turned her back toward him and launched into her spiel with a middle-aged woman leaning on the bar.

By the time the ship anchored at the dock, Jenny's cheeks ached from hours of smiling and pitching. She pulled Valerie aside. "Time to hand out the goodies."

"Is everyone ready to leave?"

"I'm guessing the limos lined up at the dock are a clue." They maneuvered a glass and chrome cart to the gangway and handed departing guests elegant gold bags—each filled with a box of chocolate truffles, a bottle of expensive wine, and a black and gold brochure promoting the new business.

By midnight, the gift bags were distributed and the limos departed. Jenny stretched her arms over her head and yawned. "I believe we hit a homerun."

"You definitely caught one guy's attention." Valerie motioned toward a young man seated on the aft deck's blue and white cushions. "He kept his eyes on you all night."

"Who is he?"

"Peter Wallace."

"Same Wallace—"

"As the yacht's owner. He's single. Go work your magic."

Jenny glanced sideways at the dark-haired young man balancing a glass of wine in his left hand. His right arm stretched across the back of a cushion. An ankle rested on his knee, revealing his sockless foot in tan deck shoes. "I bet he's never worked a day in his life."

"Why should he? His daddy and granddaddy are both rich. I'll cover for you. It'll give me time to cozy up to Derrick."

"The waiter?"

Valerie nodded. "He'll do until my snag-a-rich-guy plan pays off."

"You're hopeless."

"You mean, hopeful." Valerie nudged her. "Go and turn on your Jenny charm."

"I might as well." Jenny meandered to the bench. "I appreciate your father letting us launch the business on his yacht."

"My dad and your boss are buddies from way back."

She sat catercorner to him. He wasn't as handsome or as muscular as Sam, but good-looking. "I'm Jenny Collins."

"The brains behind this affair." Peter's grin widened. "You started out slow before transforming into the most brazen flirt on board."

Had he watched her the entire evening? "You mean business promoter."

"Whatever you call it, I'm guessing your technique, as well as your exceptional party fare, will land a half dozen jobs by the end of next week."

"An informed projection or wild guess?"

"Little of both. I haven't seen you around town."

Like she'd hang out with his crowd. "I moved up from Georgia a couple months ago."

"Too bad for Georgia. Lucky for South Carolina." He lowered his arm from the back cushion. "How about I buy you a glass of free wine."

"Thanks, but I need to help my crew clean up."

"Okay, until next time we end up at the same party, Miss Jenny Collins."

Fat chance of that happening, unless he attended one of her catered events. "Why do you assume I'm not married?"

"No ring on your left hand."

He noticed. Maybe they would connect socially. "Nice to meet you, Mr. Peter Wallace."

"Likewise."

Jenny stood and sashayed across the deck to the grand salon. Inside, she passed André relaxing on a sectional sofa, drinking brandy and smoking cigars with Peter's father. She approached the two men. "Thank you again, Mr. Wallace. I'm confident tonight's launch will lead to dozens of successful events."

He chortled. "More cash for my pal's bloated coffers."

André lifted his chin and blew a smoke ring. "Perhaps I'll expand my empire and open a gentleman's cigar and brandy lounge."

The yacht owner nodded. "There's an idea worth pursuing."

Offended by André's blatant refusal to acknowledge her presence, Jenny spun and strolled away with every ounce of dignity she could muster. One of these days she'd attract an investor, open a first-class restaurant, and give her boss serious competition.

Chapter 33

Jenny poured a glass of orange juice, dropped onto the sofa bed, and stared at the envelope from Lou. Maybe she should wait and open it later. Better to read it now. She ripped the envelope open and removed the single sheet of paper.

Dear Jenny,

Fall is beginning to show in Madison. Soon all the colors will change. Here at the coffee shop, folks complained about us serving the same quiche every week until Madge gave one of your recipes a try. It's a mystery how she ends up with a dish so different from yours. She doesn't much cotton to fancy cooking, so maybe she self-sabotages.

My daughter came back from overseas and accepted another big promotion. Executive vice president. Seems she'll never slow down long enough to give me a grandchild.

Sam still comes in every morning. He puts on a good front, but I can tell he misses you like crazy. We all wish you a lot of success in your new catering adventure. At the same time we hope one day you'll bring your skills back home. In the meantime, stay well and safe.

Love,
Lou

Jenny dropped the letter onto her lap and stared at the blank wall over her rented dresser. Maybe she should ask Paul to ship her sunflower painting and her guitar to Charleston. Best to leave both behind. Like she'd left Sam. Besides, she could buy another painting, and the catering business left little time for guitar plucking.

After penning a postcard to Lou, Jenny dressed and headed to work. Five hours after arriving, she and Valerie rolled two carts loaded with trays of hors d'oeuvres from the van through a gate beside a grand King Street home.

Valerie pushed her cart onto a brick patio. "Fancy backyard."

Memories of Lou's surprise birthday party came to mind as Jenny eyed dozens of round tables, their white cloths flowing to the ground. Unlike the wicker chairs and mason-jar center pieces in Paul's backyard, gold fabric covered every chair. Elaborate floral centerpieces with candles glittering in expensive cut-glass containers shouted sophistication and old money.

"This is the kind of engagement party I want." Valerie pointed to the string quartet positioned between two makeshift bars. "Complete with high-brow music and cute bartenders."

"You'll definitely need to snare a rich guy to pull that off."

Valerie tucked her hair behind one ear, revealing a dangling rhinestone earring brushing her neck. "If you let me ditch this catering jacket, I could pass as one of the guests."

"Not while you're minding a buffet table."

"How about after the guests scarf down all the food?"

Jenny nodded toward the host and hostess emerging from the house with their daughter and her fiancé. "I suggest we concentrate on pleasing the folks footing the gigantic bill."

Valerie rolled her eyes. "One of these days, an event will pay off."

"Hopefully, for both of us. Right now, it's time to go to work." Jenny nodded toward the right. "You take that table. I'll work the other one."

While dusk descended on Charleston, guests—some Jenny recognized from other catering events—arrived and mingled. When folks meandered to her table, she tuned into their conversations, listening for names and bits of useful information she could use to expand the business.

"I'm not surprised they hired the best caterer in town."

Jenny turned toward the familiar voice. "Fancy seeing you here. Are you friends with the bride or groom?"

"Both." Peter Wallace grinned. "Although the bride and I had a thing going a couple years back."

"Which means you have a big decision to make."

"About?"

"Which side of the aisle to choose during the wedding."

"Good point." Peter moved closer. "One decision I've already made, I don't intend to let you escape before I offer you a drink. So, what do you say?"

"Hmm, I'll deliberate and reveal the verdict and sentence a bit later."

"You're both judge and jury. Smart move." He loaded his plate.

Jenny's gaze followed him as he stopped at the bar before joining a group of peers. She didn't run in his circles, and the way women clung to him made it clear he didn't need to troll for female companionship. Maybe she should keep her distance. Unless...was it possible he held the key to her future? After all, Valerie said his family was swimming in money.

She envisioned an upscale, downtown restaurant comparable to Le Champagne—owned by world-renowned Chef Jenny. Frequented by Charleston's elite and discerning tourists. Why not use her feminine wiles to turn him into an investor?

As the party wound down and the crowd thinned, Peter wandered over with a drink in hand. "What's the verdict?"

"I'm ready for a break."

"What's your pleasure? Wine, beer, or a fancy cocktail?"

"Ginger ale on the rocks. I'm technically still working."

"A lady with integrity."

She removed her catering coat, revealing a white form-fitting tee shirt.

His eyes drifted down her body, then back to her face. "Wow, now you look more like one of the guests."

Jenny tucked her hair behind her right ear. "All I need is a pair of sparkly earrings."

"Do you want me to ask the bride-to-be to lend you a pair?"

"I'll settle for a generous tip."

He touched her arm. "If I booked one of your gigs, I'd take good care of you."

"Do you go above and beyond to please all your lady friends?"

"A select few." He winked and nodded toward his right. "Wait for me over there."

"Perfect spot to get acquainted." Jenny moseyed to an empty chair, kicked off her work shoes, and slipped into southern-belle mode.

Peter returned, placed two drinks on the table, and sat facing her. "So, who is Jenny Collins, and how did she end up in Charleston?"

She crossed her leg over her knee. "A southern-born gal who's drawn to towns known for exquisite dining and refined ladies and gentlemen."

He chuckled. "You obviously haven't experienced Charleston's wild side."

"There's still time. Now it's your turn. Who is Peter Wallace and what keeps him here?"

"A man with a sizable inheritance, thanks to a generous grandfather."

Jackpot. "Lucky you."

He sipped his drink. "And Charleston holds me hostage because it's my hometown and the perfect environment for an aspiring novelist."

Jenny reached for her ginger ale. "You're the first author I've met. What do you write?"

"Suspense from a southern perspective."

"Like alligators and swamps, or grits and gravy?"

"More like mayhem, murder, and magnolias."

She twirled her foot in a lazy circle. "Are you a free-spirited writer who lives in a loft above a trendy bar, or a refined gentleman occupying a Charleston-style mansion?"

"Let me buy you dinner tomorrow night, and following a decadent dessert, I'll show you where I hang out."

Step one accomplished. "You've made me an offer I can't refuse." Jenny finished the ginger ale and slipped her shoes on. "For now, I need to finish earning my fee and a big fat tip."

"A lady has to earn a living." He grinned. "Tell me where you live, and I'll pick you up at six."

"Better yet, I'll meet you at the restaurant."

"Smart. Don't trust the man until she finds out more about him."

"And where he lives."

"Give me your number, and I'll call to tell you where to meet."

Jenny pulled a business card from her pocket and handed it to him. Eager to entice him to open his wallet and offer far more than a generous tip, she leaned down and kissed his cheek.

He moved. His lips brushed hers.

Jenny straightened. "Until tomorrow, Mr. Aspiring Author." While returning to her buffet table, she envisioned Sam watching her from across the lawn. Someone grabbed her arm.

"Seems tonight we both lucked out." Valerie pointed her thumb over her shoulder. "Tomorrow I'm meeting one of the groomsmen for lunch. And you, girlfriend, scored big time. I'm guessing Peter asked you for a date?"

"Dinner tomorrow night."

"If you snag him, you'll have it made."

"I'm not looking for a long-term relationship. Besides, my heart belongs to someone back in Georgia." Heat rushed to Jenny's cheeks. Had the words tumbled off her tongue, or had she just imagined saying them?

"Well, goodness gracious, girl." Valerie planted her hands on her hips. "What are you doing way up here in South Carolina?"

Jenny looked away. *Running away from the past.*

Chapter 34

S am bit into his hamburger and eyed his sister and grandpa sitting across the table in Madison Chop House Grill.

"All this talk about real estate and the coffee shop." Sandra dug her fork into her salad. "You two don't fool me one little bit."

Her grandfather swallowed a bite of his reuben. "What are you implying?"

"You're avoiding the giant gorilla in the room. Or more precisely the infamous Jenny Collins and my brother's crusade to lure her back."

Sam's eyes widened.

"Don't play all innocent with me, Sam. George told me all about your letters. How many are you up to now?"

"Does it matter?"

She pointed her fork at him. "Jenny running off isn't remotely like Grandma leaving Grandpa after she lost a baby."

His grandfather's sandwich froze halfway to his mouth. "Who told you?"

"Grandma. Years ago, one night after Ted and I had a big fight. She claimed you wrote her a couple dozen love letters before she came to her senses."

Sam nodded. "Twenty-seven to be exact."

"Look, I know you both think I'm meddling." Sandra sighed. "The fact is, you're right. Because you're my brother and I want what's best for you." She tapped her phone, then pushed it across the table. "This is my nurse friend who wants to meet you."

"No way I'm letting you set me up on a blind date with some chick."

"Not even a smart, drop-dead gorgeous woman?"

Sam shook his head. "Forget it."

"Why are you so all-fired stubborn. Even if Jenny finds her way back, she's not who you think she is." Sandra pushed her salad aside and locked eyes with Sam. "Are you aware she's never held a job longer than seven months?"

"How do you know?" He narrowed his eyes. "You pulled strings and checked up on her, didn't you?"

"Why do you suppose she moves around so much? Because she's ambitious?"

"You didn't answer my question."

"Or maybe because she can't control her urges." Sandra's features grew rigid. "Did she bother to tell you she had a DUI and spent the night in jail before she moved here?"

"You had no right—"

"Maybe she can't stay away from booze."

Sam diverted his eyes. "She doesn't drink anything stronger than sweet tea."

"Maybe not around you. And even if she somehow managed to stay on the wagon, it doesn't mean she won't tumble off again."

Her grandfather clasped his hand over Sandra's. "No matter how much you love your brother, digging into Jenny's background was wrong."

"Do you have any idea how many addicts show up in my emergency room over and over again?" Her voice wavered. "Jenny's not good enough for Sam, Grandpa."

"That's not for you to decide."

"Maybe you need to talk some sense into him." Sandra pulled her hand from beneath his. "Unless you're encouraging him."

"Try to understand—"

"What? That he's smitten with a pretty stranger who shows up in town after her license was suspended for drunk driving?"

"Enough!" Sam threw his napkin on the table. "You're my big sister, and I love you. That doesn't change the fact that what I do with my life is my business. Not yours. So, knock it off." He pushed off his seat and stalked out of the restaurant.

As he turned away from downtown, Sandra's revelations exacted conflicting emotions. He knew Jenny had a past. But drunk driving? What other details had she kept secret?

Sam wandered past a church. All humans carried burdens in their souls. Didn't everyone deserve second chances? Had he driven her away? Pushed her too hard? Did she drink while she was alone?

He glanced across the street at a political banner stretched across pillars supporting a home's porch roof. On which side of the political fence did Jenny stand? Had she registered to vote? Or had she moved around too much to bother with civic duty?

He turned onto the sidewalk leading to the restored building housing the Madison Morgan Cultural Center. Another site he and Jenny could visit together. If she ever found her way back. He climbed the stairs to the brick entry porch and peered through an arched opening at the circular lawn and artwork. Why had Jenny responded to his letters with nothing more than a postcard? Maybe he was wrong about her feelings for him. Or maybe another man had already replaced him.

He climbed down and walked to a historical marker mounted on a metal post adjacent to the sidewalk. An elderly gentleman walking his dog approached. "How's it going, Sam?"

"Can't complain. How's your wife?"

"Feeling better today."

"Good to hear."

The man passed on by.

Sam glanced over his shoulder at the local who had married his high-school sweetheart decades earlier. Maybe he needed a new approach with Jenny. No more 'your pal' endings to his letters. He crossed the street and stepped up his pace. When he arrived at the stairs leading to her apartment, he climbed up to the stoop, removed the key from under the mat, and unlocked the door.

A battle ensued inside him between invading Jenny's privacy and discovering the truth about Sandra's claims. What did he expect to find inside? If she still struggled with a drinking problem, she wouldn't leave liquor behind. Would she? After crossing the threshold, he flung open cabinets and drawers. Nothing out of place. No booze.

Curiosity led him to the bedroom. He opened the closet. Empty. He moved to the dresser and peered into the first three drawers. Nothing there. He gripped the bottom drawer knobs. As he pulled it open, an object rolled forward and clanged against the wood. His chest tightened. He lifted the bottle of wine and stared at the golden liquid. Was this the pain she ran from? The past that haunted her?

Sam carried the bottle to the bathroom, screwed off the cap, and tipped the bottle over the sink. As he watched the contents disappear down the drain, a two-thousand-year-old phrase about truth setting you free popped into his head. Maybe Sandra's interference gave him what he needed to bring Jenny home. He tossed the empty bottle in the trash, scrambled from her apartment, and headed toward his office.

He set his phone on the desk. Maybe he should call Jenny. Except she hadn't responded to any of his previous calls. Forget the phone. Sam removed a sheet of stationery from his desk drawer and stared at the blank page. What could he write to let Jenny know how much he cared and that her past didn't matter?

Chapter 35

Jenny laid her fork across her plate in an iconic Charleston restaurant. "I'm too full to eat another bite."

Peter planted his forearms on the table. "Does that mean I'm off the hook for a fancy dessert?"

"Are you counting your pennies?"

"More like eager to show you where I hang out."

She mirrored his position. "Will I end up impressed or disappointed?"

"That depends on what you consider impressive."

Any place that didn't reek of alcohol and dirty clothes. "How far away is your bachelor pad?"

"A short drive, or a brisk walk. Your choice."

"Hmm, think I'll opt for the ride."

"Good decision." After signaling the waiter and paying the bill, Peter slid Jenny's chair away from the table and offered his arm. "Your chauffeur awaits."

And if she played her cards right, her investor.

Peter escorted her to his late-model silver convertible.

"Nice sports car."

"This is the first Jaguar I've owned." He opened the passenger door. "Is it okay if I leave the top down?"

"Definitely." She slid onto the leather seat.

"Next stop, my place."

During the drive, Jenny focused on the scenery while mentally reviewing her plan. Tonight, she would lay the groundwork, then wait for the right moment to make her pitch.

"We've arrived." He aimed a remote at an ornate gate and drove onto a single-lane driveway between two tall brick houses built close to the front sidewalk.

"You obviously don't live in a loft."

"The house dates back a century." He rounded the rear of the car and opened her door. They walked to the front and up three steps to a black door and beyond to a covered veranda stretching below a second-story balcony. "Welcome to my bachelor pad." He pointed to an elaborate fountain and wrought-iron furniture adorning the patio. Shady trees and a high stone wall shielded the outdoor space from the sidewalk and side street.

"Are you impressed or disappointed?"

"I'll hold my opinion until I've seen the inside."

"Prepare to be surprised." He escorted her across the threshold, through the foyer, and into the front room.

Jenny eyed the white walls, modern furniture, and abstract paintings which stood in stark contrast to the coffered ceilings and lavish decorative molding. "Interesting décor. Based on the courtyard, it's not what I expected."

"I'm inspired by contrasts."

Like inviting a poor caterer to dinner instead of a woman in his social circle?

He moseyed to a sleek buffet with a white marble top. "Would you prefer an after-dinner drink or something stronger?"

"Nothing for me."

"Mind if I indulge?"

Jenny shrugged. "Suit yourself." She strolled to a painting featuring an explosion of nondescript, drab colors. Nothing like the sunflower painting she'd left in Madison. "I don't understand abstract art. What is this supposed to mean?"

Peter held a short glass half filled with dark gold liquid. "It's called *The Illusion.*"

Her brows furrowed. "Illusion of what?"

"The answer lies in the viewer's interpretation. To me it represents the deception poor people have about wealth and happiness."

Jenny fingered the narrow black frame. "Are you saying the two are incompatible?"

"Depends on whether the money is inherited or earned. I fall into the first category but aim to tackle the latter."

"As a writer?"

"My family has connections with a major publishing company."

If money couldn't buy happiness, maybe it could buy success. She spun away and wandered to another painting. "In addition to writing, I expect you're a wise investor."

"I suppose." Peter followed her. "This is my favorite piece."

Jenny stared at the canvas, white with random splotches of bright colors. "Seems the artist couldn't decide what to paint."

Peter laughed "Maybe you're right. I do own one traditional work of art. Want to see it?"

"Why not. Maybe I'll understand what the artist intended the viewer to see."

He set his glass on an end table and led her up the stairs to a bedroom decorated in traditional style.

She nodded toward the still-life painting above the four-poster bed. "There's no denying that artist painted a basket of fruit." She moved closer. "The detail is amazing. It's almost three dimensional."

"My grandmother willed each grandchild a piece from her collection. This one's worth a fortune."

Lots of family money. "I assume this is a guest room."

He moved closer. "For my more traditional visitors."

"I see. And how would you describe me?"

He pinched his chin between his thumb and index finger. "I'd say ambitious and adventurous."

She tilted her head. "I'm guessing your bedroom isn't traditional."

"Good guess." He slid his arm around her shoulders and led her across the hall into a large room.

"Wow." Jenny turned in a slow circle while eyeing the dark-charcoal walls and platform bed covered with a white spread tucked under the thick mattress. An abstract painting of gray cubes filled the space above. A white love seat and glass coffee table completed the arrangement. "A world without color."

Peter lifted a remote off the nightstand and aimed it toward the windows. The pale gray curtains parted. "The color comes from nature." He opened the French doors leading to the balcony above the entry porch.

Jenny stepped outside and ran her fingers along the wrought-iron railing. "Great spot to start the day."

"Or end it."

She leaned back against the railing. "When the mood strikes you to write, where do you go?"

"I'll show you." He reached for her hand and opened the French doors leading to the adjacent room. "Welcome to my office."

She entered the space awash in shades of gray and white. A bland abstract painting hung on the wall behind a slab of polished black slate serving as a desk. Nothing like Sam's colorful office or his beautiful sunrise painting. Why think of him now?

She pulled her hand from Peter's and pointed to a laptop sitting in front of a white executive chair. "Do you let anyone read your work in progress?"

"A couple of close friends. Maybe one day, I'll give you a glimpse."

"Know what I'd like right now?"

Peter's face inched close to hers. "Clue me in."

"A tour of your patio before you drive me home."

"So soon? The night's still young."

"Not for a caterer who has to show up at work at the crack of dawn."

"I'll continue the tour outside on one condition." His eyes met hers. "You agree to see me again."

Confident she had taken a giant step towards securing her future, she flashed a smile. "How could I turn down a handsome, gifted author."

"Saturday night. Dinner here."

"It's a date."

Chapter 36

Jenny stared at the unopened envelope lying on the table. Another letter from Sam. Why had it arrived today of all days? She could ignore it until after her date with Peter. What if he had urgent news about Paul or Lou? Ridiculous. He'd call. Except she hadn't answered any of his phone calls or responded to his voicemails.

She grabbed the envelope, ripped it open, and removed the letter. Her stomach quivered as she dropped onto the sofa.

Dearest Jenny,

There are historical events which remain as relevant today as they were thousands of years ago. One of those is the phrase, "You will know the truth, and the truth will set you free."

The night you joined us at Paul's dining room table and responded to Sandra's relentless probe into your past, my heart ached for you. I hoped I could help you move beyond painful memories and accept my family as yours.

Today, Sandra told me and Grandpa that she had learned the truth about your past. Your DUI. The reason you refused to drink anything stronger than sweet tea. The reason you kept your car parked and rode a bike to work. Maybe the reason you ran away.

Nothing I learned changed my feelings for you. When you find the courage to come back to me, I promise to cherish you with every fiber of my being. Until that moment, know that you are deeply loved.

Yours forever,

Sam

The letter slipped from Jenny's fingers and fluttered to the floor as she fought off the nausea threatening to erupt. How could she possibly respond? A shudder ripped through her as buried memories surfaced. Sandra had uncovered the result, not the source of the bitter truth. She retrieved the letter, stuffed it back in the envelope, and dropped it in the dresser drawer with the others.

Jenny trudged to the single window in her tiny apartment. A sensation akin to a dozen fluttering butterfly wings assailed her chest as she gazed at the street five stories below. There was only one way to convince Sam she wasn't worthy of his love and devotion. She changed into her red dress, spritzed a healthy dose of perfume behind each ear, and rode the elevator to the ground floor. Outside, a young man approached. His eyes traveled over her from head-to-toe moments before the Jaguar pulled to the curb.

Peter slid his sunglasses down his nose. "Wow, you look gorgeous."

"You're not bad yourself, Mr. Aspiring Author." She slid onto the passenger seat and crossed her leg over her knee, letting her skirt reveal three inches of thigh.

"I'm guessing we're in for an exciting evening."

Jenny flashed a smile and buckled her seatbelt.

He pulled away from the curb. "I'm not much of a cook, but I'm a wiz at grilling. Especially prime filet mignon."

"My favorite cut of beef." Images of Sam grilling steaks on his patio skated across her mind. She tuned Peter out as she struggled to tamp down the guilt niggling at her conscience. Peter Wallace was Sam's ticket to freedom, and to hers.

"...what do you think?"

"Sorry?" Jenny uncrossed her leg. "Mental vacation."

"It's not important." He turned the corner, aimed the remote at the gate, and eased onto his driveway. "I hope you don't mind eating outside."

"Perfect night for alfresco dining." She'd made the same comment to Sam on the way to their first date.

Peter opened her door and held out his hand. "Shall we?"

Jenny tucked her hair behind her right ear revealing a dangling earring and placed her hand in his.

He squeezed her fingers.

Her pulse accelerated as they made their way to his private patio. She ran her hand along glass covering the wrought-iron table while breathing in the vanilla scent from candles glowing in three hurricane holders.

Peter pulled a wrought-iron chair away from the table.

She lowered onto the thick cushion.

He lifted a bottle from a silver chiller. "Champagne is the perfect accompaniment for our appetizer." He removed the cork, filled two flutes, and handed her a glass. "To new beginnings."

Like Sam's sunrise painting.

He tapped his glass to hers.

Jenny eyed the bottle. Dom Perignon. Expensive. Her focus shifted to her flute. Mesmerized by bubbles cascading up the golden liquid, she curled her fingers around the stem. One drink would help her stop thinking of Sam and give her the courage to follow through on her plan. She sipped then lowered the glass and kept her eyes trained on Peter while the crisp liquid slid down her throat.

"How's the Champagne?"

"Delish." She swallowed another sip of chilled courage. "What's the appetizer?"

"Oysters with pecorino."

"Fancy for a guy who claims he can't cook."

"Not for a master griller." He opened a cooler and transferred oysters on the half shell to the grill.

As she watched Peter work his culinary magic, a comment uttered by her mother found its way to the surface. 'Men easily fall prey to beautiful women who are smart enough to use them for their own gain.' Jenny lifted the glass to her lips and swallowed another mouthful. Halfway through the appetizer, he refilled the flutes. She polished off the second glass. "You're right about oysters and Champagne. Perfect combination."

"I'm glad you approve." After finishing their first course, Peter placed two steaks on the grill. "Back in a sec." He dashed toward the porch. Moments later he returned and placed a bowl and one bottle of wine beside the cooler and the second on the table.

"Yummy-looking salad."

"Like the one you ordered during our first date." After uncorking the wine, he poured a small amount, swirled, and tasted. "Excellent Chateau Lafite-Rothschild."

"Sounds expensive."

"Set me back three-hundred smackers."

Good. He had money to burn. "I've never tasted an expensive French wine." Why had she revealed that fact? She'd just pegged herself as a woman way out of his league.

Peter tipped the bottle over her glass. "Good wine is one of life's many pleasures."

For a man with a fat bank account. Her eyes focused on the ruby-red liquid.

"Best to let it breathe before tasting."

"Always." She swirled her glass. If she refused to sample the wine, she would disappoint Peter. Especially after he'd spent a fortune to please her. Besides, she could handle a few sips during dinner.

Peter plated the salad and returned to the grill to flip the steaks. "First time I've fixed dinner for a professional chef. I hope I won't disappoint you."

"If the entree is anything like the oysters, you'll impress the dickens out of me." She swallowed the first sip of wine. Amazing what three-hundred bucks would buy. "Do you treat all your lady friends to such extravagance?"

Peter grinned. "Only a select few."

Like a poor caterer planning to hit him up for a boatload of cash. Jenny giggled at the notion and swallowed another sip.

Peter glanced over his broad shoulder. "How do you like your steak?"

"Slightly north of rare." Wasn't that Sam's description the night she helped him plan Lou's surprise birthday party?

"In that case, they're ready." Peter carried the main course to the table. He sat across from Jenny, cut a piece of steak, and popped it into his mouth without bowing his head. "This might qualify as the best steak in Charleston."

She tasted. Not as good as Sam's. Why couldn't she stop thinking about him? Peter was the new man in her life.

"What's the verdict?"

"I'd say you earned the title of grill master."

"Quite a compliment coming from a pro."

Jenny cut another piece of steak. "How many bottles of expensive wine do you keep on hand?"

"Enough."

Jenny followed each bite with a sip of wine to escalate her courage and weaken her defenses. A fling with Peter would give her everything she wanted and end her infatuation with the man she loved. She dismissed a momentary spark of integrity and swallowed the last drop.

Peter refilled her glass and opened the second bottle. For dessert he served chocolate cake and more red wine.

Concerned that her slurred words would soon render complete sentences difficult, Jenny tilted her head. "I've been thinking 'bout your investment stragedy." She giggled. "I mean strategy. The thing is, I have this plan to open my own restaurant. The problem is I don't have any money."

"Difficult task without funds."

She set her wine glass on the table and stumbled through her idea. When finished, she tilted her head. "So, what do you think?"

Peter stared at her for a long moment. "Sounds like you're hitting me up for a loan."

"An investment." She reached across the table, bumped her empty glass, and sent it crashing to the ground. "I hope that cost way less than the wine."

"The expensive crystal stays indoors." Peter moved beside her and reached for her hand. "Why don't we enjoy an after-dinner drink and watch the sunset from my balcony."

Jenny's head spun as she lifted off the chair and leaned against him. "Sorry, I almost tripped."

"You stood up too fast." He wrapped his arm around her waist and guided her across the veranda to the front room. After plucking a bottle and two aperitif glasses from the bar, he escorted her up the stairs, through his bedroom, and out to the balcony.

Jenny dropped onto the double chaise and shook the fog from her head. "I remember you saying you like ending the day out here."

He poured two drinks, handed her one, and settled beside her.

She swallowed a mouthful of the sweet liquid. "Tastes like dessert."

His arm slid behind her neck.

Jenny closed her eyes, hoping the world would stop spinning. Images of Sam sitting at Lou's counter raced across her mind, then everything went dark.

Chapter 37

J enny's fingers probed a cold cloth pressing her temples as she willed the fog in her head to clear.

"Welcome back among the conscious."

She forced her eyes open and squinted at bright sunlight beaming through the window. "What time is it?"

"Little after nine." Peter tilted a silver carafe over a mug sitting on the nightstand.

Relieved she still wore her red dress, Jenny blinked and removed the cloth. Her head pounded as she pushed up on her elbows. One glance at his guest room made it clear what had happened. "Did you carry me in here?"

"You were in no condition to walk." He slid pillows behind her back and handed her the mug. "Seems you don't handle alcohol too well."

She cradled the drink and breathed in the rich coffee aroma. "What happened after I—"

"Passed out cold?"

Jenny nodded.

"I made sure you wouldn't throw up and choke, then I went to bed. Alone. In *my* room."

Heat mingling with shame stung her cheeks. She leaned back and sipped the bitter black liquid. "I didn't mean to imply anything."

"Like I'd take advantage of a comatose woman?" He dipped the cloth into an ice bucket and wrung out the excess water. "I suspect you'll need this."

"Thanks, for being a gentleman."

"Are you shocked or disappointed?"

"Relieved and grateful." Jenny pressed the cloth to her head. "I grew up with an alcoholic mother."

"Are you blaming her for your lapse of judgement?"

"You don't understand. Until last night, I hadn't had a drink since my father died."

"Why last night?" Peter's eyes narrowed. "Did you figure a few belts would give you the guts to ask me for money?"

"I thought...if we, you know—"

"You've misread me, Jenny." He walked across the room and slumped onto a wingback chair. "For starters, I found you fascinating and enjoyed your company. It's obvious you pegged me as an easy target."

"That's not...exactly true."

"Either it is true, or it isn't. Second, even if I considered your idea a good investment, I couldn't possibly loan you the money."

"Because I made a fool of myself?"

He shook his head. "I'm what you call a poor rich man. My substantial inheritance is tied up in a trust fund that doles out a monthly allowance. Barely enough to fund my lifestyle and an occasional splurge."

"Like the wine?"

"You're catching on. Seems my grandfather expected me and my sister to do more than live off his money. Which is why I'm writing a novel."

"I had no idea."

He shrugged. "Why would you?"

Jenny swung her legs over the side of the bed and set the mug on the nightstand. "I think I need to find the bathroom."

"Careful." Peter dashed to her side. "I don't want you falling and cracking your head open." He gripped her arm and led her to an open door. "Do you want me to wait for you?"

She shook her head. "I'm fine."

"That's debatable."

"Honest." She forced a smile. "I need a few minutes to freshen up."

"Fair enough. When you're ready, come down to the kitchen and I'll fix us something to eat." He held her gaze for a moment then walked out.

Jenny stumbled into the bathroom. She clutched the pedestal sink and stared at her image—smudged mascara, bloodshot eyes. Disgusted by her appearance and behavior, she splashed cold water on her face before rinsing the acrid taste from her mouth. To keep her reputation intact among Charleston's elite, she needed to patch her relationship with Peter. If there was anything left to fix.

She squared her shoulders, returned to the guest room, and retrieved the coffee mug. Afraid she'd lose her balance, she gripped the handrail as she maneuvered down the stairs. At the bottom, she paused to let the dizzy sensation pass. The scent of bacon led her to the kitchen.

Peter stood facing the stove. "You'll find aspirin and a glass of orange juice on the table." He glanced over his shoulder. "I figured you'd need them."

"From experience?" Jenny swallowed two pills and eyed the platter of toast and bacon.

"I've suffered through my share of mornings after. Mostly in college." He spooned scrambled eggs onto two plates and carried them to the table.

She reached for a slice of toast. "How many dates have you nursed back to sobriety?"

"You're the first. Don't worry, your lapse will remain our secret."

"Am I also the first woman you dated outside your circle?"

He swallowed a bite of scrambled eggs and stared at her for a long moment. "I have a question for you."

"Okay."

"Who is Sam?"

She choked, grabbed her glass, and swallowed mouthfuls of orange juice. "How do you know about him?"

"This morning before you opened your eyes you mumbled his name more than once. Said you'd never stop loving him."

Jenny slumped back in her chair. "He's a guy I met in Madison."

"Is he the reason you moved here?"

"Does it matter?"

"I don't pretend to be an expert in the romance department, but I do know something about regret." He set his fork down and slathered jam on his toast. "At the beginning of my senior year in college, I fell for a beautiful, brilliant pre-med student. You remind me of her."

Was she the reason he'd asked her out?

"After one wild spring break, short-sighted Peter Wallace—who partied through school with barely a C average—decided a woman dedicated to her career didn't qualify as a candidate for a serious relationship. I still regret letting her go."

"Sometimes we do what we think is best for the other person."

Peter retrieved his fork. "Or make foolish decisions that impact the rest of our lives."

His comment cut Jenny to the core. Her brows knitted together as she pushed her plate aside.

"Upset stomach or a bad case of regret?"

"I think it's best if we remain friends but don't date anymore. Not because you can't loan me money."

"Because you're in love with Sam?"

She diverted her eyes. "It's complicated."

"Life is complicated."

Way more than he could possibly imagine.

Chapter 38

Sam slumped on the sofa in his dark living room, nursing a beer. Six days had passed since he'd mailed the latest letter to Jenny with no response. Had admitting he knew about her DUI embarrassed or angered her? He swallowed the last of his beer, slammed the bottle on the end table, and glanced at the mantel clock. Five minutes 'til midnight. Another day gone without Jenny in his life. He pushed up and trudged to his second-floor bedroom. Maybe it was time to accept defeat. He set his phone on the nightstand, peeled off his clothes, and dropped onto his king-size bed.

Hoping a mindless program would lull him to sleep, he turned on the television. At some point he drifted off, until his ringing phone jolted him awake. Four A. M. He blinked and eyed the caller ID. Beads of sweat evaded his upper lip as he answered. "What's wrong, Madge?"

"Sorry to wake you, Sam. I've been pounding on the coffee shop door for five minutes. Lou hasn't responded, and she's not answering her phone. I don't want to make a big deal and involve our sheriff if she simply overslept."

"You were right to call me. I'll check on her. Let me know if she shows up." Sam pulled on jeans, a sweatshirt, and sneakers, then pocketed his phone and raced to his car. Could Lou have overslept? Maybe she fell. He sped through abandoned streets and slammed on his brakes in front of Lou's house. A light illuminated her front porch and cast shadows on the manicured lawn. He dashed to the door and rang the bell three times. No response. He tried the doorknob. Locked.

His adrenaline spiked as he raced around the corner of her house and swung open the picket-fence gate. He tried the patio door. Also locked.

Light shone from a lamp on the kitchen counter. Desperate, he searched for a key and found one hidden under a rock on the patio's edge. He unlocked the door and stepped inside, relieved an alarm hadn't shattered the silence.

"Lou, it's Sam." He turned on the lights and searched every room on the main floor. No sign of his friend. He sprinted up the stairs and spotted dim light spilling from an open door. A dog whimpered. Sam swallowed past the lump in his throat and entered the bedroom. He found Lou, wearing a flannel nightgown. Lying on the floor. Conscious. Unable to speak. Buttons lay beside her. "Hang on, sweetheart. Help is on the way."

Sam dialed 911, then held her hand and talked to her until the paramedics arrived. Tears trickled as he watched them position an oxygen mask over her mouth and nose before wheeling the gurney into the hall. His phone vibrated. Madge. "She's on the way to the hospital. I'll keep you posted." He pocketed the phone, scooped Buttons into his arms, then dashed downstairs and raced to his car. The ambulance backed out of the driveway, its lights flashing, the siren silent. He followed close behind.

How could this be happening? Other than his grandpa, Lou was the healthiest senior in town. A shudder ripped through his body. He pulled into the hospital parking lot, pressed his palms together, and whispered a prayer. The moment the EMTs pushed the gurney into the ER, he cracked the windows, then left Buttons and rushed inside.

After providing information to the admitting nurse, Sam slogged to the waiting room. He popped a pod in a coffee dispenser, hoping a shot of caffeine would ease his rigid neck and shoulder muscles. How long had she lain helpless on the floor? Should he find her phone and call her daughter or wait for a diagnosis?

Sam gripped the cup of steaming hot liquid in one hand and paced, pausing every few minutes to swallow a mouthful of the bitter liquid. Nothing like Lou's. He glanced at the clock. In ten minutes, customers would begin showing up for their morning dose of donuts, cinnamon buns, and coffee. Someone had to take charge. He called George. His friend cried, then volunteered to take care of Buttons and stand outside the coffee shop to spread the word.

Sam resumed pacing, imagining mornings without listening to Lou's take on the local news. He stopped beside a window and eyed the first hint of dawn creeping over the horizon. Jenny loved Lou. Maybe he should call and beg her to come home.

He drained the rest of his coffee and clutched his phone. The worse the news, the better the chance she'd return. The prospect of using Lou's tragedy to lure Jenny back to Madison released a bitter taste on his tongue and pain in the back of his throat. He crumpled the empty cup and hurled it into a trash can. If that's what it took to bring her back, so be it.

Exhausted, Sam pocketed his phone, dropped onto a chair, and propped his arms across his thighs. He hung his head and silently prayed for Lou's recovery.

"Thank goodness you found her in time."

He sat up straight and stared at his sister. "What happened?"

"Lou suffered a right-hemisphere stroke. Serious but not massive." She sat beside him. "With time and rehabilitation, it's likely she'll regain the full use of her left side and enjoy a full recovery."

"How much time?"

"Hard to tell. We'll know more in a couple of days." Sandra picked at a fingernail. "She'll need a reason to fight. We need to contact her daughter and encourage her to hire someone to keep the coffee shop open."

"That's one possibility." Sam hesitated. "Or I could call Jenny and ask her to return."

"The woman who abandoned Lou? You're not thinking rationally."

"Maybe I'm not, or maybe I want her to come back for selfish reasons. Regardless of what I want, one fact remains. Jenny is the only person who can step in and manage the business."

"It's obvious your mind is made up." Sandra stood and smoothed her white coat. "After the way she treated Lou *and* you, chances are one in a million she'll ever set foot back in this town."

"You might be right. Either way, the decision is hers, not yours or mine."

"If you ask me—"

"I'm not."

Sandra released a long sigh. "At least call Lou's daughter."

"After I call Jenny." He dashed outside, pulled his phone from his pocket, and stared at the name topping his favorites list. What made him think Jenny would answer his call or respond to a text? He dashed to his car and tossed the phone on the passenger seat. This mission was too important to leave to chance.

Chapter 39

Jenny stood at the worktable in the catering kitchen preparing crème fraiche and caviar tartlets for the evening event. After her fiasco with Peter, she'd been forced to alter her plan. Make Le Champagne Catering the best in Charleston to attract an investor whose money wasn't tied up in a trust. At least she had that going for her.

Valerie hummed to the upbeat music playing in the background while icing a cake. When the song ended, she sidled over. "When are you going out with Peter again?"

"I'm not."

"Uh-oh. Did he fix a lousy dinner?"

"Nothing like that." Jenny sighed. "Like I told you before, I'm not looking for a romantic relationship."

"Because of your Georgia *friend*?"

Jenny rolled her eyes. "Give it a break, Val."

"Geesh, you're sensitive. And when did you shorten my name?"

Jenny softened her tone. "When we became good friends."

"So, girlfriend, what really happened between you and Peter?"

"Nothing."

"I get it. You don't want to talk about it."

"What gave you that idea?" Jenny focused on the tartlets.

One of Paul's name-that-tune wins began to play.

"Hey there, handsome." Valerie's voice rose above the music.

Now what? Had one of her boyfriends wandered in to disrupt them? "Who are you talking to?"

She pointed her spatula toward the door. "Him."

Jenny turned. She blinked.

He moved closer. "Hello, Jenny."

"Sam." Her pulse pounded in her ears. "What are you doing in Charleston?"

Valerie glanced from Jenny to Sam. "Oh, my gosh. You're the mystery man from Georgia."

Sam's pained expression released alarm bells in Jenny's head. "What's wrong? Did something happen to Paul?"

"He's fine. We need to talk." He nodded toward the door. "Out there."

Jenny wiped her hands with a paper towel and followed him to the front. "You're scaring me. What's going on?"

"It's Lou." He relayed the details.

She dropped onto a chair. "Please, tell me she'll recover." Her voice trembled.

He pulled a chair beside her. "You know how important the coffee shop is to her."

"It's her whole life."

"Lou loves you as much as she loves her own daughter. My sister believes she needs a reason to fight her way back to health." Sam locked eyes with her. "What I'm trying to say is she needs you to come back to Madison and keep the coffee shop open."

Was Lou the only reason he wanted her to return? "What about Madge? Can't she take over?"

"She's a nice enough lady, but she's barely able to manage quiche, much less run a business. Look, I know I'm asking a lot."

Sitting a foot from the man she loved made her ache for his touch. How could she handle seeing him every day, knowing they could never have a romantic relationship? "I don't know. My career is on a roll. I have new friends—"

"For Lou's sake, will you consider the move?" His eyes pleaded.

Jenny nodded.

"I'll wait."

"I need more time. Please. I don't want the pressure."

"All right." Sam stood. "Don't take too long." His tone hinted of desperation.

She pushed up, mustering every ounce of will power to keep from rushing into his arms. "Go back home, Sam. I'll call you when I've made a decision."

He turned toward the front door then hesitated. "You know Lou's not the only one who needs you."

Jenny fought back tears. "Don't make this more difficult..." Her voice cracked.

"I'll wait for your call." He walked out.

Tears she had kept at bay spilled. She wiped her cheeks with the back of her hand and returned to the kitchen.

"No wonder you're crazy about that guy. He's gorgeous." Valerie looked up. "What's wrong?"

"Lou is in a bad way."

"He drove all the way from Georgia to deliver the news?"

"She's more like a mother than a friend. I need time to think."

"I've got you covered." Valerie embraced her. "Take all the time you need."

"Thanks, Val, I owe you." Jenny draped her chef coat over a chair, donned her sweater, and reached for a tissue. She blew her nose while making her way to the front door. Outside, the late afternoon sun cast long shadows on the sidewalk and street. A cool breeze nipped her cheeks. She meandered to the corner and turned toward the harbor.

Her heart raced as she entered Waterfront Park, circumvented planters surrounding a massive fountain, and settled on a bench facing the water. Images of Lou lying in a hospital bed unleashed an earthquake-sized shiver. Jenny pulled her knees up, wrapped her arms around her shins, and breathed in the salty sea air. She propped her chin on her knees and forced her eyes to focus on her surroundings. A jogger passed by. A woman dressed in sweats talked on her cell phone while walking her dog. A cruise ship anchored at a dock. Everything seemed normal. Except for one undeniable fact. Sam had turned her world upside down once again.

Jenny's focus shifted to the water. Waves rippled across the surface. A seagull swooped down and snared an unsuspecting fish. A fisherman sitting in an aluminum boat cast a line, providing competition for the hungry gull.

Reality slammed Jenny's chest like a sledgehammer. If she abandoned the catering business, André would make sure she'd never again find work in Charleston. He'd destroy any chance for her to find an investor. On the other hand, if she ignored Sam's request and Lou failed to recover...how could she live with the regret? She sighed heavily, lowered her feet to the pavement, and pushed off the bench.

Jenny headed south to the end of the park and cut over to East Bay Street. She stood on the corner and eyed the row of townhomes painted in a rainbow of pastel colors. How many future catering clients lived on this street? Did Valerie have the skills and dedication to manage the business if she left town for a while?

She strolled to White Point Garden and wandered along the paths to a gazebo perched in the center of the park. A young couple stood arm in arm at the railing, whispering to each other. Memories surfaced of Sam's arms wrapped her around her the afternoon lightning bolts and torrential rain held them captive in the Town Park gazebo.

Her chest tightened as she spun and walked up Meeting Street. By the time she returned to work, her head pounded with pain and her heart ached. At least she had moved one step closer to making a decision about her moral dilemma.

After Jenny walked out of Le Champagne Prestige Catering and headed up the street, Sam sat in his car, parked halfway down the block. His heart urged him to race after her and tell her how much he loved her. How much he needed her. Only steely self-control forced him to keep a firm grip on the steering wheel until the urge passed. When she turned the corner and moved out of sight, an ache attacked the back of his throat. The way she had referred to new friends hinted she had met another man.

His pulse accelerated as he pulled away from the curb and braked at a stop sign. He peered down the side street and spotted Jenny walking away from him. Should he follow her? Find out where she was going or who she had arranged to meet? The prospect of stalking the woman he loved churned his gut. As much as he wanted to stay in Charleston and press her for an answer, he understood she needed time alone to sort through her emotions. After all, he had blindsided her.

A horn blasted from behind.

He glanced in the rearview mirror at an impatient driver then stole one more glimpse of the woman he loved before turning in the opposite direction. As he drove through town and onto Interstate 26, an overpowering sense of dread weighed heavy on his chest. Maybe he had misjudged Jenny's feelings for him.

Memories of the day she announced her move to Charleston raced through his head. Was a new job the real reason she'd fled Madison? Or something more profound? Perhaps fear she would fall victim to her addiction? Now she knew that he knew. Maybe shame kept her from responding to his last letter. Sam pounded the steering wheel with his fist. What made him think writing it had been a good idea?

He eyed the upcoming exit. Perhaps he should turn around, go back, and explain that his love was unconditional. Bad idea. She had to find her way back to him on her own terms.

With each passing mile, fear that he had lost Jenny forever escalated. By the time he pulled into his driveway, anger and despair had triggered pounding pain in the back of his neck. He released his grip on the steering wheel and trudged to his back door. His only option was to find enough patience to wait for Jenny's call.

Chapter 40

Jenny leaned close to the bathroom mirror and stared at the dark circles under her eyes, thanks to a torturous night reading and rereading every letter from Lou and Sam. At some point in the wee hours of the morning, she had stopped teetering between staying in Charleston and returning to Madison. Now she had to make good on her decision. She splashed cold water on her face and changed into her chef uniform. On the way to work, she stopped at a coffee shop and purchased two take-out cappuccinos and cinnamon rolls. Dark clouds hinted of rain as she scurried two more blocks and met Valerie at the door. "I brought your favorite morning indulgence."

Valerie sniffed. "Cinnamon rolls. What's the occasion?"

"We need to talk."

"Are you sweetening me up to fire me for flirting with the clientele?"

"Hardly." Jenny handed her the goodies and unlocked the door. "About yesterday."

"When Sam, your mystery man, showed up? Sounds like a cute song title." Valerie followed her into the kitchen.

Jenny sat on a worktable stool and pointed to the one beside her. "Sit with me."

"Uh-oh, I *am* in trouble." Valerie settled beside her and pulled a cinnamon roll from the sack. "So, what's up boss?"

"Despite the fact that you have your eye on every eligible bachelor—"

"Available and rich, mind you."

"What I'm trying to say is I believe you have the experience and skills to run this entire show."

"Maybe when André promotes you to president or something." Valerie's eyes widened as if a light bulb had suddenly flicked on. "Oh my gosh. This is about the lady in Madison who's like a mom, isn't it?"

"She needs me, Val."

"For how long?"

"Couple of months. Maybe longer."

"Have you told André?"

"Not yet. I want you to go with me when I break the news."

"You know that man scares the dickens out of me." Valerie licked icing from her fingers. "Would you believe he made me work for free for a week to prove I could handle this job?"

"That's what he does, and you obviously passed the test. Now you need to prove you're ready to take over for me."

"How do you propose I make that happen?"

"Tomorrow morning, present a plan to André showing how you'll expand his business."

"Are you kidding me?"

"Nope." Jenny sipped her coffee. "When we wrap up today's event, I'll help you put it together."

"Do you really think I can pull it off?"

"Without a doubt."

"Imagine that." Valerie grinned. "Me an honest-to-goodness businesswoman."

"Who also knows how to charm the socks off rich folks."

"I'll do it." Valerie popped off her stool. "First we have to make today's event one of our best."

"See? You're already thinking like the boss."

Jenny stood beside Valerie on the sidewalk in front of André's restaurant. "Remember to approach him as if you already have the job."

Valerie patted her laptop. "Thanks to you, I'm raring to go."

"Not quite." Jenny's gaze zeroed in on her friend. "Whose plan are you presenting?"

She rolled her eyes. "Mine."

"That's right. You need to own it and pitch it like a pro."

"Yes, boss."

Jenny planted her hands on her hips. "Yes, who?"

"My good friend who knows I deserve a big promotion."

"Now you're ready." Jenny led the way to André's office and knocked on the door.

"*Entrez.*"

"It's showtime," whispered Jenny.

Valerie squared her shoulders, held her head high, and stepped inside. "Today is your lucky day, Chef André."

Jenny cleared her throat and closed the door.

Valerie pulled a chair close and set her laptop on his desk. "I'd like to share a strategy I developed to expand Le Champagne's reach and influence, sir."

André's brows pinched as he glanced from one woman to the other. "All right." He laced his fingers. "You have my attention."

As Valerie revealed her presentation and began her rehearsed spiel, Jenny's mind drifted to the morning she had first walked into André's private space—nervous, yet confident her charm and cooking skills would win him over. Now her friend had stepped up to prove her worth and ease the burden of an unexpected announcement. She blinked and eyed André's passive expression.

Valerie scrolled to the final page. "As you can see, this plan will expand Le Champagne's influence beyond Charleston."

"Remarkable." He lifted his chin. "I hired two smart chefs."

"Yes, you did." Jenny pulled a chair up to the desk. "Which is why Valerie has the skills and experience to manage Le Champagne Catering."

André's eyes narrowed. "Why do I have the impression something else is going on?"

Time for 'get Jenny off the hook' part two. "You're an astute business observer, Executive Chef André. The thing is, yesterday a friend called me with bad news. My...mother suffered a stroke. She desperately needs me to come home to Madison and keep her coffee shop afloat until she's well enough to return to work."

His stare intensified. "Are you offering your resignation?"

"Given the fact that I don't know how long she'll need me, I think it's best to turn the reins over for a while."

He unlaced his fingers and leaned back. "Your mother, you say?"

It was only a little fib, and Lou did claim her as a daughter. Jenny drew in a deep breath and nodded.

André's focus shifted to Valerie. "Other than your proposal, what makes you think you can replace the woman I handpicked to manage my catering business?"

"Well, sir, because Jenny is way more than my boss. She's an excellent teacher and role model. Plus, she spent the last few months teaching me everything I need to know to keep the business running smoothly."

"I see." André shifted his focus to Jenny. "Before I hand over the reins, I need you and Chef Valerie to hire an assistant."

"Yes, sir. One more thing. I'd appreciate you writing a recommendation letter for my professional portfolio."

"Come see me after you accomplish your final task." He flicked his hand toward her. "Now pardon me, I have important work to finish."

Valerie retrieved her laptop and followed Jenny through the kitchen and dining room to the front sidewalk. "Yippee, now I'll have an even better inside track to the rich and powerful."

"You handled yourself like a pro. I had no idea you'd learned so much."

"There's a doggone good brain under all this blonde hair. Besides, what if I fall in love with some good-looking, sexy guy who's too broke to support me in the manner to which I'm aspiring?"

Jenny laughed. "There's a plan you can take to the bank."

"Now we need to hire someone almost as talented as you and me."

"Piece of cake for the two smartest catering gals this side of the Mississippi."

Chapter 41

Jenny's eyes followed the young man who had accepted their offer as he walked toward the exit. The moment Prestige Catering's front door closed behind him, she high-fived Valerie. "Finally, after interviewing fourteen candidates, we have a good hire."

Valerie nodded. "Lucky for me, he's smart and good-looking."

"Perfect credentials for a caterer. Plus, you won't miss a beat when I leave."

"Except I'll miss you like crazy." Valerie curled a lock of hair around her finger. "Who am I gonna talk to about all the good-looking, rich men we run across?"

"You'll find someone."

"If you ask me, when Lou recovers, you should come back to Charleston. André would take you back in a heartbeat. I know I would. Unless Sam gives you a reason to stay in Madison."

Jenny shook her head. "Impossible."

"Hmm. You protested a bit too fast."

"Don't read anything into my quick response. I've already decided to leave Madison as soon as Lou is well enough to manage without me." Jenny zipped her culinary knife case closed. "I guess this is goodbye."

"I've never managed a business all by myself..." Valerie's voice drifted off, her eyes pleading. "What if I have questions or need advice?"

Jenny placed her hands on her friend's shoulders. "Believe me, you're more than ready to take over, and when you implement the plan you presented to André, our little catering business will expand to amazing new heights. In fact, I'm predicting you'll need to hire more staff before the end of the year."

"You're right. Still, promise to keep your phone turned on in case I need you?"

"Cross my heart. Right now, I'd best scoot on out of here before we both break down in tears."

Valerie embraced her. "Thank you for everything."

"You go knock the socks off Charleston's elite, girlfriend."

"I'll do my best." Valerie released her.

"I know you will." Jenny shouldered her purse, tucked her knife case under her arm, and walked out of Le Champagne Catering. Outside, she breathed in the cool fall air. During her stroll to André's restaurant, a bittersweet sensation tugged at her heartstrings. Tomorrow she would leave new friends behind and abandon the most prestigious position she'd ever held. For once in her life, she had put another person's needs ahead of her own.

When she arrived at Le Champagne, she paused at the entrance. Would this be the last time she'd ever walk through downtown Charleston? She forced her anxiety aside and made her way to André's office. She breathed deeply and knocked.

"*Entrez.*" He motioned her to take a seat. "What's the status on a new hire?"

"You'll be pleased to know that an exceptional young man with excellent educational credentials accepted Valerie's offer. He's young and eager to prove his skills."

"Practical experience?"

"He worked as a line chef in Beaufort after he graduated with a two-year culinary degree." She named the restaurant.

"I know the executive chef. Good place. Now I suppose you're expecting me to write a letter of recommendation."

He had promised. "Any word from a world-class chef will be a big plus for me."

"You're quite the charmer." He opened a drawer, lifted a manila folder, and handed it to her. "I wrote it yesterday."

"Really?"

"I knew you'd come through."

Jenny blinked away astonishment as she opened the folder and removed a letter typed on Le Champagne stationery. Her hand pressed to her chest as she read the first sentence. She continued reading three glowing paragraphs praising her talent as a chef and touting her business acumen. "Wow. I'm honored. What I mean is...you've managed to blow my socks off."

"Such an interesting phrase." André chuckled and leaned forward. "I'm aware that my entire staff sees me as demanding. Those who understand the restaurant business are keenly aware that thriving in the culinary world requires toughness and perfection."

"You definitely mastered the art of perfection."

"Yes, I have." His eyes laser-focused on hers. "Perhaps you are unaware of the depth of my admiration." His French accent disappeared. "You are willing to do what many people aren't—walk away from a promising career and put your family first."

Stunned by his comment, she considered telling him the truth about Lou.

"If I had done what you're doing years ago, I wouldn't be divorced from my wife and estranged from my twenty-two-year-old daughter."

His shocking revelation rendered Jenny speechless. She couldn't tell him Lou wasn't her mother. Not after he'd allowed her a glimpse into his soul.

"However, there is no point in dwelling on the past. What's done is done." André's accent returned. "The future belongs to those of us who demand nothing less than perfection." His phone buzzed. He glanced at the screen. *"Excusez-moi,* I must take this call. I wish you the best life has to offer, Chef Jenny." As always, his emphasis was on the last syllable.

"Thank you, Chef André." She placed the letter in the folder. "For everything."

He nodded then dismissed her with a hand wave.

As she wandered from the kitchen, through the dining room, and out to the sidewalk, her heart swelled with new respect for the man whose unique approach delivered results. Maybe one day she would find her way back to South Carolina.

When she arrived at her building, she rode the elevator to her floor and unlocked her apartment. Eager to complete one final task before turning in the key, she opened her chef portfolio and slid André's letter into the empty sleeve opposite a copy of a Le Prestige Catering menu. Mission accomplished. After stashing her envelope of cash into the next-to-last sleeve, she placed the portfolio and knife case in her suitcase, zipped it closed, and set it on the floor. In five hours, she would return to the garage apartment and her beloved guitar. Tomorrow, she would visit Lou and figure out how to manage the coffee shop while encouraging Sam to fall out of love with her.

Chapter 42

Sam clutched his phone in his right hand and trudged into his grandpa's office. "She's on her way."

"Who's on her way where?"

"I've written a letter every week since Jenny moved away. She responded with three-sentence postcards. Except for the last one I wrote the day Sandra told us about her DUI." Sam slumped onto a leather easy chair. "I drove to Charleston to ask Jenny to return to Madison. She refused to commit. Not one word from her for five days." He held up his phone. "Then, out of the blue, she sends me a text telling me she's driving back today."

"Why all the doom and gloom?" His grandpa pushed a contract aside. "She's coming back."

"For Lou. Not me."

"Does the reason matter?"

A burst of air escaped Sam's lungs. "The way she said, 'I have friends' when I told her Lou needed her—" He shook his head. "I suspect she met someone."

"You can't draw conclusions based on one comment."

"What if I'm right?"

"What if you're wrong?"

Sam massaged the back of his neck to ease the ache inching up to his skull. "I don't know if I can deal with another cat-and-mouse game—seeing her every day, not having a clue where I stand."

His grandpa pointed to a photo of his wife sitting on the corner of his desk. "If I had given up on your grandmother after she left me, you wouldn't exist."

"That's not the same. You and Grandma were married."

"You can't let your pride get in the way."

"One wrong move and I'll destroy any chance I have with Jenny."

His grandpa's eyes trained on Sam's. "Act like nothing has changed between you two. Show her how much you care."

"How?"

"You'll figure it out."

"Up to this point, nothing I've tried has worked." Sam tapped his fingers on the chair's arm. "And now, thanks to my last letter, she knows that I know about her DUI. What if I overreacted and she doesn't have a problem with alcohol?"

"All the more reason to *show* her how much she means to you."

Sam stopped tapping and stared at his grandpa. "Maybe you're right."

"No maybe about it. You love Jenny too much to give up without a fight."

"What if I lose?"

"You won't."

"What makes you so sure?"

"Faith."

Sam eyed his grandmother's picture. Maybe the time had come to try a new approach with Jenny. He popped up and headed out, ready to take the first step.

Weary from a five-hour drive and mind-numbing anxiety, Jenny parked in Paul's driveway and spotted her bike propped against the garage door. A reminder that Sam, Paul, and Sandra knew about her struggle with alcohol. She'd returned for Lou, so what anyone else thought about her didn't matter.

Jenny popped the trunk, hauled her duffel up the stairs, and retrieved the key from under the mat. Inside, she breathed the sweet scent of flowers wafting from an arrangement of yellow roses sitting on the coffee table.

She carried the duffle to the bedroom, set it beside the dresser, and opened the bottom drawer. Empty. She opened every drawer. Nothing. Had Paul or Sam found her wine and tossed it out? Her jaw tightened as she returned to the main room and eyed the roses. No sign of a note. Her eyes drifted to the guitar case leaning against the wall under the flat-screen television. She sat cross-legged on the floor, removed the Gibson, and stroked the smooth wood. After adjusting the keys, she played one of her favorite songs.

A knock. The front door inched open. "Welcome home."

Her heartbeat accelerated.

"I figured you'd need help moving back in." Sam walked in with her suitcase and picnic basket in hand. "First time I've heard you play."

She leaned the guitar against the wall. "After all these months, I'm kind of rusty."

"Sounded good to me." He set the suitcase on the floor and the basket on the dinette table. "I stocked the kitchen with a few essentials."

Why did he make it so easy to love him? "Thanks for the food and the roses."

"How'd you know they were from me?"

Jenny pushed off the floor. "Lucky guess."

"Roses were the closest I could find to sunflowers. Did you have a chance to visit Lou?"

"Not yet. How's she doing?"

"She started rehab today."

"Does she know you asked me to keep the coffee shop open?"

"The last time we spoke, you left me hanging. So, I haven't told anyone except Grandpa." Sam locked eyes with Jenny. "I'm curious. Why didn't you respond to my last letter?"

She diverted her eyes, lifted her copy of *The Scarlet Letter* off the shelf, and fingered the leather cover. "We agreed to remain friends, right?"

"We did. There's one big problem. Falling out of love isn't easy."

She had to make him believe she didn't love him. "Who tossed my wine?"

"The bottle you left in the dresser?"

"So, you're the one." Jenny slammed the book on the shelf and glared at him. "What's the matter, Sam? Are you afraid I'll go off the deep end and drink myself into a stupor?"

"I admit I knee-jerk reacted to the news about your...you know."

"Say the words, Sam. Say what you think I'm straddled with. An alcohol addiction."

He placed his hands on her shoulders. His eyes probed hers. "Why won't you let me love you, Jenny?"

"Because women like me aren't lovable."

"What do you mean, women like you?"

"Women who drink too much."

"You're not a drunk."

"No?" Her tone rang harsh. "Then you tell me why after I read your last letter I drank enough to pass out and wake up in a man's bedroom."

Sam's brows pinched. "In his bed?"

She couldn't lie. Not now. "His guestroom. Fully dressed." She pulled away and faced the bookcase. "Turns out he was more of a gentleman than I was a lady."

"Is that the only time, since we met that you—"

"Got a snootful?" He needed to know all the ugly truth. "The day I learned my father had died, I ended up in a bar. That night I drank so much the bartender held my car keys hostage. Kelley had to rescue me. That's the reason I didn't return to Madison until the following morning." She shuffled to the window and stared at his car parked beside hers.

He followed. "I want to help you, Jenny."

"I'm not a charity case."

"That's not what I'm saying."

"How can I make you understand?" Jenny faced him. "I only came back because Lou needs me."

"Do you want me to take you to see her?"

"After everything I've told you?" Her voice faltered.

"That's what friends do."

She drew every ounce of strength to resist wrapping her arms around his neck and kissing him. "I need a minute to freshen up."

"Take all the time you need."

Jenny darted to the bathroom and splashed cold water on her face. Her eyes drifted to her image in the mirror as truth hit home. Resisting Sam would take far more will power than staying sober. She squared her shoulders and returned to the main room.

Sam stood beside the bookcase, plucking a guitar string. "One of these days will you teach me how to play? No strings attached."

She rolled her eyes and managed a half smile. "You're definitely one of the good guys."

"That's a better description than 'interesting.' I have something for you." Sam set the guitar on the floor and slid his hand into his slacks pocket. "Hold out your hand."

Jenny's eyes narrowed to a slit. "Why?"

"You are one suspicious woman."

"A personality trait fine-tuned by my mother."

Sam held up a key. "You'll need this to unlock the coffee shop. Do you want to go to the hospital in your car or mine?"

"Yours. I've driven enough for one day."

Ten minutes later Jenny's breathing accelerated as they walked into Lou's hospital room. She gripped the railing on the empty bed. "What if Lou suffered another stroke? Or worse?"

Sam placed his hand over hers. "You're not wild about hospitals, are you?"

Painful memories sent a quiver ripping through her limbs. "Not my favorite place." She pulled her hand away from the railing and settled on the bench stretching below the window. "Maybe your sister is cranky because she spends most of her time taking care of sick and injured people."

"It's more like problem-solving is her thing, which is why she chose emergency medicine."

"Does she know her number-one problem is back in town?"

Sam sat beside her. "Long before you moved to Madison, Sandra designated herself as our family defender. I suppose it makes sense, since a defense attorney raised her, *and* she married one. Despite her flaws, she's a brilliant, and believe it or not, a caring doctor."

"You didn't answer my question."

"Unless she saw us walk in, I doubt she knows you're here."

Jenny picked at a hangnail. "She's likely to blow a fuse when she finds out."

"If keeping the coffee shop open speeds up Lou's recovery, my sister might warm up to you. If you stick around for a while."

"Don't count on that happening."

"Sandra's attitude adjustment or you staying in town?"

Jenny shrugged. "Neither. I mean both."

"I suppose a guy can hope." He nodded toward the door. "Here comes our favorite patient."

A young man wearing light blue scrubs pushed Lou's wheelchair into the room. "Our gal did herself proud today."

Jenny's throat tightened as she watched him swivel the footrests from under Lou's feet, then lift his patient from the chair to the bed.

"Are you comfortable, Ms. Johnson?"

She waggled her right index finger at him. "Like I keep telling you, Andy, my friends all call me Lou."

Jenny pressed her hands to her lips, surprised at how well Lou spoke. Other than dark circles under her eyes, she looked the same as she had before her stroke.

"Yes, ma'am, Ms. Lou. Did you notice a couple of visitors sitting over there by the window?"

"Well, I declare." A smile lit Lou's face. "Look who's found her way back home."

Jenny rushed to the bed and grasped Lou's left hand. "It's good to see you looking all perky."

"On my right side anyway."

Andy clutched the wheelchair handgrips. "Won't be long before we have your left side working as well as the right. You'll be as good as new in no time."

"My good-looking physical therapist is a hard-driving optimist who slap wears me out."

"Twice a day starting tomorrow." Andy backed the wheelchair toward the door.

"Double the torture." Lou faced Jenny. "How long are you in town, honey?"

"As long as you need me." She stroked Lou's limp hand.

Sam moved to Jenny's side. "Our gal plans to open the coffee shop and keep it going until you're ready to return."

Lou eyed Jenny, her brows pinched. "What about your catering job?"

If she told her the truth, would it help Lou recover or make her feel guilty? She couldn't risk causing her one moment of anxiety. "I'm taking a leave of absence for as long as necessary."

"My goodness, you have a considerate boss."

"Chef André understands the situation. About the coffee shop, how much can I expect from Madge?"

"Besides her showing up on time and chatting up the customers, she's mastered donut making."

They continued to talk until Lou's eyelids grew heavy and her speech slowed. "Sorry." She yawned.

Jenny leaned over the railing and kissed her cheek. "I'll come back tomorrow and give you an update."

"Thanks…" Lou's eyes closed.

"I love you, Lou," Jenny whispered, then straightened and walked out.

Sam caught up with her as she passed the nurses' station. "Are you really taking a leave of absence, or did you fudge the truth for Lou's sake?"

"All you need to know is I can stay until she's a hundred percent."

"Are you saying you don't have a job to go back to?"

Jenny huffed. "You're reading too much into my comment."

"Whatever the facts, I'm glad you're here. For Lou's sake."

"So am I."

He pressed his hand to her back as they made their way to the first floor and out to the parking lot. "How about letting me take you to dinner?"

"Are you inviting me on a date?"

"Now who's reading too much into a comment?" He aimed his key at his car, unlocked the door, and started the engine. "Treating you to a meal is my way of thanking you for showing up."

"Oh."

He opened the passenger door. "What's your answer?"

She slid onto the seat. "I haven't had a bite to eat since six this morning."

"I'll take that as a yes." Sam closed her door and rounded the front of the car.

Jenny glanced at his profile as he settled on the driver's seat. If only she could erase her past and undo what she had done. She turned toward the side window and spotted a young woman lifting a toddler from a stroller. Her only option was to discourage Sam without breaking his heart. Starting tonight.

Chapter 43

Frustrated by Jenny's endless prattle about her latest adventures, Sam turned onto his grandpa's driveway and parked beside her car.

"Sorry if I talked your ear off."

"I'll survive."

"No need to walk me up. I know the way." Jenny's face lit as Duchess bounded toward the car. "My best pal in the whole world." She slid out, crouched, and wrapped her arms around the dog's neck. "I missed you like crazy."

"Outranked by a dog," Sam mumbled.

Jenny peered through the window. "Did you say something?"

"Nothing important."

"Thanks for dinner, Sam." She dashed toward the stairs. "Come on, girl. Bet I can find a treat for you."

Duchess padded behind her.

"Maybe I need to develop a taste for dog biscuits," Sam murmured before responding to a tap and lowering his window. "Hey, Grandpa."

Paul leaned down. "You're not the only one excited to see Jenny."

"I spent the last two hours getting an earful about Charleston. According to Jenny, it's darn near perfect, and everyone who lives there is loaded with talent and infectious charm. Either she can't wait to go back, or she's working overtime to brush me off."

"Seems you'll need to win her over a little every day."

Sam tapped his fingers on the steering wheel. "Do you suppose she'll give me half a chance if I adopt a dog?"

"Not a bad idea. Want to join me for a brandy?"

He shook his head. "I'd be lousy company, not to mention I'm exhausted."

"In that case, go home and get some rest. I'll see you in the morning."

"Good night, Grandpa." Sam backed out of the driveway. Maybe a goodnight's sleep would improve his mood. A block from home, Sandra's car parked on the street came into view. So much for peace and quiet. He parked in the detached garage behind his house and trudged past the fireplace anchoring the patio, geared for a confrontation. Inside, he found his sister sitting at the kitchen table, clutching a bottle of water. "I'm guessing this isn't a friendly visit."

"When were you planning to tell me?"

He tossed his keys on the counter and grabbed a beer from the fridge. "Who clued you in? Lou or one of your spies?"

"Did you tell Jenny a sob story about Lou needing her, or did you tell her the truth?"

"That is the truth." Sam twisted the cap off the bottle and sat across from her.

"Don't feed me that line of malarkey. You wanted her to return because you refuse to let her go."

"You've nailed it, Doc." He downed a long swig and swiped the back of his hand across his mouth. "You'll be thrilled to know she walked away from a great job because she loves Lou, not me."

Sandra's gaze softened. "I don't understand why you continue allowing her to break your heart."

"Tell me something." He set the bottle on the table with a loud snap. "What would you have done if Ted snubbed you after you'd dated him for a couple of months?"

"I for doggone sure wouldn't have chased after him."

"Even if deep down you knew you could never love anyone else?"

Sandra fingered her diamond wedding band. "Comparing my husband to Jenny isn't fair."

"Why not?"

"Because Ted isn't tainted by a troubled past."

Sam folded his arms across his chest. "Your comment doesn't reflect a Christian attitude."

"Don't try to guilt-trip me, Sam. The truth is, I care about the alcoholics who end up in my ER. At the same time, I don't deny one crucial fact. They are all slaves to their addiction." Sandra stood, flattened her hands on the table, and leaned toward him. "You need to face reality and abandon your misguided feelings for Jenny before she smashes your heart into a million pieces."

"Have you finished?"

"For the moment."

"Good." He grabbed his bottle. "Because I intend to drink the rest of my beer without listening to a meddling relative."

"Fine." She grabbed her purse and stomped out.

Seconds after the front door slammed and shook the walls, Sam carried the bottle upstairs and set it on his bathroom vanity. He turned the shower on, hoping warm water would calm his anger and ease the tension sending ripples of pain across his neck and shoulder muscles.

A rolling sensation attacked Jenny's gut as she stared at the unopened suitcase sitting on her bed. Spending the entire dinner grossly exaggerating her life in Charleston hadn't come easy. Especially when Sam's pained expression and glazed stare hinted that her comments cut deep.

She unzipped the suitcase, removed her chef portfolio, and sat on the edge of the bed. Duchess licked her chops and plopped her head in Jenny's lap. She stroked the dog's muzzle. "You know I'm pushing Sam away because I love him, don't you, girl?"

The dog's tail slapped the floor in a rhythmic motion.

"I knew you'd understand."

Jenny flipped to the latest entry and read every word, relieved she hadn't embellished the truth when she shared André's accolades with Sam. Maybe she should use her experience and skills to ramp up the coffee shop and extend the hours. Except the extra work could make life too difficult when Lou returned. A decision for another day. She stared at the cash she'd manage to save before closing her prized possession and setting it on the dresser.

After unpacking her clothes, changing into pajamas, and sending Duchess home, Jenny crawled into bed. As she sniffed the sheets, a rain-washed spring morning came to mind. A yawn escaped as she closed her eyes and imagined new life for the little coffee shop the locals touted as their favorite morning hangout. The last image tiptoeing across her brain before she drifted to sleep was Sam sitting at Lou's counter smiling at her.

Chapter 44

J enny slipped out of her chef coat and switched the classical music to country pop. "It's time to welcome folks back to Lou's Coffee Shop."

"My goodness, I'd best put these in place." Madge lifted a tray of fresh donuts off the stainless-steel worktable and shuffled out of the kitchen.

Jenny pressed her lips tight to hide her frustration over the woman's painfully slow pace. But as Lou had said, at least she showed up on time and baked delicious donuts. Jenny removed keys from a hook and carried them to the front. Seconds after unlocking the door and flipping the sign from closed to open, George crossed the street. "Good morning, early bird."

"Nine days without my regular morning routine and I'm as grumpy as an old codger who forgot to drink his prune juice."

She laughed. "I missed you, George."

"We all missed *you*, Jenny. I hope you stick around this time."

"Until Lou is back to her old self."

George moseyed to his favorite stool. "Morning, Madge. You're looking mighty spiffy."

"Why thank you." She pushed a mug of coffee to him then fluffed her hair. "Do you fancy my new style?"

"I swear you don't look a day over fifty."

"You really think so?" Madge giggled. "Imagine that. I'm younger than my youngest daughter."

Jenny subdued a laugh and moved behind the counter to transfer donuts from the tray Madge had abandoned to the display cabinet. "I assume you're still a coffee and cinnamon-roll kind of guy, George."

"Unless you fixed one of those quiches that tastes like pie."

"As a matter of fact, I did. Special for you. Madge, bring our favorite customer a slice from the kitchen, with a side of banana bread."

"Coming right up."

George stirred a packet of sugar into his coffee. "Lou told us you had a job fixing fancy parties for highfalutin rich folks over there in Charleston."

"We catered to a discerning clientele."

"Bet they liked your fruit-free pies."

"Indeed, they did."

Madge returned and set a plate on the counter.

George's eyes widened. "What's that green thing sitting on top of my pie?"

"Goodness gracious, George." Madge handed him a fork. "Haven't you ever seen a slice of kiwi?"

"Is it some kind of fancy fruit?"

"Taste it and find out for yourself."

Jenny rolled her eyes and suppressed a giggle.

Her favorite policeman walked in and moseyed over.

"Good morning, Matt."

"Morning, Jenny. Heard you were back in town." He settled on a stool beside George and set his cap on the counter.

"For the time being." Jenny poured him a cup of coffee. "What can I bring you?"

"One of those cinnamon buns. How's Lou doing?"

"She's coming along." Jenny plated a bun.

George swallowed a bite of quiche. "One day soon we'll show up and find Lou standing behind the counter as if nothing ever happened. Right, Jenny?"

"Absolutely."

As customers drifted in, Madge tended to those opting for tables while Jenny served and chatted with old friends at the counter. Despite her determination, she found herself keeping an eye out for Sam. She hadn't heard a peep from him since talking his ear off during dinner. Maybe he had finally come to his senses about her. Isn't that what she wanted? By ten o'clock, knots had invaded Jenny's stomach. Maybe Sam was busy with clients.

She was wiping the counter in front of his empty stool when movement at the door caught her eye.

Sam strolled in and claimed his spot. "Looks like business is booming."

His smile turned her brain to mush as she continued swiping the cloth across the surface.

"I think that spot's plenty clean by now."

"What? Oh." She pulled the cloth away. "You want coffee?"

"Is it as good as Lou's?"

"Close." George motioned for a refill. "No offense, Jenny. Truth is, no one brews coffee like Lou."

"None taken." She topped off George's coffee and filled a mug for Sam.

He added sugar and tasted. "He's right. It's almost as good as Lou's."

The man dressed in overalls sitting beside George wiped his fingers with a napkin. "Miss Jenny did right good with the cinnamon buns, but don't tell Lou I said so."

Jenny placed a bun on the counter and pushed it to Sam.

"Looks as good as Lou's." He cut a chunk with his fork. "I plan to visit her later today. Do you want to go with me?"

If she said yes, would it give him false hope about their relationship?

He paused the fork halfway to his mouth. "No strings. Just two pals visiting a friend."

If she turned him down, would everyone within earshot think she didn't care about Lou? "Sure, why not."

"I'll pick you up at four." Sam's eyes remained focused on Jenny as his fork reached its target.

Jenny raised her right shoulder and turned away, trusting the physical snub would send the message her mouth refused to convey. After Sam finished eating and paid his bill, her eyes followed him as he slid off his stool and strolled out. Why hadn't he turned to steal a glance?

She shifted her focus back to the counter and noticed George smiling at her. "What?"

"It's like old times. Watching you and Sam playing goofy games."

"Give it a break, George." She switched roles with Madge and spent the remainder of the morning away from the counter.

Jenny sat on the bottom step chewing a fingernail while eyeing the entrance to Paul's driveway. Why hadn't she called Sam and begged off? After all, she could drive to the hospital in her own car. She could text him with some sort of excuse. His car turned onto the driveway. Too late. She pushed off the step and waited for him to ease to a stop.

Determined to avoid eye contact, Jenny slid onto the passenger seat and buckled her belt.

Sam backed onto the street. "By now, I suspect Lou knows all about the coffee shop reopening."

She shrugged. "I suppose."

"Good old George is happy you're taking charge."

"He knows I'm only staying until Lou is back on her feet."

"Understood."

Jenny clasped her hands in her lap and turned her head toward the side window.

"What's wrong?" Sam drove onto Main Street.

You made me fall in love, that's what's wrong. "It's been a long day, so humor me and skip the mindless chitchat."

"Not a problem." His tone hinted of a clenched jaw.

Uncomfortable silence hung heavy. The moment Sam parked, Jenny bolted from the passenger seat and headed straight toward the hospital entrance.

Sam caught up with her halfway across the parking lot. "I don't know what I've done to tick you off, but one thing I do know, Lou doesn't need you storming into her room with a giant chip on your shoulder." He gripped her elbow. "Either ditch the attitude or march right back to the car, and I'll drive you to your apartment."

Her feet froze in place. He was right. Lou deserved better.

"What's your decision?"

Jenny refused to face him. "Sorry, guess I'm a bit anxious."

He touched her arm. "I understand."

What did he understand? That she still loved him? That his touch ignited a passion she found impossible to ignore?

"Tell you what, in lieu of kissing and making up, how about we call a truce and go visit the lady we both love?"

Everything about Sam made her love him more. "Agreed." She remained silent while they made their way to the entrance and up to Lou's room.

A smile lit Lou's face the moment they walked in. "Two of my favorite visitors. I hear you reopened the coffee shop this morning."

Jenny pulled a chair close to the bed. "Everyone misses you, especially your coffee and friendly conversation."

A half hour after they arrived, Andy showed up with a wheelchair. "Time for your afternoon rehab, Miss Lou."

"You mean torture treatment?" Lou grinned. "Tell George and everyone I'm making good progress, Jenny."

"Will do."

Andy helped Lou to the wheelchair and pushed her out.

Jenny and Sam walked in silence as they returned to his car. After sliding onto the driver's seat, he turned to her. "How about letting me treat you to dinner on the way home. A peace offering of sorts."

No more dinners alone. "Invite your grandpa to join us for take-out burgers and milkshakes, and I'm game."

"Safety in numbers?"

He had that right. "More like a pleasant meal among friends."

"Why not." His words failed to mask his disappointment.

Jenny pressed her hand to her stomach hoping to ease the stab of guilt rippling through her.

Chapter 45

Two weeks after Jenny began managing the coffee shop, she entered Lou's hospital room to find her sitting on a recliner holding greeting card in her right hand while exercising her left. "Wow, at this rate you'll be back to work in no time."

"Seems the good Lord isn't ready for me to retire quite yet." Lou aimed the front of the card toward Jenny. "You're the first to see what my Sara sent me."

Jenny sat on the edge of the bed and read the message. "Congratulations, you're a grandmother." Her eyes widened. "Oh my gosh, your daughter's pregnant?"

"She's due in seven months. I had resigned myself to going to my grave without ever holding a grandchild in my arms." Lou pressed the card to her chest. "Now I'm more motivated than ever to recover."

"That's great news for all your coffee-shop buddies."

Lou lowered the card to her lap. "According to George and Madge, business is better than ever."

"It's clicking right along. Which brings me to an idea that's been percolating."

Lou chuckled. "Let me guess, after two weeks you're itching to add fancy new menu items."

"Actually, I've floated a concept by some of your most loyal customers."

Lou laced her fingers and steepled her thumbs. "What wild notions are bouncing around in your pretty head?"

"I'm thinking we should stay open 'til two and serve lunch. We could start out simple. Sandwiches. A couple of salads. Maybe a soup of the day and fresh-baked pie."

"A mite ambitious considering Madge isn't what you'd call a whiz in the kitchen."

"I've noticed." Jenny flattened her palms against her thighs. "Which means I'd have to hire another chef, someone who'd accept minimum wage to start."

"Interesting idea." Lou paused. "Except, how do you expect to attract anyone with a lick of skills who's willing to work for peanuts?"

Jenny drummed her fingers on her right leg. "I don't know yet."

"You'd best figure that out before you go making any changes."

Jenny stopped drumming. "Are you giving me the go-ahead?"

"On one condition. You stick around as long as it takes."

"To do what?"

"That's for you to figure out."

Jenny noted the twinkle in Lou's eyes. "Why do I have the feeling you're not talking about the coffee shop?"

"Lots of folks besides me are pleased as punch you're back in town. There's George, Paul, our customers, and a few more."

"You're not exactly subtle."

"Neither are you. Your expression suggests you know what, or should I say, who I'm talking about."

"You're a treasure, Lou. I missed you more than anyone."

"You keep telling yourself that, honey." Lou winked. "Whether you admit it or not, we both know who pulls your heartstrings."

"Sam's right about you working overtime as Cupid. Enough about your alter ego. Do you mind if I put the word out about needing help?"

"Hmm." Lou pinched her chin between her thumb and index finger. "Maybe you won't need to." She nodded toward the bedside table. "Be a dear, press the Perkins' number, and hand me my phone."

Jenny complied.

Lou raised her phone to her ear. "The call's going to voicemail. Hello, dear friends, it's Lou. Give me a jingle after you listen to this message. I want to talk to you about Jacko." She set the phone on the chair.

"Who's Jacko?"

"The Perkins' grandson, Jacob."

"Interesting nickname."

Jenny spun around as Andy swung the door open and pushed a wheel-chair into the room. "Time for my favorite patient's afternoon therapy."

"I suspect that's the line you use with all your patients." Lou eyed Jenny. "I'll text you as soon as I hear from the Perkins. When you talk to them, ask how Jacob's nickname came about."

"Talk to them about what?"

"The solution to your manpower problem." Lou leaned forward. "About my new Grandmother status, I'll text all my friends after Andy brings me back from the torture chamber." She waved over her shoulder as Andy pushed her wheelchair into the hall.

Two hours after Jenny left the hospital, she read Lou's text. "Jacko's meeting you at the coffee shop in twenty minutes for an interview. Keep an open mind about him. Beyond the surface, he's a good kid."

Who was this guy? Five minutes after she settled at the counter, a tall, lanky young man with his hair pulled into a ponytail walked in. "I'm Jacob. Most folks call me Jacko." He extended his tattoo-covered right arm. "Thanks for agreeing to interview me, ma'am."

Jenny gripped his hand and stared at the double barbed-wire tat encir-cling his neck. Her eyes shifted to the gold cross earring dangling from his left ear, then to his pierced eyebrow and nose ring. What was Lou thinking? She released his hand. "You're...um—"

"Not what you expected?"

No kidding. Jenny cleared her throat. "Did you bring a resume?"

He pulled a sheet of paper from his jeans pocket and handed it over. "As you can see, I worked three different jobs as a short-order cook in Atlanta. Hamburgers, eggs, fries—stuff like that."

She noted the end date of the last job. "Looks like you haven't worked in more than two years."

He sat on the stool beside her. "Because I've been in prison, ma'am."

Lou sent her a criminal? "For what?"

"I was a dumb kid who got in good with a guy who drove an expensive car and made tons of money selling drugs. I figured why sweat over a hot stove for little pay when a few drug deals would make me big bucks. Which it did. Until I got caught and spent every dime on a lawyer who didn't do squat to keep me out of jail. Oh, you don't need to worry about me being a druggie. I never touched the stuff. Anyway, after I was released, I moved back in with my grandparents. Now I'm ready to set my life straight."

Jenny propped her elbows on the table, rested her chin on laced fingers, and eyed Jacko. Another damaged soul needing a break. "Lou seems to trust you."

"I'm a fast learner, and I promise to work hard."

No doubt he'd work for minimum wage. "Are you willing to show up at four every morning?"

"Yes, ma'am."

Why not give him a chance. "In that case, welcome to the team."

His face lit with a grin. "Thank you, ma'am."

"You can call me Jenny. One more thing. How'd you end up with the name Jacko?"

"The whole town knows about that story. When I was sixteen, me and some of my buddies blew up a bunch of Halloween jack-o'-lanterns. That caper landed me in a heap of trouble." He held up both hands and splayed his fingers tattooed with the word faith on one hand and logic on the other. "Good news is I didn't lose any body parts."

"That is good news." Jenny slid off her stool. "Because you'll need all ten fingers to learn what I'm about to teach you." She led him to the kitchen for his first lesson in baking cinnamon buns.

Chapter 46

A week after the coffee-shop hours and menu expanded, Sam added a noon lunch break to his morning routine. Seeing Jenny twice in one day and noticing how frequently she glanced in his direction kept his emotions in turmoil. Especially after she had refused his dinner invitation for the third time. He bit into his sandwich.

Jenny approached. "What do you think of the Reuben?"

Did she really care what he thought? Sam swallowed. "Best I've ever tasted."

"Thanks to Jacko."

"Giving him a chance to turn his life around proves you have a heart."

"Why wouldn't I?" Jenny's eyes narrowed. "He's a decent guy who deserves a fair shot."

Sam smirked. "Unlike a realtor with a clean record?"

George set his glass on the counter. "What's with you two, squabbling instead of kissing and making up?"

"Give it a break, George." Sam pushed his glass toward Jenny. "All I'm saying is she cares."

Jenny stared at him. "Are you looking for a refill or absolution?"

"A little of both."

She grabbed a pitcher and refilled his sweet tea. "Have you talked to Lou today?"

"Grandpa visited her this morning. Says she's chomping at the bit to return to work." Sam squeezed lemon into his tea. "With the extra hours and workload, she'll need you to stick around for a while."

Jenny set the pitcher on the counter. "What makes you think I'm planning to leave any time soon?"

"Given your inclination to job hop, I'm guessing it's a distinct possibility."

"In case you're wondering, every move I've made advanced my career and added to my portfolio."

George cleared his throat. "Sorry to butt into your little tiff again, but I'm thinking you two had best steer clear of that subject."

"You're a smart man, George." Jenny refilled his lemonade. "Sam would do well to heed your advice."

Sam pointed his sandwich at George. "To show my appreciation for your words of questionable wisdom, lunch is on me."

"Well now." George smacked his hand on the counter. "Since Sam's paying, bring me a big slab of apple pie and make it à la mode."

"While you're at it, Chef Jenny." Sam squared his shoulders. "Bring me a slice without ice cream and make it to go."

She placed her hands on her hips. "What's wrong, Sam? Did you botch a big real estate deal?"

He glared at her. "I don't botch deals."

Madge wandered over and stood beside George. "What has Sam and Jenny all hot and bothered?"

"Lover's quarrel."

"We're not lovers...ugh." Jenny scowled.

Madge touched George's shoulder. "You're right, and it's a doozy."

"Know what?" Sam pulled his wallet from his back pocket, removed three tens, and slapped them on the counter. "Forget the pie and keep the change. You'll need it when you hightail it out of town again."

Sam slid off his stool, stalked out, and headed straight toward his office. When he arrived, he sent the front door banging against the wall beside the window.

Mary looked up. "Uh-oh. Did you and Jenny have a lover's spat?"

"What's with you people?"

"Oh dear, it must've been a humdinger."

Sam clenched his jaw, dashed to his office, and slammed the door shut. He dropped onto a leather easy chair and stared at the sunrise painting. New beginnings. What a joke.

His grandpa walked in and sat beside Sam. "Either your door slam shook the building, or an earthquake tipped the Richter scale."

"I've had enough. Seeing her every day. Pretending she's nothing more than a friend while George and every other busybody consider us a couple."

"Folks don't let go of notions easily."

"It's time to set everyone straight." Sam bolted to his feet and turned Jenny's photo facedown on his desk.

"You need to give her a little more time."

"I've given her all I have to give." He rounded the desk and dropped onto his chair. "If she ever decides to yank our so-called relationship out of the ditch, she'll have to make the first move. Until that happens, I'm staying out of her way."

"Can't say I blame you, although I suspect you still believe Jenny is worth your effort. So, take my advice, and don't let your ego rule your emotions."

"This isn't about my pride."

"Uh-huh." His grandpa pushed up and strode out.

Sam plucked Jenny's photo off the desk. Everything about her touched his soul. Yet nothing he had tried seemed to penetrate the wall she had built around her heart. Instead of giving up, maybe he needed a new tactic. Something to appeal to a different set of emotions.

"This is for you, Jenny." He placed her photo in the bottom drawer, logged onto social media, and searched for the nurse Sandra wanted him to meet. He found her Facebook page. At least his sister was right about her looks. Maybe a beautiful redhead was his ticket to Jenny's heart. His finger hovered over his keyboard. What if his plan backfired and destroyed their friendship? He snuffed the spark of doubt niggling his brain, clicked his mouse, and sent a friend request.

An hour later Sam's office phone rang. He answered. "What is it, Mary?"

"A woman named Lisa is on the line, she wants to talk to you. Says she's Sandra's friend."

A twinge of guilt pricked Sam's conscience. Maybe he should forget his plan and decline her call. His eyes drifted to the bottom drawer. Desperate times called for desperate measures. "Send her call through."

"Yes, I'm clued in." Did everyone in town know about Sam's date with the redhead? Jenny rolled her eyes and wandered away from yet another customer who wanted to make sure she'd heard the news. She glanced at the vacant stool at the end of the counter—third day in a row Sam hadn't shown up. Didn't he have the decency to face her and admit he had moved on? Except why should he? After all, she'd made it clear where he stood with her.

Following three more hours of telling customers she knew about the redhead, Jenny locked the front door and retreated to the kitchen where Jacko was busy scrubbing the stainless-steel worktable. "Have I told you what a great job you're doing?"

He swiped the back of his hand across his sweaty brow. "One thing I learned about prisoners. They either carry a big chip on their shoulders or learn from their mistakes and turn their lives around. You trusting me with this job made the second choice easier. Which is why I ditched the earring and the nose and eyebrow rings without you asking."

Jenny's admiration for her tattooed chef had escalated with each passing day. "You're an amazing young man and an inspiration."

"One day I'll find a way to help other ex-cons deal with their bad decisions. Everyone needs to know their pasts don't have to define the rest of their lives."

At least he'd found the courage to overcome his bad decisions, which seemed to pale in comparison to hers. "I have something for you, Jacko." She removed cash from her apron pocket and placed it in his hand.

He stared at the gift. "It's not right to take the money you earned."

"Without you working your tail off back here, there wouldn't be any tips." She folded his fingers over the bills. "Starting tomorrow, I'll handle kitchen duty for a couple hours while you wait tables and earn your own tips."

"You know some folks don't like a guy who looks like me."

"Nonsense. Your smile and positive attitude will win them over." She hung her apron on a hook beside her chef coat. "You've done enough work for today, so scoot on out of here and I'll lock up."

"Thank you, Miss Jenny."

She returned to the dining area and envisioned the space repurposed as a café. Fresh paint. Updated tables and chairs. Jenny sauntered to the window and wiped a smudge off the glass. Maybe an outdoor seating area under a canopy. What was she thinking—this was Lou's place not hers. She dismissed the pipe dream. Besides, she'd already told Sam she planned to move on as soon as Lou no longer needed her. Now she needed to make him understand that she was pleased he'd begun dating the redhead.

Jenny returned to the kitchen, locked the back door, and climbed onto her bike. During the short ride to his office, she waffled between facing him today or riding on by. Would Sam believe her or see through the lie? When Gibson Real Estate came into view, the overwhelming desire to see him won out. She parked her bike on the sidewalk fronting the office. With her hand on the door handle, she glanced across the street at the autumn leaves fluttering in the cool breeze. Memories of dancing with Sam, their bodies close, flooded her mind. She squeezed her eyes shut until the image vanished then she walked inside.

Mary looked up. "Hey, girl, I hear Lou's eager to return to work next week. She is one amazing woman. If you're looking for Sam, he's taking a few days off to visit his parents over on Lake Oconee. Their gorgeous home is a perfect getaway resort." Mary's brows knitted. "I'm surprised he didn't tell you."

Like he hadn't told her about the redhead. "I've been busy, with Lou gone and all. It's good that Sam's taking some time off."

The office phone rang, commanding Mary's attention and giving Jenny the excuse to leave. She climbed onto her bike and rode through the park. Had Sam gone to his parents alone or with the redhead? Surprised by the pang of jealousy sending shockwaves through her limbs, she continued to ride through the streets until a semblance of reason returned and eased her damaged ego.

Chapter 47

Jenny climbed onto a stepladder, reached overhead, and hooked the end of a rainbow streamer to a ceiling tile. She tossed the roll to Jacko who completed the crisscrossed array of streamers decorating the coffee shop. When she climbed down, her focus shifted to Sam, standing on the sidewalk under the glow of the streetlight, helping George hang a *Welcome Back, Lou* sign across the front window. The prospect of facing him for the first time since he'd returned from his parents' home churned her stomach. How should she act? Should she mention the redhead? Did it even matter?

Madge set a platter of fresh-from-the-oven buns on the counter, sending cinnamon and vanilla aromas wafting across the space. "That makes four dozen. Do you think we'll have enough before we serve lunch?"

Jenny nodded. "Plenty, considering we're opening an hour later than normal this morning."

Madge arranged a stack of paper plates beside a tower of disposable coffee cups. "Free sweets and coffee to celebrate Lou's return is likely to draw a big crowd."

Footsteps striking the tile floor followed a sudden draft. George closed the distance from the door to the counter ahead of Sam and slid onto his favorite stool. "Mind if I sample the goods before the crowds arrive?"

Madge poured him a cup of coffee and plated a roll. "Reward for helping hang that sign. How about you, Sam? Do you also want to taste test?"

"No thanks." He settled on his stool. "But I'll take a cup of coffee."

George emptied a packet of sugar into his cup and pointed his spoon at Sam. "Where've you been for the past few weeks?"

"Busy working and taking time off." Sam caught Jenny's eye. "Looks like life's been treating you well."

She shrugged. "Like you, I've kept plenty busy."

His eyes remained trained on her while he cradled his coffee cup in both hands. "Lou's grateful for all you've done to keep the place going."

Was Sam also grateful or had he regretted asking her to return? "It's the least I could do." She turned her attention to Jacko backing in from the kitchen.

The young man pivoted and set a decorated sheet cake, scribed with *We Love You, Lou*, on the counter. "One red velvet masterpiece to welcome the boss home."

George pointed his cup toward Jacko. "Who made all those pretty little flowers fancying up that cake?"

"I did." He pushed up his sleeves to his elbows, revealing his inked forearms. "With the cake-decorating kit Miss Jenny bought."

"No kidding? Who'd have guessed a guy who could deal with all the pain those tattoos represent had an artistic flair?"

Sam grinned. "Sounds like you're speaking from experience."

"Vietnam War tattoo." George tapped his left bicep. "After all these years, it doesn't look quite the same as it did back in the day."

Another cool draft sent Jenny to the front door to greet the first of a steady stream of new arrivals. Despite keeping her back aimed toward the counter as she welcomed each guest, she couldn't resist glancing in Sam's direction. Each time she eyed his profile, her breath hitched. In the past, her glances frequently caught his eye. Now he barely seemed to notice her.

"We hear our grandson has taken a liking to baking."

Jenny turned and faced Mrs. Perkins. "Wait 'til you see the work of art he created. It's almost a shame to cut it." Movement outside drew Jenny's attention.

George's shrill two-fingered whistle quieted the crowd.

Paul parked his wife's sports car in front of the coffee shop, dashed to open the passenger door, and held out his arm. Lou, looking elegant in a colorful tunic over black slacks, stepped onto the curb. A broad-brimmed red hat sat atop her shoulder-length hair. Applause and cheers erupted as Paul escorted her inside.

Jenny moved behind the counter and stole another glance at Sam. He motioned her over. Her heartbeat accelerated as she approached. "Doesn't she look fabulous?"

"Lou's a survivor." He leaned forward. "She's also a woman in her seventies recovering from a stroke. Don't let her take on too much too fast."

"I'll do my best." She paused. "Now that she's returning, are you planning to add visits back into your daily routine?"

"I've missed tapping into Lou's intel."

Jenny avoided eye contact. "Is that a yes?"

He pushed his empty coffee cup toward her. "Have you missed me?"

Jenny refilled his cup, determined not to open that door again. "Every customer is important."

George tapped the counter in front of Sam. "Some folks are more important to her than others, if you get my drift."

Jenny set the coffeepot on the warmer. "Know what, George? You're the only person who makes that big a difference around here. In fact, the day you stop showing up, the whole place is likely to go under."

Sam guffawed. "Guess you're right, George. Some customers are way more valuable than others."

"Don't let her kid you, Sam."

"She's made her sentiments perfectly clear." Sam slid off his stool and joined the crowd surrounding Lou.

George shook his head. "I don't understand today's young couples. In the good old days, when a guy met a gal he fancied, he courted her and worked to convince her parents he was a good catch. When the time came, he popped the question."

"How many times do I have to tell you that Sam and I aren't courting?"

"I'm starting to get the picture."

"It took you long enough." Jenny's eyes followed Sam as he embraced Lou and walked out of the coffee shop.

"How about seconds?" George slid his empty plate to her. "Despite Sam's new lady friend, you can count on Lou making it her mission to get you two back together."

And there it was, the truth about Sam and the redhead. "Some missions are impossible." Jenny plated another cinnamon bun.

"Not according to *Mission Impossible*. My second favorite TV show back in the sixties." George dug his fork into the bun. "*Twilight Zone* topped the list."

Mission impossible in the twilight zone. Jenny rolled her eyes. An appropriate description for whatever was going on between her and Sam.

Chapter 48

Jenny zipped her leather jacket, climbed onto her bike, and headed to town fifteen minutes earlier than normal. The moment she pedaled to the back door, the light shining through the rear window and the classical music playing in the kitchen made it clear Lou had already arrived. Inside, she found her boss breaking eggs into a large bowl. "You didn't have to come in this early."

"There's no need to fret about me overdoing, honey. If I end up a wee bit tired, I promise to take a break. After all, I want to stay healthy so I can spend years spoiling my grandbaby."

"Another reason to let your staff shoulder most of the work." Jenny hung her jacket and purse on a hook and donned her chef coat.

"Speaking of staff, yesterday during my welcome-back party, I heard lots of good comments about Jacko."

"He's an amazing young man."

Lou added flour and sugar to her bowl. "He's also living proof that people can prosper after making bad decisions."

"Some people," Jenny mumbled while removing a set of quiche pans from the cabinet.

"Sorry, honey, the music drowned you out. What'd you say?"

Grateful Lou hadn't heard, Jenny set the pans on the worktable. "No matter how hard I tried, my coffee never measured up to yours."

"I spent years perfecting my technique. You couldn't be expected to master it in a few weeks." Lou stirred oil and vanilla into her bowl. "According to George, until yesterday Sam hadn't shown up for a couple of weeks."

Jenny peered at Lou, surprised she had abandoned her no-chatter routine. Had she heard about Sam and the redhead, or was she fishing? "You know how busy Sam gets with work. Plus, he took some time off to visit his parents. With you back behind the counter, I suspect he'll return to his regular morning routine."

"I might call on you to help me take care of customers for a couple of days."

"Anything you need."

The back door swung open, emitting a blast of cool air. Jacko darted in wearing the chef coat Jenny had purchased for him. "Glad to see you back, Ms. Lou. Miss Jenny's been teaching me a lot about cooking and taking care of customers."

"You're making quite an impression, young man."

Jacko's shoulders squared. "I had to go through some tough times before landing in a good place."

"At some point, we all do." Lou whisked her ingredients. "I've learned that the valleys we struggle through enable us to reach the peaks God has in store for us."

Listening to Lou and Jacko's chatter sparked a flicker of hope in Jenny's soul. If Lou could recover from a stroke and Jacko could thrive after a prison term, maybe one day she could find the courage to move beyond her past and find peace.

When Madge arrived, the chatter continued until Lou unlocked the front door. By the time dawn lit the morning sky, George had taken up residence on his stool, and Matt had set his police cap on the counter. Jenny divided her time between helping Madge wait tables and finalizing lunch offerings.

The moment Sam showed up, conflicting emotions sent her scrambling to the kitchen to hide out, until Lou wandered in and hung her apron on the hook. "It's time for you to take over counter duty, honey." She faced Jenny and winked. "I'm pacing myself until my energy is back one hundred percent. Besides, you have work to do out there."

Jenny knew Lou well enough to recognize an ulterior motive lurked under the surface. "Promise you'll go home early and rest?"

"After I spend a few minutes with my pal, Jacko, I'll call it a day. Now scoot before someone needs a coffee refill."

"I'm on it." When Jenny walked into the dining area, one glance told her everything she needed to know about Lou's intention. A pretty woman with long red hair cascading down her back, sat catercorner to Sam, chatting with George. Curiosity curtailed the wave of jealousy washing over her as she moved to the end of the counter. "How about introducing me to your friend, George?"

Before he could respond, the woman extended her hand. "I'm Lisa, and you must be Jenny."

She stared at the woman whose blue eyes matched her hospital scrubs. "Welcome to Lou's Coffee Shop." She accepted her hand and held it with an iron grip.

"Thanks." Lisa maneuvered her hand away from Jenny's and wiggled her fingers. "I've planned to come in ever since Sam's sister claimed this is *the* place to hang out and meet new friends."

"I assume you work in the ER with Dr. Sandra?"

Lisa nodded. "I was on duty the morning the EMTs brought Lou in. We're all thrilled at the progress she's made." Lisa placed her hand on Sam's arm. "Thanks in part to this amazing guy, she'll regain her full strength in no time."

Could she have been any more obvious?

"A lot of people are responsible for Lou's recovery." Sam kept his eyes focused on Jenny while moving his arm away from Lisa's hand. "Including Jenny coming back to keep the coffee shop up and running."

"Don't be modest, Sam." Jenny forced a wide smile. "After all, you're responsible for bringing me back to Madison." She shifted her gaze to Lisa. "Can I bring you a slice of mouthwatering quiche or maybe some coffee cake?"

"No thanks. I stopped by on my way to the hospital to thank Sam for a lovely dinner last night. As a bonus, I'm also meeting Lou's number-one helper." Lisa broke eye contact with Jenny and patted George's hand. "And this fascinating gentleman." She slid off her stool and touched Sam's arm again. "I'll see you later."

Jenny's eyes remained glued on Lisa as the woman sashayed out the door. "My, goodness, that nurse missed her calling. She should have been a surgeon since she's so adept at operating."

Sam burst out laughing.

George meowed.

Jenny flipped her hair and moved to the other end of the counter to chat with an arriving customer.

The unrelenting fingers of regret clamped Sam's chest and shoulder muscles. What made him think jealousy would send Jenny running into his arms? Especially after Lisa showed up following three casual dinners to make *her* intentions clear.

"Nurse Lisa's a real looker." George clutched his coffee cup. "But, if you ask me, she can't hold a cake full of candles to Miss Jenny."

"Don't give me a hard time, George."

"All I'm saying is you shouldn't settle for second best." George leaned forward and motioned to Jenny. "I'm ready for a refill."

She grabbed a coffeepot and moseyed over. "Is Lou's coffee as good as you remembered?"

"Every bit."

"How about you, Sam?" Jenny finished filling George's mug. "Has your cup also run dry?"

"In the event you're wondering, I never asked Lisa to show up."

"Well now." She looked him square in the eyes. "It seems the most eligible bachelor in Madison has attracted a gorgeous woman who has sunk her hooks into him."

George chuckled. "You nailed it, Jenny."

"Stay out of this, George," Sam and Jenny said in unison.

George held up his hands. "You two aren't fooling anyone."

Sam reached across the counter and gripped Jenny's arm. "We need to talk. Privately. Meet me out back in five minutes."

She pulled her arm away. "I'm working."

"The coffee shop can spare you for a couple of minutes." He paid his bill, walked out, and made his way around the corner to the coffee shop's back door. How should he act if she bothered to show up? He paced. Angry? Hurt? Sam paused and glanced at his watch. Five minutes had come and gone. He resumed pacing. What should he say about the nurse? Six minutes. Should he give up and walk away? Eight minutes.

The back door swung open. "You're gonna wear a path in the pavement." Jenny stepped off the stoop.

Sam's pulse accelerated as she moved close. "Lisa's a friend, nothing more."

"You don't owe me an explanation." She paused. "It's time we both face reality."

"What reality are you talking about, Jenny? The fact that we love each other? Or that we're playing some ridiculous cat-and-mouse game?"

She broke eye contact. "We both know it's only a matter of time before I leave Madison again."

"I don't understand why."

Jenny stooped and plucked a twig off the pavement. "The reason's not important."

Riddled with frustration, Sam gripped her shoulders. "What do you want me to do, Jenny?"

"Please, Sam, forget about me." Her eyes pleaded. "For my sake as well as yours."

Fear of losing her forever cut deep and overpowered his desire to gather her in his arms. Yet as long as a glimmer of hope remained, he refused to give up. He released her shoulders and touched her cheek.

Her jaw tightened.

Sam swallowed his pride, then turned and walked away.

His touch tugged on Jenny's heart. She opened her mouth to call out and beg him to come back. The words failed to form. Her eyes followed him until he disappeared around the corner. She stood frozen. Had his silence meant he'd finally given up?

Jenny folded her arms and massaged her biceps to ward off a sudden chill. Now what? Her gaze drifted to the kitchen door. She couldn't return to the coffee shop counter and face probing questions from George and Madge. With a heavy sigh, she entered the kitchen and found Jacko spooning coleslaw beside a Reuben.

Madge lifted the plate off the counter while eyeing Jenny. "Is everything okay?"

"Fine and dandy, like wine and candy." Where had that come from? "Know what, Jacko?" Jenny removed her apron and slipped into her chef coat. "You deserve a break from kitchen duty. I'll take over 'til closing."

"You sure?"

"Positive. Now get out there and earn yourself some good tips."

"Yes, ma'am. I mean, Miss Jenny." He followed Madge out of the kitchen.

Jenny gripped the counter to steady her trembling hands. Somehow, she had to come to grips with reality. Her quest to drive away the only man she'd ever loved had finally paid off.

Chapter 49

A week after Jenny's confrontation with Sam, his haunting words and the anguish of him walking away had evolved to a sense of relief. Lou had returned to the coffee shop full time, and most days Sam only showed up for breakfast. All seemed normal as Jenny hummed along to the upbeat classical song playing in the background.

Jacko pointed his spoon at Jenny. "You're in a good mood."

Madge grinned. "I'm guessing she and Sam are two black-eyed peas in a pod again."

Jenny rolled her eyes and slid a third quiche into the oven. "I'm amazed at your stamina, Lou. You're like your old self, even better."

"Honey, a little ole stroke can't keep this tough southern lady down for long."

"That's the truth." Madge slung a towel over her shoulder. "Like George says, we mature ladies have a certain savior-faire."

Lou set a mixing bowl in the sink. "I'm surprised he knows what that means."

Madge giggled. "I think he read it in an ad."

"George is a cool guy." Jacko wiped his hands with a paper towel.

"Not to mention a permanent fixture around here." Lou removed a pan of cinnamon buns from the oven.

Jenny marveled at Lou's shift from her no-conversation policy during her morning routine to her new daily jovial chatter. Funny how a brush with death could change one's perspective.

A ring rose above the chatter.

Madge pointed to Jenny's purse hanging on a hook. "Sounds like your phone."

Jenny's heart pounded at the memory of another pre-dawn call. She pulled her phone out and stared at the screen. Jill. "I have to take this." The cool pre-dawn air sent a chill racing through her as she stepped out back and answered. "What's wrong?"

"She's gone, Jenny. Our mother's dead. The EMTs found her. Seems she had enough self-control to call 911 before her heart had all the abuse it could take."

Stunned, Jenny dropped onto the stoop and stared at the star-studded sky. "We need to make arrangements."

"You mean you need to make arrangements."

"No way I'm letting you bug out on me this time. Besides, if she bothered to leave a will, you're most likely named as the executor."

A heavy sigh resounded through the phone. "I suppose it's not fair to saddle you with this burden. I'll schedule a flight for tomorrow. Will you reserve a hotel room?"

Jenny struggled to remember the available credit on her one and only charge card. If she had to, she'd dip into her savings. Again. "I'll take care of it."

"Good. I'll text you my arrival information along with a list of things to do." Jill paused. "Somehow, we'll muddle through this and put our past behind us once and for all."

"Thanks, Jill. I couldn't manage without you." Jenny returned to the kitchen.

"Bad news?"

"My mother died."

"Oh, honey." Lou wrapped her arms around Jenny. "I'm so sorry."

"I'll need a couple of days to take care of everything."

Lou stepped back. "You take all the time you need. Madge, Jacko, and I will cover for you if you need to leave now."

"It's best to keep working." Jenny dropped her phone in her purse. "When the coffee shop opens, don't mention it to anyone. I don't want to deal with a bunch of questions."

Lou nodded. "Understood."

For the remainder of the morning, Jenny's emotions volleyed between relief and guilt for not shedding a single tear. Memories of her childhood haunted her while she struggled to focus on customers. By the time the coffee shop closed, her head pounded with pain. She returned to her apartment and downed three aspirin. After reserving a hotel room, she opened her closet and stared at her limited wardrobe. What should she wear to a funeral for a woman who spent her life making her daughters miserable? She chose the only outfit that made sense.

Her phone pinged a text from Sam. "I'm sorry to hear about your mother. Call if you need me."

At least they were still friends. She texted back. "Thank you, Sam. I'm fine." She yearned for him to hold her and shield her from the pain. If only she hadn't gone to that liquor store all those years ago. Jenny forced the memory back into its hiding place and finished packing.

Following a night interrupted by nightmares, and a long drive to the Atlanta airport, Jenny dashed from the parking deck to the terminal. She hadn't seen her sister since she'd fled San Diego to take a chef job in San Francisco years earlier. Other than the call about their father, she could count on one hand the number of times they'd spoken. How should she greet the woman who was more a stranger than a sibling?

Sweat popped out on Jenny's upper lip when Jill emerged from the escalator. She waved her over. "You haven't changed much since I last saw you."

"A few pounds heavier, thanks to delivering two eight-pound babies in two years. You're a little thinner than I remembered, but you're still the pretty sister."

They headed to baggage claim.

"Have you been to their house?"

"Not since our dear old dad died."

"I have to admit that the idea of stepping one foot in that place makes my skin crawl."

"Lucky for us the wicked witch won't be around to order us to our room or threaten us with annihilation." Jenny eyed dozens of bags crowding onto the carousel. "It wouldn't surprise me if our mother left us a nasty note accusing us of driving her to drink and ruining her life."

"If we find one, we'll light it on fire and watch it turn to ashes." Jill pulled a suitcase off the carousel and released the handle. "Speaking of ashes, are you okay with having her body cremated?"

"It doesn't matter to me one way or the other."

"Good. We have one decision settled."

Except for comments about the weather and crazy drivers, the sisters remained silent during their drive to Norcross. When Jenny turned onto their parents' driveway, Jill gasped. "I can't imagine anyone wanting to buy this eyesore. Their neighbors left a key under the doormat. At least Dorothy had enough sense to give them access."

"You still refer to her by her name?"

Jill reached for the door handle. "She doesn't deserve to be called Mother."

Jenny popped her trunk and removed a package of trash bags before she and Jill made their way up the mold-stained walkway. She unlocked the front door. Inside, mounds of dust covered every surface and hung heavy in the air. Empty liquor bottles littered the living-room floor. The stench of alcohol and years of neglect accosted them.

Jenny covered her nose and mouth with her hand. "It's worse than the last time I was here."

Jill opened the front windows, letting in a wisp of fresh air. "How could she live like this?"

"She didn't live. She existed."

"If I'd had any inkling she'd left the place in this shape, I wouldn't have arranged for a real estate agent to show up tomorrow afternoon."

Jenny's jaw dropped. "Are you kidding me?"

"My return flight is in five days. I don't have time to dillydally."

"In that case we'd best start cracking." Jenny pushed her sleeves up to her elbows.

"Our first task is to find a will."

"Unless you want to spend all five days in this madhouse, I suggest we multi-task and search while we clean."

"You're right."

Jenny dove into the demanding tasks of bagging trash, vacuuming, and scrubbing away years of dirt while keeping her eyes peeled for anything resembling a last will and testament. When she walked into the kitchen, she squeezed her eyes shut at the painful memory exploding in her head. A loud crash jolting an eight-year-old from sleep. Clinging to her twelve-year-old sister's arm as they crept down the hall to the kitchen. Cabinet doors flung open. Broken glass littering the floor. Their mother standing beside the kitchen sink barefoot, accusing their father of pouring her booze down the drain. Hurling an empty bottle at him, missing his head by inches. The scream when the woman who called herself their mother stepped on a piece of broken glass. The crunch under their father's slipper-clad feet as he rushed to lift her into his arms. The trail of blood from the kitchen to their bedroom.

A hand touching her arm startled Jenny. She opened her eyes.

"You're remembering that night, aren't you?"

"Yeah."

"Tell you what, we've been working like crazy women for hours without a bite to eat." Jill batted a fly away from her face. "How about we take a break and order a pizza."

"Great idea."

After placing the order, Jenny settled on the living room couch and propped her feet on the coffee table. "A lot of painful memories live in this room."

"Not all bad." Jill sat beside her. "Do you remember Miss Edna?"

"Who?"

"The lady who took care of us."

Jenny's brows arched. "We had a nanny?"

Jill nodded. "She took care of me when Dorothy went away, before you were born and both of us after."

"Away where?"

"All I know is one day a sweet, white-haired lady showed up and Dorothy didn't. Miss Edna called us her precious babies. She played with us, read us stories, and baked cookies. I called her our fairy godmother."

Jenny picked at a loose thread on the worn upholstery. "She rescued us from the wicked witch of the south."

"I remember Miss Edna coming back when Dorothy left a second time. Probably rehab." Jill paused. "When she returned, she stayed away from booze for a while."

"How long did she stay sober?"

"Best I can remember, a couple of months." Jill stared straight ahead. "Until one morning during a nasty storm, she ordered me to take you to our room and lock the door to keep you safe. In my mind the thunder came from monsters stomping in our yard, waiting to break in and snatch us away. That day she plummeted from sobriety and left me, a five-year-old, to take care of my baby sister. Funny how those are the only memories from my pre-school days that stuck."

"Too bad Miss Edna didn't replace our mother permanently."

A fly landed on the coffee table.

"Stay perfectly still." Jill moved in slow motion, gripped a magazine, and slammed it on the unsuspecting fly.

"Good shot, sis."

"I'm not sharing one smidgen of pizza with an uninvited visitor."

"Perfect timing." Jenny popped up at the ring of the doorbell.

"Do you need some cash?"

"No thanks." Jenny pulled bills from her pocket. "My treat."

After devouring the pizza, Jenny clutched a handful of garbage bags and led the way down the hall to their parents' closed bedroom door. She gripped the doorknob. "Be prepared for a shock."

"At this point, nothing would surprise me."

"I'm not talking about the mess." She opened the door and pointed to the dresser. "Over there."

Jill covered her mouth and nose with her hand and gawked at the array of framed photographs.

"A shrine to the woman who existed in our father's mind."

"He abused her."

Jenny raised her brows. "How did you know?"

"I paid attention." Jill lowered her hand and turned away from the dresser. "I can't imagine anyone sleeping in here with this terrible odor."

"A sober person couldn't." Jenny caught sight of two legal-size envelopes taped to the headboard. She grabbed the first envelope and ripped it open. "It's a hand-written will, dated two weeks ago."

"Dorothy must have known she was knocking on death's door." Jill reached for the second envelope. "She left this for you."

Jenny's hand trembled as she stared at her name and the word private scrawled across the front. She folded the envelope and stuffed it in her pocket.

"Aren't you curious enough to open it?"

"No." Jenny scooped a pile of clothes off the floor, held her breath to avoid the stench, and stuffed them into a garbage bag. No way she'd open that envelope and succumb to a non-verbal tongue-lashing from the woman who even in death continued to haunt her.

Chapter 50

Sam gripped his mug and breathed in the rich scent of Lou's signature coffee while eyeing her across the counter. "I don't understand why Jenny hasn't reached out to us."

"I remember way back when my mom passed. Taking care of all the details sapped my energy. Besides, Jenny and her sister need time alone to mourn their mother's passing."

"You do know she considers you more of a mom than her own mother."

"Doesn't matter, she still has to grieve."

Sam took a sip of coffee. "I found details about the funeral on the internet. It's tomorrow. We should send flowers and show up."

"I'm not sure she wants us there. Besides, she'll need our support more after she returns."

"*If* she bothers to come back." Sam broke eye contact and stared at the dark liquid in his mug. "Do you remember what happened after Jenny's father died?"

"Yeah," George piped in. "She left town for a better job."

Lou removed her reading glasses and pinched the bridge of her nose. "That's what she claimed."

Sam looked up and caught Lou's eye. "That makes two of us who doubted her story."

"Hey, you two naysayers." George set his mug on the counter. "Jenny came back."

"Now that Lou's fully recovered, she's likely to take off again."

George knuckled Sam's arm. "Unless you plan on marrying one of our local gals, you'd best give Jenny a doggone good reason to stay put."

"Well, shut my mouth." Sam snapped his fingers. "Why didn't I think of that?" His tone screamed of sarcasm.

George's gaze shifted from Sam to Lou. "Sounds like the town's number-one bachelor might need more help in the romance department."

Sam scoffed. "One thing I don't need is *two* senior citizens playing cupid."

"Know what, George?" Lou refilled his coffee. "I think our boy knows what he's doing."

"Thanks for the vote of confidence, Lou." After swallowing his last drop of coffee, Sam removed cash from his wallet and slapped it on the counter. "I'll see you two tomorrow."

"You're not coming back for lunch?"

"Why would he?" George snickered. "Jenny's not here."

Sam ignored the comment and walked out to the crisp autumn air. Mountains of doubt weighed him down as he meandered toward his office. Despite Jenny's refusal to notify him or anyone else about the funeral, wouldn't attending show he still cared? He stepped up his pace, crossed the street, and entered Gibson Realty's reception area.

"Good morning, Sam." Mary's cheery tone failed to lighten his mood.

"Uh-huh."

"Oh dear, you're missing Jenny—"

"You're not my shrink, so lay off."

Mary clucked her tongue. "My, my, he doth protest a bit too much."

"Sorry, Mary." He released a heavy sigh. "I have a lot on my mind."

"I understand."

Sam walked into his office, dropped onto his executive chair, and gazed at Jenny's photo. Should he send flowers, show up at the funeral, or do nothing? He swiveled toward the sunrise painting. Only one decision made sense. He removed his phone from his belt and pressed a number.

Jenny propped her hands on her hips and glared at Jill's not-so-subtle headshake. "What's your problem?"

"Is that what you brought to wear to the funeral?"

"What's wrong with it?"

"A sexy red dress?"

Jenny lowered her hands. "It beats the heck out of the somber outfit you're wearing."

"I suppose black is a bit much." Jill removed a hot pink skirt and jacket from the closet and held it up in front of the mirror. "Is this better?"

"Much. Except we'll clash."

"At least we'll give guests something to talk about. If anyone bothers to show up."

Twenty minutes later they entered the funeral home and followed music to a small chapel. Jenny stopped beside the open doors and stared at the guest book displayed on a stand. She counted three names—their mother's next-door neighbors and Kelley. "Her passing hasn't exactly drawn a crowd."

"At least we're here."

After signing the guest book, they entered the chapel, walked to the front, and slid into the pew beside Kelley. Jenny touched her friend's arm. "Thank you for coming."

"I'm here for you and your sister." Kelley peered around Jenny. "Fancy outfits. Looks like you two are celebrating."

Jill smoothed her skirt. "In a way we are."

Jenny's focus shifted from a colorful floral arrangement in front of a podium to the funeral director entering from a side door. A man wearing a three-piece navy suit accompanied him.

The funeral director approached their pew. "Ladies, meet my pastor."

The silver-haired gentleman leaned down and extended his hand to Jill then to Jenny. "I'm sorry for your loss."

"We appreciate you presiding over a funeral for a woman you've never met."

"Your mother is a child of God who deserves kind words spoken about her."

Jenny stifled a snicker. He had obviously never met Dorothy Collins. "Seems not more than a handful of guests will hear your comments."

"Funerals are as much for the family as the departed."

"That's me and Jill, so we might as well begin."

The pastor straightened and nodded toward the back. "After the new arrivals are seated."

Who else would bother to show up? Jenny turned and pressed her hand to her chest.

Jill glanced over her shoulder. "Do you know those people?"

She nodded and swallowed the lump rising in her throat. Lou, Paul, and Sam walked up the aisle.

Kelley leaned close to Jenny. "Your Madison support team. Who's the distinguished older gentleman?"

"Sam's grandfather."

Lou smiled at Jenny as she slid in the pew behind her. Paul and Sam settled beside Lou.

Jenny's heart swelled as she turned toward the front.

The pastor moved behind the podium and faced the audience of eight. "We are here to celebrate the life of Dorothy Collins."

Jenny tuned out the pastor's words and surrendered to images of the three people sitting behind her. Even though she hadn't wanted them to come, she was glad they cared enough to drive all the way from Madison. Somehow, she had to let them know how much it meant without sending the wrong message to Sam. She closed her eyes and let images from her life in Madison play in her mind like a favorite movie.

"At least he kept the service short and sweet." Jill's comment disrupted her mental musings.

Jenny blinked. "Is it over?"

"Thankfully, yes." She stood and turned toward the pew behind her. "I'm Jill, Jenny's sister. I assume you three are her friends?"

Paul smiled. "It's a pleasure to meet you, Jill. I'm Paul Gibson."

Jenny swiveled. "Paul's my landlord, Sam's his grandson, and Lou's my boss."

"Don't let her kid you." Lou stood. "Jenny's more like my partner."

Sam's eyes found Jenny's and lingered. "Are you okay?"

"Yeah." Except she had yet to shed a single tear. She aimed her thumb over her shoulder. "The flowers. From you three?"

"Plus all your friends back at the coffee shop." Lou moved into the aisle.

Jenny choked back tears. "Tell them thanks for me."

Sam smiled. "You can thank them yourself when you return."

She looked away.

Jill shouldered her purse. "We appreciate you coming, and thank you for sending flowers."

"I suspect you and Jenny have a lot to take care of." Paul moved into the aisle. "So, we'd best be heading back to Madison."

Jenny's sideways glance caught Sam's fleeting glimpse of her seconds before he followed Lou and Paul down the aisle.

Kelley nudged her. "Sam is still wild about you."

Jill's eyes widened. "He's your boyfriend?"

"A friend." Jenny faced Kelley. "Jill and I are going to lunch before I drive her to the airport. You're welcome to come with us."

"Unfortunately, my afternoon schedule is full."

"The busy life of a psychologist, listening to tortured souls spill their guts." How many of Kelley's patients had families as messed up as hers and Jill's?

Kelley stood. "If you're available later today, we'll talk."

"As a patient and shrink, or friends?"

"A little of both. My next appointment is due in thirty minutes." Kelley followed Jill and Jenny into the aisle. At the exit she embraced Jenny. "I'll call you this afternoon, and we'll decide where to meet." She tucked her purse under her arm and headed to the exit.

Jill released a long sigh. "I'm glad it's over."

The funeral director approached carrying a white box. "Your mother's ashes. Who should I give them to?"

Jill pointed to Jenny. "My sister will take them."

Jenny accepted the box and waited for the funeral director to leave them alone. "Why me?"

"Because I don't want anything in my home that reminds me of her. You do with the urn whatever you want. Right now, I'm in the mood for a big juicy hamburger with a side of fat fries."

"There's nothing like a funeral to whet one's appetite for greasy cuisine."

"It seems Dorothy is still bringing out the worst in us."

"Her most noteworthy talent." Jenny guffawed as they walked through the lobby and out the front door. She set the box in her trunk then drove to a steakhouse and settled across from Jill. After ordering, she caught her sister staring at her. "What's wrong? Is my lipstick smudged?"

Jill hesitated. "There's something I've needed to tell you for a long time."

"Another memory about our mother?"

"Not exactly. Do you remember the day after I graduated from high school and shared my plans to move away?"

Jenny nodded. "I begged you to take me with you."

"You have to understand, I had five hundred dollars in my wallet and no plan other than moving as far from Georgia as possible. Every mile that bus traveled chipped away my guilt. By the time I arrived in San Diego, I had convinced myself that you possessed the strength to survive on your own. Truth is, I was terrified I would turn out like our mother." Jill's voice quivered. Tears pooled. "What I'm trying to say is I'm sorry I abandoned you."

"You escaped the only way you knew how. So did I. The day Dorothy chased me to my room with a butcher knife, I was terrified she'd stab the life out of me. That's when I packed a bag, climbed out the window, and ran to Kelley's house. I lived with her family for two years."

"Maybe now we can both bury our pasts." Jill wiped her tears with a napkin. "And I can tell my daughters you're their aunt."

Jenny stared at her sister. "Who do they think I am now?"

"A friend from my high-school days."

She shook her head. "We have one screwed-up family."

"Now, minus the two chief screwups." Jill sniffled and leaned back. "Do you remember the sign we hung on the front door the first Halloween after Henry took that long-distance driving job?"

"The one that said, 'the wicked witch lives here, if you knock, she'll capture you and eat your brains for breakfast'?"

"That's the one." Jill laughed. "We kept all the candy for ourselves. Dorothy was too drunk to realize it was Halloween, much less that we conned Henry into buying all our favorites."

Jenny reached across the table and touched her sister's hand. "I want us to stay in touch."

"So do I. First, I want to hear everything that's going on in your life."

While enjoying lunch, Jenny shared details about her career, avoiding comments about Sam. During the drive to the airport, she listened to Jill rave about her family. By the time she pulled to the curb outside the airport terminal, she understood she had lost a mother and found a sister. "Thank you for leaving your husband and daughters to trek across the country."

"Together we closed the final chapter in our tragic story." Jill stepped out and closed the door. After removing her luggage from the back seat, she leaned down and peered through the open window. "I love you, sis, and hope one day you'll fall in love with a wonderful man and create a couple of cousins for my daughters."

Jenny swallowed hard. "I love you too."

"You take care, little sister." Jill straightened and pulled her bag away from the car.

Jenny gripped the steering wheel. Her gaze followed Jill until she disappeared into the terminal. For the first time in her life, she envied her sister.

Chapter 51

Jenny drove her car into the hotel parking lot, climbed out, and caught sight of a plane flying overhead. Was it Jill's flight? When would she see her sister again? Maybe she should move back to California. No, that was too far away from Lou. And Sam. She made her way to her room to wait for Kelley's call.

After changing into jeans and a sweatshirt, she switched on the television to ease her growing anxiety. An hour passed. She paced, fighting the urge to escape to the hotel bar. Just one drink. She plopped on the edge of the bed and tapped her foot. If Kelley failed to call soon, she'd forget about meeting her and drive back to Madison. While flicking through program options again her phone rang. Jenny plucked it off the night stand. "About time you called."

"Sorry, last minute emergency patient."

"Are you in the mood to psychoanalyze your most challenging patient, who, by the way, is stone-cold sober?"

"Where are you?"

"Hilton, Peachtree Corners."

"I'll meet you out front in fifteen minutes."

"See you in a few." Jenny waited until the last minute to ride the elevator to the ground floor. She dashed outside seconds before Kelley pulled under the canopy.

Her friend glanced at her as she slid onto the passenger seat. "How did everything go between you and Jill?"

"Are you on the clock?"

"I'm asking as your friend."

"Way better than I expected." Jenny buckled her seatbelt. "Jill apologized for running off to California and leaving me behind."

"Oh my gosh, that's huge." Kelley drove out of the parking lot and merged into traffic. "When do you head back to Charleston?"

"Guess I forgot to tell you. I moved back to Madison a few weeks ago."

"Why am I not surprised?"

Jenny relayed details about Lou's illness and recovery.

"She's one tough lady."

"Truth is, Lou no longer needs me."

"Are you planning to leave Madison?"

Jenny's jaw tensed. "Returning to the coffee shop was a big step backwards."

Kelley turned into another parking lot.

Jenny peered at the dense woods beyond the pavement. "Where are we?"

"Jones Bridge Park. Let's take a walk."

They climbed out and headed toward the whisper of rushing water. When they arrived at the river, Jenny plucked a twig off the ground. "Do you remember shooting the Hooch back in the day?"

"Tubing down the Chattahoochee—a rite of passage for every local teenager."

"Those were good times." Jenny snapped the twig and let the pieces fall to the ground. "My mother left a sealed envelope in her bedroom. My name's scribbled on the front. I couldn't open it."

"Afraid?"

"Terrified."

"Understandable."

Jenny wandered to a bench facing the river that snaked through Atlanta's suburbs.

Kelley followed and sat beside her. "What's going on with you and Sam?"

Maybe it was time to reveal the truth. "I need to tell you something that happened after you left for college." She hesitated. "I've never told anyone what I'm about to share. It's the reason why I can never fall in love with Sam or anyone." Her eyes remained fixed on the river while she revealed the deep, dark secret.

When she finished, Kelley sandwiched Jenny's hand between hers. "You've carried that burden alone far too long. It's time to let it go."

Words failed to form as Jenny's eyes followed a branch floating downstream in the river's current.

"Your silence speaks volumes."

Jenny bolted from the bench and raced toward the river.

Kelley caught up with her and gripped her shoulders. "Please, Jenny."

"If you're worried about me jumping in the water to drown my sorrows, forget it."

"Will you promise me you won't end up in a bar tonight or any other night?"

"Alcoholics aren't known for keeping promises." Jenny pulled away and headed toward the path.

Kelley fell in step beside her. "I care about you."

"I know, and I promise to give sobriety my best shot. Right now, I'm exhausted and need to return to the hotel."

"Fair enough. About your revelation, you need to tell Sam."

Jenny shook her head. "I can't."

"You mean you won't."

"Either way, he's better off not knowing." Jenny stepped up her pace.

"I know that's what you believe, but if Sam was suffering from a painful incident from his past wouldn't you want to know?"

"I don't want his pity. So don't try using psychology to convince me to change my mind."

They remained silent while returning to Kelley's car. When they arrived back at the hotel, Jenny refused her invitation to dinner. She kissed her friend's cheek. "Thanks again for being here for me."

"I'm always here for you."

"I know." Jenny climbed out, rushed inside, and made a beeline to the elevators. When she arrived on her floor, she scurried to her room, grateful she understood enough about her addiction to recognize the triggers. She shoved her clothes into her suitcase and raced to the parking lot.

An hour and a half later, Jenny drove onto the exit ramp to Madison. Her eyes shifted to the gas gauge needle that had dipped below empty twenty miles ago. She pulled into the gas station. While filling her tank, the monkey she had managed to keep off her back since her last binge dug its fingers into her flesh. Revealing her secret to Kelley hadn't diminished the heart-wrenching regret that remained lodged in her soul. She capped the gas tank and stared at the convenience-store window. One purchase. Preventative medicine.

She walked inside and bought a cheap bottle of wine. The threat of another DUI kept her from uncapping it while driving. By the time she parked in Paul's driveway and popped her trunk, the urge to drink had passed. Jenny tucked the bottle under her arm and dragged her suitcase and the box securing her mother's ashes up the stairs.

Inside the dark apartment, she switched on the overhead light and set the box and the wine on the coffee table. Should she leave the urn out of sight or remove it from the box? Even a mother as damaged as Dorothy deserved some measure of respect.

She reached into the box. The moment her hands curled around the cold metal urn, a dull ache attacked the back of her throat. The woman was dead. She could never again spout hateful words. Jenny carried the urn to the bookcase and placed it beside her copy of *Great Expectations*. Tomorrow she would decide what to do with the ashes.

Desperate for rest, Jenny tucked the wine under her arm and eyed a floral arrangement sitting on the dinette table. She blinked back tears as she read the words scrawled on a notecard.

Whatever you need, I'm here for you.
Love, Sam

If only Sam had come into her life years ago. Before Max. She trudged to the bedroom and collapsed onto the bed. Within moments sleep triumphed over mind-numbing exhaustion.

Jenny bolted upright in the dark room, drenched in sweat. Her pulse raced. The vivid nightmare of her mother's ashes spinning in a tornadic funnel inches from her face sent her dashing from the bedroom. Terrified, she switched on the overhead light. Relieved the urn hadn't mysteriously moved to another spot or tipped over and spilled its contents, she trudged to the refrigerator and stood in front of the open door to allow the frigid air to cool her feverish brow. She grabbed a bottle of water, took a long drink, and slogged back to the bedroom. Would her mother ever stop haunting her? She switched on the bedside lamp.

Maybe the nightmare served as some sort of sign. Jenny dug deep for a measure of courage as she eased away from the nightstand, knelt beside her suitcase, and unzipped the side pocket. She removed the sealed envelope. Her breath came in shallow spurts. She peeled back the flap and pulled out her mother's letter. Her hand trembled as she unfolded the single sheet of notebook paper and forced her eyes to focus on the words.

Dear Jenny,

Somehow, I know my life is hours away from ending. I don't want to go to my grave carrying a lie in my heart. First thing you need to understand is that today, for the first time since you were a baby, I haven't had a drop to drink. Facing death is a sobering event. Who knows? Maybe during my final moments on earth, my life will flash in my head like some sort of movie, and I will find peace. Unless I end up drunk, which is more likely than not. Sorry for rambling. It's not easy for an alcohol-soaked brain to stay focused.

Back to why I'm writing this letter. One day after Jill turned three, Henry doubled over with pain. Sick as a dog. Turns out he had a burst appendix. His spending two days in the hospital gave me the chance to escape. I left your sister with a neighbor and drove to a bar where I met a man. He was ordinary-looking, but dressed like a million bucks. We hit it off big time and I ended up spending the next five months living in his fancy penthouse, drinking champagne and expensive wine.

Until the day cops smashed his door down and hauled us both off to jail. Turned out I was shacking up with a big-time gangster wanted for murder. After grilling me for hours, the detectives decided I had nothing to do with his crime. They released me. I had no place to go. So, I called Henry and begged him to take me back. I didn't tell him I was pregnant until I could no longer hide my condition.

I'm telling you this because if you ever decide to bring a child into this world, you need to know that Henry isn't your father. One more reason why you and Jill are different.

I don't know how to end this except to say, maybe one day you'll find it in your heart to forgive me for laying this final burden at your feet. Although I wouldn't blame you if you went to your grave despising me for the curse I passed on to you.

Since I'll be dead when you read this, I'll say my goodbyes and wish you a far better life than mine.

Your Mother,
Dorothy

A shudder ripped through Jenny's body. The only letter her mother had ever written to her revealed a heartbreaking truth. She was the daughter of an adulterous drunk and a murderer.

Forgive.

"She doesn't deserve forgiveness." Jenny crumpled the letter and hurled it across the room. How long before Sandra dug up that truth? An overwhelming urge to drink sent her scrambling to the dresser. She grabbed the wine bottle from the bottom drawer, dashed to the living room, and caught sight of the urn mocking her from the bookcase. She hurled the bottle across the room. It struck the kitchen cabinet and shattered.

In a rush of adrenalin, she yanked the urn off the shelf and scurried to the bathroom. A wave of nausea buckled her knees and sent her sinking to the floor. Her cheeks burned with shame at the mental image of her mother's remains swirling in a pool of water as they flushed down the toilet.

Jenny clutched the urn to her chest and returned to the living room. She dropped onto the love seat and rocked back and forth. Where would Dorothy want her ashes scattered? In a park? A lake? On a sidewalk in front of a liquor store? She set the urn on the coffee table and stared at the river of wine snaking across the kitchen floor.

Nausea gripped her as she cleaned up the mess. Desperate for sleep, she plodded to the bedroom, crawled into bed, and pulled the covers up to her chin. She closed her eyes and struggled to clear her mind. Each time she came close to dozing off, Dorothy's letter returned to haunt her. The truth of her existence clarified one undeniable fact. Her days in Madison had come to an end. This time she needed a logical reason to leave, something based on a semblance of truth. Her mind raced with possibilities until a solution crept in, and exhaustion plunged her into a deep sleep.

Chapter 52

Sam strolled into the coffee shop at the first hint of dawn and settled on his stool. "Morning George."

"Sam." George swallowed a bite of cinnamon bun. "How was the funeral?"

"Short."

"And small." Lou filled a coffee mug and set it in front of Sam. "Only nine people, including the preacher."

George scowled. "If you ask me, funerals are overrated. When I pass on to glory, invite everyone to come here for free coffee, donuts, and cinnamon buns. Call it George's last happy hour."

Sam's brows furrowed. "As far as I could tell, neither Jenny or her sister cried during the service. What kind of mother would fail to elicit a single tear?"

"See what I mean about funerals?" George aimed his fork at Sam. "People are expected to get all weepy-eyed and if they don't, folks think something's wrong."

Lou leaned on the counter. "It's likely Jenny grieved before the service."

"Maybe. Speaking of Jenny." Sam peered around Lou. "Where is she?"

"Taking the day off. You can talk to her tomorrow."

"If she doesn't hightail it out of town like she did after her father died."

"Things are different now."

Sam caught Lou exchanging glances with George. "What's going on?"

Lou pushed her glasses up her nose. "What makes you think something's happening?"

"I haven't parked my behind on this stool all these years without learning how to read you two."

George shook his head. "What's with the younger generation, being all suspicious?"

"Maybe because life's way more complicated than it was way back when we were in our thirties."

"Yeah, all that internet stuff must have these young folks' brains all fouled up."

"Enough already." Sam slid off his stool and pulled his wallet from his back pocket. "It's obvious neither of you are gonna clue me in."

Lou pulled his mug close. "You didn't finish your coffee."

Sam set a dollar on the counter. "That ought to cover what I drank."

George shook his head. "You're in a mood."

"You bet I am." Sam shoved his wallet in his pocket and strode out. Halfway down the block, he glanced over his shoulder. Had he overreacted and misread Lou's glance at George? Maybe fear that Jenny was days away from leaving town for good had clouded his judgment. He longed to talk to her and ask point-blank if she planned to stay in Madison. Sam unclipped his phone, pulled up his favorites list, and stared at her name. Was she taking the day off to rest or to pack?

Sam glanced skyward. "I'm leaving her in your hands, Lord," he whispered.

He pocketed his phone and continued walking, hoping he would have one more chance to earn Jenny's trust and capture her heart.

Sun streaming in through the bedroom window nudged Jenny awake. She swung her legs over the side of the bed and plucked her phone off the nightstand. Surprised she had slept past three, she trudged to the bathroom. After splashing cool water on her face, she walked to the kitchenette and poured a glass of orange juice.

Eager to launch her plan, she moved to the sofa and pressed Valerie's number. Her foot bobbed until her friend's voice interrupted the ring. "Hey, girl, how's everything going down in Georgia?"

"Lou's back full time and working circles around the rest of us." Jenny eyed her chef portfolio lying open to André's recommendation letter. "Which means I'm ready to return to Charleston."

"What happened with Sam?"

Jenny eyed her mother's urn sitting on the bookcase. "Fact is, I'm free in more ways than one. How's the catering business going?"

"Way better than I expected, thanks to the plan you helped me develop. Would you believe that André gave me the go-ahead to hire one more person? Oh my gosh, are you calling because you want your old job back?"

"You're my friend, Val. No way I'd ever make such an underhanded move. However, if you haven't filled the position, would you consider interviewing me?"

"Are you saying you wouldn't mind me being in charge?"

"Why would I?" Jenny sighed. "I need a job and you need an experienced chef you won't have to waste time training. So, what do you say? Are you willing to give it a go?"

"That depends on your answer to two important questions. First, how soon can you get yourself back up here?"

"By the end of the week. What's your second question?"

"A couple of weeks ago, I moved into a two-bedroom, two-bathroom apartment. I need a roommate and you need a place to live. Are you willing to move in and share expenses fifty-fifty?"

Jenny's mind drifted back to California and her one female roommate. Why wouldn't an arrangement with Valerie work as well as her previous experience? "Sounds like a good deal for both of us."

"Wow, it turns out today's my lucky day. By the way, the apartment is furnished. All you'll need are towels and linens for a double bed."

"Got it." Relief fused with angst the moment Jenny ended the call. Now she faced the next task—sharing the news with Lou, Paul, and Sam. Best to get on with it before her heart overruled her brain. She grabbed her keys, dashed downstairs, and drove the short distance to her first destination. When she parked at the curb, images of the only other time she had visited Lou's home loomed large—the night Sam and Paul showed up for a surprise farewell dinner. Given the way she had treated Sam, the likelihood of that happening again seemed far-fetched at best. She breathed deeply, made her way to the front porch, and rang the bell.

Lou swung the front door open and wrapped her arms around Jenny. "I'm glad you made it back safe and sound."

Jenny's chest tightened as she stepped inside and followed Lou and her border collie to the kitchen. She inhaled the intriguing scents wafting in the air. "Tomato, onion, and cumin. Homemade chili?"

"Vegetable soup." Lou pointed to a chair. "Have a seat." She poured two glasses of lemonade and sat beside Jenny. Buttons sprawled on the floor under the table. "Did you accomplish everything that needed doing for your mother?"

"All except selling the house." Jenny eyed the cheery space featuring yellow walls and updated stainless-steel appliances. "I have some important news."

"So, do I. You go first."

Jenny hesitated until fear she would back out overrode her curiosity. "This morning I learned the catering business I launched is expanding."

"I'm not surprised."

How could she make Lou understand? "You know advancing my career is important to me. Unfortunately, the opportunities in Madison are limited. Which is why I've accepted an offer to return to Charleston and pick up where I left off."

Lou remained silent for a long moment. "Remind me about your ultimate career goal."

Jenny's failed attempt to extract a loan from Peter skated across her mind. "One day I plan to open my own restaurant."

"Th same goal I had years ago. Does it matter where?"

Why was she asking? "I suppose a shack out in the boonies wouldn't do."

"Good point." Lou leaned forward. "For years, my daughter's ambition and fierce independence kept us thousands of miles apart. It's amazing how God's gift of a child opens doors." Lou wrapped her fingers around her glass. "My Sara is facing a difficult pregnancy, given her age and all. She needs me to help her through the next few months, and after the baby is born, I'll need to help care for my grandchild while she returns to work.

What I'm trying to say, is I've decided to sell my business and move to Texas."

"Leave Madison? How will the coffee shop survive without you?"

"I have it all figured out." A smile crinkled the skin around Lou's eyes. "I want you to purchase it and live your dream right here while I'm living mine out west. Spending however many years I have left on this earth with my daughter and grandchild is a blessing beyond anything I ever imagined." She touched Jenny's hand. "Especially knowing I'm leaving my business in good hands."

"I appreciate you thinking of me, Lou." Jenny pulled her hand away while mentally counting the small amount of cash she had managed to save. "The truth is my fifteen-year-old car is my only asset, and I don't have a lick of credit. Which means, unless I win the lottery, I couldn't possibly come up with the money."

"Not a problem, honey. You have an investor."

"No way I'm taking money from Sam or Paul."

"Goodness gracious, you're quick to jump to conclusions." Lou chuckled. "The investor willing to bankroll you is none other than George."

Jenny's jaw dropped. "Are you talking about our George? The guy who spends half the day sitting at the counter drinking coffee and eating cinnamon buns?"

Lou nodded. "Years ago, he invested wisely in a couple of stocks and is—in his words—loaded with dough."

Images of a downtown café sporting her name danced in Jenny's imagination. "Who else knows about your plans?"

"All my conversations with George have been private. For now, only the three of us know about my move and the sale."

Jenny turned away from Lou. If she declined, how many years would it take to find another investor for another property? If she accepted, could she see Sam every day and ignore her feelings? What about letting Valerie down?

"I understand this is a big decision, honey, with a lot at stake." Lou patted Jenny's arm. "Will you promise to give my proposal serious consideration?"

She owed Lou that much. "I'll sleep on it and give you my answer by noon tomorrow."

"Good. Now I insist you stay for dinner and enjoy my Saturday night special—Grandma's veggie soup and my melt-in-your-mouth, grilled cheddar cheese and bacon sandwiches."

Jenny hesitated.

"I promise not to say or do anything to sway your decision."

"In that case, how can I refuse such an intriguing gourmet meal."

Chapter 53

Sunday morning, rain pelting the roof and the wind rattling the window jarred Jenny awake. A gaping yawn and heavy eyelids urged her to pull the covers up and surrender to more sleep, until her promise to Lou overruled her body. She climbed out of bed and massaged her arms to warm her chilled skin. Determined to decide her future by noon, she moved to the kitchen and popped a pod in her coffee maker.

The rich scent of cappuccino escaped as the milky liquid filled her sunflower-adorned mug. She clutched it in both hands to absorb the warmth, returned to the bedroom, and sat on the edge of the bed. While sipping the brew, her eyes drank in the view. The furniture that once belonged to Sam's parents. The walls she had painted pale blue. If she stayed in Madison, she'd need to buy a couple of paintings to liven up the room. Maybe some throw pillows for her bed and some pretty curtains.

Her eyes landed on the rain-splattered window before shifting to the crumpled sheet of paper lying beneath. Her mother's letter. She shuddered at the prospect of reading it again. Except maybe she'd missed something. She laid her cup on the nightstand and inched toward the window.

Jenny picked the letter off the floor and smoothed the creases. Her eyes froze on the last line. *Since I'll be dead when you read this, I'll say my goodbyes and wish you a far better life than mine.*

The message collided with heart-wrenching memories of her childhood. In the hours before her death, had the woman found enough decency to pen a note to guide her daughter's future? Isn't that what Lou had offered? A chance for a better life? How could a job in Charleston compare to living her dream in a town she had come to love, among people she adored?

Jenny faced the window and stared at her car parked in the driveway below. The pounding rain had evolved into a gentle shower. If she poured every ounce of energy into transforming the coffee shop into a café, her feelings for Sam would eventually disappear. Wouldn't they? Besides, Lou was counting on her to preserve her legacy.

A fluttering sensation skipped through her chest as she spun around and dropped the letter on the bed. She plucked her phone off the nightstand and pressed a number.

"Hey, Jen," Valerie's yawn hinted the call had awakened her.

"Sorry to call so early. Something has come up." Jenny shared Lou's good news and George's offer. "I hope you're not too disappointed."

"You and me not sharing an apartment is a bummer. But goodness gracious, girl, you're going to achieve your dream without having to snag some rich guy. Unless George expects something in return. If you know what I mean."

Jenny pictured George bantering with Lou. "He's a sweet old guy who considers the coffee shop his home away from home."

"Hmm. I'd say you won the lottery without buying a ticket."

"I'm gonna miss sharing an apartment with you, Val."

"Me too. We absolutely must stay in touch. Especially since you're on my bridesmaid list. In case you're wondering, I've already picked out the dresses. They're to die for."

Jenny laughed. "Is this an official announcement or wishful thinking?"

"I have my eyes zeroed in on a good prospect. I'll keep you updated."

Anticipating Valerie's curiosity about Sam could kick in any moment, Jenny ended the call with a promise to send photos of her new venture. She carried her mother's letter to the living room and placed it between two pages in *The Scarlet Letter*. Somehow that seemed appropriate, even humorously wicked.

Eager to reveal her decision, Jenny dressed and drove to Lou's. The door opened seconds after she rang the bell.

"It's half past ten, which means you've made a decision." Lou motioned Jenny inside.

"I only have one question. How soon can we meet with George and work out the details?"

"Come with me." Lou linked her arm with Jenny's and led her toward the scents of cinnamon, vanilla, and freshly brewed coffee.

As they rounded the corner, Jenny gawked at George sitting at the kitchen table.

He set his fork down. "It seems the new owner of Lou's Coffee Shop isn't intimidated by a little rain."

"How'd you know?"

"I'm not what you'd call up to snuff when it comes to fancy food or kiwi." George tapped his fingers against his forehead. "But there's enough brainpower in this noggin to know you're a smart young lady who recognizes a good deal. In case you're wondering if I aim to meddle, rest assured I'm way past itching to get involved in the nitty gritty of running a business."

"You can count on me to deliver a good return on your investment."

"Paying me back isn't near as important as a promise to keep the counter and my favorite stool in place."

"Cross my heart."

George stood and extended his hand. "In that case, we have ourselves a deal."

"Indeed, we do." Jenny grasped his hand. Now one niggling task remained. She had to make Sam understand that her decision to stay in Madison wouldn't change her resolve to keep their relationship permanently parked in friendship mode.

Chapter 54

A week after Paul hosted a going-away event rivaling Lou's surprise birthday party, Jenny helped Sam load two boxes marked family photos in Lou's ten-year-old sedan. "Years ago, when I drove to California by myself, I slept in rest-stop parking lots and showered at truck stops."

Sam closed the trunk. "A sense of adventure or lack of cash?"

"I barely had enough money to buy gas and food."

Lou ambled across the driveway. "You were a courageous young woman to head out on your own."

"So are you. All the same, promise you'll stop driving before nightfall."

"I know. You and Sam are worried about an old lady falling asleep behind the wheel." Lou traced an x on her chest. "I'll keep you posted."

"And no sleeping in parking lots."

"Heck no." Lou smiled. "I'm looking forward to checking into a fancy hotel and taking a long hot shower."

Jenny embraced Lou. "I miss you already."

"You can count on me returning every once in a while. After all, I'll want to visit all my friends and see firsthand what changes you've made to the coffee shop."

Jenny released her and squatted to pet Buttons, while keeping her eye on Lou. "In the meantime, we'll stay in touch?"

"Every day." Lou placed her hand on Sam's arm. "Thanks for leasing my house to that nice young couple. Turns out I couldn't deal with selling the coffee shop *and* my home all at once."

He nodded. "A wise decision to have a place to live when you decide to move back home."

"Maybe when my grandchild goes off to college. That is, if I'm still kicking in my nineties."

"I'm betting we'll all celebrate your hundredth birthday." Sam winked. "With you moving four states away, I'll have to find a new source for my daily dose of local news."

"George will fill that void. One thing distance won't change is me playing cupid 'til you're settled down and married."

Sam chuckled. "You're a hopeless romantic."

"You mean hopeful." Lou nodded toward the porch. "Now, go get that suitcase and load it in my car while I say goodbye to my girl."

"I'm on it."

Lou turned to face Jenny. Her smile accentuated the wrinkles around her eyes. "You're a beautiful young woman with a bright future, and I'm tickled to leave my little coffee shop in your capable hands."

"Thanks to you, I'm days away from living my dream."

"You know I love you like a daughter, which is why I'm fixing to give you some motherly advice." She grasped Jenny's hand. "I've experienced the satisfaction and pride of owning a successful business. But I also know that a career pales in comparison to the pure joy of a deep, loving relationship with your soulmate."

"I—"

Lou pressed her finger to Jenny's lips. "When we keep our hearts and minds open, honey, everything works out in God's timing. Promise me you'll find a way to break down the wall you've built around your heart. It would be a shame for you to miss out on the life He wants for you."

Silence enfolded the moment as Jenny struggled to keep her tears at bay. "I promise," she whispered.

"You know that pledges daughters make to their mothers should be kept." Lou kissed her cheek.

Jenny averted her eyes as painful memories surfaced and clarified the truth. As much as she loved and admired Lou, her past had forced her to make a promise she could never keep.

Sam hoisted Lou's suitcase onto the back seat. "All set."

"The time has come for me to head out west." Lou coaxed Buttons into her car then slid onto the driver's seat and lowered the window. "I'll text you both when I stop for the night. In the meantime, I wish you all the best that life has to offer." After blowing a kiss, she backed into the street and drove away.

Tears escaped and spilled down Jenny's cheeks as guilt and a deep sense of loss kindled inside. She hadn't shed a tear when her mother died, yet saying goodbye to Lou in the wake of a lie unleashed a torrent of emotions. "She served as the coffee shop's heart and soul. It won't be the same without her."

"The end of one season always ushers in the next." Sam placed his hands on Jenny's shoulders. "It's time to forge a new future and transform the coffee shop to fulfill your vision."

Desire bubbled up like fizz in a soda can at Sam's touch. Had he overheard Lou's comments? Jenny inched away. She had to keep her mind focused on work. "I'd...um...appreciate your opinion on my plans. I mean, given everything you know about real estate and marketing. Not to mention your take on Madison's vibe and the coffee-shop customers. That is, if you don't mind. Unless, of course, you're too busy."

"That's some sales pitch." Sam chuckled. "I have a proposition."

Jenny narrowed her eyes.

"No need to act suspicious. If you treat me to lunch, I'll give you my best assessment."

Discussing business over a meal made sense, right? Especially if she paid. "Sounds like a fair trade."

Sam slid his arm around Jenny's shoulders. "Did I mention the deal includes dessert?"

"As long as your description of dessert means an item from the menu."

Pleased his touch hadn't triggered a cringe, Sam grinned. "I'd prefer a kiss, but I'll settle for chocolate cake."

"Wise choice." Jenny pulled away. "There's no need to take two cars. Leave yours here and I'll drive."

"Lunch and chauffeur service? How lucky can a guy get?"

During the short drive to the restaurant, Sam focused on Jenny's profile while listening to her prattle on about applying everything she had learned in culinary school. After they settled in a booth and ordered lunch, she ticked off key points to generating profits in the restaurant business.

"Sounds like you've nailed the basics."

Her head tilted. "Are you surprised?"

"Impressed." As Sam noted the sparkle in her eyes, his heart swelled with joy. Knowing she no longer had a reason to leave Madison gave him the courage to wait as long as it took to win her over.

Chapter 55

A cool pre-dawn breeze tousled Jenny's hair as she stood on the sidewalk, wearing a new white chef coat trimmed in black bearing the café's logo. She ran her fingers along the glass top on one of three tables under the new green and white striped awning. Her heart swelled as she eyed *Jenny Lou's Café* illuminated by the streetlamp, scribed in an arc across the front window. She stooped and used white chalk to write breakfast and lunch specials on the slate sandwich board poised beside the door. Satisfied, she straightened and brushed chalk dust from her fingers.

Inside, she paused in the newly decorated dining area lit by overhead recessed lighting.

An upbeat instrumental tune created a welcoming mood. She gazed at two enlarged photos hanging opposite the entrance. One of Lou cutting the ribbon during the coffee shop's grand opening, and to the right, the picture of her and Jenny posing in front of her living-room fireplace. Two women from different generations who gave birth to their dreams in the same space decades apart.

The front door opened, emitting a waft of cool air. Jenny's heart skipped a beat at the sight of Sam carrying a vase filled with sunflowers and baby's breath. "A congratulations gift from Gibson Realty."

"Oh my gosh." She pressed her palms together. "Where did you find sunflowers this late in the season?"

"Special order to celebrate today's grand reopening." He set the vase on the counter and moved to her side. His arm brushed her shoulder. "Are you apprehensive or excited.?"

"Little of both, I suppose. Mostly excited." She nodded toward the painting covering the wall opposite the counter—a field of sunflowers poised under a morning sky. "The mural turned out great, don't you think?"

"There's no mistaking your favorite flower."

"Do you think it's too much?" She pressed her hand to her chest. "Maybe I should have chosen a framed picture or more photos of Lou."

"Way too subtle. Besides, the mural makes a statement about the new owner."

"What kind of statement?"

A smile lit Sam's face. "That she's a visionary with a bold sense of style."

"That's a way better description than 'interesting.'"

"Glad you approve. I hear you hired another server."

She nodded. "The new menu requires me to spend more time in the kitchen."

"Does that mean Chef Jenny won't spend hours charming George and other loyal counter customers?"

"Anyone can charm, but only a select few can create mouthwatering cuisine to delight the senses."

Sam chuckled. "Think I'll add 'confident' to my description."

"To tell you the truth, I'm more nervous than I expected. Replacing one of the town's favorite citizens is a monumental task."

He slid his arm around her shoulders. "Think of this as the next chapter in the coffee-shop story."

The chapter that included her falling out of love with him. "Thanks for the pep talk." She pulled away and straightened one of the new chairs at a white four-top table. "You're a good friend, Sam."

A gust of cool air announced another arrival. "Morning, folks." George meandered in and stood beside Sam. "How do you like the way our gal fancied up the place?"

'Our gal' was Lou's phrase.

Sam kept his eyes focused on Jenny. "I expect she'll deliver a good return on our investment."

What did he mean by *our* investment? "The grand opening begins in twenty minutes. While you two carry on, I'll check the progress in the café's nerve center." Jenny entered the kitchen as Madge loaded the last yellow gift bag sporting the café's logo onto a chrome cart.

Jacko removed quiches from the oven, adding bacon and cheddar aromas to vanilla and cinnamon scents. "Slick move, giving the first hundred customers half a dozen fresh-baked cookies."

"Each a different flavor," added Bonnie, the perky young waitress hired two days earlier.

"A thank you and an enticement." Jenny glanced at her watch. Eighteen minutes before opening. Her breathing accelerated as the minutes ticked by. She understood that the coffee-shop regulars were accustomed to Lou's presence and appreciated her personal touch. Somehow, she had to strike the right balance between cooking and socializing.

At six straight up, Jenny wiped her damp palms with a towel. She filled her lungs and slowly released the air to slow her pounding pulse. "Madge, I want you to serve the table customers and Bonnie the counter folks while I welcome our guests." The women followed her as she pushed the cart into the dining room.

Jenny found her investor greeting Officer Matt. She moved the cart close to the front door and handed Matt a gift bag. "Welcome to Jenny Lou's Café." She linked arms with both men and escorted them to the counter. "As our first guest and one of the town's heroes, breakfast is on the house." She nodded toward Bonnie. "Take good care of Officer Matt, while George keeps him company."

Sam approached Jenny when she returned to the front door. He leaned close. "Well done."

"What?"

"The way you took control and assigned George to counter duty."

She glanced back toward the counter. "Do you think he noticed?"

"I'm guessing he's relieved." Sam lifted a gift bag off the cart and removed a waxed-paper bag holding a chocolate chip cookie. "Your newest signature creation?"

"Try it and tell me what you think."

He removed the cookie releasing chocolate and brown sugar scents. "It definitely passes the sniff test." He bit into the cookie. "Hmm." He tasted again.

"Well?" Jenny tapped her foot.

"You want my honest opinion?"

Her eyes widened. "What's wrong? Is it too sweet? Not enough chocolate?"

Sam's face inched close to hers. "Truth is, it pales in comparison to a kiss from a beautiful woman." He winked. "However, as far as cookies go, it's a mouthwatering masterpiece."

His comment reduced her brain to mush. Should she pretend she hadn't understood the kiss comment or respond with humor? Maybe make a cutting remark? Before her words could form, Sam gestured toward the door. "More customers have arrived."

Jenny grabbed a gift bag and spun around to greet the Perkins and escort them to their preferred table beside the window. After touting Jacko's contributions to the grand opening, she left them with Madge. While scurrying to greet the next arrivals, her eyes drifted to Sam sitting on his stool at the end of the counter. Bonnie handed him a coffee mug. She leaned close. He laughed.

Had her new hire taken to flirting with Sam? Why wouldn't she cozy up to the town's most eligible bachelor? Jenny squared her shoulders and turned back toward the entrance while vowing to pour every ounce of energy for however long it took to ensure Jenny Lou's Café's success.

The moment Bonnie stepped away, Sam shifted his gaze to Jenny. He marveled at her transformation from flirtatious waitress to gracious business owner. The woman who had swept into town, broke and desperate, had become an admired member of the community.

George nudged his arm. "You're grinning like a cat burglar who made off with a bagful of diamonds."

"She's amazing." Sam's eyes continued to follow Jenny. "Her passion. How she makes everyone feel special." The way she no longer cringed when he touched her.

George lifted his coffee mug. "I don't know how Jenny did it, but the coffee's as good as Lou's."

Madge stepped in from the kitchen and stopped between Sam and George. "Some things haven't changed. You two are still claiming your favorite spots. Not that I'm complaining."

"You're looking mighty spiffy this morning." George nudged Madge's arm. "With your fancy new apron and all."

"Jenny had it special made." She smoothed the pale-yellow fabric adorned by a single sunflower. "I think it's real pretty." She glanced toward the newest arrivals. "Duty calls. I'll talk to y'all later."

Sam chuckled at George craning his neck toward Madge as she sashayed away. "Seems I'm not the only guy fascinated by a pretty lady."

"Madge isn't bad for her age."

Sam shook his head. "That description makes 'interesting' seem like a raving compliment."

"So, I'm a little rusty." George turned back toward the counter. "Now that Jenny's here permanent, are you two gonna start courting again?"

"Are you adopting Lou's role as my personal dating service, or are you as nosey as all get out?"

"Yep, you're fixing to pop the question."

"I assume you mean asking her for a date."

George grinned. "For now."

Chapter 56

As had been true every day since the café's grand opening two months ago, cinnamon and brown sugar aromas wafted through the kitchen. Jenny removed three apple pies from the oven and set them on cooling racks.

Jacko flipped a sandwich on the grill. "Makes my mouth water."

"Lou's grandma's secret recipe."

Bonnie breezed in and handed Jenny an order. "I don't know which is more popular, the Monte Cristo sandwich or the dill potato salad. Either way, today's lunch special is a big hit. Oh, and Sam wants to talk to you."

"About what?"

"He didn't say."

Jenny wiped her hands with a towel, straightened her chef coat, and strolled from the kitchen. One glance around the café confirmed another day of booming business. She meandered to the end of the counter and faced Sam. "Back so soon? Are you here for lunch or more bits of information?"

"Take a look at this." He tapped his phone and slid it across the counter. "Jenny Lou's Café has a four-plus rating on Yelp, with twenty-seven reviews."

George snickered. "Isn't yelp the noise a dog makes when someone steps on its tail?"

Sam laughed. "That too."

Jenny's eyes widened as she scrolled through eight weeks of comments. All posted four or five stars. "Wow." She pushed the phone back to Sam.

He propped his arms on the counter. "It's a big deal, considering the short amount of time since your grand opening."

George squared his shoulders. "Our gal knows her stuff."

"Indeed, she does." Sam's grin sent a twinkle to his eyes. "In my opinion, this calls for a celebration."

Jenny tilted her head. "Sparklers and fireworks?"

"Even better. A break from your demanding schedule."

"Are you offering to take over my chef duties?"

"Just tonight. Dinner at my house. I'll pick you up at seven." Sam clipped his phone to his belt and slid off his stool. "Gotta run. I have an appointment with a prospective buyer." He dashed to the door before Jenny had a chance to refuse.

She trilled her lips and caught George smiling at her. "What?"

"R and R along with a nice dinner?"

"What makes you think I plan to show up?"

He shrugged. "Why wouldn't you?"

Good question. "Know what, George?" Jenny planted her hands on her hips. "I can't come up with a single reason why I shouldn't go."

"Atta girl."

Madge sidled up to George and eyed Jenny. "Did you say yes?"

"Good grief." Jenny rolled her eyes. Had everyone sitting at the counter heard Sam's invitation? She dropped her hands to her side and returned to the kitchen.

"What'd Sam want?" Bonnie plucked a plate off the counter and backed toward the door.

"To show me reviews. All positive."

Jacko plated a Monte Cristo sandwich. "Jenny Lou's is rocking."

"Indeed, we are." She ran her palm along the worktable's stainless-steel surface. The idea of spending time alone with Sam in his home unleashed a confusing mix of anticipation and anxiety. Why not enjoy a relaxing dinner with a pal? After all, she had managed to keep their relationship in the friendship column. Hadn't she?

After escorting his newest client to the front door, Sam wandered into his grandpa's office and sat across from him. "I wrote a contract for one of our historic homes, above asking price."

"Good going." He pushed his laptop aside. "Did Jenny accept your invitation?"

"I didn't give her a chance to refuse."

His grandpa laced his fingers behind his neck and leaned back. "I still say you're taking a huge risk."

"The timing seems right. The café's thriving, and after reading all the positive reviews, Jenny's in a good mood. Not to mention we're getting along better than ever." Sam propped his ankle across his knee and fingered his sock. "Even so, I'll play it by ear."

"Women are difficult to read."

"I've spent enough time with Jenny to tune into her moods."

"I suppose jumping in with both feet is the best tactic. No matter how she reacts, the café will keep her here."

"Another reason not to wait."

"Good point." His grandpa unlaced his fingers and leaned forward. "By the way, I'm leaving for the lake in an hour to spend a couple of days with your mom and dad."

"Tell them hi for me, and don't mention tonight."

"Not a word."

"I'll fill you in when you return. For now, I have a lot to do before dinner." Sam lowered his foot and headed out humming a tune he'd last heard during the concert in the park all those months ago.

Chapter 57

Jenny flung open her closet and stared at her wardrobe. What would a lady wear to dinner with a guy friend? Red dress? Too sexy. Jeans and a sweatshirt? Too casual. Opting for cute and comfortable, she donned a white pull-over, a jean jacket, and black jeans. After choosing gold hoop earrings, she fingered her only bottle of perfume. Chefs never wore fragrance while working, and she'd had few occasions to indulge. Besides, her outfit screamed casual acquaintance, so why not tonight? She spritzed behind each ear before a bout of common sense could change her mind.

Jenny scooted from her bedroom, plucked a yellow gift bag off the coffee table, and headed down the stairs as Sam turned onto the driveway. Second thoughts about dinner at his home sent a quiver rippling through her stomach. Maybe she should beg off. Except a last-minute refusal might send the wrong message. Best to relax and enjoy the evening. She filled her lungs and willed her anxiety away while walking to his car. "Right on time." She slid onto the cool leather seat.

"Glad you dressed warm."

"Are we dining al fresco?"

Sam nodded. "Perfect time to enjoy the sunset before cold weather moves in later tonight." He backed onto the street, drove the short distance, and parked in his driveway.

Soft jazz drifting from outdoor speakers greeted Jenny as Sam pressed his hand to her back and escorted her to the patio. A blaze crackled in the free-standing fireplace. A pair of candles and a floral centerpiece adorned the round glass-top table. "Nice setting." She handed him the gift bag. "A little thank you for the invitation."

He pulled tissue from the bag. "Jenny's mouthwatering cookies."

"All six flavors."

He set the bag on the table, opened a bottle, and filled two Champagne flutes. "Alcohol-free sparkling cider." He handed one to Jenny.

She stared at the bubbles cascading up the golden liquid. Was his choice a statement about dining with an alcoholic or a considerate gesture?

Sam tapped his glass to hers. "Cheers to Madison's newest successful restauranteur."

"And to one of Jenny Lou's most loyal customers." She sipped. "Good choice. The drink and the venue." Movement behind Sam drew her eye. "It appears we have company."

Billie bounded across the yard clutching a sheet of yellow construction paper. Sam leaned down and scooped him into his arms. "What's up, Buddy?"

He held the paper up. "I drew a picture for you."

"Wow, is that you and me?"

"Uh-huh. Playing catch."

"Sorry for the interruption." Billie's mother approached. "He scooted out before I could stop him."

"It's hard to wait when a little guy has a special picture to share with his pal." Sam accepted the gift and set the child down. "How about we play catch tomorrow after church?"

"Okay."

Jenny's eyes shifted from Billie holding his mother's hand as she led him home, to a pair of long shadows cast across the patio. Hers and Sam's. Standing close, yet so far apart.

Sam set the drawing on the table and aimed his glass toward the sky. "There's something magical about sunsets."

Dismissing the regret churning her stomach, Jenny gazed at the orange and pink colors painting wide swaths across the western sky.

"Like the painting in my office, they represent the promise of new beginnings."

Desperate to keep the mood locked in friendship mode, Jenny nudged Sam's arm. "Is the best steak east of the Mississippi on the menu or have you expanded your culinary horizons?"

"Why mess with a winner. Although I'm counting on my lemon pota-toes and grilled asparagus to tantalize your taste buds."

"Oh my." She exaggerated her southern accent. "How can a lady resist such enticing cuisine prepared by a real-estate tycoon?"

He grinned. "Wait 'til you see dessert."

"Another store-bought pie?"

"You'll see." He winked. "First, it's time to put my master-chef skills to work." He placed two filets on the grill. "Is slightly north of rare still okay?"

"Perfect." She closed her eyes, delighting in the scents of fresh rosemary, garlic, and balsamic vinegar while imagining Sam preparing a meal for another woman. Someone like Billie's mother. A woman who deserved his love. Fearing her feelings had drifted too close to the surface, she launched into a monologue about the café until Sam sent her to the kitchen to fetch the bowl of lemon potatoes warming in the oven.

She carried the dish to the patio as Sam plated the steaks and asparagus and set them on the table.

"Smells amazing. Like last time."

He pulled her chair out then sat across from her.

She bowed her head, anticipating when he had finished his silent bless-ing. When she looked up, he was smiling at her. "Maybe next time I'll say it out loud."

"That would be nice."

"Check your steak to make sure it's okay."

She cut a slice. "Perfect."

During dinner Sam entertained Jenny with humorous stories about growing up in a small town. She shared tidbits from the year she'd lived with Kelley's family, and the few happy memories from her childhood. By the time they devoured their steaks, Jenny trusted their relationship remained steadfast in the friendship category. She laid her fork down and leaned back. "You definitely tantalized this chef's taste buds."

"Dessert's still on the menu."

She patted her tummy. "I don't think I can squeeze in one more bite."

"Wait here." He gathered the plates and walked inside.

Jenny's ears tuned into the music accentuated by the pop and crackle of burning wood. She moved close to the fireplace to ease the sudden chill from a gust of cool wind. A log split and fell into the ash.

"Are you cold? Do you want to go inside?"

She turned toward Sam. "I'm fine now." She eyed a white bakery box sitting on the table. "A store-bought cake instead of a pie?"

"Not just any cake." Sam reached for Jenny's hand and led her back to the table.

"You do know it's not my birthday."

"I do." He scooted his chair close to hers, opened the box, and lifted a heart-shaped cake decorated with a sunflower motif. *To the chef who stole my heart* was scribed in chocolate.

Her chest tightened.

"I've waited a lifetime for this moment." Sam pulled a small black box from his pocket.

Jenny pressed her left hand to her mouth.

He dropped to one knee and opened the box. "Jenny Collins, I love you with all my heart. If you marry me, I promise to cherish you and spend the rest of my life making you happy."

Her pulse pounded as she lowered her hand and splayed her fingers.

Sam slid the ring onto her finger.

She stared at the princess-cut diamond sparkling under the glow of candlelight. Words failed to form.

Sam stood and gathered her into his arms.

Jenny's knees grew weak and threatened to buckle.

He held her tight. His lips brushed her ear. "The day you arrived in town was the luckiest day of my life."

She remained silent, basking in the warmth from his body. The scent of his skin. The strength of his arms holding her against his chest. Until the past holding her captive reared up and exploded in her mind. She pushed back. "I've been awake since three this morning...guess I've run out of steam."

"Do you want me to drive you home?" His tone hinted of concern.

Jenny gazed into his eyes, devastated that the moment that felt so right was so wrong. "Please."

Sam stroked her cheek. "Tomorrow we'll announce our engagement to the entire town." After snuffing out the candleflames and placing the cake in the box, he escorted her to his car.

As Jenny slid into the passenger seat, a shiver cascaded through her body. She closed her eyes and bit her lower lip to stop the rush of tears threatening to escape.

The moment he braked in front of Paul's garage she climbed out. A gust of cold wind clawed her face as she climbed the stairs and plucked the key from under the doormat.

Sam followed. He touched her shoulder.

She spun and stared up into his eyes. It wasn't too late to say yes. To welcome him into her heart. To invite him to come inside and let him make love to her.

"You swept me off my feet the day you first walked into my office." He brushed a lock of hair away from her cheek. "I hope our first child is a girl who's the spitting image of her beautiful mother."

His words ripped a hole in her heart. "Thank you for a lovely evening, Sam." Her voice cracked. She turned away. Her trembling fingers fumbled with the lock.

Sam's breath warmed her cheek as he grasped her hand and helped her slide in the key.

Her breathing accelerated.

"I want your voice to be the first I hear tomorrow morning. Call me the moment you wake up."

She nodded, knowing tears were seconds from erupting. "Good night, Sam," she whispered.

"Good night, my love." Sam hesitated before pulling away and descending the stairs. At the bottom step, he turned and peered at the empty landing. He returned to his car and eyed the apartment's dark windows. Was Jenny too tired to turn on the light? Should he go back upstairs and comfort her?

He gripped the door handle. If his grandpa hadn't chosen this weekend to spend with his parents, he could ask his opinion while enjoying a brandy.

Sam slid onto the driver's seat and backed into the street. After parking in his garage, he trudged to the patio and dropped onto a chair in front of the fireplace. While eyeing the dwindling flame he mentally replayed the evening. Jenny's cheerful demeanor. The way she smiled when he talked about growing up in Madison. Her stories about living with Kelley's family. The moment he dropped to one knee. The way Jenny's mouth opened then closed without responding. Had she been on the verge of saying yes? Had he asked her to marry him? No. He'd said *if* you marry me.

Sam released a heavy sigh, then carried the cake box to the kitchen and set it on the counter. Maybe he should call her. What would he say? How about giving me an answer? The night he proposed to his former fiancée she had squealed with delight and said yes more than once. That hadn't turned out so well.

At least Jenny hadn't told him no. He removed a beer from the fridge and pried off the cap. All she needed was a good night's sleep. Tomorrow he would give her a dozen roses, propose again, and wait for her answer.

Chapter 58

Jenny stepped inside and listened to Sam's footsteps striking the stairs. She waited to hear a car engine before willing her feet to move through the dark space. The full moon cast an eerie glow on her bedroom floor. She pulled down the shade.

Tears she had held at bay erupted. She sniffled and swiped her fingers across her cheeks as the all-too familiar urge forced her to open the drawer and dig beneath her sweaters. Her fingers wrapped around the courage she had hidden the night she drove home from her mother's funeral. She yanked the wine bottle from the drawer, twisted off the cap, and took one long swallow.

Her eyes shifted to the top of her dresser. She slammed the bottle down. Her hand inched toward her treasured chef portfolio. Jenny opened to the last entry—a menu from Jenny Lou's Café. Scrawled across the top were the words she'd written three days earlier. *At last, my dreams have come true.*

Her heart leapt to her throat as she fled to the living room. She switched on the light, dug her phone from her purse, and pressed Kelley's number.

"Jenny. Are you okay?"

She swallowed hard. "I didn't see it coming. Maybe I ignored the signs. We watched the sunset paint gorgeous colors across the sky. He served grilled steaks. For dessert...a heart-shaped cake."

"Sam proposed, didn't he?"

Jenny's breath caught. "I don't know why I let him slip the ring on my finger."

"Sam loves you—"

"He doesn't know what I've done."

"You have to stop running from your past, Jenny. Tell Sam. Let him decide."

"I love him too much to ruin his life."

"You won't."

Jenny stared at the sunflower painting on the wall behind the sofa. "Yes. I will."

"Please, listen—"

Why had she called Kelley? Nothing she could say would change her mind. "You're a dear friend and I love you. I'll call you in a couple of days."

"Jenny—"

"Good night, Kelley. Sweet dreams." She dropped her phone in her purse and splayed her left hand. The diamond sparkling like brilliant fireworks sent second thoughts skittering across her mind.

Desperately needing another drink, she fled to the bedroom and grabbed the wine. She hesitated. Kelley's words the night of her mother's funeral bubbled up and tugged at her conscience. "Find courage in the strength of your character." What strength? She lifted the bottle and swallowed a mouthful.

A sense of shame forced her to cap the wine and set it on the dresser. She switched on the bedside lamp and removed a sheet of stationery and an envelope from her nightstand. As she stared at the blank page, memories of the evening washed over her like a warm spring shower. Maybe she should heed Kelley's advice and tell Sam about her past. No. The truth would force him to stay with her out of pity. She gripped a pen and searched for the right words.

Dearest Sam,

This is the most difficult note I have ever written, and you are the most amazing man I have ever met. Yet, I am forced to reject your proposal. Not because I don't love you. Believe me, I do. With all my heart. It is the depth of my love which forces my decision. If I stay in town, we will forever be haunted by what could have been. Therefore, I am leaving one last time. Please forgive me and find a woman worthy of your love.

Also, apologize to George for me and tell him I will pay back every penny I owe.

Wishing you a life filled with happiness,

Jenny

Her heart ached as she read the note and blotted the teardrop smudging her signature. She folded the paper, slipped it into the envelope, and scribed Sam's name on the front. Her head pounded as she slid off the ring and dropped it in with the note. With trembling fingers, she laid the envelope on her pillow.

Jenny slid to her knees and pulled her suitcase and duffel bag from beneath her bed. She rushed to fill them with her meager belongings. The last item she added before zipping the suitcase—her portfolio. Her ticket to starting over...again. In a new town, miles away from Sam. She took one more drink, capped the bottle, and slid it back in the drawer.

She carried her suitcase and duffel to her car and stashed them in the trunk, then returned to her apartment to collect her remaining possessions. Her shoulders and arms screamed with pain as she locked the door and slid the key under the mat.

She trudged down the stairs and set her picnic basket, guitar, and her mother's urn beside the duffel. After glimpsing the apartment one last time, she closed the trunk and slid behind the steering wheel. The bike propped against the staircase caught her eye and unleashed a torrent of emotions.

Jenny tossed her purse and phone on the passenger seat and backed out of the driveway before her heart could overrule her mind. Her pulse pounded as she drove away from town on a dark stretch of road. The all-too-familiar craving for a drink raised its ugly head. Why hadn't she brought the wine?

She gripped the steering wheel praying for the urge to pass.

A ping drew her attention. She reached for her phone. A text from Sam. Telling her how much he loved her. Tears filled her eyes. Should she turn around? Confess the truth? After all, didn't he deserve more than a goodbye note?

A blasting horn startled her. Blinded by bright headlights, she jerked the steering wheel hard to the right as memories of another dark night loomed large. The truck slammed into her rear bumper sending the car tumbling out of control. The deafening sound of crushing metal and shattering glass exploded around her. Images from her past flashed across her mind at warp speed...until the world around her faded and turned black.

Chapter 59

Jenny floated in a vast black void. A dim light crept into the darkness and grew brighter. Her body drifted to the edge of a long, straight path, like a butterfly landing on a petal. Air warm as a spring morning brushed her cheeks. At the far end of the path, a beacon shone through misty clouds.

A hand—its body lost in the haze—reached out. "Come with me, Jenny." The gentle mail voice beckoned. "Someone is waiting to meet you."

She submitted with abandon. Fingers curled around her hand and led her along the path. The clouds faded and vanished. Brilliant colors surrounded her, as if she stood inside a kaleidoscope filled with thousands of shimmering, precious jewels. She breathed in the sweet essence, like that of a rose, but infinitely more fragrant. The sounds of a thousand violins in perfect harmony kissed her ears.

The hand released hers and slipped away. Jenny turned in a slow circle, marveling at the majestic surroundings and indescribable beauty. A sense of wonder delighted her senses and awakened every nerve in her body. She had come home.

A figure floated toward her, more spirit than flesh. Yet somehow the apparition seemed familiar—someone she had met but couldn't place.

"Welcome to my world." The young girl's melodious voice radiated love.

"It's magnificent."

"My world is like no other."

"I should have come here years ago." Memories bubbled up, diminishing Jenny's joy. "The night I—"

"It wasn't your time."

Jenny stared at the girl's hazel eyes and delicate features. "Do I know you?"

"I live deep in your subconscious."

Confusion muddled Jenny's brain. "Tell me your name."

A serene expression formed on the ethereal face. "I don't have a name."

"How is that possible?"

"I was gone before I left my mother's womb."

Jenny's heart pounded as she stared at the mysterious figure. She blinked as confusion gave way to clarity. In one profound moment, she understood. She pressed her hand to her chest as her heartbeat slowed. Tears of joy filled her eyes. "You are my child."

"Yes. You are my mother, and I am your daughter."

Jenny's elation dissolved into heart-wrenching regret. She buried her face in her hands as bitter tears of sorrow cascaded down her cheeks. "I am so ashamed. How can you ever forgive me?"

A hand touched Jenny's shoulder. "Your father has forgiven you."

She lowered her hands and spun toward the voice that had led her along the path. Jenny gazed into eyes filled with deep understanding and heart-warming compassion. "Are you—"

"I am who you think I am." He gently spun her to face her daughter. "It's almost time to say goodbye."

Jenny reached out to touch daughter's hand, grasping at air. "Why can't I touch her?"

"Because you are not part of this world."

"Then why am I here?"

"To discover the time has come to *forgive* yourself and your mother."

Jenny swallowed the lump rising in her throat as memories bubbled to the surface. She turned toward the voice. "Yours is the mysterious whisper I heard.

"Yes. Your daughter has one request before you leave."

"Why can't I stay here with you and my daughter?"

His hand lifted off her shoulder. "Because your life on earth has just begun." He faded into the mist.

Jenny's heart filled with love as she turned and gazed at her daughter's beautiful face. "What question do you want to ask?"

"If you had brought me into your world, what would you have named me?"

Jenny closed her eyes as a recurring dream she had never shared with a living soul surfaced. Holding a tiny baby wrapped in a pink blanket. Kissing her sweet face. Fingering a bracelet with a girl's name, before the child faded away. "Grace. I would have named you Grace."

"You have given me a beautiful name I will cherish forever. I love you, Mother."

"I love you with all my heart, sweet girl." The light around Jenny dimmed. Grace drifted away. "Please don't go. I don't want to lose you again."

"You will never lose her." The gentle voice behind Jenny filled her with hope. "Until you meet Grace again in eternity, go live your life. Someone who loves you with all his heart is waiting for you."

Darkness descended and enveloped Jenny. She drifted back to the empty void. Pain emerged and invaded her body. Light penetrated her eyelids. Her eyes fluttered open. She squinted at the overhead light fixture. The hum of medical equipment secured to stands towered above her. Tubes and wires attached to her body.

"Please come back." Sam's voice was filled with angst. "I promise to let you go."

"She's coming around." A woman's voice. Familiar. Sandra, dressed in scrubs, leaned over a railing. "Can you hear me, Jenny?"

She blinked away the fog of confusion. "Where am I?"

"Intensive care."

"You've been unconscious for hours." Sam lifted her hand to his lips and kissed her fingers. "I love you with all my heart, Jenny. Enough to let you walk out of my life forever if that's what you need to do."

"You found my note?"

He swallowed. "Yes."

"I need to explain."

Sandra touched Jenny's arm. "Right now, you need to rest."

"Not until I talk to Sam." She lifted her head. "Please."

"All right." Sandra raised the bed to a semi-sitting position. "Call me if she begins to drift away, Sam." She walked out and closed the door.

Jenny's heart pounded as she gazed deep into Sam's eyes. The time had come to reveal the truth that had tormented her soul and robbed her of happiness. "The story I'm about to tell you began a long time ago." She filled her lungs and slowly released the air. "Three months before my high school graduation, I took a waitress job in a family-owned Italian restaurant. Max, the owner's son, worked as the executive chef. He was the most handsome and worldly man I had ever met. Nothing like the immature teenage boys I'd hung out with. When he asked me for a date, I felt grown up and desirable."

Jenny coughed. "I need a drink."

Sam grabbed the water and held the straw to her lips.

She let the cool liquid slide down her parched throat then pushed the glass away. "After a couple more dates, I believed we were destined to be together. The perfect couple. When Kelley left for college, I moved out of her parents' home and into Max's apartment. Everything seemed perfect until—" Jenny closed her eyes as the painful memory solidified. "This is the hard part, Sam."

He held her hand.

She opened her eyes. "One night after work, we cuddled on the living room couch watching a movie. When it ended, I knew I couldn't wait any longer." Her voice was barely above a whisper. "I wrapped my arms around his neck and told him we needed to start planning our future. Open our own restaurant. Get married. Max laughed and said the only future he planned with me involved a lot of hot sex."

Her mouth went dry. "I need another sip."

Sam held her glass.

She swallowed. "When I told him I was pregnant, he jerked my arms away from his neck and bolted to his feet. His face turned beet red. He raised his fist. I closed my eyes and braced for a blow." Jenny's voice cracked. "The words he screamed hurt far worse than if he had hit me. He said a stupid teenager with a disgusting drunk for a mother would never saddle him with her careless mistake."

"He had no right."

"The truth is, I lied to him about being on the pill."

"That doesn't matter—"

"Let me finish. When I tried to explain his responsibility, he threw me out. An overwhelming sense of shame and anger drove me to the nearest liquor store. I bought a bottle of vodka, walked outside, and swallowed a mouthful. The bitter taste seemed appropriate. I sat on the curb and guzzled more to numb the pain. The world began to spin out of control. I closed my eyes and pictured Max saddled with a lifetime of guilt for abandoning me. After swallowing the last drop, I managed to push off the curb. My knees threatened to buckle. My vision blurred. Approaching headlights blinded me. I dropped the bottle." Her breath caught. "When it shattered...I staggered in front of the oncoming car."

"Jenny—"

She pressed her fingers to Sam's lips. "I woke up in a hospital with a concussion and four broken bones. No longer pregnant. All these years, I've carried the guilt of destroying my child's life and not my own. When you proposed, I ran away to keep you from discovering the truth about me. Then something miraculous happened."

A smile she could not contain spread across Jenny's face. "What seemed like moments after that truck slammed into my car, I drifted into eternity. An indescribable place filled with peace and immeasurable beauty. While there, I met her and I discovered I had destroyed her body, not her spirit. After all these years, I finally gave her a name. I named my beautiful daughter Grace."

Sam's face inched closer.

"That divine experience changed me. For the first time in more than a decade, I'm at peace."

He stroked her cheek.

"There's more. That night I lost more than my baby. The damage destroyed too much. I can never have another child. I love you with all my heart. You're the perfect man for me, Sam. The truth is, I'm not the right woman for you."

"Is that why you ran away?"

Jenny nodded. "To spare you the pain of committing to a woman who can never give you the family you deserve." She touched his cheek. "I won't hold you to your proposal, and I'll understand if you let me go once and for all."

Sam's eyes filled with tenderness. He kissed her fingers. "At this moment, I love you more than I have ever loved anyone. With every fiber of my being,

I know that we belong together. I want to spend the rest of my life with you by my side. Loving you. Caring for you."

Memories of Sam's relationship with little Billie floated up. "What about children?"

"We'll adopt a child, or two, or however many our hearts desire. What can be more beautiful than giving one of God's precious abandoned babies a warm, loving home." He slid his hand into his pocket and withdrew the ring she had left in the envelope. "Jenny Collins, will you do me the honor of becoming my wife and spending the rest of eternity with me?"

As she gazed at the diamond sparkling under the overhead light, the last shred of shame and regret dissolved like hail melting in the sun. She wrapped her arms around Sam's neck and pressed her cheek to his. Her tears mingled with his while her heart danced with joy. "Yes. A thousand times, yes."

Chapter 60

Sunshine flooded Jenny's bedroom as her eyes fluttered open. She spread her fingers, delighting at the sight of her engagement ring sparkling in the sun's rays. Her gaze drifted to her wedding gown hanging on the closet door. Three weeks before the big day, she faced one final step on her road to a new beginning. She plucked her phone off the nightstand and pressed Sam's number.

"Good morning, future Mrs. Gibson. Are you ready for breakfast?"

She strolled to the window, relishing the sun caressing her cheeks. "Give me half an hour, Mr. Wonderful."

"I'll count the minutes."

"Me too." Eager to complete her mission, Jenny showered and dressed. After donning a ball cap, she placed three items in a cardboard box and carried it down the steps.

Duchess bounded off Paul's deck to greet her with an enthusiastic tail wag.

"Hey, girl. Are you loving this gorgeous spring morning?"

Her canine pal responded with a muffled bark moments before Sam turned onto the driveway and parked beside her car.

Jenny placed the box on his back seat.

Sam dashed to the passenger side and drew Jenny into his arms. "Today's a big day."

She nuzzled his neck, relishing the scent of his musky aftershave. "Twenty-two mornings from now, I'll wake up beside you."

He stroked her back. "A moment worth waiting for."

Duchess stood on her hind legs and plopped her paws on Sam's arm.

"Seems Grandpa's four-legged child is jealous of a little competition." He released Jenny, sending the dog's front legs dropping to the driveway.

"Don't you worry, girl." Jenny patted Duchess' head. "You're still at the top of my list."

Sam shook his head and playfully rolled his eyes. "Second place to a mutt."

"A pedigreed mutt, I'll have you know." She kissed Sam's cheek. "At least you're the only pal whose bed I'll share."

He winked. "Lucky me."

A whistle from Paul sent Duchess scrambling back to the deck while Jenny slid onto the front seat. Sam returned to the driver's side. "Breakfast at your place or the competition?"

"My team's expecting us to show up."

Five minutes later they walked into Jenny Lou's Café and settled at the only vacant table, beside the wall mural. As Jenny's gaze swept across the sky painted above the field of sunflowers, a warm sensation kindled inside. "This is the happiest painting in Madison, maybe all of Georgia."

"Definitely a great choice."

"Sam's right." Madge set two filled coffee mugs on the table.

Jenny opened a sugar packet. "How's everything going in the kitchen?"

"The new cook—I mean, chef—you hired knows her stuff. Still, me and Jacko are glad you're only taking *one* day off a week until your wedding." Madge pulled her order pad from her apron pocket. "What can I bring you two lovebirds?"

After Madge took their orders and stepped away, Sam reached across the table and held Jenny's hand. "Have you told your staff about your plans to take every Monday and Tuesday off?"

"Not yet. I'll bring them up to speed after our honeymoon." From the corner of her eye, she spotted George moving toward them. "I think we're about to have company."

"Morning, you two." Jenny's financial backer sat beside her and set his coffee mug on the table.

Sam grinned. "What's up, George?"

"Got a letter from Lou. Says she's coming to your wedding." He leaned forward. "Have you heard the latest?"

They listened to his take on the local news then engaged in light-hearted conversation while enjoying the breakfast special. As soon as they finished eating, Sam paid the bill. "Nice talking with you, George." He pushed away from the table and stood. "It's time for us to leave."

"More wedding planning?"

"Something like that." Jenny held Sam's hand and spoke to customers while they made their way to the door. Outside, she breathed in the crisp air and geared herself for their next destination.

Half an hour later, Sam parked in a circular driveway. "Are you sure about this?" He reached across the console and touched Jenny's arm.

Gazing at Sam's parents' elegant house on the large, wooded lot fronting Lake Oconee brought memories of the first time she'd entered their home. The night his parents welcomed her into the family. "It's the only move that makes sense."

"All right then." After climbing out and retrieving the box from the back seat, Sam opened the passenger door.

Jenny stepped onto the pavement and adjusted her ball cap. A warm spring breeze fluttered her shirt as they strolled to the backyard and followed the stone path leading downhill to a dock. When they arrived, she slipped out of her tennis shoes and relished the warm wood under her feet as they passed the moored pontoon boat and sat on the dock's front edge. Sam set the box down and settled beside her.

"I love this cove. It's so peaceful." As Jenny's eyes swept across the panoramic view, her mind wandered to the moment she'd lost sight of Grace and plunged back into the grey void. "My mother spent most of her adult life in a dark room, shackled by her past and poisonous notions about life and men."

Sam slid his arm around her shoulders and pulled her close.

"Jill and I had her body cremated for convenience. Now I understand there was a deeper, more meaningful reason. Rather than resting in a dark casket buried under layers of dirt, she deserves to float free in sunshine and fresh air."

Jenny reached into the box and wrapped her fingers around the cool metal surface. She lifted the urn and removed the cap. "I forgive you, Mother, and release you from the dark into the light." She tilted the urn and watched her mother's ashes drift to the shimmering lake and float on the gentle waves. "Dorothy Collins, your body is finally free."

Sam squeezed Jenny's shoulder. "Are you?"

"Almost." She removed her mother's letter from the box and read it one last time. "Today, I am letting go of the past and accepting one undeniable fact. No matter who my parents are, I am a child of God, loved unconditionally for eternity." Jenny struck a match and held the flame to the corner.

As her mother's confession turned to ash and sailed into the wind, Jenny squeezed Sam's hand. She knew beyond the shadow of a doubt she had finally won her lifelong battle with guilt and despair.

Chapter 61

Jenny sneaked a final glance in the freestanding mirror before following her attendants—dressed in floor-length gowns the color of ripe peaches—from the dressing room to the church vestibule. She breathed in the sweet scent wafting from fresh flowers and tuned in to music drifting from the sanctuary.

"Your wedding is the most anticipated event since Lou's surprise birthday party." Sandra adjusted Jenny's veil flowing down her back. "It took me a while, but I finally realized you're a perfect match for my brother and the only woman who can make him happy. Plus, having a professional chef in the family is a welcome bonus."

"Especially if you love crab cakes." Kelley leaned down to help Jill and Valerie fan out Jenny's bridal train. "Jenny's are hands down the best on the planet."

"No kidding?" Jill straightened. "Seems I still have a lot more to learn about my little sister."

Jenny smiled. "We have a lifetime to catch up. Especially since your sweet daughters now know we're sisters."

"Have I told you how much my girls adore their Aunt Jenny and Uncle Sam?"

"The handsome guy from Georgia, who captured my friend's heart after all." Valerie moved in front of Jenny. "Can you believe in six weeks you'll be one of my bridesmaids?"

"Thanks to your snag-a-rich-guy plan?"

"Hardly." Valerie grinned. "I chose love over money."

"Smart choice."

"Oh, and I'm catering my own wedding. After all, Le Champagne Prestige Catering is the best in Charleston."

"Thanks to your business savvy." Jenny embraced her. "I'm glad we're friends, Val."

"Me too, girlfriend."

The front door opened, emitting light from the streetlamps. "You ladies all look beautiful." Paul approached Jenny. "Especially the bride."

"Other than your grandson, you're the most charming man I've ever met."

"I'm happy to take second place." He winked. "I talked to Lou. She's thrilled you asked her to sit in the front row."

"You know I've adopted her as my mom, and you're more like my dad than my grandpa-in-law." She placed her hand on Paul's arm. "I'm honored you're walking me up the aisle."

He patted her hand. "I wouldn't have it any other way."

The wedding coordinator slipped in from the sanctuary and handed each attendant a bouquet of white roses tied with shimmery ribbon. "We're ready." She opened the double doors.

The music changed.

Valerie stepped into the aisle.

Jenny stretched to kiss Paul's cheek. "Thank you for everything you've done for me and Sam."

Sandra began her stroll.

Paul patted Jenny's hand. "Duchess will miss showing up at your apartment every afternoon."

"You know you can walk her to my new home any time."

Jill followed Sandra.

Paul grinned. "I'd like that."

As Kelley moved into the aisle, the attendant placed a bouquet of miniature sunflowers and white roses in Jenny's hand. "It's time."

Jenny's heart drummed in her chest as she stepped into the sanctuary and gazed at guests filling every seat. Friends spun to watch her stroll toward the man she loved. She turned her eyes skyward and imagined Grace peering over the edge of a thick white cloud blowing kisses and whispering, *I love you, Mom.*

Sam entered the sanctuary from the side door, followed by his dad, brother-in-law, George, and a close friend. He stopped at the end of the railing and turned to face the guests, equally seated on both sides of the aisle. His mother, niece, and nephew sat on the right. Lou, her daughter and granddaughter, Jill's family, and Valerie's fiancé sat on the left. His eyes shifted to the vestibule door. The procession began. He smiled at each of Jenny's attendants as they moved into position.

The music morphed to the bridal chorus. Sam's breath caught in his throat at the vision of his bride, stunning in a white strapless gown. The diamond-studded cross dangling on a delicate gold chain, and the two-carat diamond earrings—his birthday gift—reflected the light but paled in comparison to her radiant glow. As she moved toward him, their eyes met and locked.

When his grandfather placed Jenny's hand in his, her irresistible smile and sparkling eyes filled his heart with so much joy he believed it might burst. He caressed her cheek before turning to face the minister.

After they each recited their vows, the minister introduced them as husband and wife.

The room erupted in applause as Sam kissed his bride and breathed in the intoxicating scent of her perfume.

Kelley handed Jenny the bridal bouquet while Sandra and Jill straightened her train.

Jenny slid her hand around Sam's bicep for their stroll down the aisle.

The newlyweds joined the bridal party gathered in the vestibule and exchanged hugs before yielding to the photographer's instructions. Following a series of poses, the attendants and family members headed to the reception venue, leaving the newlyweds to pose alone.

Sam pulled Jenny close. "When's the last time I told you how beautiful you are?"

"Five minutes ago." His bride's face lit with an irresistible smile as the photographer snapped a candid photo.

"What about how much I love you?"

"Hmm. I think six minutes." She stole a kiss.

"Great shot," said the photographer.

Following another half hour of posing, the bride and groom climbed into a white limo. Sam reached for Jenny's hand and kissed her fingertips. "You've made me the happiest man alive, Mrs. Gibson."

"Thank you for never giving up on me."

He kissed her. Deeply. Passionately.

When their lips parted, she gazed into his eyes. "Oh my. Maybe we should skip the reception."

"The good news is we're spending our first night as a married couple upstairs in the hotel's honeymoon suite."

Jenny wrapped her arms around Sam's neck. "I want to spend every night for the rest of our lives sleeping by your side."

He stroked her cheek as the limo pulled to the curb in front of the James Madison Inn. The driver dashed around the rear of the vehicle and opened the passenger door.

Sam stepped out and held out his hand. "Are you ready to greet our guests?"

She accepted. "Lead the way, Mr. Love of My Life."

Sandra met them at the ballroom entrance. "My overeager brother kissed the color right off your lips." She grinned and handed Jenny a tissue, a mirror, and her lipstick. "I figured you'd need a quick repair before making an appearance."

"Thanks, sis." Jenny wiped away the smudge and reapplied her lipstick. "Is this better?"

"Perfect." Sandra opened the door and signaled the three-piece band and the female vocalist. The music changed to "The First Time Ever I Saw Your Face."

Sam nestled Jenny's hand in his as they stepped into the grand salon. His heart swelled with pride as the crowd greeted them with a standing ovation. He led Jenny to the dance floor and pulled her into his arms. "This moment is for you, the mysterious woman who swept into town, stole my heart, and ended my carefree life as a bachelor."

"When I first drove into Madison, I thought an empty gas tank led me here. Now I believe divine intervention along with a subtle nudge from my heavenly father brought me to this town and into your arms." She wrapped her arms around his neck.

Their bodies moved as one to the music. The moment the song ended, a guest's comment, "theirs is a match made in heaven," reached Sam's ears. Sensing Jenny had also heard, he whispered, "They have no idea how true that comment is."

Jenny glanced toward the ceiling and winked. "Someday we'll tell the children we adopt the story about their sister. The story of Jenny's Grace."

Thank you for reading *Jenny's Grace.* If this is the first of my stories you've read, I invite you to check out the first book in my award-winning Willow Falls women's fiction series. https://www.amazon.com/dp/B07J R5CKZB/

All of my paperbacks are available online or at your favorite bookstore.

A Note From the Author

Jenny's Grace, a fictional story with fictional characters, was inspired by a beautiful young woman. She was a gifted chef who drifted in and out of our family's lives before she departed this world for her eternal home. We remember her fondly and miss her signature crab cakes. Yes, they were real, and the best we've ever tasted. We are comforted knowing one day we will see her again and perhaps delight in her culinary expertise.

Some of the settings in Madison and Charleston are places my husband and I have visited. Both are wonderful, walkable towns filled with fascinating history and friendly residents. It's fun to include real locations in my stories. I also enjoy creating fictional sites, like Willow Falls.

I'd love to send you two short stories and keep informed about my upcoming books. Simply go to:

https://www.subscribepage.com/pat-nichols-newsletter

A Special Thank You

Authors never travel their journeys alone.

To my beta readers, Pat Davis, Carlene Dunn, Bev Feldkamp, Kitty Metzger, and Kathy Warner, thank you for taking the time to read my manuscripts and providing feedback and suggestions. You make me a better writer.

To my friends at American Christian Fiction Writers North Georgia Chapter, thank you for your inspiration and for providing excellent speakers willing to share their experiences and knowledge. To my friends at Word Weaver's International Greater Atlanta Chapter, thank you for your exceptional critiques and encouragement.

To my readers, newsletter subscribers, and launch team, thank you for joining me on this journey.

To all who posted or plan to post reviews on Amazon, Goodreads, BookBub, and other sites, thank you for taking the time to share your thoughts. Your reviews are the best way to thank authors.

To my amazing family, thank you for being the wind beneath my wings.

To the citizens of Madison, Georgia, and Charleston, South Carolina, your beautiful towns inspired me to choose both as settings for Jenny's Grace.

Above all, I thank God for His amazing grace, unconditional love, His Son, and the gift of eternal life.